MURDER LIKE CLOCKWORK

Also in the Marchfield Square series

10 Marchfield Square

MURDER LIKE CLOCKWORK

NICOLA WHYTE

Cover design by Patrick Sullivan and Jared Oriel
Cover images by Shutterstock.com: Anastasiia Gevko (type); sergio34 (wood texture); jekson_js (knife)

Union Square & Co.
Hachette Book Group
1290 Avenue of the Americas, New York, NY 10104
unionsquareandco.com
@unionsqandco

First Edition: May 2026

Union Square & Co. is an imprint of Grand Central Publishing, a division of Hachette Book Group, Inc. The Union Square & Co. name and logo are registered trademarks of Hachette Book Group, Inc.

Print book interior design by Rich Hazelton

Library of Congress Cataloging-in-Publication Data has been applied for.

ISBNs: 978-1-4549-5843-7 (paperback), 978-1-4549-5844-4 (ebook)

Printed in Canada
MRQ-L
10 9 8 7 6 5 4 3 2 1

For Andrew & Mia

1

Celeste

Celeste van Duren sat in front of her picture window and looked out over Marchfield Square. Her square. The private little enclave left to her by her dear father, which she and Leonard had hoped would be a safe haven for those in need.

The afternoon sun glinted off the windows of the upper apartments, but Celeste barely noticed, her eyes fixed on the door of Flat 10. It was a delightful property, she knew, in spite of all that had occurred there. Anyone in their right mind would snap it up. Londoners couldn't afford to care about things like murder, especially not when it concerned a two-bedroomed maisonette with a private garden to the front, glimpses of Battersea Park across the river from the back, and a landlady who kept the rent artificially low. It would be leased in half an hour, if she'd only put it on the market.

Except that she couldn't. Celeste did not consider herself unduly sentimental, and self-doubt was not a feeling that had bothered her much in her life. An upper-class background and forty years of international travel would do that to a person. But now here the feeling was, standing in the doorway of 10 Marchfield Square, asking her if she'd lost her marbles.

She sighed.

"You won't get inspiration from up 'ere," said Dixon, setting the tea tray down on the table between the armchairs. "You need to get out and meet people. That's how you used to do it."

"You think I've forgotten?" she snapped. Celeste never forgot anything, and certainly not the good old days, when she or Leonard would happen upon some desperate, unhappy soul and bring them back like a stray dog. Giving someone a safe and secure home and watching them blossom into the person they were meant to be was the most good Celeste had done in her life. Which was saying something, all things considered. "That's not how the world works anymore, Dixon. It's all websites and advertisements now. Besides, the old way wasn't infallible either, or have *you* forgotten?"

"That was different," said Dixon, pouring out her Earl Grey. "Remember, before the Gleads moved in, there was Victor and Captain Gordon. Then, Joe and Manny, Sarah and her little boy, and Audrey and Mei. And before them, there was Lewis. Nothing wrong with your judgement in any of those cases. The Gleads just happened to turn up after Lenny's funeral, when neither of us were at our best. I'm as much to blame."

That silenced her. She could no more blame Dixon than she could blame her beloved Leonard, but the fact remained, Celeste had been arrogant and made a serious error of judgement. An error that had resulted in death.

Dixon handed her the teacup before settling into the second armchair, a mug of strong brown tea in one hand, a shortbread cookie in the other. Celeste sipped her tea and counted silently, smiling when Dixon dunked his shortbread for exactly three seconds. Military precision in everything, even dunking.

"You're right, of course," she said eventually. "I'm proud of what we've done here, Gleads notwithstanding. Bringing everyone together. And hiring Lewis and Audrey to solve the crime turned out to be the making of them both."

Dixon snorted.

"I'll say. A cleaner and a crime writer, besting the police. I knew Audrey was sharp, but Lewis? That were a surprise."

"I'm choosing not to be offended that you doubted me, Dixon," said Celeste, in her haughtiest voice. "They worked well together, as

I knew they would. She quite brought him out of himself. I shouldn't be surprised if we saw him at the May Day picnic this year."

They sat side by side, eyes scanning the square and the buildings beyond, the tower of Chelsea Old Church just visible, backlit by a cold yellow sky. Down in the courtyard, Captain Gordon sat on his usual bench with his usual newspaper, his only acknowledgement of the freezing February weather the burgundy scarf around his neck. The other residents were either still at work or snug in their homes, avoiding the bitter winds and icy temperatures that had plagued London for weeks.

"What about Flat 6?" asked Dixon. "No murders there."

Celeste reached for her own piece of shortbread.

"It's not the murders, it's what they represent."

"You've lost your confidence," he said. "You need to get back on t'horse."

Three months ago, she would have taken her valet to task for that statement, correct or otherwise. Especially if he was correct, come to think of it. But now she just sighed again and turned back to the window.

"It will come, Dixon," she said, as the afternoon sun hit the top of the buildings on one side of her beloved Marchfield Square. "There's no rush, is there?"

"No," he said, his voice quieter than before. "No rush at all."

But as they sat in their respective armchairs and gazed out of the window, the teapot cooling on the table between them, Celeste knew they were thinking the same thing. When all was said and done, how much time did an eighty-two-year-old really have?

Not as much as she'd like.

2
Audrey

Audrey Brooks enjoyed her walks home these days. London was enduring a long, dry, cold snap, a welcome change from the more common seasonal rain, and the new wool coat her flatmate, Mei, had given her for Christmas kept her comfortably warm, even as the icy wind bit her cheeks and whipped her hair out from under her hat.

The hat—a sunny yellow pom-pom hat—had also been a present, from her neighbour, Lewis. It clashed horribly with her green eyes and chestnut hair and did nothing for her pale complexion, but she liked it anyway, amazed that such a ferociously happy item had come from the most unwhimsical person she knew.

She was a fast walker and glanced up at St. Luke's to check the time as she passed, heavy cleaning bag knocking against her leg. At four o'clock, she was later than usual but should still have time for a bit of quiet before Mei got home from work. Mei was her best friend and Audrey loved her, but that decompression time, alone in the flat with a cup of tea, was the part of her day she looked forward to the most.

A few minutes later, she crossed onto Pickering Lane and spotted a black cab parked near the side entrance to Marchfield Square, the curbside rear door open. Mekhala Hetherington stood to one side, bundled up in a thick winter coat, watching as a young man carefully guided her husband's wheelchair backwards down a ramp and onto the pavement.

"Thank you," said Philip to the cab driver, adjusting the position of his chair and sitting up straighter. He, too, was wearing a heavy coat, but he pulled the scarf away from his neck as he rolled his shoulders. "Never quite enough headroom in these cabs."

"Sorry, Mr. H," said the cabbie, crouching down to put the ramp away.

"I'm not blaming you, Clayton," said Philip. "You're very considerate. There's a reason we always book you for our outings."

"Hello, both," said Audrey, fumbling in her pocket for her keys. "Good day out?"

"Hello, Audrey," said Mekhala, smiling. Her black hair was shot through with grey, but her smile was bright and youthful. "We've been to the National Gallery. It's the last day of their Neo-Impressionist exhibition, and it was quite wonderful."

"Just in time, then."

"And, of course, once you're there, you might as well see everything else," said Philip. "Do some sketching. Make a day of it."

"Get some inspiration, you mean?" asked Audrey, raising an eyebrow, and Philip chuckled.

"Maybe, maybe."

"Right, that's me done, guys," said the cab driver, closing the rear door and giving them a big smile. "You take care, and I'll see you soon."

"Thanks, Clayton," Mekhala called after him, and as the Hetheringtons waved the cab off, Audrey swiped her key fob against the panel on the gatepost and held the gate open for them.

"A good lad, that," said Philip, as he wheeled himself into the square.

"Seems it," said Audrey. "Glad you had a productive day."

They headed down the flagstone path, the low winter sun blinding when they reached the courtyard. As the Hetheringtons made for their flat on the ground floor of the big house, Audrey turned off to her side of the square, where Captain Gordon sat on his bench, doing one of the sudoku puzzles in *The Times*, a scruffy little dog at his feet.

"Afternoon, Captain," said Audrey as she drew near. He looked up and smiled, his grey moustache bristling with the movement. "How are you today?"

"Fair, young Audrey, fair," said the Captain. "Been anywhere interesting today?"

"No, not really," she said, crouching down to scratch the dog behind the ears. It rewarded her with a crooked-toothed smile. "Just the usual, plus a new Sharelet in Sloane Square."

"A Sharelet?"

"It's a holiday app," she explained. "People rent out their homes or, in this case, second homes, to make extra cash. There's loads of them in London now."

"Sounds dreadful. Still, Sloane Square, eh?" He put a number in the grid. "Nice to see new places."

Audrey laughed, and he chuckled with her. Neither of them had been outside London for years now, as evidenced by the fact that they exchanged the same pleasantries at the same time and place most days.

"Damned cold today," the Captain went on. "Still, it's good for the heart, I expect."

"It isn't good for the heart," scolded Audrey, gently. "Heart attacks are twice as likely to occur when the weather is cold, and you've already had one. You should do your puzzles inside."

"Nonsense," he said, slapping the paper against his knee. "It's heat that's bad, I'm sure. And if you'd like, it's dashed dull inside, and Muffin likes it out here."

Everything felt different in Marchfield these days. While a certain amount of tension had now disappeared, there was a general feeling that the square had also lost some of its personality, as though it was leaking out of the empty apartments.

A movement at the far end of the garden caught her eye, and she saw Roshan Jones, the gardener, on his way to the tool shed, which was concealed by hedges near the more impressive front gates on March Street. Roshan glanced across the lawn and raised a hand in greeting before disappearing once again into the shrubbery.

She said goodbye to the Captain, carrying on down the path to the steps at the end of the mews. The sound of children's television floated out from next door's open window as she climbed up to the first floor, and as she let herself into Flat 7 and closed the door behind her, she dropped her cleaning bag onto the mat and exhaled.

Home sweet home.

"Hey," Mei called out. "In the kitchen!"

Surprised, Audrey went through and found Mei sitting at the dining table, surrounded by strewn papers, open files, and a pile of sticky notepads. She'd changed out of the neat black suit she'd been dressed in that morning and was now wearing a heavy-knit cardigan over pyjamas.

"Hey," said Audrey, unbuttoning her coat. "What are you doing home? It's not even five yet. And why are you in your pyjamas?"

Mei pulled a face.

"I had an awful client meeting in Ealing with one of the partners after lunch, and he insisted we share a cab back to the office. I had to listen to him drone on and on about how everyone deserves representation, even the super-rich and super-guilty, and by the time we were past the roadworks at the top of the bridge, I just wanted to scream. I realised if I got out of the cab, I could be home in ten minutes and still have a job in the morning, so that's what I did." She breathed out heavily and rubbed the crease between her eyes. "Sorry, I know this is your quiet time."

"Don't be silly," said Audrey, who could count on one hand the number of times Mei had left work early in the four years they'd lived together. She hung up her coat, then returned to the kitchen and put the kettle on. "Cup of tea?"

Mei shook her head.

"No thanks, no more caffeine for me today. I'm jittery enough."

Audrey took a mug from the cupboard and the milk from the fridge, glancing at Mei across the counter that divided the kitchen from the little dining area. Her head was bent over a document, glossy black hair almost touching the table, and while her right hand wrote busily, her left lay on the table, clenching and unclenching.

"What's wrong?" asked Audrey.

Mei looked up.

"Hmm?"

"You're stressed. And not in the usual I've-got-a-stressy-job way. What's up?"

Mei dropped the pen and put her head back for a moment, looking at the ceiling. She let out another long breath.

"Just this case I'm working on. As a solicitor, I genuinely believe everyone deserves a good defence. I do, I truly do. But this guy . . . he might be the exception."

"Why, what's he done?"

"I won't say too much," said Mei. "Except that it's financial."

Audrey frowned.

"You've defended worse cases, surely?"

"I know, but . . . he's so arrogant. Thinks he should be able to do what he wants because he's clever and other people are stupid." She rubbed her eyes again. "I don't know. Maybe Sofia's lectures are starting to get to me."

"Ah." The kettle flicked off, and Audrey turned away to make her tea. Mei's detective girlfriend had strong opinions on defence lawyers. "You still can't agree on that? I was sure you'd win her round in the end."

"So was I. But she seriously thinks we shouldn't try quite as hard to win if we believe they're guilty. I mean, entire cases have been overturned because the defence wasn't doing their job properly! It's a fundamental human right, and you'd think a detective sergeant would understand why."

"I know," said Audrey, soothingly, swishing the teabag around in her mug with a spoon. "So what's the problem with this guy?"

"There are no extenuating circumstances, that's what. He knew exactly what he was doing, and nobody made him do it either. He was a very rich man who wanted to be a little bit richer." She snorted. "You know he was on holiday last week? While we were trying to prepare for his case, he went skiing! And the worst thing is, he seems to think he's already won. I've no idea why. I told him juries don't automatically bestow the benefit of the doubt on tailored suits and Rolexes, but he just smiled at me." She sighed and pinched the bridge of her nose. "Anyway, I'd had enough today, and Dominic going on and on about justice just tipped me over the edge. I'm working on some other cases to cleanse my palate." She gestured at the chaos in front of her. "People who actually deserve to be acquitted."

"You think he will?" Audrey took a scalding sip of tea and winced. "Be acquitted, I mean?"

"Probably. People like him never get what they deserve, do they?"

"No, I guess not."

A subdued silence filled the room, Mei looking at the mess of papers in front of her, Audrey staring out of the kitchen window, mug clasped between her hands.

"God, I'm so rude," Mei said, breaking the silence. "How was your day?"

Audrey shrugged.

"Same old, same old. Cleaned the Demsky place first thing, which was nice because one of the kids had had a fingerpainting party, so I got to try out my new Zabimax spray on her kitchen wall. Worked brilliantly, and she was really grateful. I managed to fit in that new holiday lease in Sloane Square at lunchtime, so they could take some pictures for the website. Didn't take long, but it'll be a little extra cash. Then I did the Williams house, as usual, where she followed me around, also as usual. I can't work out if she thinks I'm going to break something or steal something, but after two years, you'd think she'd cut me some slack."

"Who've you got tomorrow? Lady Muck?"

"Lady Macintyre, yes. Then the Russian house in Belgravia."

"You work for some weird people. I can't believe you clean that place every week."

"And wind the clocks. Mr. Petrov loves his clocks. They switched my days because of the winding schedule, apparently. Something about the mechanisms. There's a lot of antiques in there, and it does get dusty, but yeah, it's not very interesting."

"What a waste of a house."

"I know. And it gives me the creeps—sometimes it feels like someone else has been there, except nothing's ever different. But the company must be checking on me somehow. Hidden cameras maybe, or the alarm logs?"

Mei shuddered. "Looks like tomorrow will be fun for both of us then."

"Worse for you, I think," said Audrey. "Shall I do pasta for dinner?"

Mei smiled. She loved her carbs.

"You're an angel. Just what the doctor ordered."

3
Lewis

Lewis McLennon swiped his key against the gatepost with one hand and was loosening his tie before the gate had even swung open. He moved a lot faster these days, partly to make sure he could keep up with Audrey, who walked everywhere as if she were late for a meeting, but mainly because he needed to get home as quickly as possible and stay there for as long as possible. His agent had given him a deadline.

His agent! A deadline!

Thanks to his sabbatical from the nightmare that was his recruitment job, he'd finished the first draft of his new book in record time and sent it to his agent, Felicia, just before Christmas. It had taken her more than a month to read it, busy as she was with her more successful clients, but when she had, she'd been excited.

A return to form, she'd said. Better, even. His dialogue had improved no end, apparently, and she liked the addition of the optimistic female sergeant as a foil for his cynical detective inspector. Gave extra depth to the whole thing, she said, which Lewis found odd, as he'd intended the character to be rather annoying. She liked it though; that was all that mattered.

He'd ducked out of work early today and waved to Captain Gordon as he passed. The old man was sitting on his usual bench, doing the crossword or something in his actual, dead-tree newspaper. Lewis had once told him that he could do his puzzles on a computer, but the Captain had just scowled and said that was cheating. Lewis had declined to ask why, lest passing the time strayed into actual conversation. Thanks to Audrey, who insisted on keeping him apprised of the comings and goings of everyone in the square, he was dangerously close to becoming involved in the community as it was without adding pensioner IT support into the mix. He'd heard something about a May Day picnic, too, but he had no intention of setting that precedent. Although, now that he thought about it, could the improvement in his dialogue be down to the fact that he'd actually been talking to people recently? Something to think about.

He walked across the courtyard, where the last of the afternoon sunshine was fading, past Celeste's door and the Hetheringtons' ground-floor studio with its big windows. Even to Lewis, who had never paid much attention to his neighbours, the square felt different now. Quieter. He should make the most of it, really. Celeste was bound to rent out the empty flats soon, and then there'd be new people to avoid.

He let himself into his flat and in five minutes had changed out of his hated suit, scruffed his curly hair free of the product he used to neaten it for the office, and made coffee, noticing as he did so that he was nearly out of the blend Audrey had given him for Christmas. She'd thought she was being funny, buying him a subscription from a company called Coffee Snob, but the coffee had been exceptional. He'd have to get some more.

He dropped into his executive leather desk chair, which was finally paying dividends now that he was writing again, and wiggled the mouse to wake his computer.

He'd received Felicia's edits on Monday, and while her email held a warning—his last book had done so poorly, finding a publisher for his new one might be difficult—he was desperate to get the thing polished and sent back to her before she thought better of it.

He still couldn't believe how quickly he'd written the first draft. It had just poured out of him, like it had been there all along. Shaking things up had made all the difference.

Although, he checked himself, he probably shouldn't call what had happened last year "shaking things up." Audrey wouldn't like that. She made it clear, whenever they went for coffee, that she still found the whole thing upsetting. He nodded and frowned in what he hoped were the right places, but he didn't really understand. It had been a few months, after all, and it wasn't like they were family. What was there to still be upset about?

He opened up Felicia's notes, and a shiver ran across the back of his neck as he read the first line again. She loved the chemistry between the two characters and thought they had series potential. She wanted to see where they went next.

The recurring fantasy of telling his irritating boss that he was quitting his job played out in his mind, but he shut it down. He couldn't get ahead of himself. Even if Felicia did think this might be his best work, nothing could happen until she'd found him a publisher, and she couldn't do that until he'd finished this draft. First things first.

Focus.

Of course, underlying all the unfamiliar positivity was a very familiar fear: that lightning wouldn't strike in the same place twice, and now the real-life case was solved, he might run out of inspiration again, like last time. He was hardly going to be called on to investigate another murder, was he?

He shook his head to clear the negative thoughts, then rolled his shoulders. Edits first, new ideas second. He was back in the saddle now. Totally on top of it.

Everything was going to be fine.

4

Audrey

The next day was Thursday, and as usual, Audrey ate her lunch early, sitting on a bench in Ebury Square Gardens, bundled up against the cold. January had been bitter, but February had arrived with even more unreasonable temperatures, and she wasn't due at the Petrov house for ages. Her cleaning bag lay at her feet, and her cold hands were being warmed by a cup of hot soup, poured fresh from her Thermos. A blackbird hopped across the grass in front of her, scratching fruitlessly at the hard ground, while the sound of traffic mingled with the birdsong in the bare-branched trees above.

She'd finished at Lady Macintyre's by eleven and walked from Cadogan Place to the tiny park in Belgravia to have her lunch. Nothing reminded Audrey as sharply of how she was perceived by her clients so much as their insistence on her arriving and leaving according to her hours, regardless of the weather or whether anyone was home. She must leave Lady Mac's by eleven and take care not to arrive at Beaton Gardens until twelve, so she took a short detour to eat in the only public park in the area, wishing for the umpteenth time there was somewhere warm she could sit and wait without having to spend any money.

Soup finished, she fumbled the top back onto the flask with frozen fingers and checked her phone. She still had more than half an hour to kill, and the Petrov place was less than ten minutes away.

God, she was so cold. She squeezed her hands together in an attempt to get some warmth into them, but as every ounce of heat had long since left her body, there was no transference to be made.

Bugger it. She'd been the perfect cleaner for more than a year, so why should she stand around in the freezing cold for the sake of thirty minutes? And maybe this was a good way to check if Trinity Property Management was, in fact, spying on her. She'd be early, and if the company or Mr. Petrov had a problem with that, they'd no doubt let her know.

She picked up her cleaning bag and set off with an angry spring in her step, either the cold or her indignation making her walk faster than usual. There was a brisk wind, forcing the cold even deeper into her coat, and a few minutes later, as she rounded the corner of Beaton Gardens, a gust of wind blew apart the trees and shrubs on the other side of the railings, and she caught a glimpse of the private garden beyond.

A dishevelled man in a dirty but warm-looking padded coat stood beneath the trees on the other side of the railings, looking right at her. His face was puffy, his eyes red, and there was a strange pink tinge to the lower half of his face. She jumped back, but the wind had already dropped, and the greenery fell back into place, concealing the man from view.

Unnerved, she scurried over to number thirty-five and began rooting for her keys. She'd only ever seen one person in the residents' garden before, an elderly man walking a dog, and something about this man's appearance alarmed her. The coat had looked expensive, but he himself was unkempt, with a stubbly chin and windswept blond hair, his eyes heavy with shadows to the point of looking bruised. Perhaps he was just having a bad day. Rich people had those, too, presumably.

After dropping the keys twice from her icy fingers, she managed to get them in the lock and, finally, opened the door.

The alarm started beeping immediately, a loud, urgent tone that set her nerves further on edge. She dropped her bag onto the marble-tiled floor and keyed in the code. With an electronic chirrup, the alarm disengaged.

She took off her coat and scarf and hung them on the coat stand, then slipped off her shoes, shivering as the underfloor heating began to work its magic on her freezing feet. She crouched down and placed her hands against the tiles, letting the heat creep through her body, relieved that Mr. Petrov didn't have to scrimp on his heating like everyone else. The house maintained a carefully controlled temperature at all times, the property agent had explained, partly to stop the pipes from freezing during long periods of absence, but mainly to protect the artworks. Mr. Petrov was a keen collector of art and antiques. From time to time, the agent had informed her, she'd be required to prepare the place for the family to come and stay, but after eighteen months on the job, that had never happened. She wondered if it ever would.

After a few minutes, she'd warmed up enough to put on her cleaning shoes and start work. She went to the kitchen to get the vacuum cleaner from the utility room, then returned to the hall to collect her bag, but as she moved to pick it up, a noise stopped her in her tracks.

She paused, listening. A metallic noise, followed by a soft bang, floated down to her, like a van door closing, somewhere far away. She relaxed. Probably a vehicle outside.

The Petrov house wasn't as grand as some in the neighbourhood, but it was still a single unit, whereas many of the larger properties had been divided into flats. The basement was an empty wine cellar, while the ground floor contained a large kitchen-diner, utility room, and cloakroom. Audrey always started at the top of any property, working her way down to ensure she left everything as clean as possible, so with her bag in one hand and the vacuum in the other, she set off up the stairs.

The first floor consisted of a wood-panelled study and one enormous reception room, zoned with furniture into sitting and dining areas, while on the second floor, two bedrooms led off the cream-carpeted landing. She carried on up, however, until she arrived on the third and final floor, the master suite. The master bedroom was vast, decorated in white and gold and complete with en suite bathroom, home gym, and a dressing room bigger than their lounge at home, with a view across the private green space that gave Beaton Gardens its name.

Audrey parked the vacuum on the landing and went to clean the en suite first, a spacious, light-filled ode to white marble, with gold taps at the sink and the claw-footed bathtub, and a golden-headed waterfall shower behind a wall of glass. She sprayed and wiped the already-spotless surfaces with resigned dissatisfaction, going over the floor with her travel mop before turning her attention to the bedroom.

She dusted the ornaments on the bedside cabinets and wound the clock on the polished dressing table before wiping down all the furniture. Then she vacuumed, lifting the eiderdown on the bed to clean beneath it and tucking it in neatly when she was done.

She was about to vacuum the landing when the clocks began to strike, so she stopped work, waiting and listening. Clocks were a particular favourite of Mr. Petrov's, and there was one in every room, each with its own chiming pattern. Audrey took great care with their winding and setting, and she enjoyed hearing them all chime together, discordant though it was. An orchestra performing for her ears only. Mr. Petrov didn't know what he was missing.

But she'd never heard the clocks strike fully twelve before. Being true to her scheduled arrival time, she'd only ever heard the fading peals at midday, followed by them striking one, two, or three as the afternoon progressed. Today it sounded different, although she didn't know why. Perhaps the midday chime had extra notes she'd not heard before.

When the last note of the Whittington chime from the clock in the study died away, she went back to her cleaning, vacuuming the top floor before carrying everything down to the second. She checked her phone. Still half an hour ahead of schedule. Maybe she should go a bit slower, make sure she left closer to her usual time. She didn't know whether the agent was able to monitor the alarm, and she didn't want any quibbling over her hours.

She sighed. She didn't know why she was so paranoid about this place. Something about the emptiness got to her; it just never seemed quite right.

Ding-ding-ding.

She paused. Another clock was chiming, somewhere nearby. She checked her phone again. Four minutes past twelve. That wasn't right.

The tiny bells kept ringing, belatedly chiming midday, and Audrey turned her head, trying to locate the source. She opened the door of the bedroom nearest to her, but the clock on the bedside table was silent, its face showing the correct time. She made for the other bedroom, grasping the door handle just as the final note sounded.

She opened the door and stopped, frozen to the threshold.

The back room was occupied. Had been occupied, anyway.

Painted simply in Mr. Petrov's preferred gallery-wall white, the bedroom was the most sparsely furnished in the house. Audrey didn't know if Mr. Petrov had a family, but if he did, she guessed they hadn't been expecting to use this room. There was an antique wooden bed dressed in an enormous white sheet that spilled onto the polished oak floorboards, while the bedside tables were plain, bearing old-fashioned fringed lamps. The only decoration in the room was a framed still life hanging above the cast-iron fireplace and the brass-and-rosewood clock on the mantel.

Or at least, it had been the only decoration. As of right now, it had been comprehensively decorated by a not-insignificant amount of blood.

A chair stood beside the floor-length window, which overlooked the back garden from a wrought-iron Juliet balcony. It was covered by another white dust sheet, but sitting upright on top of the sheet was a man, head tilted down onto his blood-soaked chest. Blood spattered part of the wall and the sheet over the bed, and still more pooled strangely on the glistening floorboards, where a plastic sheet beneath the chair wrinkled with the weight of the liquid. The air smelled of meat and metal, and the clock on the mantel ticked steadily, although Audrey could barely hear it through the ringing in her ears.

Someone had been murdered in Mr. Petrov's house. For a second, Audrey couldn't think at all, and then all she could think was, when? Had this man been alive when she'd entered the house?

Was the killer still in the house?

Audrey's head started to spin, and she pushed away from the door. She had to get out.

She tried to run, but her legs were suddenly mired in treacle, and it seemed to take forever to reach the floor below. There was no air in her lungs, and as she cleared the landing and rounded the staircase, heading for the ground floor, she thought she might pass out before she got there.

Then there was the marble floor of the hall and her shoes by the door. She grabbed her coat and wrenched the door open, staggering out onto the front steps with a cry of relief. The door slammed shut behind her, and she finally stopped when she reached the pavement, gripping the iron railings with one hand as she fumbled for her phone with the other.

"Police," gasped Audrey, trying to get her breathing under control as the call connected. She was safe now, safe outside. Why couldn't she breathe? "And an ambulance. Thirty-five Beaton Gardens. Someone's been murdered, and I think the killer's still inside. Please, come quickly."

5
Lewis

"Yes, it's a very competitive salary. May I ask what you're earning in your current position?"

Lewis listened with half an ear as the person on the other end of the line lied about her income. They always did, and he'd long since learned the tell-tale signs of someone hoping to get a big pay rise: the "erm erm erm" as they tried to think of a convincing number, followed by the soft sigh of relief when they thought they'd pitched it about right. He couldn't blame them, really. He'd do the same in their position.

Although if someone phoned him up and tried to offer him a different recruitment job, he'd probably burst into tears.

"Well, I'm not sure you could earn *more* than that in the current climate," he explained to the liar on the phone. "That's very much the top end for that particular role, but you never know. How long have you been in the position?"

He rubbed his eyes as the woman, whose name he'd already forgotten, told him her work history in a long-winded stream of jargon. He blinked at the screen and typed in a few words. Phrases like "team management" and "sales targets," which he vaguely understood, but also terms like "gantt scheduling" and "dynamics processing," which he wasn't 100 percent sure were real but dutifully typed in anyway.

"That's great," he said, when she'd finally finished her nonsense poem. "We have lots of employers looking for those skills. I'll send some details over to you. Can I just confirm your email address?"

He read the woman's email address back to her and, after a few more scripted pleasantries, ended the call.

As he pushed the button and watched the dreadful email compile itself using the company's AI software, he wondered if the job had always been this bad or whether it just felt worse after his sabbatical. He certainly seemed to hate it more, which he really hadn't thought was possible. Or maybe it was Audrey, who seemed absurdly happy to go off to work every day and clean other people's houses. What he wouldn't give for a job he liked.

Or just one he didn't despise.

"Lewis, mate?" called his boss from his glass-fronted office on the other side of the room.

"Yes, mate?" he replied, loathing himself just a little bit more.

"You coming out for drinks tonight? Head office has given me a kitty for team-building. Thought we'd try the Lincoln Sports Bar off Millbank. Watch a bit of football while we're there."

Oh, God, the team night out. Nothing made Lewis angrier than the company's so-called staff morale drinks. No pay rises, even though food prices and energy bills had gone through the roof and staff were quitting all the time because they couldn't afford to live in London anymore. No biscuits in the office, or decent coffee in the kitchen, or an occasional bonus for filling high-commission positions. They didn't even fork out enough to pay for a meal, just an expensive monthly pint in a shit pub with the same boring people he was forced to see every day.

There wasn't a kitty in the world big enough to improve his morale.

"Wish I could, mate," he said, a liar among liars. "But I've already got plans."

"Ah, too bad. You didn't come last month either. Maybe next month, yeah?"

"Yeah, definitely."

His boss disappeared back into his box, and Lewis returned to his screen, resisting the urge to bang his head on the desk.

He needed another distraction. Something to stop him from thinking about all this empty noise in his life. It didn't have to be another crime, just something more interesting than this. Like pot watching or paint drying.

He glanced at his phone and thought about texting Audrey, but she'd be at work right now. Besides, he couldn't think of anything to say.

He sighed.

It was the job, he knew it was, making him paranoid about failure. The idea that this might be his life, forever. Spending his days typing incomprehensible things into a database and calling people who didn't want to speak to him. No wonder he was worried about inspiration.

But then, lack of inspiration was how he'd ended up in this job in the first place, wasn't it? That and the books that hadn't sold.

After the runaway success of his first book, everyone had expected the next to be another smash hit, but it had taken him too long to write, struggling with what his agent had laughingly called "difficult second album syndrome."

She wasn't laughing for long.

The book hadn't had many reviews, but they were all lacklustre—not unkind, just underwhelmed—and when his third book had sunk without trace, he'd found himself unable to write, second-guessing every idea, every character, every sentence, staring at the screen for hours on end, watching the cursor blink. Until he'd run through all the money, of course, and then he'd had to take a job just to make ends meet. A temporary job, in recruitment.

Four years ago.

His mobile lit up.

THE CLEANER: Can you get out of work? Could do with your help. 35 Beaton Gardens.

He blinked. Audrey needed his help? Since when? And that address was in Belgravia. He went through there sometimes, on the bus. He picked up the phone to message her back, wondering what was going on, and then realised he didn't care what the problem was—he'd leave work for literally any reason.

He tapped on his boss's door.

"Steve? I've got a senior person over in Belgravia who won't talk on the phone. HR director. Is it okay if I run over and buy her a coffee?"

Steve looked impressed.

"Yeah, mate." He nodded. "In-person meet. Nice move. Be back before end of the day though, yeah?"

Lewis grabbed his phone and his jacket from his desk and was on the move before anyone could stop him, typing a reply to Audrey as he went.

6

Audrey

Audrey sat on the curb opposite Mr. Petrov's townhouse, her back to the railings of the residents' garden, and watched the front door. She'd been out there fifteen minutes, and while the fear remained—a pulsing, nauseating horror in the pit of her stomach—the adrenaline was wearing off. She was cold, very cold, and anxious, wondering why it was taking so long for the police to arrive.

Once she'd explained that she was safely out of the house, on the street and in broad daylight, the urgency of the call handler's questioning had changed. She'd been assured the police weren't far away, but as the minutes ticked on, she was starting to wonder if they were coming at all. What could be more urgent than a murderer potentially still on the scene?

So she'd texted Mei, asking her to come and meet her—or rather, she'd meant to text Mei. In her panic, she'd accidentally texted Lewis instead, and she cursed herself when he replied.

FLAT 5 GUY: On my way.

Damn. She could really have done with Mei's support, but it didn't seem right to pull both her friends out of work just for a bit of emotional hand-holding. And, if she were being entirely honest, Lewis would probably get a kick out of this, emotionally stunted, crime-obsessed weirdo that he was.

She kept going over the scene in her mind, but now she was worried. What if the man hadn't been dead? What if she could have helped him? She should at least have checked for a pulse before she ran out.

She wrapped her arms around herself, noticing for the first time that she was still wearing her white cleaning shoes instead of her street shoes. She'd have to wash them when she got home, make sure she wasn't treading mud into her clients' houses.

Or blood.

A single trill from a siren made her jump, and she looked up to see a police car driving sedately down the street. About time. She jumped to her feet, and the car pulled in outside thirty-five, lights flashing.

Two uniformed police officers, one male and one female, got out.

"Are you the one who called this in?" asked the female officer as Audrey approached.

"Yes," she said. "I've not seen anyone leave the house since I came out, but they might have got out another way."

"Slow down, miss," said the male officer. "I'm PC Yassin, and this is PC Wade. Can you tell us what happened?"

"Yes, sorry." She took a deep breath. "I'm Audrey Brooks, and I clean here every Thursday. Twelve 'til three. The owner's abroad, and the house is empty. I came in to clean as usual, and everything seemed fine. I started on the top floor, but then I came down to the next floor, and that's when I found him."

"Found who?"

"The man. The body. He's in a chair in the back bedroom. Blood everywhere." She swallowed the lump in her throat. "The blood looked wet, and I thought the killer might still be in the house, so I ran, but he might still be alive, mightn't he? I did ask for an ambulance but . . ."

"It's all right," said PC Wade soothingly. "You did the right thing. Do you still have keys to the property? PC Yassin and I will go and check the scene now. If the victim's alive, we'll notify dispatch, and it'll be upgraded to a priority one."

"Okay." Audrey nodded, taking out the keys. "Yes, I can let you in."

She led the officers up the steps to the front door and unlocked it with trembling fingers. The house was eerily silent without the alarm beeping, but she stood aside for them.

"Where are we going?" asked PC Yassin in a low voice, drawing his Taser from his belt.

"Second floor," said Audrey. "Back bedroom. The first floor is the lounge."

He nodded.

"Wait here, please."

Audrey watched from the front door as the two officers disappeared up the stairs, listening to their footsteps overhead as they climbed the next flight to the second floor.

The distant sound of a door opening and closing. They must have checked the front bedroom first. Then a second door opening. Audrey held her breath.

Footsteps on floorboards. Murmured voices. A creak. A door closing.

More footsteps, softer this time and muffled by stair carpet. They must be going up to the master bedroom, maybe to clear the property, make sure no one was hiding. Audrey's heart thudded as she waited, the draught from the front door keeping the chill at her neck.

Footsteps again, heavy now, and a few moments later, PC Ward and PC Yassin reappeared on the staircase.

"Well?" she asked, as they joined her in the hall. "Is he dead?"

The constables exchanged a look.

"Is who dead?" asked PC Ward, folding her arms.

"The man! The man in the chair."

"There is no man in a chair," said PC Yassin, holstering his Taser. "Every room is empty."

Audrey looked from one to the other in shock.

"But . . . the blood."

"No blood either," said PC Wade. "If this is a practical joke, it's a very poor one."

"A joke?" She blinked at them. "I don't—come on, I'll show you." Audrey pushed past the officers and took the stairs two at a time, heading straight for the back bedroom, but when she opened the door to the crime scene, she pulled up short.

The room was empty.

Not *empty* empty. The bed was still there, under its sheet, but the sheet was now white again, and all traces of blood spatter were gone from the wall. There was no plastic on the floor, with blood congealing in pools—just clean, polished oak, as she'd left it the week before. The chair was still by the window, but the sheet and the blood-soaked body that had previously occupied it were nowhere to be seen.

"What the hell?"

7
Lewis

Beaton Gardens was one of the most expensive addresses in the most expensive area of London. The houses were tall terraces, with white stucco frontages and portico entrances. The street ran in a loop around the central, private garden enclosed by black iron railings, and every house appeared to have at least five floors, including the basement. Some were double-fronted, others—including number thirty-five—single-fronted, and therefore, Lewis guessed, were smaller.

Although *small* was a relative term in this case.

The door to thirty-five stood open, and Lewis felt a stab of fear as he saw Audrey and two police officers on the front steps. Was Audrey all right? What had happened?

"You realise we can charge you?" one of the officers was saying, while the other said something about a false alarm into her radio. "Wasting police time?"

"I'm not wasting your time." Audrey glared at the officer. "There was a murder here, and someone's cleaned it up!"

"What?!" Audrey and the two officers turned towards Lewis, and he marched down the path towards them. "There was a murder?"

"Yes," said Audrey.

"No," said the male officer.

"Who are you?" asked the female officer.

"Lewis," said Lewis.

"He's my friend," said Audrey.

The officers looked at each other, shrugged, then turned back to Audrey.

"Look," said the female constable, sounding kind. "Sometimes people imagine things. Maybe you watched a crime drama last night or read a book that described a house similar to this, and you had a kind of . . . imaginary flashback." Audrey opened her mouth but the policewoman held up a hand. "We'll have to write this up, obviously, but we won't call it a prank, so you won't get in trouble. But you mustn't let this happen again, okay? Next time, check your facts before calling 999."

"Check my facts?!" Audrey became shrill. "How long would you like me to stay in an active crime scene exactly? Ten minutes? Twenty? Maybe an hour, just to be really sure the murderer has a chance to kill me too? Would that be enough of a fact for you?"

"Hey!" said the other one, his voice holding a warning. "We're letting you off, but don't push it. There's nothing here. No blood, no body, no nothing. That's the only fact there is." He looked at his colleague. "Come on, we need to get back."

Lewis stood to one side to let the officers pass and watched as they returned to the patrol car. He waited until they were safely inside to speak.

"Did you say murder?" he asked, turning to Audrey as the car started up. "What the hell happened?"

Her cheeks were red and her eyes fierce as she faced him. For a moment, he thought she wasn't going to answer but then she grabbed his sleeve.

"Come on."

She pulled him into the house, heading for the stairs, taking them two at a time all the way up to the second floor. All Lewis had time to see was beige carpet and white walls until she opened the door to a small, sparse bedroom at the end of the landing.

"Half an hour ago, there was a body in this room. A dead body. In that chair by the window."

Startled, Lewis turned and looked around. It was a modest, light-filled room, painted white, with a small fireplace against the chimney wall and a double bed opposite, draped in a white sheet folded neatly over the pillows, as if it were a hotel. A chair upholstered in white and gold fabric stood in front of a large window. The room looked clean and tidy, with no sign of a disturbance. It smelled fresh, too, almost fruity, although there was another smell underneath, one he couldn't put a name to.

"This room?"

"Yes. I think his throat had been cut. There was another sheet over the chair, and it was covered in blood, and there was something on the floor too—plastic, I think—with so much blood on it . . . "

"Jesus. Where is it now?" Then he remembered. "Wait, they said there wasn't . . . "

"That's the thing." She took a deep breath. "I ran, okay? I called the police, and I waited outside for them. When I came back inside, the body was gone. The body, the blood, the lot. The only thing that's different is the clock."

"The clock," he repeated, looking to where she was pointing. An old-fashioned clock in a shining case of reddish wood stood on the mantel of the iron fireplace. He checked his watch. "It's slow."

"Exactly. I always wind the clocks—they keep pretty much perfect time—but when I got here, this one was four minutes behind. So the body's gone, the room's been cleaned, but the clock is still slow."

"I don't understand."

"Neither do I. The police think I'm lying, or else I'm mad and hallucinated a violent crime scene—and don't you *dare* suggest that I did, McLennon."

He held up his hands.

"I wasn't going to!"

He paused, thinking. Although she often had what he considered to be an overemotional response to things, Audrey wasn't hysterical, and she'd seen at least two dead bodies that he knew of without losing it. And one thing he did know was that she would never have called the police unless she had a very good reason.

"How long have you worked here?" he asked, walking around the room.

"Eighteen months."

"Where's the owner?"

"Russia, I think. His name's Anton Petrov."

Lewis crouched down by the chair, examining the legs for any sign of scratches or blood. There was nothing.

"How often does he come here?"

"Never."

"You clean an empty house?"

"Every week. Clean the house, dust the antiques, wind the clocks."

He looked out of the window, angling his head to see past the little balcony. There was another below and a single-story extension to the ground floor, but it would be impossible to get a body out that way. The garden was small, hemmed in on all sides by the neighbouring properties and the one behind. To say it was overlooked would be an understatement. He tried the window, but it was locked.

"The sheet over the bed had blood on it, so it must have been replaced," said Audrey, and now she sounded unsure. "It's got creases, like it's fresh out of the package. And it's smaller. The original was huge and draped onto the floor. I had to gather it up to vacuum underneath."

He walked around the bed, looking at the crisp white sheet that barely reached the floorboards. It did indeed have a regular pattern of sharp creases across the fabric.

"Is that normal? For you to clean empty houses?"

"No. This is the only empty place I clean. I haven't got mixed up."

Sharp, as always. She definitely wasn't losing it. He knelt down by the fireplace, examining the edges where the iron hearth met the floorboards and where the mantel met the wall. Then he smiled.

He got to his feet. Audrey's shoulders sagged.

"You think I hallucinated, don't you? You think I'm going mad."

"Nope," he said, grinning at her surprise. "I believe every word you've said. I think someone took away the body and cleaned the room while you were outside, waiting for the police."

Her eyes widened.

"Why? How do you know?"

"Because they missed a bit."

8

Audrey

Lewis pointed to the underside of the mantelpiece, and Audrey crouched down for a better look. There, on the white-painted iron, was a collection of small, red-brown splashes.

She squinted up at the marks.

"Why are you so sure that's from the crime scene?" she asked, reluctantly. "Someone could have banged their head or cut their hand on the fireplace."

"See the shape of the droplets? They're fat at one end and thin at the other because they arrived at speed, all travelling in the same direction. The only way that could happen is if the blood sprayed towards the fireplace." Lewis flung his arm out to the side. "Like that. If someone had cut themselves, it would more likely be a smear or a smudge." His dark eyes glittered with excitement. "That's blood spatter."

"Great," she said, standing up and sighing with relief. "Well done. Now we can get the police back. Forensics. They can swab it, or whatever they do."

Lewis's face fell.

"Oh. Are we not . . . ?"

"Not what?"

"You know . . . investigating?"

She stared at him.

"This is a matter for the police," she said. "Besides, what's to investigate? We've no body, no suspects. Where would we even start?"

"Start by working out how they did it. The plastic sheet means somebody knew it was going to get messy, and only a seriously organised outfit could get a body and a crime scene cleaned up in under twenty minutes with you standing outside."

"That sounds like an excellent reason to hand it over to the police. No way am I getting mixed up in anything involving a 'seriously organised outfit.'"

"I thought we'd talked about air quotes," said Lewis, frowning his disapproval. "And aren't you curious as to how they pulled it off?" His expression became sly. "How they got rid of all that blood, so clean and so quick?"

She glared at him. Up to that moment, she'd been mostly concerned with proving she hadn't imagined a murder, but now that he'd mentioned it . . .

"Well, *now* I am, yes. But look, you didn't see him. The body, I mean. You don't cut someone's throat in the middle of an argument, do you?"

"No. They must have brought him here specifically to kill him. I wonder why." He considered. "Any chance the body was the owner? Mr. Petrie?"

"Petrov. I don't know, I've never seen him."

He looked at the clock on the mantel, which had always been one of Audrey's favourites. Set in a rosewood case there were intricate brass flourishes laid into the wood, while the yellowed clockface had an engraved brass centre with keyholes for winding.

"What do you think it would take to put a clock like this out of time?"

"No idea," she said, with a shrug. "I just wind the damn things. To be off by four minutes though, either the pendulum would have to be stopped and restarted, or else it had a bump big enough to knock something out of whack. That might slow the pendulum enough to gain some extra time. I don't know."

Lewis studied the clock.

"So this little bit of paint on the corner might be from someone knocking it into the wall?"

Audrey joined him at the fireplace and looked to where he was pointing, at a tiny flake of white paint clinging to the corner of the casing.

"That wasn't there before."

They looked at the wall behind the clock, where the smallest scratch was visible on the paintwork. The clock had to have scuffed against it at some point.

Lewis took a photo of the clock, then carefully turned it around and opened the case, ignoring Audrey's worried hiss. Inside was a delicate pendulum set against a brass backplate engraved with fleurs-de-lis and the words "Henry Massy, London".

"How long before you need to be out of here?" he asked, taking another picture.

"Two hours."

He nodded, closing the clock case and turning it the right way round again.

"Let's have a poke around. There might be a photo of your boss somewhere."

"Lewis . . . "

"It'll put your mind at rest, if nothing else," he said, in a manner that in no way suggested he cared about her peace of mind. "Got any gloves?"

With a sigh, she went out into the hall to get her cleaning bag. After discovering her and Lewis wearing Marigold rubber gloves during their last foray into crime-solving, Mei's girlfriend, DS Sofia Larssen, had thought it funny to give Audrey a box of powder-free, examination-grade disposable gloves as a Christmas present, but she'd put them in her cleaning bag anyway. After all, you never know.

As she offered the box to Lewis, his eyebrows shot up.

"Good for cleaning, are they?" he asked, swiping two from the box.

"Shut up."

She led him up to the top floor, noticing that the police had left track marks on the carpet. She'd have to vacuum again. She watched from the door as he took in first the dressing room, then the master bedroom, filled with the ornate wooden furniture that made the space gloomy and took ages to dust, then disappeared off into the bathroom. She felt her anxiety rise the moment he left her sight, imagining the killer, hiding in the waterfall shower, slashing at the first person they saw.

"Nothing in there," said Lewis, reappearing at the door. "It's all very white, isn't it?" He paused, looking at her. "Are you all right? You've gone pale."

"Yes, I'm fine," she snapped. "You'd be pale, too, if you thought there might be a killer behind every door."

He nodded but continued his prowling, apparently unperturbed by such imaginings. He opened every drawer and cupboard, looked under every scrap of furniture, working his way down until they were back in the living room.

The living room had more furniture than any other room, including a comfortable-looking damask-covered suite, several uncomfortable-looking antique armchairs, and an obscene number of mahogany end tables. There was the fabric-covered card table that was a nightmare to dust, a walnut chessboard, two brass ashtrays on tall twisted stems, a Chippendale grandfather clock between the two windows overlooking the gardens, and enough table lamps to light a small village.

"Don't touch that!" she warned, as he reached out to the golden ormolu clock on the bedside table. "They're sensitive. Doesn't take much to knock them out."

He withdrew his hand and shrugged.

"Nothing personal here at all. Who are these people?"

"I'm starting to wonder that myself," said Audrey, leading him back towards the stairs. "The agent who hired me said Mr. Petrov was a financier who was rarely in the country, but that the house was full of things that needed taking care of."

"The things being . . . ?"

"Clocks, mainly. But the antiques and the furniture also need cleaning. Lots of twiddly bits and polished finishes. Dust can ruin antiques, if it sits too long."

"Every week though? To look after clocks? The man must have more money than sense."

"I don't know how much you think I earn, but spending three hours a week on a cleaner wouldn't make a millionaire blink, let alone a billionaire."

"Which is it? Millionaire or billionaire?"

"No idea. But if he wants to pay me to come in and wind his clocks, that's his business."

"You don't remember seeing any photos before? Nothing about the family?"

"No," she said, looking around the room. "But I don't go rooting around in their cupboards."

"What's that room?" asked Lewis, standing by the door and pointing down the hall.

"The study."

"Excellent!" He marched off down the hall. "If there's anything to find, it'll be in there."

The study, for some reason, made Audrey even more uneasy. The back wall was lined with shelves stuffed with old-looking books, while a huge mahogany desk inlaid with green leather stood in front, a glass-shaded reading lamp on one side and a large leather office chair tucked underneath. The only ornament in the room was a framed silver coin on the wall and the glass-domed clock with the Whittington chime, which stood in the middle of the bookshelves.

"There's nothing in here," said Audrey, lingering by the door. "Just books. Hey, what are you doing?"

"Investigating," said Lewis, peering into the top drawer of the desk. "No point doing half a job . . . ah-ha!"

Triumphantly, he pulled a silver frame out of the drawer and handed it to her. It held a black-and-white photo of a family, where a dark-haired man with a flattish nose had his arm around a woman. She had a sweater knotted around her shoulders and looked to be a little younger than him. In between them, pressed together and smiling shyly at the camera, were two young children. The boy was tall and thin, his face partially obscured by his mother's dark curls, while the girl was younger and a little rounder, with dimples in her cheeks and bright, happy eyes. They appeared to be at the seaside, the ocean stretching behind them to the horizon, although the lack of any kind of landmass was disorienting. Perhaps, she thought, looking at it a moment longer, they were on a boat. Didn't all rich people have boats?

"Is that him?" prompted Lewis. "The victim?"

"No." She shook her head, relieved. "He was stockier, and shorter, I think. And his hair was a kind of sandy brown."

"So assuming the man in the photo is Mr. Petrov, then at least we know it wasn't him. He can go on the suspect list now."

"Suspect list? Lewis, we can't—"

"Whoever brought the victim here to be slaughtered must have had some knowledge of, or connection to, your Mr. Petrov."

"Maybe. But—"

"First, we need to identify the victim. And draw up a list of everyone who might have access to the house. That will narrow the field."

"Lewis—"

"Then there's the modus operandi. If we can work out how he was killed, we could compare that to other cases and other killers."

"*Lewis.*"

"And the cleaning. Getting rid of the body is hard enough, but getting rid of the blood? That can't be easy. You can be in charge of—"

"Lewis!"

"What?!"

She looked at him, and his eyes were wide and animated. He was looking forward to investigating, she realised. He was *longing* to investigate. He was, in fact, already investigating.

And he assumed she'd be investigating too.

"Fine." She let her shoulders drop. "We'll look into it. But—" She raised a finger as he broke into a smile. "I'm going to call Sofia."

"Sofia?"

Audrey rolled her eyes.

"DS Larssen? Blond? Beautiful? Works for a grumpy DI who'd gladly Taser you if he saw you again?"

He folded his arms.

"Why me? You found just as many bodies as I did."

"You have a way about you," she said shortly. "But we need to get the police back. There's a dead body out there somewhere, and it needs to be found. We're going to need all the help we can get."

9

Lewis

Lewis tried to keep his enthusiasm to a minimum. There he'd been, worried about inspiration, and another real-life crime had dropped into his lap.

After inspecting the empty wine cellar, they'd relocated to the clean, white echo chamber that was the kitchen. Lewis walked about, looking in the cupboards, while Audrey leaned against the marble-topped island, looking antsy.

He paused in front of a pristine coffee machine, a shining monolith of stainless steel bristling with dials and nozzles that looked like it had never been used.

"Do you know how much these cost?" he said, awestruck. "I bet the crema would be incredible."

"Don't even think about it."

"Think about what?"

"You know what I'm talking about." He ran a gloved finger around the temperature dial. "Step away from the machine, coffee nerd."

He grinned but stepped back, shooting it one last, longing glance.

"Would you like me to leave you two alone?" she asked, but as he opened his mouth to reply, the doorbell rang.

"About time," he said. "Although based on our last experience, I don't think it's going to help. She'll probably think you imagined it too."

Audrey shook her head.

"I don't think so. She's been around ours a lot lately. She'll know I'm not going to waste her time."

"Has she?" Lewis was surprised. "Been around yours a lot?"

There it was again, the "are-you-kidding-me?" expression he'd come to know and hate.

"You cannot have forgotten that she and Mei are dating?"

Couldn't he?

"I wouldn't say I'd forgotten," he said, after a beat. "But I also wouldn't say that I'd *not* forgotten." He ignored the incredulous shake of Audrey's head, then followed her down the hall to the front door, which opened to reveal DS Sofia Larssen.

"Hey," said Audrey, standing back to let her in. "Thanks for coming."

"Gets me out of the office" was all Sofia said in reply. Her smooth blond hair and sharp grey suit did not suggest a person who'd already been at work for hours. She looked past Audrey to Lewis. "Hello, Mr. McLennon."

"Hello, DS Larssen."

"How uncomfortably formal," said Audrey, brightly. "We'll get right to it, shall we?"

"Yes, please," said Larssen. "Take it from the top and leave nothing out, starting with whose house this is."

Audrey gave her the full story.

"And the burglar alarm was on when you arrived?"

"Yes. But it only covers the entrances and exits. You could move around the house, and it wouldn't go off."

"Did you bring a swab kit?" asked Lewis. "For the blood?"

Larssen frowned but took a pair of latex gloves from her pocket.

"I did, although I'm surprised you don't have your own." She looked pointedly at Lewis's gloved hands. "You seem pretty well equipped already."

"I had them with me," said Audrey.

"Ah. I suppose I'm to blame for that," said Larssen, giving a wry smile. She put on her own gloves. "Right then. Take me to your crime scene."

Audrey led Larssen up the stairs to the back bedroom, Lewis following behind. She opened the door to let Larssen go first and they waited while she looked around the room.

"Describe the scene you found for me," said Larssen, her tone measured. Lewis couldn't tell whether she was taking this seriously or not.

"That chair," began Audrey, pointing to it, "was covered in a sheet. There was a man in it, with his head tipped forward, blood all down his front. There was blood spatter on the sheet over the bed and the wall near the window, and plastic on the floor, with blood all over it."

Larssen's eyebrows disappeared beneath her blond fringe, blue eyes wide.

"And then?"

"I thought the killer was still here, so I ran. But when the police arrived, less than twenty minutes later, the room looked like this."

She waved an arm at the spotless room and looked anxiously at the detective. Larssen remained silent as she walked around, however, only pausing by the window to sniff the air, before dropping to the floor to inspect it.

"Floor's dry," she said, standing again. She turned to look out the window, scanning the gardens up and down the street before turning back to the room. "Show me the blood you found."

"Under here," said Lewis, crouching down in front of the fireplace.

Larssen joined him, peering up to where he pointed. Then she looked back towards the window, her eyes narrowed, as if trying to work something out. Without saying a word, she took photos of the fireplace and the blood spatter, then removed a little plastic bag from her pocket and took out a sample tube, unscrewing it to get to the swab. She took a tiny bottle from the bag, putting a single drop of liquid on the end of the swab, then reached up and delicately rolled the swab against the fireplace before returning it to the sample tube.

"That's the sample," she said, sealing the plastic bag and returning it to her pocket. "Now let me see if I can get a presumptive. No point wasting the lab's time if it isn't even blood."

Lewis snorted.

Larssen ignored him but took a second swab of the underside of the mantelpiece, then shuffled several bottles from hand to hand as she put a drop from one, then a drop from another, onto the swab.

"There might not be enough to be conclusive," she said, adding a drop from the last bottle, "but hopefully . . . "

They watched the tip of the swab turn bright pink, and Lewis smirked.

"Human blood," said Sofia, and her note of surprise wasn't lost on Lewis. "It could have got there in a number of ways, but still. I'll run the sample through the databases, see what comes back." She returned the bag to her pocket, then looked around the room again. "I don't know what's harder to believe: that you imagined a dead body or that someone could clean a crime scene that fast and that thoroughly. For there to be just a few drops of blood . . . "

"I know," said Audrey. "And when I figure out how they did it, you'll be the first to know."

Lewis frowned.

"Second to know," she corrected.

Larssen spun around.

"You're not trying your hand at police work again?"

"It isn't technically police work," said Lewis quickly. "Unless you open a case. And you still don't believe her, do you?"

"I—that is—" Larssen's cheeks reddened. "It's not that I don't believe you, Audrey, but you must see that it'll be hard to prove anything happened here."

"I know what I saw."

"I'm sure you do. But eyewitness accounts are notoriously unreliable, even minutes after the fact. And this is uncorroborated. There's no one else to back you up."

"What about the blood sample?" asked Lewis. "That's evidence."

"Assuming the person whose blood this is, is in the database, we'd need to try to track them down. But the likelihood is, they won't be, and then we're nowhere."

"In other words," said Audrey, "you can't take my word for it. Until that body surfaces, you can't investigate. But they were here when I was here, Sofia. Whoever did this knows that I know."

"But if we find some evidence, you'll see she was telling the truth," said Lewis, cheerfully. "Then we can work together."

"We don't work with civilians," said Larssen.

"You're not wor—" began Lewis, but Audrey silenced him with a look.

"You're right," said Larssen, after a moment. "I can't stop you looking into it right now. But if what happened here was as you describe, it would take some dangerous people to pull it off. Far better to wait for the lab to come back, see if we get a hit."

"How long will the lab take to come back?"

"Seventy-two hours probably. Maybe longer, because it's not linked to an open case."

"Seventy-two hours is a long time to wait and see if a killer comes after me."

There was an uncomfortable pause.

"All right," said Larssen, with a sigh. "I'll pop this sample in to Forensics but I warn you, it won't be a priority. There's an ongoing gang turf war that's causing a processing backlog."

"Whatever you can do," said Audrey.

"How did you come to meet Anton Petrov, anyway?" asked Larssen, as they went back downstairs. "You'll need to let him know, I suppose."

"I didn't," said Audrey. "Never have. I'm employed by an agency, Trinity Property Management. Celeste put me on to them. They look after hundreds of properties all over London."

They reached the hall and Larssen paused by the front door.

"Honestly, Audrey," she said, shaking her head. "I'm really hoping this is nothing. A momentary hallucination or a trick of the light. I'll have a lot of questions to answer otherwise."

Lewis thought there were plenty of questions already, but he stayed silent.

"I understand," said Audrey, opening the door and smiling in a way Lewis thought was unnecessarily apologetic. "I really do appreciate it."

They watched as Larssen walked down the path to the street, where her car was parked. Audrey closed the door and leaned her back against it.

"That was painful," she said. "But at least she took the swab. Now what?"

10
Audrey

"The property company," began Lewis, the second Audrey turned away from the door. "That's a whole load of suspects right there! They'll have keys, floorplans, alarm codes . . ."

Audrey frowned.

"That's . . . a good point actually," she said. "Trinity will have a key. And they know what time my shift is. They were very specific about it."

"What do you mean?"

"They said I had to clean between twelve and three. No earlier, and no later. They said the clocks had to be wound at the same time each week and implied they'd know if I didn't keep to my time. I always assumed there was a camera somewhere, but I've never spotted one."

Lewis glanced around, as if trying to spot any concealed devices.

"We should talk to them first," he said. "If there are cameras, then they should be able to show us what happened and who was here. And the alarm will have logs, so if someone disabled it—someone who wasn't you—they should have a record of that too. What happens if you do get here early?"

"I've never tested it," said Audrey, thoughtfully. "Today was the first time I've ever been earlier than midday."

"So there could be a murder here every week, and as long as they were out by eleven fifty-nine, you'd be none the wiser?"

She gaped at him.

"Why would you say that?" she half-shrieked. "I have to come back here, you know!"

"Just thinking out loud. You have to admit, an empty property makes a perfect crime scene, doesn't it? Plenty of time to clean up, and only the cleaner to notice anything amiss. Why else be so funny about your time-keeping?" He nodded and she watched him make a note in his phone. "It's something to consider."

"Sofia's right that I'll have to tell them, though." She turned and looked up the staircase, chewing on her lip as she thought. "I really don't like leaving without cleaning. What if I just finished running the vacuum round?"

Lewis opened his mouth then shut it again. He was silent for a moment.

"If you'd just pulled off the most impressive cleaning job in history," he began, "would you avoid coming back to the scene and trust that you'd got it all first time? Or would you return at the earliest opportunity and make sure you hadn't missed anything?"

She considered this. Someone else had access to the property. Someone who'd had to clean up a lot of blood very quickly. Would they be so confident in their work that they wouldn't return?

"I'd come back," she said at last. "If I could. Especially if I might have left evidence behind—something that could send me to prison. If I were able to get in and out without anyone knowing, then yes, I'd definitely come back."

"Right," he said. "In which case, anything we don't get now, we have to assume will be removed once we go. We can't dust for fingerprints and we can't swab for trace . . . "

She beamed at him.

"But we can empty the vacuum cleaner! Good thinking, Batman. I empty the bag every week, so anything in it will be new. There might be hairs or fibres. I can vacuum every room, and we can take the contents with us to look at later."

"There were some sandwich bags in the kitchen. We can save the contents by room."

Audrey scampered upstairs and returned with the vacuum cylinder, and, standing over the sink in the utility room, they managed to empty the contents into a sandwich bag, which Lewis labelled "Top Floor" with a Sharpie. Then began the complicated and messy process of Audrey vacuuming every room inch by inch, using almost every attachment she could to ensure she didn't miss anything.

"How can there be this much?" Lewis complained, as they emptied the vacuumed contents from yet another floor into yet another bag. "No one lives here!"

"There's always something," said Audrey. "But lots of people have been up and down the stairs today. Just the basement to do now."

Lewis sat at the kitchen island, clearly bored, watching Audrey as she went over every inch of tiled floor and skirting board.

"Do you always clean like that?" he asked, as they funnelled the contents from the basement into the final bag. "Or is it because it's a crime scene?"

"I am being especially careful," she said, tapping the side of the cylinder to empty it. "I don't want to leave anything behind. But I think I'm usually pretty thorough." She put the cylinder back into the vacuum and carried it to a cupboard in the corner. "Right, that's done. Ooh, wait, is it mop day?"

"Mop?!" Lewis was outraged. "Mop what? The place is spotless!"

"The floors, of course. Anything that's not carpeted." She pulled her phone out and checked it. "No, that's next week. That's lucky. It's past three and I should really be out."

"Shit. I should have been back at work ages ago."

They returned to the hall, where Audrey changed her shoes and packed up her bag, squeezing the sandwich bags full of dust in between her cleaning products.

"Are you going straight home?" asked Lewis, as they put on their coats.

"I thought I might drop in at the Trinity offices first. Sloane Square isn't far out of my way."

"I think I'll come with," he said. "If that's okay?"

"Sure. Won't you get into trouble at work though?"

He shrugged and for a moment she thought she saw a gleam in his eye. Was he still hoping he'd be fired?

"I said I was meeting a client. I'll think of a reason for being so long. Come on. Let's get out of here."

11

Lewis

They'd only walked a few steps down the street when the door to number thirty-four opened, and a man came out of the house with a small black-and-tan spaniel on a lead. Lewis gripped Audrey's arm.

"A neighbour! We didn't think of that."

"Think of what?"

"Excuse me?" he called, rushing towards the man, who stopped in his tracks on the front step. He was probably in his seventies, bald on top with grey hair at the sides clipped close to his skull. He was wearing beige chinos and a pink shirt beneath a Barbour jacket, his belt disappearing at the front beneath the roundness of his stomach.

"Can I help you?" asked the man. He had a Scottish accent, and his eyes darted suspiciously from Lewis to Audrey and back again.

"Hi," said Audrey, before Lewis could speak. "Sorry to bother you. I'm the cleaner for next door? Number thirty-five."

"Oh, aye?"

"I don't suppose you noticed anything out of the ordinary this morning? Anyone coming or going?"

Lewis sighed. There was vague, and then there was *vague*.

"Something was removed from the property," he said. "At around midday. Did you hear anything?"

"A burglary?" The man looked alarmed. "This morning?"

"Possibly," said Lewis. "We know they didn't come out the front, but we were wondering if they could have taken anything out through the back? Perhaps you saw or heard something?"

The man shook his head while the spaniel strained at the lead, trying to reach Audrey, who dropped her bag on the ground.

"All these gardens are walled," he said. "Only way out's through the front. And the management company won't allow us a video doorbell." He tutted. "Privacy reasons, they say. Who'd wan' tae burgle a holiday house? Is it not empty?"

"Not entirely," said Audrey, crouching down to play with the dog. "Aren't you a little sweetheart? Yes, you are! Oh, look at your eyes."

"So nothing then?" prompted Lewis, doing his best to ignore the baby voice coming out of his fellow investigator. "No strange noises or people you didn't recognise?"

"No more'n usual."

"What about the other side?" he pressed. "Thirty-six. Do you know them?"

"Aye, a little, but they're away. Dubai, I think."

"I saw a man in the residents' garden earlier," said Audrey. "Fair hair. Big coat. Looked a bit worse for wear. Does that sound like anyone who lives round here?"

"Can't say I know. Not many people use the garden in winter, 'less they've a dog." He looked thoughtfully down at Audrey. "Do you work for yourself or an agency?"

"Both." She kept fussing the dog. "I have a mix of clients."

"Only, the wife and I could do wi' a cleaner. We used to have one, but she retired, and we've had two this past year, and the latest just left the country. We're only a flat, mind, no' a whole house."

"Erm. Okay, sure." Audrey stood up, suddenly flustered. "Could you give me your number, and I can give you a call later?"

The man patted his coat pockets, of which there seemed to be many, eventually fishing out a card.

"Here you are. We'd need you to keep to time. Fixed hours, none o' this turning up when you fancy. I suppose it doesn't matter so much wi' these oligarch houses, but it does when it's a family home."

"Of course." She took the card and glanced at it. "Mr. Forrest-Ross. Nice to meet you. I'm Audrey Brooks."

He smiled then, and his eyes twinkled.

"You've nice manners, anyway. You'll give me a ring then, aye?"

"Aye. I mean, yes. I will."

They watched him cross the road with the dog, heading towards the garden.

"Why did that feel like I was being told off for something?" asked Audrey. She handed Lewis the old-fashioned calling card on linen stock. It simply read *Julian Forrest-Ross, 34 Beaton Gardens, London SW1* and then a phone number.

"Because you're paranoid," he said, passing it back. "Anyway, it wouldn't be a bad thing to have a reason to talk to him again, would it?"

She pulled a face but didn't argue, picking up her cleaning bag again.

"Come on," she said. "It'll be getting dark soon."

The walk was almost pleasant as they passed through the smart residential streets, polished brass gleaming against shining black doors, but Lewis spent most of it composing a text to his boss to explain his ongoing absence.

> Steve,
> Heading over to their office on Sloane Square to meet some more people. Might not make it back before five. Will update you tomorrow.
> Lewis

Technically, the only lie he'd told was that Audrey was a senior HR person who'd invited him for coffee, but as she was self-employed, that would make her the most senior person and, therefore, in charge of HR. However, she also worked for Trinity Property Management, and they were heading to Trinity's offices, so if he bought her coffee on the way home, then was any of it actually untrue?

By the time they reached Sloane Square, Lewis's conscience was entirely clear.

12
Audrey

It took less than ten minutes for Audrey and Lewis to reach the corner of Sloane Square and Lower Sloane Street, a busy junction in the middle of a designer shopping district, with honking traffic and jostling pedestrians all trying to navigate a three-way crossing. Everyone was wearing huge coats and warm hats and trying to avoid ice on the pavements. Overhead, the sky was pale grey through the leafless branches of the trees.

Audrey led the way, away from the high-end brand shops and down Lower Sloane Street, where everything immediately became quieter. To the right, ornate red-brick mansion blocks lined the street, while to the other side, at the farthest end of the handful of commercial buildings near the square, stood Trinity Property Management. It had a glass shop-style frontage, with photos of expensive-looking properties displayed in the windows.

"Right." Lewis turned to her. "Obviously, you're their employee, so you'll need to take the lead, but stick to the matter at hand. We want to know about alarm logs, security cameras, and whether anyone else has access to the property."

"I'm an independent contractor." She glared at him. "And I know what we're doing."

He held the door for her and followed her inside, to where a bored-looking young woman with blond hair sat behind a desk opposite the door. There was a large staircase to the left of the desk, while in the corner by the window, some upholstered chairs had been arranged around a glass table.

"Hi," said Audrey to the woman behind the desk, taking off her pom-pom hat. "Is Felix Casetti in?"

The woman looked them up and down.

"I'll see if he's available," she said, reaching for the phone. "Name, please?"

"Audrey Brooks," said Audrey. "It's about 35 Beaton Gardens."

The woman's eyebrows went up, but she pressed a couple of buttons, tapping her fingers on the desk as she waited for someone to answer.

"Audrey Brooks here to see you," she said, turning her chair away from them. "She said it's about Beaton Gardens . . . "

There was a pause, then she spun the chair back around and replaced the receiver with a brittle smile.

"He won't be a moment."

They stepped away from the desk to stand awkwardly near the window, but in less than a minute, footsteps on the stairs made them look up.

A tall, slim man in a grey suit trotted down the stairs, flashing a smile at the receptionist as he passed. Felix Casetti, who had interviewed Audrey for the job, was good-looking in an average kind of way, with wavy dark-blond hair and dark eyes. He made straight for her with a confident grin, although he faltered a little at the sight of Lewis.

"Audrey, hey," he said, then looked at Lewis with something approaching annoyance, which was odd because Lewis hadn't even spoken yet. "And this is?"

"This is Lewis McLennon."

"Hi, Lewis," said Felix, and this time the smile was fake. "Felix Casetti. Great to meet you."

"Likewise," said Lewis, shaking his hand.

"What can I do for you both?"

"It's about the Petrov house in Beaton Gardens," Audrey began, wondering how to explain it. "Something happened this afternoon. Someone was there. Or had been there."

"A break-in?" asked Felix, worried. "Was anything stolen?"

"I don't think so, but the alarm was on, so I wondered if it could have been someone from Trinity?"

"Of course not." Felix began playing with his tie. It had a tie pin. "What are we talking about then? Damage? Some kind of mess?"

"Yes," said Audrey, emphatically. "A big mess. It was horrible."

"So . . . you did overtime? Is that what this is about?"

"No!" Audrey was offended. "But, you see, the police can't investigate unless we have proof someone was there, so I was wondering . . ."

"The police?" Felix took a step back. "Why would you go to the police?"

"Because of the break-in?"

"But you said nothing was stolen."

They stared at each other for a moment, Felix's head angled in confusion.

A shadow passed the window, and the receptionist coughed, loudly enough that they all turned to look at her. She nodded towards the street door, and a second later, a man in an expensive three-piece suit walked in. He wasn't particularly striking—average height and average build, with brown hair greying at the temples—but Felix straightened up at the sight of him.

"Hello, Steph," said the man, approaching the desk. "Any messages?"

"None, Mr. Waverley," said the receptionist.

"All right, thank you." The man glanced over to where Felix, Lewis, and Audrey were standing. "Felix," he said, by way of greeting, eyes raking over the group. "Sorry if I've interrupted."

"Not at all, Roland. Miss Brooks here is one of our cleaners. And this . . . " Felix gestured to Lewis but couldn't seem to find the words. "Why are you here?"

Lewis opened his mouth to reply, but Audrey jumped in.

"Lewis is acting for Celeste van Duren on behalf of Mr. Petrov," she fibbed, flashing an embarrassed smile at Waverley. He was clearly the boss. He looked distinguished, although perhaps not as old as the grey hair would suggest. "Celeste is the one who connected me with your company. Lewis works in recruitment." She hoped that sounded vaguely professional, if not entirely logical.

"Oh?" Roland Waverley moved away from the receptionist and joined them, holding out his hand to Lewis, who shot a quick, surprised glance at Audrey. "You know Anton Petrov?"

"Yes," said Lewis, turning pointedly away from Felix to shake Waverley's hand. "Lewis McLennon. When Audrey discovered the situation at the house, she called me as well as the police. We didn't want to worry . . . Anton until we knew exactly what had happened, but the police aren't able to take it any further without evidence of the intrusion."

"Situation at the house?" Waverley looked at Felix. "What situation?"

"Miss Brooks cleaned the house at Beaton Gardens today, and apparently there was a bit of a mess," explained Felix. "She . . . uh . . . called the police and Mr. McLennon here. I'm trying to get to the bottom of it."

"You should have come to us before the police," said Waverley.

Now Audrey's hackles were up. *What was wrong with these people?*

"There appeared to have been some sort of altercation," she said, choosing her words carefully, considering there was no evidence to back her up. "There was . . . blood."

"Jesus!" Felix was startled. "You never said anything about blood." He looked at Waverley, who seemed just as alarmed.

"You can see why we're taking it so seriously," said Lewis, gravely.

"Yes. Yes, of course. Wow." Felix nodded, then turned abruptly to Audrey, face full of concern. "Are you okay? That can't have been pleasant."

He put his hand on her shoulder in what he clearly hoped was a sympathetic manner, and she saw him glance at Waverley again.

"It was a bit of a shock, but I'm all right."

"Good." He smiled and nodded in a way that made her think of politicians. "And you got it all cleaned up okay? Do you need any special cleaning stuff? We'll pay if you do."

"There's no trace left," she said. "Don't worry."

"You seem a most efficient young lady," said Waverley, approvingly, and she felt momentarily bad for taking credit for someone else's work. "But we can't have people breaking into our properties, Felix. Especially not to commit violence. We'll look into this at once."

"Yes, of course." Felix smoothed his tie again. "I'll take a look at the security footage, shall I, Roland? See what we can find. I'm sure it's just bad luck, someone taking advantage of an empty property. Maybe I'll pop round myself and do an inventory. Make sure everything's still there and as it should be."

"Good man."

"So there *are* security cameras?" asked Lewis.

"Oh yes. We have at least one camera in all our properties. Can't be too careful."

"That's great," said Audrey, suppressing a shudder at discovering this previously unknown surveillance. "I arrived at eleven thirty, and whoever did this was still there, so you'll need to check the whole morning at least. They may have snuck out sometime between twelve and twelve thirty after I went out to wait for the police. I'm happy to help you go through it."

"Woah, woah!" Felix put his hands up, looking horrified. "You're not supposed to go in until twelve. I was very specific."

"It was a one-off," she said defensively. "I was outside already, and it was absolutely freezing, so I went in. Lucky I did, or you might not know anyone else had been there."

The expression on Felix's face suggested he didn't agree with this sentiment. "Well, you really shouldn't. We have everything organised precisely. We need to know who's where and when."

"Why?" asked Lewis, sharply. "What's it matter if the cleaner is half an hour early?"

"It just does," said Felix, tugging at his shirt sleeves. He was also wearing cufflinks, she noticed. "I think perhaps it would be best if we suspend cleaning Beaton Gardens for a few weeks. Give us time to look into this and make sure the property's secure. What do you think, Roland?"

"That's not necessary at all," said Audrey hastily, as her heart rate sped up. She couldn't afford to lose a job, not when she was only just getting her finances back on track. "I promise, I'll be fine."

"I wouldn't want to put anyone at risk," said Felix, firmly. "Roland, do you agree?"

"Oh." Waverley blinked, discomfort evident on his face. "Well, I suppose this is your area, Felix. If you think it's best."

"I do."

"But the antiques!" Audrey looked from Felix to Waverley. "And the clocks. They need regular maintenance. Mr. Petrov is so particular."

"I'll square it with Mr. Petrov," said Felix, holding up his hands to bring an end to the discussion. "But we can't have you going in and out until we know what's gone on there. I'm sorry, but you're to stay away from the house until further notice. Now, was there anything else? I have a call."

Audrey looked helplessly at Lewis, who shrugged, and a wave of anger washed over her. He had no idea what it was like for her, none of them did, how hard it was to manage on such a low income. And now, because some showman of a murderer thought they could make a fool of her, she'd just taken a pay cut!

"No, nothing else," said Audrey, trying not to let rage make her cry. "But could you send over the security footage if you find anything?"

"Or logs from the alarm?" added Lewis. "So we can reassure Mr. Petrov."

"If we find anything, we'll be in touch with Mr. Petrov," said Felix, glancing at Waverley. "It's his property. We can't deal with middlemen, no offence."

"None taken," said Lewis, in a tone that suggested offence had, in fact, been taken.

"Thank you for coming in," said Waverley, shaking hands with them both. "We appreciate you bringing this to us."

"One more thing," said Lewis suddenly, as Waverley turned to go. He reached into his pocket. "Mr. Waverley, as you're here, I don't suppose I could give you my details, could I?" He offered him a business card. "I'm sure a successful company like this is often recruiting. If you find yourself with any positions you need to fill, please, give me a call. We can connect you with the best in the business."

Bemused, Waverley took the proffered card politely while Audrey barely had a chance to pick up her cleaning bag before Felix escorted them past the pucker-mouthed receptionist and out the street door into the cold. As the door swung shut behind them, Audrey could just make out Felix and Waverley through the glass, walking up the stairs together.

"What a smarmy git," said Lewis. "He's definitely going on the suspect list."

"I assume you mean Felix," she said. Daylight was starting to fade, and at the near end of the road, Sloane Square glittered with moving lights and the approach of rush hour. "I cannot believe he just fired me."

"He said it was only temporary. And you'll still get paid, right?"

She rubbed the bridge of her nose.

"No, Lewis." She took a deep breath and tried to stay calm. "I will not get paid. Independent contractors don't get paid if they don't work."

"Shit." She watched as the information sank in and his expression became dark. "That bastard!"

She almost laughed at how comforting she found his anger and felt some of her anxiety drain away.

"I did just tell them I found a crime scene, so I suppose it's not entirely unreasonable. And they didn't take the keys, so hopefully it won't be permanent."

"Good point, we might need those. If we can figure it all out quickly, they'll have no reason not to reinstate you. And if Celeste got you the job, she'll have the lowdown on Petrov. Plus, it'll cheer her up to have another mystery to think about."

"Cheer her up?"

"Yes. Haven't you noticed? She's not been herself lately."

Audrey was silent for a moment, remembering how many times in the last couple of months she'd asked Celeste if everything was all right. She mentally kicked herself.

"Of course I've noticed," she lied. "I'm just surprised *you* have. And what was all that with the business card? I didn't even know you had business cards."

"Let's just call it an alibi," he said, checking his watch. "It's past four. No point going back to the office now. Come on, let's head home. I'll carry that, if you like?"

He took her cleaning bag from her, and they walked back via King's Road, talking through possible motives for murder. Lewis was remarkably cheerful, considering the interview had been worse than a bust, but after the day she'd had, she definitely wasn't complaining.

He even bought her coffee on the way home.

13

Celeste

Celeste was reading quietly in the gallery nook when the doorbell rang, an electronic replication of the chimes that had rung in the big house when she was a child. Dixon, in the process of clearing away the afternoon tea things, looked up in surprise.

"It must be Lewis," said Celeste, as the sound faded away. "He's the only one who drops by unannounced."

The mantel clock had not long chimed half past four, and the vast space of the open-plan penthouse floor was growing dark. Dixon was halfway to the door when the bell rang again, and Celeste smiled as he muttered, "Definitely Lewis."

She pushed back her chair but stayed seated, ready to receive her visitor. Dixon reached the door and, after looking at the video camera, pushed the button on the intercom.

"Lewis *and* Audrey," he said, surprised.

Celeste heard the buzzer sound through the speaker. A minute later, Dixon opened the door just as the pair came clattering up. They entered the apartment, and what peace remained was shattered at once.

"But it's what lifts are for," complained Lewis, trying to get his breath back as they entered from the hall.

"It's two flights of stairs. You cannot be that unfit."

"You're denying the lift from fulfilling its one and only function. My fitness doesn't come into it."

"Hello to you too," said Dixon, folding his arms. Much to Celeste's amusement, they stopped bickering at once.

"Sorry," said Audrey, unbuttoning her coat and eyeing the teacups on the table beside Celeste's armchair. "Have we interrupted?"

"Not at all," said Celeste, waving them over to the dining table. "Dixon was just about to start preparing supper. Come and sit down."

Audrey sat on one of the velvet-cushioned chairs while Lewis draped his coat over the chair opposite before sitting. He glanced at Audrey. Whatever this was, it must be her story to tell.

"To what do I owe this unexpected pleasure?" asked Celeste as Dixon took a seat beside Lewis. "You look like you have news."

"Something happened at work today," began Audrey. "And we thought you might be interested to hear it. It's about the house in Beaton Gardens . . . "

Listening was a skill Celeste had learned well, and she watched as Audrey spoke, leaning across the table in her earnestness, gaze drifting to Dixon from time to time, including him in the tale. Celeste kept her reactions to a minimum, but even so, she was unable to keep from flinching when Audrey mentioned the body.

Lewis added a few interjections, adding certainty to the parts where Audrey seemed less sure—the blood spatter and the lack of interest shown by the police—but when she was done, Audrey sat back and looked anxiously from Celeste to Dixon, eyes flickering with fear. Fear of what she had found? *Surely not, Audrey, after everything you've been through.* Fear of not being believed?

There was silence for a moment, and Celeste was sure Dixon was running the same analysis she was.

"That is quite the puzzle," she said at last. "Could you describe the man in the chair?"

"I didn't get a long look, but he was white, with light brown hair. Kind of messy. Average height, maybe? Not tall, anyway, and a stocky build. His clothes were all dark. Looked about sixtyish."

Celeste allowed herself a sigh of relief.

"Do you know how they removed the body without you seeing?"

"No idea," said Audrey. "We went to speak to the people at Trinity on our way back, to ask if they had any security cameras, but they said they wouldn't share it. They, uh . . . got a bit funny about Lewis being there and . . . well, I sort of dropped your name, along with Mr. Petrov's. I hope you don't mind."

"Mind, dear?"

"Yes. I didn't want to put you in an awkward position with Mr. Waverley."

"I'm afraid I don't know this Waverley person at all, it's Anton that I know." Celeste smiled at Audrey's surprised expression. "I was a friend of his wife's, in point of fact, but she's gone now, and Anton and I keep in touch. Letters, mainly, and Christmas cards. We had dinner last time he was in London, and he was quite agitated because his cleaner had stopped winding his clocks. He asked if I knew of someone who could be trusted to be diligent, so, of course, I gave him your name."

"Oh. Well . . . thank you."

"He passed it on to Trinity, and I put you onto them. I'm sure he won't mind you grilling them. In fact, I'll call him myself. He'll be most aggrieved to hear what's happened. The property will need to be secured at once."

Audrey and Lewis looked at each other.

"You don't think he could be involved?" asked Lewis.

"Anton? Killing a man in his own house? I shouldn't think so."

"I don't suppose he has his own cameras installed?" asked Lewis. "At the house, I mean. Has he ever mentioned anything like that?"

"Not to me, dear, no," said Celeste, smiling. "He's rarely in town, so when we do meet, we tend to talk about old times, not home security. If I had to guess, though, I'd say Anton wouldn't scrimp on a thing like that. He does so love his antiques."

"Could you ask him? When you talk to him?" asked Audrey, then bit her lip. "You don't think it sounds . . . ?"

"Impossible?" Celeste finished for her. "Yes, and I'm absolutely thrilled for you."

Audrey blinked. "Pardon?"

"I'm delighted you two have found another case to work on. I have complete faith you'll get to the bottom of it."

For some reason, Audrey didn't seem to find these sentiments encouraging, but Lewis laughed.

"DS Larssen thought she was seeing things."

"That's not—" began Audrey.

"DS Larssen prefers to believe the evidence of her own eyes and ears," said Celeste. "I admire that. But while I'd be prepared to accept that Lewis, as our resident crime writer, might imagine a crime scene, that doesn't extend to you." She ignored Lewis's indignant huff. "If you saw a body in Anton Petrov's house, then there was a body in Anton Petrov's house. No question about it."

Audrey's eyes welled up, but she blinked and bit her lip hard enough to make her mouth flush red. She glanced across at Dixon, who nodded. While not always entirely truthful, Dixon was a fundamentally honest person, and as such, his opinion often mattered more than everyone else's.

"Have you told Mei?" asked Dixon. "What does she make of it?"

"She's not home yet," said Audrey, shifting in her seat. "I'll tell her as soon as I see her, though, assuming Sofia hasn't already." She muttered the last bit, and Celeste knew why. Mei Chen hadn't been supportive of her roommate's first murder investigation, and hearing this secondhand was bound to make matters worse. Celeste knew that Mei meant well, but there was a fine line between safe and stifled. Girls and their friends.

She took a deep breath, batting away memories that threatened to sink her into melancholy.

"It's a fascinating problem, isn't it?" she said. "How could a person remove a body from a house in broad daylight without being spotted? I'd have waited for cover of darkness, myself."

"You'd have to hide it on the premises in the meantime, though," added Dixon. "And why an upstairs room, instead of the ground floor? Making life hard for yourself."

"Good point," said Lewis. He turned to Audrey. "Maybe we can interview more of the neighbours."

"And the man in the residents' garden," added Audrey. "He was definitely suspicious."

"How marvellous," said Celeste, clapping her hands. "If there's anything Dixon or I can do to help, please let us know. What an exciting development."

Lewis nodded his agreement, but Audrey frowned.

"A man's dead. He could have family. Someone waiting for him to come home. It's not exciting, it's tragic."

"A circumstance can be both those things, my dear. There's no shame in acknowledging it." Dixon gave a discreet cough, and Celeste got to her feet. "Do let me know how you get on, won't you? I want regular updates."

"Of course," said Lewis, pulling his coat from the back of the chair. "I knew you'd be curious."

"And you were right." She ushered them towards the door. "How are the edits going, by the way?"

"Oh, fine, I think. Hard to tell at this point."

"And Audrey? Usual time tomorrow?"

"Eight thirty, sharp," said Audrey, giving a little salute.

"Wonderful."

They let themselves out, and Dixon and Celeste stood in the near-darkness of the hall, listening as the footsteps on the stairs faded into nothing. They looked at each other.

"A new investigation," said Celeste.

"Could be dangerous," replied Dixon. "If the killer saw Audrey. And she's lost a job because of it."

"Yes, poor thing. Still, I'm glad to see them communicating better."

"All that bickering?"

"But the looks between them, Dixon. They're starting to understand each other."

Her valet said no more but walked over to the picture window and stood gazing out into the gathering darkness. Celeste joined him, and as Dixon stared at the waning Snow Moon, already bright and rising above the indistinct lights of the skyline, Celeste looked down into the courtyard, where Lewis and Audrey were saying their goodbyes. Tendrils of mist were beginning to appear, and Roshan's immaculate lawn glistened, which, if the clear sky and drop in temperature were anything to go by, meant another frost was on the way. She watched as they parted, heading for opposite sides of the square, Lewis's ground-floor flat to the left of the big house, Audrey and Mei's first-floor maisonette to the right, their journeys illuminated by pools of orange light cast by the Victorian streetlamps.

"Will you go?" she asked, watching Audrey climb the steps up to Flat 7. The lights were already on.

"Aye," said Dixon.

"You should take the car. It's too cold to be out for long, and who knows how late it might be?"

"All right. I'll call the garage. Shall I get someone to come in?"

"No need to fuss, dear." She paused, glancing around the square before sitting down in her armchair. "Although perhaps if the Captain is free . . . He's good at theorising." She looked up at her valet. "I'll also see if I can get hold of Anton. I do hope he's not in any trouble."

Dixon's expression remained neutral.

"Petrov's no fool."

"No." Celeste sighed. "Certainly not."

"I'll start on supper," said Dixon, turning on the lamp closest to her chair. "Call if you need owt."

He returned to the kitchen, leaving Celeste alone in front of the now-black window, the outside world rendered invisible by the light from the lamp. She stared at nothing, her mind whirring against the reassuring clatter of Dixon in the kitchen.

It was a puzzle all right, a very satisfying one, and she could certainly use an interesting diversion to take her mind off things.

As long as it didn't get complicated.

14
Lewis

Back in his flat, Lewis changed quickly out of his work clothes and sat down in front of the computer, shivering in spite of the central heating and the thick hoodie he'd just thrown on. The cold air had hit him as he'd left Celeste's, waking him up and clearing his mind, and he wanted to knuckle down while the last of the caffeine hit worked its magic.

As usual, the only light in the room came from his computer and the warm glow from the square that shone into his tiny kitchen and spilled out onto the living-room floor. He never saw the point in turning the lights on. His furnishings were pretty basic, and everything he wanted to look at was on his computer anyway. Why waste electricity?

Instead of opening up his novel, Lewis opened a new document and began making notes on the afternoon's events, starting with Audrey's alleged time frame of events.

He paused, fingers hovering over the keys. Why had he thought "alleged" there?

It wasn't that he didn't believe what Audrey had said—he did. It was just that he had the distinct feeling things weren't as they'd seemed.

He typed.

Questions:

Who is the dead man? Why was he killed? And by whom?

Is it really possible to remove a body and clean up a crime scene in 15–20 minutes? If so, how?

Why an upstairs bedroom instead of the ground floor? Makes it much harder to remove the body.

Why didn't they deal with Audrey when she arrived? They'd already killed one person, why let her start cleaning? Did they see her and let her leave? Or did they return to the property by chance just after she left?

If they weren't there when she arrived, then how did they get into the property and out again without her seeing?

The neighbour hadn't seen or heard anything or anyone, which suggested the killer had stayed in the house. Had they been holed up with the body, watching him and Audrey the whole time? Or had they left the property by some other means?

He added to the document.

Tunnels? Check floor plans.

That would probably be easy. People on TV shows were always accessing building plans. Tunnels weren't likely, really, but people in Belgravia were always building underground. Car parks, swimming pools, home cinemas. He'd read an article about how homes in London were now plagued with structural issues and subsidence because of it.

If they were hiding, then where? Where did they stash the body?

Why that house? There must be hundreds of empty houses in London, most without a regular cleaner. Is Petrov involved? (Add to suspect list.)

Felix Casetti: He was very shifty about Audrey's start times and upset at the idea of the police being called. Worried about his professional reputation or something else? (Add to suspect list.)

If not Casetti, could someone else at Trinity be involved?

Why was Audrey suspended? Waverley seemed surprised by that decision. Was Casetti really trying to keep her safe, or did he want to stop her discovering something more?

He sighed. He knew it wasn't his fault Audrey had been suspended from Beaton Gardens, but he felt guilty anyway. She couldn't afford to lose any part of her income, and who knew how long it would take them to reinstate her? He shook his head to release the thought. Just another reason to solve this quickly.

What else?

Scruffy man in the residents' garden. Was he watching the house or just looking for somewhere to sleep? Could he have seen something? How to track him down?

Even if you're confident you can clean up a crime scene in 20 minutes, why wait until just before the cleaner is due to do so? The house is empty six and a half days a week. Why make life hard for yourself?

And the final question, the one he had been thinking over and over:

What if the police had taken 10 minutes to get there instead of 20?

A few minutes either way, and Audrey could have walked into a completely different situation, a thought that made him squirm inside. And if the police had been quicker, they would have found the remains of the crime scene themselves, and this whole investigation would be in their hands instead.

He didn't like that thought either.

He read the questions back and smiled. Another murder to investigate. How lucky could a guy get?

15

Audrey

"Of course I believe you," said Mei, throwing up her hands. "That's not the point!"

Mei had gotten home early again. Audrey had found her in the kitchen, leaning against the counter while typing furiously into her phone. Now they were sitting at the kitchen table, Mei still in her work clothes, facing off about what she was calling "another dangerous situation."

"Then what *is* the point?" asked Audrey. "The police didn't believe me. Even Sofia didn't, not really. But somewhere, there's a body waiting to be discovered, and I know where he was killed!"

"But why does it need to be more than that? When the body turns up, the police will be able to link the two things, and you don't need to get involved."

"Someone committed murder in my client's house—and cleaned it up right under my nose! They made a fool of me, and I lost my job because of it. I'm already involved."

"No, you're not." Mei reached across the table and took Audrey's hands in hers. "Don't you get it? They were prepared. They were professional. What do you think they'll do to you if you start poking around?"

"You think I don't know that?"

"Then why?"

"Because I have to know."

"Know what? Who he is? They might have dropped the body down a sewer or out at sea by now. You might never know!"

"How they did it."

"You said they cut his throat?"

"I mean, how they cleaned up the scene so fast."

Mei gaped at her for a moment, then pressed her forehead to the table and swore.

"What?" demanded Audrey.

Mei lifted her head again. "This is about *cleaning*? Are you out of your mind?" She punctuated the question with jabs of her hands. "Are you actually out of your actual mind?"

They stared at each other for a moment, then Audrey laughed.

"Yes," she said. "Possibly to both questions. It's mostly not about the cleaning, but it is a bit. You've no idea, Mei. The place was spotless. They'd removed virtually all trace in under twenty minutes. If I'd done that, I'd consider it a professional triumph. They made me look stupid. Crazy. I can't help it. I have to know how they did it."

"Give me strength." Mei massaged her temples. "I don't need this right now, Audrey. I do not need this."

"Why? Is that horrible client still giving you trouble?"

"The horrible client . . . has disappeared."

"'Disappeared' as in run off?"

"I don't know. Maybe. He didn't show up for this morning's meeting, and no one could get hold of him. His assistant didn't know where he was and said she hadn't heard from him since yesterday afternoon." Her fingertips moved from her temples to her brow, and now that Audrey was looking at her properly, she could see that the shadows under Mei's eyes had darkened.

"I thought you said he was going to get off."

"I said *he* was confident he'd get off. Maybe he's so sure of himself that he's gone away for the weekend, but we're due in court on Monday, so to miss the final briefing is a level of arrogance I just don't understand. Dominic was beside himself. All the cases he's taken to trial, and this has never happened before."

"What happens if the client's not back in time for the court hearing?"

"Depends. We'll talk to the Legal Adviser's Office tomorrow and try to get a contingency plan together. If we can find a mitigating circumstance for his absence, we can request an adjournment while we try and track him down. The alternative is that we file an application to proceed without him present, but the judge may just issue a warrant for his arrest. Whichever way you look at it, it doesn't look good."

"He might still show up, though?"

"That's what I'm hoping, but it's a massive distraction when we're supposed to be prepping for court, and in spite of everything, I didn't have him down as stupid. I spent the entire day trying to find him, calling all sorts of places, interrogating his assistant for every last detail of his life . . . Plenty of people would be happy to see him out of the way, but not before his trial. They'd lose any chance of reparation then. I just have this nagging fear that something untoward's happened to him."

Audrey's mind started racing.

"Maybe it has," she said slowly. "What does he look like?"

Mei got the inference at once and narrowed her eyes.

"That is definitely putting two and two together and making five, Auds. I meant more like an accident or a family situation, not getting his throat slit by a professional killer in a house owned by a mysterious Russian."

"He's not mysterious, he's a friend of Celeste's. Humour me. Please."

"You're ridiculous." Mei sighed. "Fine. Middle-aged. Medium height, medium build, bit of a stomach. Blond hair and dark brown eyes."

"What kind of blond?" asked Audrey. Dark blond could look light brown in the right light. And with blood on the floor to distract you . . . "Dark or light?"

"Blond! You know, yellow. Straight. Smoothed over in a preppy way. Thinning a bit."

"Ah, right." Audrey relaxed, half-disappointed. "Yeah, this guy wasn't thinning. His hair was a bit shaggy."

"Glad we cleared that up. Is the Russian really a friend of Celeste's?"

"Yep."

"I hope it wasn't him in the chair."

"There was a picture in the office. Didn't look like him."

Mei nodded, then caught herself and frowned, burying her face in her hands.

"I can't believe this is happening again. Remember six months ago, when life was simple?"

Audrey gave a weak smile. Mei's life might have been simple, but hers had been anything but. Trying to make ends meet on a cleaner's wage, with her rent supplemented by her landlady's generosity and a hefty overdraft. And that was just the shameful background noise to the daily stress of trying to fit in as many clients as possible within the hours they'd let her into their homes.

"Not really," she said and stood up, ignoring Mei's look of surprise. "It's past seven. We should eat. You okay with soup? I can't be bothered to cook now."

"Yes, of course. Sorry, I didn't realise the time. I didn't mean to leave it for you."

She'd rattled her friend, Audrey realised, and no wonder. She'd spent the last four years avoiding excitement, partly out of fear and partly because she was broke, telling everyone, including herself, that she liked a quiet life. It was easier than telling the truth, especially to Mei, who never hesitated to cover Audrey's share whenever she so much as hinted at financial difficulties. She could hardly blame Mei for believing her when she'd downplayed her money troubles for so long.

"I know," she said, smiling for real this time. "I don't mind. You go and put your feet up. Stick the *Tarzan* soundtrack on or something. Relax."

"Sure?"

"I'm sure."

With a last concerned look at her friend, Mei left the room, and Audrey went to open a can of soup.

Once it was on the stove, she opened the Notes app on her phone, where she'd written up everything she could remember about the afternoon's events. That was something she'd learned from Lewis, and she had to admit, it was useful.

She stirred the soup with one hand and typed with the other, hoping she hadn't missed anything. She scrolled up, reading back what she'd written earlier.

> White male, average height, stocky build. Sixtyish. Sandy brown hair, bit scruffy, clean-shaven. Long-sleeved black T-shirt, black trousers, black shoes.

She sighed. She couldn't have written a more generic description if she'd tried. The clothing bothered her, for some reason, but she couldn't put her finger on why. It hadn't seemed natural somehow, more like a uniform. But she'd been so busy looking at the blood and the body that she hadn't fully registered much else, and being flooded with the adrenaline of terror hadn't helped either.

The soup began to bubble, so she put down her phone. No more talk of murder this evening, or the killer who could even now be looking for her—just dinner with Mei and something trashy on TV.

Everything else could wait until tomorrow.

16
Lewis

Lewis stared at the computer screen, a bowl of instant noodles cooling on the desk beside him. His agent's notes had made perfect sense last night, but this evening he couldn't make head nor tail of them.

He read the highlighted passage again, but to no avail. He sighed, reached for the bowl, and turned his chair away from the screen.

He glared at the darkened room. Why couldn't he focus?

The meeting with Celeste was swimming across his mind. Something had been said that had raised a flag with him, but whatever it was, he'd lost it in the general flow of conversation. That was the problem with Audrey's way of dealing with people, there was always so much chaff.

He forked lukewarm noodles into his mouth, barely tasting them as he replayed the interview. Was it about the cameras? No, Celeste hadn't known anything about that. But she did say Petrov was unlikely to have scrimped on security. Then she said something about removing the body in broad daylight, and Dixon had agreed.

Yes, that was it. As a rich man with valuable possessions, Petrov would invest in his security, but Beaton Gardens was entirely populated by rich people. Richer than Lewis could imagine, probably. And those people wouldn't hold back on security either.

They knew the body hadn't gone out the front door, because Audrey was watching the entire time, and the neighbour had said there was no way out the back, except to other houses, which would run the risk of being picked up on other security measures from the other properties. Even if they'd somehow hacked into Petrov's system, they'd have then had to hack into the many different systems in use in the vicinity, which was an awful lot of trouble to go to when you could just arrange to commit your crime somewhere else. And even if you managed to pull that off, it surely wasn't possible for anyone to ensure that the entire population of Beaton Gardens, including staff and passersby, was absent during the time in question.

He spun back to the computer, shoving the now-empty bowl to one side, and started searching for a satellite view of Beaton Gardens. He zoomed in and out, scanning the road and the one behind from every angle, walking up and down virtual streets until his vision blurred. He couldn't see any way through to the back gardens from the street, apart from through one of the houses.

Whichever way he tried, he couldn't get round it. There were too many variables. Too many chances. If you'd gone to all the trouble of planning the perfect execution to an almost unfathomable degree, would you leave your exit plan to chance?

No.

He didn't know how and he didn't know where, but Celeste was right: The body had been in the house or else close by the whole time. It had to have been. The perpetrators were waiting for darkness to take it out.

He checked his watch. Ten to eight. Eight was practically still daytime in the city, in terms of people coming home and going out, plus the businesses that operated all hours of the day and night. If you were waiting for both dark and quiet, you'd need to wait until the small hours, unless you were particularly clever.

Which they clearly were.

They'd need a van, most likely, and how late could a van show up on a quiet street in Belgravia without raising eyebrows? No later than ten, surely?

Heart pumping, he grabbed his phone and typed a message to Audrey before running into his bedroom to get changed. When he returned, dressed in his warmest, darkest clothing, he saw five messages from Audrey stacked up on his screen.

> **THE CLEANER:**
> Stakeout?? What for?
> They won't come back to finish cleaning tonight. You need full daylight for a proper inspection. Besides, it's literally 0 degrees.
> Seriously, we're not doing this.
> You'd better not be putting your coat on. I am NOT going on a stakeout!
> LEWIS!!!

He swiped the messages away and shoved the phone in his pocket, pulling on his coat and adding a hat and gloves for good measure. She was right about one thing.

It was freezing out there.

17
Audrey

"I can't feel my feet," said Audrey, shuffling back and forth on the pavement. The cold had long since penetrated her new warm coat, and no matter how tightly she squeezed her arms to her sides, she couldn't generate any more heat.

"I can't feel my face," said Mei into her ear.

They'd taken turns circling the block that made up the west side of Beaton Gardens, looking for any potential points of exit near or behind the Petrov residence. There didn't seem to be any way of accessing the gardens except through the house, but that didn't preclude the killers taking the body from one garden to another and exiting through a different property. They'd set up a group call and separated, Lewis taking a corner at the rear of the block; Mei the same view, but from the front; and Audrey the diagonally opposite corner closest to number thirty-five. They'd been standing about for almost two hours.

"How many more times are you going to tell me you're cold?" Lewis huffed down his phone. "It's a cold night, and we're all cold. I think we've made that clear."

He was standing on the junction of Lyon Street and Beaton Place, staking out the houses that backed onto Mr. Petrov's as well as the properties on the west side of the block, and Audrey could hear a regular stream of traffic in the background. In contrast, she stood in relative quiet beside the garden railings on Beaton Terrace, a quiet road that ran from north to south along the eastern side, bordering the private garden in the middle. A thick hedge grew into the railings around the park with shrubbery behind, and a tree overhung the path just enough to add to the density of the shadows, allowing her to stand and watch two points of approach while shrouded in darkness.

"I'm not cold, Lewis, I'm frozen to the bone," said Mei, her chattering teeth audible through their earpieces. "How much longer do we have to stand here?"

When he'd turned up on the doorstep, dressed like a burglar in head-to-toe black, Lewis had made such a big deal about needing more eyes that Mei had insisted on coming, too, although Audrey suspected that was more to do with keeping an eye on her than helping out with the case.

"I don't know, do I?" he said, sounding petulant. "I said before we left that we might already be too late. But there're still too many people about, at least at this end. I wouldn't bring the body out this way. Not yet. What about your side?"

"Traffic's been quiet on Beaton Terrace," said Audrey, looking up and down the darkened road. "Plenty of pedestrians, though. Some cabs have cut through the square without stopping, but only two people have gone inside a property. They went into number twenty-seven."

"Any lights on anywhere else?"

Audrey leaned around the railings to look down the road and saw Mei's white pom-pom hat do the same at the far end. Streetlights reflected off stuccoed façades and darkened glass, and the empty parking bays in the road glistened with the beginnings of frost.

"Twenty-eight and thirty-four this side," said Audrey.

"Thirty-nine, forty-one, and forty-six this side," said Mei. "Although I think thirty-nine might be automatic timers, because they all came on at the same time."

"Ten o'clock on a Thursday night," said Lewis. "The quietest place is going to be the front of the house. Every other angle, there'll be passersby and traffic, but you need to be a millionaire just to know someone here. They'll come out the front, I know it."

"How can you be sure?" said Audrey, her breath clouding in front of her. "We really did check everywhere."

"We thought we did," he said into her ear. "But like Celeste said, rich people don't cut back on security, and the killer or killers couldn't be sure there wasn't anyone around to see them taking the body out of the house. In daytime, that could be the postman, delivery drivers, traffic wardens, cleaners . . . This had to have been the plan: Kill him in the day, remove him at night. It's just a matter of time."

"This is stupid," said Mei. "If you're right, we could be stuck out here for hours before we see anything. If we ever do. And even if we do see something, what then? Do we perform a citizen's arrest or just watch them get away?"

"At least we'll have a description and a license plate for the police," said Audrey, as peacekeeper-in-chief. Mei and Lewis had a fractious relationship at the best of times.

"Assuming we're not dead of hypothermia by then."

Mei fell silent. The sound of traffic remained steady on Lewis's end of the call, the microphone on his Bluetooth earbuds picking up every noise around him. Audrey's own earphones were old and had a microphone on the wire, shielding her comms from the worst of the external noise by being tucked into a fold of her scarf.

Time ticked on, painfully slowly. Audrey walked up and down the pavement beside the garden, keeping to the shadows in the hope that the occupants of the houses opposite wouldn't call the police about the young woman skulking about. There were a couple of cars parked on the street outside, and the shadows inside and between them moved at the edge of her vision, making her twitchy. More than once, she thought she heard something move in the garden behind her and turned, trying to see through the shrubbery to the shrouded space beyond, but there was nothing. Nothing but mist and darkness and the secrets of the very rich.

And foxes. In London, there were always foxes.

She looked up at the terrace, the houses white, and austere, with at least two more floors than the modest-in-comparison Petrov property. Some of them had multiple doorbells, where they'd been converted into flats, and it was these where most of the lights were on. An ocean of sash windows, all overlooking Beaton Gardens; she wondered what the residents would see if they were looking. The view must be pretty good from up there.

The garden railings sparkled with delicate white crystals, and a spider's web, strung between an iron finial and one of the overhanging branches, shivered as dew turned to ice. The urgent wail of a siren cut through the night, and blue lights flashed across the junction two streets down.

"Police?" asked Lewis, in her ear.

"Ambulance," she replied, stamping her feet. She wasn't going to say it again, but, dear Lord, she was cold. Mei might have been right about the hypothermia.

By the time the bells of St. Peter's chimed eleven, Audrey's feet were somehow aching *and* numb.

"If something doesn't happen soon," she grumbled into her microphone, "I'm going to climb the railings into the garden and find a bench. My feet are killing me."

"I'm sitting on a wall," said Lewis. "But I don't think I'll ever be warm again."

"What happened to not complaining about being cold?" said Mei, sounding almost cheerful.

"Wish I had a wall," said Audrey, peering around the corner again. She watched a white van drive past the opposite corner. "Hey, why can't I hear any traffic at your end, Mei?"

"Oh, um, I keep muting myself. Keeping the line clear."

Audrey drew breath.

"You're almost as bad a liar as Lewis. Where the hell are you?"

"I'm on the corner!" said Mei at once. "I'm still at my post."

There was a scraping sound and then an *ooof* from Lewis, presumably as he clambered off his perch. Audrey heard footsteps, and the sound of moving vehicles intensified, as if he'd gone closer to the road.

"I can't see you," said Lewis. "I could see you before, in your silly hat. All I can see is a parked car."

"Well, I'm here," retorted Mei. "And I can see you. You're standing on the traffic island."

"What colour is the car, Lewis?" asked Audrey through gritted teeth, and she heard a little gasp from Mei.

"Black," said Lewis. "Why?"

"Mei Chen, are you sitting in a taxi?"

"Um . . . no?"

"You bloody are, aren't you? For how long?"

"Just half an hour or so. It was trundling past, and I sort of hailed it without thinking. I was so *cold*. I was just going to warm up a bit, but then me and Clayton got talking."

"Who's Clayton?" asked Lewis.

"The taxi driver. He's a friend of Philip and Mekhala's, if you can believe it. He was interested in what we were doing."

The heat of her outrage warmed Audrey. In the freezing air, her breath resembled smoke.

"You *told* him?"

"Well, I wasn't just going to sit here in silence, was I?"

"Of course not," snapped Audrey. "That would be weird."

"Sarcasm does not become you, Audrey," said Mei, attempting to sound dignified before adding, pathetically, "I was so cold."

"To be fair, I might have done that if I'd thought of it," said Lewis, with grudging admiration. "But you might have said."

A male voice in the background said something.

"A private-hire vehicle just turned into Beaton Gardens," said Mei, abruptly. "Heading towards you, Auds."

Stiff with cold, Audrey ducked down and crept forward, peering around the corner. A big black car with a taxi license plate was driving slowly down the road.

"It's pulling in," she said, watching as it crawled under a streetlamp and drew to a near-silent halt in the darkness outside thirty-four. "One of those big people carriers, like a van. It's parked outside thirty-four, where there's no light."

"On my way," said Lewis, and she heard him moving. "Don't take your eyes off it. And make sure you get the plate number."

"Someone's getting out," she said, hauling herself up by the ice-cold railings for a better view. "Dressed in black. They have a suitcase!"

"Where are they going?" he asked, words punctuated by the sound of heavy footsteps striking the pavement. He was running. "Which number?"

"Thirty-five," she said. "They've gone into thirty-five."

18

Lewis

Lewis ran from the junction straight up to the east corner of Beaton Gardens, where Mei was standing on the pavement between a black cab and the garden railings. The driver's side window was open and a young Black man wearing a red beanie and a padded jacket leaned out towards him.

"Clayton, I presume?" said Lewis, trying to get his breath back, and the cabbie grinned.

"You must be Lewis. I've heard a lot about you."

Lewis looked suspiciously at Mei, who waved a gloved hand at him.

"Stakeouts are boring," she said, dismissively, looking towards number thirty-five. "Until something happens."

Lewis stood behind her, stretching his neck to see over her stupid hat. The minivan was parked as Audrey had described, in the darkest point between two streetlamps, just outside number thirty-four.

"You could get a body in there, easily," he said, then looked up at the house, searching for signs of movement within. "I can't see anything happening inside."

"The downstairs windows have the blinds down," said Audrey, half-whispering into her microphone. "But none of the upstairs curtains are drawn."

"I can't see the ground floor at all," said Mei.

"Too many pillars," agreed Lewis.

"Wait, are you lot serious?" said Clayton, from inside the cab. "I thought you were having a joke with me. Spying on a boyfriend or something."

Lewis ignored him, keeping his eyes trained on the upper floors. He should have taken the long way round and joined Audrey on her corner. This one was too far away to see anything much.

"I'm gay," said Mei, without turning around. "But for future reference, Clayton, stalking is a criminal offence, and you shouldn't facilitate it for anyone, even women."

"There's a red light inside," said Audrey, her voice breathless on the other end of the phone. "First floor. I just saw it flash."

"'Flash' as in signalling?" asked Mei.

"I don't think so, it was moving. Just for a split second, and then it was gone."

"The stairs," said Lewis. "They're taking it down the stairs."

Given how cold he was, he was surprised to find a shiver could still run down his spine, but he gripped the frozen railings in anticipation. Any minute now.

"Something just moved in the hall," said Audrey. "The light changed behind the glass."

"Make sure you're out of sight," said Lewis, then turned and scowled at the giant pom-pom on Mei's hat, which could surely be seen from space. "Did you deliberately pick the most conspicuous hat you had?"

"The door's opening!" hissed Audrey, and he and Mei jostled for position by the railings, trying to see without being seen.

Lewis held his breath as two shadowy figures appeared beneath the portico of number thirty-five, dressed in dark coats and hats. The ornate glass lantern overhead remained dark, but the light from the street was just enough that they could make out something large and black standing between the two silhouettes.

"Only one person went in," breathed Mei.

"And two came out," he finished. He heard Audrey's shuddering gasp down the phone. "The killer was in there the whole time."

The smaller figure moved quickly and quietly down the front steps. Through the darkness, they heard the sound of a metal door sliding open. The other figure picked up the large, dark object by its handle and, with visible strain, hauled it down towards the vehicle.

"What is it?" whispered Audrey. "I can't see past the van."

"Suitcase," said Lewis. "Big. Heavy."

He didn't need to explain any further. They all knew what was in it.

They heard the van door close again, and the smaller figure went around to the driver's side of the vehicle and got in. The engine started, a soft purr that was barely audible over the traffic in the surrounding streets. The rear lights shone brightly, and the van reversed, readying to pull away from the curb.

Another vehicle hummed to life behind them.

"Get in," called a voice from the cab. Lewis and Mei turned at the same time and saw Clayton beckoning them. "Quick. We'll follow them."

Without thinking, Lewis wrenched open the cab door and piled in behind Mei. As the minivan drove off, the cab edged forward, and Lewis pulled down the folding seat nearest to the left-hand window.

"Stop at the next corner," said Mei. "For Audrey."

The van turned at the end of the road, heading down towards the crossroads, and Clayton turned the cab sharply onto Beaton Gardens and sped down the street after it, pulling up hard at the corner, where Audrey was nowhere to be seen. Lewis flung open the door and shouted.

"Audrey! Get in!"

She popped up from behind a parked car and ran over to the cab, leaping inside and falling onto the seat beside Mei. Clayton was moving off before Lewis had even shut the door, turning left after the van and following it down the one-way street towards the junction, where the traffic lights were on red.

The van drew to a halt at the lights, and they scrambled around inside the cab to get a better view.

The surrounding roads were still busy in spite of the hour. Taxis, vans, town cars, and lorries vied for space, their lights blinding, horns deafening. Scooters wove in and out of the traffic, stationary once again at the next set of lights, while Audrey, Mei, and Lewis sat in the cab, leaning as far forward as they could to keep the van in sight.

Another cab crossed lanes in front of them, turning tightly into the gap between them and the minivan. Then the lights changed again, and the van went on over two more junctions before stopping again beside the looming old walls of Buckingham Palace Mews.

"I'm already lost," said Audrey. "Where are they heading?"

"Victoria at the moment," said Clayton, through the speaker plate close to Lewis's ear.

The van joined an even busier road, narrowed by roadworks and flanked by cones, and the second taxi turned right while they followed the van left onto Victoria Street. Suddenly, keeping it in view became difficult as taxis and buses merged in and out of the traffic, and as they neared Victoria Station, Lewis began to panic.

"I can't see them," he said. "Where did they go?"

"Three in front," said Clayton, running through the next junction on yellow, bumper practically touching the bus in front. "That was a bit close."

"We're going to lose them." Lewis craned his neck to see past the bus.

"No, we won't," said Clayton.

"For crying out loud, stop moving about, Lewis," snapped Mei. "You're blocking my view."

The bus pulled in at the next stop, and Clayton closed the gap immediately, leaving just two vehicles between them and the minivan. Another taxi tried to squeeze between them, but Clayton tightened the gap even further, waving an apology as the driver leaned on his horn.

"That's my reputation shot," he muttered as the taxi merged in behind, beeping again.

"It's an emergency," said Audrey. "Sorry, though."

"S'all right. This is the most exciting thing to happen to me in weeks."

"Wish I could say the same. I'm Audrey, by the way. Thanks for doing this."

"No problem."

They followed the van, still two vehicles ahead, past Westminster Abbey and onto Parliament Square, where the traffic moved slowly but steadily until they came to yet another halt next to Big Ben.

"They don't seem to be in a rush, do they?" observed Lewis. "They could have gone through on yellow."

"Don't wanna draw attention," said Clayton knowingly.

The lights changed again, and they followed the van away from the Houses of Parliament onto Victoria Embankment, where, across the river, the London Eye lit up the sky, its coloured lights reflected in the Thames.

"Where the hell are they going?" asked Mei.

"Less likely to be noticed if they stick to the busier areas?" suggested Lewis.

"We all assumed they'd be heading for the river, right?" said Audrey. "Maybe they have other ideas."

On they went, past Cleopatra's Needle and Somerset House, through the Blackfriars underpass and into the city itself. The streets became darker as they moved inwards and away from the river, travelling beneath bridges and between office blocks, through areas less populated by nighttime revellers. Soon the cars between them and the minivan had turned away, and Clayton dropped back, allowing other vehicles to separate them whenever he could.

"Maybe they've spotted us," said Lewis, as they turned onto Tower Hill. "And now they're taking us for a ride."

"You'd have to be really observant to notice it was the same black cab this whole way," said Audrey.

"Lucky I flagged one down, you mean," said Mei, and even in the darkness of the cab, Lewis thought he could see Audrey narrowing her eyes.

The Tower of London came into view on their left, lit from below and glowing against the black sky. Lewis couldn't remember the last time he'd been out this far east.

"What is this, the tourist's guide to body dumping?" said Mei as they passed the walls. "This is crazy."

But the van carried on, driving up Tower Hill and turning left at the Tower Bridge junction, heading who knew where. Lewis didn't know this area of London and felt unsettled at leaving familiar territory, even in pursuit of a dead body.

Their quarry turned right onto a street lined with tall, glass-fronted buildings, then right again. There was now just a single vehicle between them and the van, and Lewis wondered how long they could keep this up before the van's occupants realised they were being followed.

"What's goin' on now?" said Clayton as the Tower came back into view. "They changed their minds?"

Lewis held onto the door handle, bracing himself against the back of the seat as he tried to keep the van in sight.

It headed on towards Tower Bridge but at the last minute indicated left, and instead of joining the line of traffic for the bridge, veered off down a side street. Flanked by the bridge's stone foundations on one side and a vast red-brick warehouse conversion on the other, the street was quiet but well lit by the lamps on the deck of the bridge above.

"Shit," said Clayton, following them in. "They're bound to spot us now."

The minivan slowed to go over a speed bump, and so the cab did, too, its speed falling well below the twenty-mile-an-hour limit the signs dictated.

"Pull in here," said Lewis, pointing at a loading bay on the left. "If they spot us, we can pretend we're passengers getting out."

Clayton pulled in. They sat, watching as the van crawled down the road ahead, the interior of the cab dark around them.

"They're bloody stopping," said Clayton, his voice muffled by the plexiglass. "Under the bridge."

The minivan waited at the end of the road, brake lights glowing red, partially obscured by a closed-up burger stand that stood beside the steps to the bridge. No one got out. Clayton turned off the engine, but not before opening his window.

"What are they doing?" asked Audrey. "It is the same van, right?"

Then the passenger door opened, and they watched as the man—and somehow Lewis knew it *was* a man—got out and went round to the door on the opposite side of the van.

They heard the faint sound of the van's side door sliding open again.

"Dammit, we can't see," said Lewis, envying Clayton his open window. "What's happening?"

"Van's blocking the view," said Clayton, shaking his head. "I can't see nothin' either."

The viewing platform at the foot of the bridge was empty and, in spite of the streetlights, shrouded in a strange, murky gloom. With the bulk of the van in the way, there was no knowing where the man had gone or what he was doing.

Traffic rumbled overhead, and the sound of horns punctuated the night with erratic regularity. Then, somewhere, a church clock began to strike midnight.

As the last toll of the bell died away, a figure emerged from the gloom beneath the bridge.

Lewis watched, heart pounding, as the man returned to the van, which began to pull away.

"Get down!" commanded Clayton, and the three of them instantly dropped to the floor, headlights sweeping across the cab's interior as the van passed up the road, going back the way they'd come.

The second the van was out of sight, Lewis wrenched open the cab door and ran down the road to the bridge, his feet sliding on icy cobbles, heading for the viewing platform. There wasn't a soul about, not even a rough sleeper taking shelter beneath the arches. He leaned on the platform's railings and looked down into the black waters slapping noisily against the supporting stonework of the bridge, then up and around, searching for cameras. This was a tourist spot, right? There had to be security cameras.

But the camera fixed to the bridge was angled backwards, pointing inside the pedestrian tunnel, and the cameras outside the darkened coffee shop were pointing straight down, covering the outside seating area. Lewis went over to the jetty, where tourist boat trips launched in the summer, and looked out at the river, lights bouncing on the surface as the currents disturbed the reflections. He went side to side and up and down the quay, searching for something—anything—that could have picked up the man or the van.

There was nothing. Not a single camera covering that corner of the quay.

They'd dumped the body at Tower Bridge, and no one had seen a thing.

19
Audrey

They stood in the shadows below the bridge, all four peering over the wall separating them from the water. No one had spoken for a full minute, and the only sound, beyond the traffic above, was the splashing of the dark water below.

"They can't have," said Mei at last. "No one would dump a body at Tower Bridge."

"I'd like to agree with you," said Lewis, sounding pained. One thing Lewis never lacked was conviction, no matter how misplaced, but he seemed genuinely unsettled. "What else could it have been? Why pick up the body and drive all the way out here if not to dump it?"

Audrey said nothing. Someone had gone to a lot of trouble to collect a large, heavy-looking suitcase from the murder scene, and Tower Bridge was the place they'd chosen to take it. London was full of rivers, not to mention canals; they could have dumped it anywhere. Darker, quieter, more obscure places. Why pick somewhere that was not only exposed but a genuine tourist hotspot, albeit in daylight and better weather?

She looked over at Lewis and found he was already watching her, waiting for her to speak.

"The tide," she said, grasping the thought as it swirled past with all the other possibilities. "The water looks pretty high, but the depths vary, don't they?"

"I don't know," he said slowly. He took out his phone, and the screen lit up his face, eerie in the darkness.

Mei and Audrey gazed upward. The spectacle of Tower Bridge, its lights dancing merrily on the black water, was at odds with the suitcase they imagined had been dropped into the depths at its feet.

"This would be the last place I'd pick," said Mei. "It's not even that dark, with all the bridge lights."

"They're pointing upwards though," said Lewis, still looking at his phone. "Creates more shadow. According to this website, it'll be high tide in half an hour. But get this: Tower Bridge seems to be one of the deepest points you can access from land in central London without having to go out to the middle of a bridge, and it gets really, really deep only a few metres out. The currents could already be washing the suitcase downriver. In forty-eight hours, it could be miles away."

There was something approaching awe in his voice, and Audrey shuddered at his ghoulishness.

"Sounds like they knew what they was doing," said Clayton, also sounding impressed. "I've lived here my whole life, and I wouldn't know where to dump a body, would you?"

"Lewis would," said Audrey and Mei at the same time, and Lewis grinned, no doubt taking it as a compliment.

"Do you think they've done it before?" asked Audrey, and the thought seemed horribly plausible on the deserted quay. "Come here, I mean. With a body."

Now they all looked up at the towers of the bridge, which loomed as if part of a sinister fairy tale.

"It's possible," said Lewis, after a moment. "Hard to know where a body goes into the Thames, though. Only where it's pulled out."

"Nahhh," said Clayton after a moment's consideration. "There'd be people sleeping under them arches, normally, and tourists are out at all hours too. They musta known it was quiet as the grave down here tonight. No pun intended."

Audrey saw Mei's white-gloved hand cover a yawn and realised she must be exhausted. Mei was a classic early bird and usually in bed by ten on a weeknight.

"We should head back," said Audrey. "We've all got work tomorrow."

"No arguments from me," said Mei, yawning again. "Clayton, any chance you can drop us back? On the meter, of course."

"Or else Tower Hill station for the night bus," added Audrey. "If you want to get on home."

"I'll run you back, no problem," he said, as they walked back to where the cab was parked. "I'm a bit wired now."

They all got inside, and a few seconds later the cab purred to life. Lewis sat back on the folding seat, awkwardly trying not to tangle his legs up with Mei's, sitting opposite.

"Sit here," said Audrey, sliding along the back seat towards Mei to make room for Lewis on her other side. "Plenty of room."

He looked embarrassed as he stumbled across the floor of the moving cab to squeeze in beside her. "Thanks. Legs too long."

"Or bum too big," mumbled Mei sleepily into Audrey's shoulder, then giggled when Audrey shushed her.

But for once, Lewis didn't react to Mei's jibing, leaning against the cab window and staring out at the city. Within minutes, Mei was asleep, and when Clayton started making conversation, it was up to Audrey to respond. Like most people, he seemed surprised that a cleaner lived in Chelsea and, also like most people, assumed she must be subletting from Mei. Unlike most people though, he didn't make her feel bad about it.

"I've got regulars who live in Marchfield Square, I was telling your friend earlier."

"I know, I saw you the other day," said Audrey. "The Hetheringtons."

"That's right." He nodded at her in the rear-view mirror as they drove back along the Embankment. "Nice place, seems like. Safe area and living with yer best mate . . . I'd be well chuffed. It's no joke rentin' right now. My mum's had to move three times in the last four years 'cause of landlords sellin' up. Now she's in some mouldy old place in Tottenham with my little brother, who has to go to the asthma clinic every month. Bloody nightmare."

Audrey had always been grateful for Celeste's generosity, but felt even more so when she heard how bad things had gotten for other renters over the last few years.

"That's terrible. How old is he?"

"Fourteen. He's had to change schools twice an' all. I do what I can to help, but I only just passed the Knowledge and had to pay for the cab, so I'm a bit behind myself, you know what I mean?"

"Yeah, I do." She really did. "Is it hard, doing the Knowledge? I read that it's the most difficult test in the world."

"Too right!" Clayton laughed. "Do you know how many streets we need to memorise in Inner London? Twenty-five thousand. And you have to know pubs, hotels, churches . . . There's a system, though, to learnin' it all. And loads of tests. That's why London cabbies are the best."

"You're not wrong there."

The roads were clearer now, so they stuck close to the river, following the Embankment back to Big Ben and then on past Westminster Abbey and along Millbank. Audrey was unable to take her eyes off the water, wondering what else lurked in its depths. How many bodies were drifting along in its currents, just waiting to be discovered?

In no time at all, they were outside the Royal Chelsea Hospital, heading towards the Physic Garden and Pickering Lane.

"Here all right?" he asked, pulling in beside the side gate to the square.

"Perfect," said Audrey, shaking Mei awake. "Thanks, Clayton, you've gone above and beyond tonight."

"Couldn't leave you all out in the cold, could I?"

Registering they were home, Lewis sat up and turned away from the window.

"What's the damage?" asked Mei, stifling another yawn with one hand while peering at the meter.

"I'll chip in," said Lewis at once.

"Me too," said Audrey, but Mei waved their offers away.

"I hailed the cab," she said, tapping her card against the machine. "Worth twice the money just to stay warm, and we weren't on the meter going out to Tower Bridge."

Clayton grinned at them from the front seat.

"Well, I've never followed anyone to a Mafia body drop before. Call it a life experience."

"Mafia?" Audrey couldn't hide her alarm. "Why do you think that?"

Clayton shrugged as best he could while twisted round in his seat.

"Dunno. Just seemed a bit casual, didn't it? Professional. Like they did it all the time."

"I think that's just in the movies," said Mei, although she didn't sound sure.

"Well, if you need anyone else tailed, give me a shout." He dropped a business card into the payment tray. "And stay safe, yeah?"

"We'll try," said Lewis, sounding cheerfully noncommittal, and opened the door to a rush of freezing air. "Cheers, mate, you're a legend."

"*Mate?*" repeated Audrey, climbing out after him and pulling her coat tight. "Since when do you say 'mate'?"

"Don't forget 'legend,'" said Mei as she slammed the door. "He definitely just said 'legend.'"

"You're both hilarious," said Lewis, breath hanging in a white cloud in front of him. "Ha bloody ha."

They watched as the cab disappeared down the road, the tarmac sparkling with frost beneath the streetlights, then Audrey swiped the entry post with her key fob.

"So what do we do now?" she asked as the metal gate clanged shut behind them. "Back to the police?"

"Definitely," said Mei, hugging herself to stay warm. "I'll give Sofia a call first thing. Hopefully they can get that suitcase out pronto, or who knows where it'll end up?"

Lewis nodded, although he looked unhappy about it.

"As long as it's still there. You'd be surprised how quickly bodies can disappear in water."

On that last worrying note, they went their separate ways, slipping and sliding across the icy flagstones to the warmth and safety of home.

20
Lewis

Tower Bridge.

Tower fucking Bridge.

He couldn't believe the audacity of it. The supreme confidence of it. Folding a dead body into a suitcase and driving it all the way to London's most iconic bridge and just dropping it into the water.

Lewis had to agree with Clayton that the entire operation had seemed as if it were just business as usual to the persons involved. And it was all done so quickly, in the shadows beneath the bridge, that someone could have been stood right next to the railings and not noticed anything but a splash until it was too late.

Given the darkness of the hour and the constant movement in and out of streetlights and shadow, he couldn't picture the two men at all and was only confident one of them *had* been a man. The passenger had been taller than the driver, with broader shoulders, but the impression could have been down to the way he handled the suitcase rather than a distinct physical attribute. That was the thing about winter clothing—it made it very difficult to determine what a person might be like underneath.

He admired them, that was the truth of it. Admired them and was annoyed by them. To clean up a crime scene in under twenty minutes was impressive, and to do it when you knew a witness was standing outside the property with the police on the way was pretty bloody ballsy. But the way they'd dumped the body was just plain *cheeky*.

What was currently causing him agitation, however, was that if he were to write that into one of his books, no one would believe it.

When he tried to get inside the mind of a criminal, he usually ended up with one of two options: someone who didn't want to be caught or someone who didn't care about being caught. The former was meticulous in their planning, going to great lengths to cover up all evidence of their involvement, if not the crime itself. The latter, however, was reckless. They either knew they could get away with it or were willing to pay the price. These guys seemed to be an unnerving mix of the two, and Lewis just didn't know which character box to put them in.

He hated it when people wouldn't fit into boxes.

He walked past his computer, in darkness on his desk. It was nearly one in the morning, so he definitely should not start writing, even though his fingers twitched to record the events of the evening. He went to get a glass of water and looked out of the kitchen window as he ran the tap. The square was dark and quiet, the limited light from the lamps making the frost look like snow. As he gulped down the water, he noticed a light still on in Celeste's apartment and idly wondered what was keeping her up so late, although, of course, it could be Dixon. Lewis liked Dixon. He didn't say much, but when he did, he said what he meant, an attribute Lewis appreciated. You knew where you were with someone like that.

He turned and paced back to the living room, thinking about the police and whether they would go fishing for the body. Mei had more chance of being taken seriously, not just because she was dating a detective but because she was a lawyer. They hadn't actually seen the body go into the suitcase, or the suitcase go into the water. The police might not be prepared to accept what they'd witnessed as reason enough to go fishing, especially given how resource-heavy water recovery was.

But then that wouldn't be the end of the world, would it? The longer it took the body to surface, the more time he had to run his own investigation. Well, him and Audrey. She was keeper of the crime scene, after all, even if she was hoping the police would take it over as soon as possible.

His mind fizzed with possibilities and new ideas. There was a sequel here, in this new mystery, he could feel it. In fact, now that he was at the computer, he should probably just write it all down before he forgot it. Get it all banked before he went back to editing . . .

He blinked, realising that not only was he already sitting in his executive chair with his hands poised over the keyboard; he'd woken the computer and opened a clean document. Ah, well. Strike while the iron is hot.

He smiled at the blinking cursor. So much for going to bed.

21
Celeste

Celeste sat up in bed, resting against four pillows plumped to perfection in pressed-silk pillowcases. The eiderdown draped over the duvet was reassuringly warm and heavy, but comfort had its disadvantages, and Celeste had dozed off several times while waiting for Dixon to return. Even now that he was back and sitting in the chair beside her bed, her eyes were still threatening to close. The perils of growing old.

"You're sure they didn't see you?" she said, blinking herself awake.

"I'm sure. I parked up before they got there, so they didn't even notice me. I thought Audrey might have clocked me once, but she were just cold and moving about. Nothing to worry about."

"And they didn't see the chap in the garden?"

"Didn't look like it. He didn't get over the railings until they were turning off."

"What about the taxi driver?"

"I kept well back. They'd have had their eyes fixed ahead anyway, on the van. And I didn't follow them down to the quay, it would've been too obvious. I waited at the top. I could see 'em parked up at the bottom, but nowt beyond."

Celeste could see Tower Quay in her mind's eye. She'd been there many times when she was younger. With Madeleine. They'd even done the official Tower Bridge tour once, for a joke.

"Do you know what they used to call that spot, Dixon? Down beside the bridge?"

"No."

"Dead Man's Hole. There are steps, you see, going down into the water, where the Victorians used to pull bodies out."

"Not put them in?"

"Not so far as I know. But then, you never know where a body goes in; that's rather the point."

"Suitcase might mean it stays down longer," said Dixon, folding his arms. "Especially as it's so cold."

"Yes, it might."

"It'll still move though. Wonder where it'll end up. Any luck with Petrov?"

"I spoke to him earlier. He's coming in tomorrow. Said he'd drop by as soon as he can. I suggested you could pick him up from the airport, but he said there was no need."

"So he could already be in the country?"

"Yes."

Celeste blinked a few more times and tried to suppress a yawn, but of course Dixon spotted it at once.

"You need yer sleep," he said, standing up. He was still in his dark clothes, and his cheeks were flushed above his beard where the cold had set in. "Audrey'll fill you in on't rest tomorrow. She'll have more than me anyway."

"All right, dear."

Dixon smoothed out her already-smooth eiderdown, then took away some of the pillows so she could lie down. She held back another yawn.

"Sorry about your evening," she said once he had placed her glasses neatly on top of her book and made for the door.

"Don't be," he said, pausing by the door. "Glad to know I've still got it."

"Pft." She gave that the short shrift it deserved. "Of course you do. Don't forget the upstairs lights, dear, will you? I left them on."

"Do I ever?"

"No. No, you never do. Good night."

As Dixon closed the door behind him, Celeste yawned delicately before settling down into her pillows. She was oddly enjoying the feeling of exhaustion, knowing that she'd sleep well tonight. It had been a while. She'd been too preoccupied with the idea of finding new tenants, and her mind would keep going back to the past, which only served to emphasise the gaping holes in her present. A late night, an exciting mystery, and Anton Petrov to boot—that was just what she needed to distract her. And Dixon on a stakeout? Positively delightful.

She smiled as she turned off her bedside lamp.

Still got it, indeed.

22

Audrey

"But this is me, not some crime writer with an overdeveloped imagination!" Mei's indignant voice carried up the stairs.

Audrey paused on the landing, not wanting to listen, but also not wanting to intrude. She checked her phone. Ten past eight. She had twenty minutes to grab some breakfast and get over to Celeste's.

"Yes, but you can't think it's a coincidence that on the same day Audrey saw a dead body, two men in a stolen van went there in the dead of night, emerging with a very large, very heavy suitcase, which they took to a dark spot near the river at high tide."

Mei's voice became shrill, and Audrey hurried down the stairs. There was no need for Mei to fall out with Sofia over this.

"I am not being dramatic!"

Audrey reached the kitchen, and Mei spun around, dark eyes flashing and a furious look on her face. She was wearing a black trouser suit, all ready to go to work. Audrey shook her head and mouthed the word *Don't*.

Mei rolled her eyes skyward and grimaced at the ceiling. Audrey could imagine Sofia's tone, calm but annoyed, and knew that would frustrate Mei even more.

"Fine," said Mei, pulling a face at Audrey. "You'd think actual witnesses would be enough to trigger the deployment of resources, but if it isn't, it isn't. Nothing either of us can do."

Audrey heard Sofia's voice rise on the other end of the phone.

"I don't see how that's our fault," replied Mei to whatever Sofia had said. "Audrey was only going to work, for God's sake, and now she might be in danger! Put yourself in her shoes. What would *you* do if you found a dead body and no one believed you?"

More listening.

"Hah!" said Mei. "You tell yourself that, but we both know you'd do the same. I only went on the bloody stakeout because of you. You were right, by the way. I had an idea while I was standing around in the cold, about where to look for Cole next . . . "

Realising the conversation had turned away from crisis, Audrey squeezed past Mei and put the kettle on, sticking some bread in the toaster and trying not to listen to the rest of the conversation.

"Well!" said Mei, when she eventually put her phone down. "Honestly!"

Audrey's toast popped up.

"What was that about a stolen van?"

"What? Oh, Sofia ran the van plates first thing. Reported stolen by a minicab driver in Brentford last night, but it turned up half an hour ago, parked further down the same street, if you can believe it." She exhaled. "Do you know what else she said?"

"I can hazard a guess. No, they won't send out divers to retrieve the suitcase; no, they can't just take your word for it; and as a bonus, 'I can't believe Audrey's dragged you into this.'"

Mei arched one perfect eyebrow.

"Almost word for word. Although she blames Lewis more than you."

"Poor Lewis," said Audrey, buttering her toast. "He's very misunderstood."

"Except by you, it seems. Anyway, I'm sorry."

That surprised her. She turned, butter knife in hand.

"What for?"

"For not understanding why you were getting involved again, but I do now. Sofia isn't exactly not believing me, but she thinks we've got the wrong end of the stick. I'm so cross."

Audrey smiled and went back to her toast.

"I can tell," she said. "And I won't say I'm not glad, but you have to see it from her point of view. Young DS gets the diving team out because her girlfriend says she *may* have seen a body dumped, and then either they don't find the suitcase or it's full of clothes or something . . . that's her career stalled for a few years. You've been so happy. Don't let this ruin things."

The colour rose to Mei's cheeks.

"God, you're so reasonable. It's sickening."

"I only do it to annoy you."

The kettle flicked off, and Audrey poured boiling water into her mug, staring out the window as the tea brewed. The square glittered with frost in the early-morning sunshine, white crystals clinging to the greenery. She knew it would be icy cold once she stepped outside, but it was very beautiful. How lucky she was to live here.

"What was that last thing you said to Sofia?" said Audrey, stirring her tea. "About having ideas in the cold?"

"Sofia told me that sitting around on stakeouts was where she got her best ideas, so I was thinking about my missing client last night—before things got interesting—and remembered he'd said something about childhood holidays on the Essex coast. If he's gone into hiding, he might have chosen somewhere familiar. It's an idea anyway."

"Seems like we're all detectives now."

"Ugh, doesn't it? Right, I'd best head off." Mei lifted her briefcase off the kitchen table. "Have a good day. And I will try Sofia again, you know. About the suitcase. I won't let it lie."

"Thanks. Good luck with your client. I hope you track him down."

"You and me both."

Audrey was halfway out the door when she remembered the bags of siphoned vacuumings still packed into her cleaning kit. The argument with Mei followed by the surprise stakeout had put them right out of her mind. She darted back inside and stashed the bags in the cupboard under the sink before heading out in a rush, crossing the courtyard at speed. Her breath clouded in front of her as she crunched over Roshan's carefully laid salt, ringing the doorbell for Celeste's just in time. Eight thirty on the dot, as always.

The door buzzed, and she pushed it open, bounding up the stairs to the penthouse door, which Dixon was already holding open for her.

"Morning," she said brightly, looking him up and down as she crossed the threshold. Dixon, always handsome in a lean, angular sort of way, somehow managed to look just as smart in jeans and a cable-knit jumper as he did in his usual suit.

He followed her through to the big room, where Celeste was already ensconced in her armchair by the picture window, reading the newspaper.

"I have news," said Audrey, approaching the nook. "We went on a stakeout last night."

Celeste immediately looked delighted, although Dixon seemed unsurprised.

"Petrov's place?" he asked.

"Yep. And guess what?" She looked from Dixon to Celeste. "You were right. They'd hidden the body somewhere in the house. We saw them bring it out!"

"How exciting!" said Celeste. "Tell me everything."

Audrey sat down in the second armchair. "It was Lewis's idea. After we'd spoken to you. We all went. Me, him, and Mei. They brought it out in a suitcase."

"Any idea where they took it?"

"We followed them in a cab. We know exactly where they took it." She grinned at their expectant faces. "Tower Bridge."

"Tower Bridge?" repeated Celeste. "How extraordinary."

"I know. Lewis was annoyed about it. I think he thought it was a bit showy."

Celeste smiled. "It is rather."

"Nice depth at high tide though," said Dixon. "Currents could have it away in no time."

Celeste nodded, and Audrey wondered how she was the only one who didn't know how bodies moved about in rivers. Must be all the crime novels they read. Celeste always had a book in hand.

"I spoke to Anton last night," said Celeste. "He was understandably concerned. I'm expecting him later this afternoon, so the more details we have, the better."

"Mei spoke to Sofia this morning. She ran the plates of the minivan, and turns out it was stolen last night and then returned. But the police won't go looking for the suitcase. Something about resources."

Celeste and Dixon exchanged glances.

"I expect it's because they can't be sure there was a body in it," said Celeste, pursing her lips. "Any excuse. In my day, they'd pull a suitcase out of the river because a suitcase shouldn't be in the river, regardless of what was in it." She tutted.

"Is that true?" asked Audrey, frowning. "I thought people chucked all sorts of things into rivers back then. And wasn't the Thames biologically dead until the seventies?"

"Pft," said Celeste, dismissing that with a wave of her hand. "All I'm saying is that modern policing leaves a lot to be desired."

"If we're on to modern policing," said Dixon with a smile, "then it's time I was off. Do you need owt before I go?"

"No, thank you," said Celeste. "Audrey and I will be just fine. I want to hear the full story, beginning to end, no detail left out." The old lady's eyes sparkled. "I'm most intrigued."

23
Lewis

THE CLEANER: Minivan reported stolen but then returned. No divers. Mei did try, but Sofia was having none of it. Celeste delighted by the stakeout. Mr. Petrov is coming to see her this afternoon. Anything specific you want me to ask?

Lewis tapped the end of his pen against his teeth and read Audrey's message for the third time that morning. No divers meant no body, which on the one hand might be a good thing, because it meant the police wouldn't interfere yet. But on the other hand, without the body, they stood next to no chance of identifying the victim. Not unless DS Larssen's blood swab came back with something.

He was also champing at the bit to go and meet the mysterious Mr. Petrov, not least because he wanted to take the lead in questioning. Audrey had a tendency to get everyone's life story, and God knows how Celeste would conduct an interview.

But he couldn't get out of work again. Not after yesterday.

He pushed the phone aside, turning back to his computer. He had a load of vacancies to type up and an inbox full of résumés to appraise and register. It was admin, really, but it was the only part of the job he didn't hate.

"Lewis?" He looked up and saw his boss leaning out of his office doorway. "Can I have a word?"

"Sure," he said, standing up.

He followed Steve into his office and shut the door behind him. "What's up?"

Steve didn't sit down but remained standing, and Lewis was suddenly worried he was about to get a bollocking.

"So I've just got off the phone with Roland Waverley."

Oh, shit.

"He said you'd impressed him," Steve went on. "He's looking to make some changes at Trinity, including a senior position. And it was strongly implied that if we do well, we could end up working with the hotel group too. Nice work, Lewis, really nice work."

"Uh . . . " *What?*

"He was wondering if you could pop over again next week, to have a word about requirements. He'll get in touch to arrange."

"Yes. Sure." Lewis nodded, trying not to look as baffled as he felt. He'd only handed Waverley the card to ease his conscience. He hadn't expected him to actually need a recruitment agency!

"Do you know much about the Waverley Group?"

"Uh . . . "

"Roland's the son of Martin Waverley, y'know, who owns the hotel chain?"

Lewis nodded.

"Well, the management company—Trinity—was Roland's baby. Started off as a separate enterprise to look after the hotel buildings, but then they expanded, took on some other chains and some high-end private properties, and now it's very successful. Between you and me, Waverley said they're considering further expansion, so you've got your timing bang on." Steve clapped him on the back. "If we can become Trinity's recruitment partner, there's a chance we can get in with the hotel group too. Martin Waverley's got to be pushing eighty. He'll be looking to retire soon enough."

"Wow," said Lewis, lost for words. "I don't know what to say."

"It's funny," said Steve, sitting down on the edge of his desk and folding his arms. "I always thought you had a side hustle or something, the way you held back in the job."

"A side hustle?"

"Yeah, you know. Something else you'd rather be doing." Steve shrugged. "It's cool if you do, man. Everyone needs something, am I right? Chris is trying to break into modelling, and Lucy's got her street-food van. I've got my YouTube channel . . . Hell, Ken's an author, for crying out loud!"

"What?" Lewis was shocked, turning to look out of Steve's half-frosted windows to where Ken, a balding, middle-aged man with a gut that rested on his thighs, sat nodding at his computer screen, illuminated headset indicating he was on a call. "Ken is?"

"Yeah. Writes something historical, apparently. But that doesn't mean he can't commit to his work as well. Take me." Steve patted his own chest. "Recruitment isn't what I imagined I'd be doing, but it's great work, and I get a real buzz from it. You've just gotta find what makes you happy."

Lewis blinked. This was all news to him. He'd always thought Steve had been born to recruitment.

"Okaaaay . . ."

"It's taken you long enough," Steve laughed, "but you showed some real initiative yesterday, and it's already paying off. I just wanted you to know that I see you. I see you trying, and I'm pleased. Keep it up, yeah? And maybe next month, you *could* come to the team drinks? No pressure, but it would help if you tried to integrate more."

"I'll bear it in mind."

Steve looked disappointed, but he nodded.

"Do your best, mate. The guys would appreciate it."

Lewis nodded and left, bewildered. He appeared to have successfully—if entirely accidentally—done recruitment and had no idea how to feel about it.

As he walked back through the cubicles, he shot a look at Ken. How had he not known that Ken was a writer? Or that Chris wanted to be a model? Now that he thought about it, though, Chris was handsome to the point of being ridiculous, and Ken did eat a lot of crisps, which should have been a clue, but even so . . . They all seemed genuinely happy in their work. The idea that there was an in-between, a state in which you could like your job yet still dream of other things, had never occurred to him.

He found this new knowledge to be oddly disconcerting, so he slumped down in front of his computer and got stuck in his work, becoming hyper-focused in an attempt to distract himself. By midday, he'd uploaded all the vacancies to the company website, and his inbox was looking reasonable. But after appraising came candidate-matching, and once that was done . . . well . . . then it was back to phoning people and speaking to them, which he loathed with a bone-deep passion.

He looked at his phone again. He had been *very* efficient that morning.

He thought for a few minutes, then stood up and walked over to Steve's office, knocking on the door.

"Yes, mate?" said Steve, grinning at him. "Landed another fish already?"

"No. Sorry. I was just wondering . . . if I work through lunch, could I knock off early today? About three? I know it's a Friday, but I've been on the waiting list for a dentist, and they just rang. They've got a last-minute cancellation, and I've not had a check-up for . . . " He stopped, trying to cement the lie with an element of truth, but came up short. "God, I can't actually remember."

"You and me both, mate," said Steve, shaking his head in wonder. "No problem. You'll make up the extra hour, though, yeah? Blimey. Roland Waverley and a dentist appointment in the same week. You lucky bastard."

24

Audrey

Cleaning 1 Marchfield Square was a slow day for Audrey, broken up by chats with Celeste and a leisurely lunch too. As she mopped the floor of the main bathroom at the end of the afternoon, she started thinking about the cleaning problem at Mr. Petrov's house. The removal of the body from the crime scene, if you were strong or had help, would take at least five minutes, maybe more, probably wrapping it in the dust sheet and carrying it out of the house or to wherever they'd stashed it in the interim. Changing the sheet on the bed would be easy, if you had a fresh one with you. Two minutes. The blood on the wall had been to one side only, and although the paint was white, it had a sort of vinyl sheen to it; cleaning that would be fairly straightforward, with the right product. An enzyme spray, perhaps. Maybe eight to ten minutes to wipe the walls down as thoroughly as they had, including the window. That was around fifteen minutes already, and she hadn't even gotten to the floor yet.

As far as she could make out, they'd have had a safety gap of less than a minute before Audrey and the police returned to the house. At the very least, she should have heard footsteps leaving or a door closing, but there'd been nothing.

With a sigh, she turned her attention back to the bathroom, rooting around in her kit for a microfibre cloth. She found another sandwich bag of grey dust and fibres in between her cleaning sprays and tucked it into a side pocket to put away with the others later. They'd have to go through them all as soon as possible, although maybe she should just hand them straight over to the police.

Assuming they ever became interested in the case, anyway.

She was just packing away her cleaning things when the doorbell rang. "Ah, that'll be Anton," said Celeste. "Be a dear, would you?"

She felt a sudden rush of nerves as she went to buzz Mr. Petrov up, hastily tidying away her cleaning bag and the mop before he reached the landing. What if Mr. Petrov was angry with her for calling the police? What if he had something to hide? What if she ended up fired instead of suspended?

"I hope Mr. Petrov isn't angry," she said as Celeste joined her in the hall to wait for the lift. "About me involving Trinity and mentioning his name."

"Don't worry," said Celeste, patting her shoulder. "I'm sure he won't mind. And if he does, you can just blame me. No one stays cross with me for long."

Not for the first time, Audrey saw a flash of something in Celeste's pale blue eyes and wondered what this little old lady had been like in her younger days. Had she always had this daring, untouchable attitude? The devilish spark? Or was it a product of old age?

The lift dinged, the doors opening to reveal a weathered-looking man of around seventy, with a flat nose and thick white hair. He was wearing a blue jumper over a white shirt, and when he saw Celeste, he smiled, brown eyes crinkling at the corners.

"My dear Celeste," he said, kissing her on each cheek. "It has been too long."

"Indeed it has," said Celeste, gripping his hands. "It's good to see you."

Audrey watched as the old friends surveyed each other with equal thoroughness, narrowed eyes taking in all the small details.

Then Celeste reached up and patted Mr. Petrov's cheek, at which point he looked away and noticed Audrey.

"Anton Petrov, this is Audrey Brooks," said Celeste. "You may know her name?"

"Ah, yes," he said. "The young lady who saw a dead body in my house." He shook her hand. "I hope you were not too scared."

"Um. No?"

Petrov nodded, and then there was a pause, in which it seemed everyone was waiting for someone else to speak.

"I think perhaps we should have some tea," said Celeste at last, her eyes still fixed on Petrov's face. "There's a great deal for us to discuss, Anton. A very great deal."

25
Lewis

It took Lewis half an hour to get back to Chelsea that afternoon, and he half-ran down Pickering Lane in his haste to get home. Petrov could have been and gone since he'd last checked in with Audrey.

As he neared the gate to the square, Lewis saw a shiny black town car parked on the street outside. He couldn't see a driver, but a man in a dark coat stood on the other side of the street, looking at the car. Judging by the purple shadow under one of his eyes, he'd either been in a fight or had some sort of accident, but either way, he was much too dirty-looking to be a chauffeur. When he saw Lewis staring at him, he turned and walked away down a side street, coughing as he went. Lewis took out his keys. The Russian must be inside already.

He swiped his fob against the gatepost and shoved his way through, cursing Audrey at the same time. Why hadn't she messaged him? He might have missed Petrov altogether!

He ran down the path to Celeste's front door, leaning heavily on the buzzer just as his phone pinged with a text.

> **THE CLEANER:** Mr. Petrov's just arrived. How far away are you?

Okay, fine. Good. Never doubted her.

The intercom crackled.

"Come on up," said Audrey through the speaker. She'd been waiting for him.

The lock-release buzzed, and he let himself in, taking the steps two at a time until he reached Celeste's landing, where Audrey was standing by the open door.

"Good timing," she said, stepping back to let him in. "They're just having a little catch-up. I'm making drinks."

She took his coat and hung it up, giving him a few seconds to catch his breath and wipe his sweaty face on his sleeve, then led him to the living area, where an older man sat on Celeste's velvet sofa. He looked perfectly at ease and smiled as Lewis walked in. This was undoubtedly the man from the photo he'd found in Petrov's study, albeit a good twenty years older.

"Lewis!" said Celeste, looking pleased. "I was hoping you'd join us. Take a seat. This is my good friend, Anton Petrov. Anton, this is Lewis McLennon. He's a writer, but he's done some investigative work for me in the past."

Lewis shook Petrov's hand, hoping his own wasn't too damp, and sat down beside him.

"Good to meet you," he said.

"And you," said Petrov.

"I was just asking Anton about his children," said Celeste. "Sabine and Jean. It's been many years since I've seen them. Sabine was married last year, I believe?"

"To a Frenchman," said Petrov. He had a deep voice and a Russian accent mixed with something else. "They're expecting a baby this summer."

"Ah, grandchildren!" said Celeste, clapping her hands together. "How delightful. Do you think you'll be a good grandfather, Anton?" The question seemed an odd one to Lewis, but Petrov laughed, a rumbling sound that echoed in the open-plan space.

"If I can stay out of trouble, then yes," he said. "Perhaps."

A soft clank made them look over to see Audrey wheeling a tea trolley across the floor.

"You keep the old standards," said Petrov to Celeste, smiling. "Like always."

"Of course."

Audrey parked the trolley beside Celeste, who nodded approval at the two pots, one a silver coffee pot, the other a china teapot.

"Shall I be mother?" asked Celeste. "Tea or coffee, Anton?"

"Is it English Breakfast?" asked Petrov. "Or do you still drink Earl Grey in the afternoon?"

"Earl Grey, dear."

"Then I will take coffee. With cream, if you have it. And two lumps."

Celeste smiled and poured some of the darkest coffee Lewis had ever seen into one of the china cups, topping it up with cream and sugar and handing it to Petrov with a silver teaspoon resting in the saucer.

"Where have you travelled from, Mr. Petrov?" asked Audrey, sitting down on the ottoman.

"From Antibes, in France."

"And how long since you've been in the UK?"

He stirred his coffee delicately.

"A little while," he said at last. "And you live here, with Celeste?"

"In the square, yes. Number seven."

"Ah. I hope you are happy here; it is beautiful for London. And how are my beautiful clocks? You have taken good care of them for me?"

"I've done my best," said Audrey, and Lewis saw her nose wrinkle for just a fraction of a second as Celeste passed her a cup of Earl Grey. Dishwater tea, she called it. "They're all keeping good time, at least."

"Except one," put in Lewis, and Petrov looked at him, bushy white eyebrows almost meeting. "The one that was at the crime scene."

"It is not damaged?" Petrov looked worried.

"No, just out of time," said Audrey. "I think it might have been knocked in the . . . incident. I didn't like to adjust it in case the police wanted to see it."

"The police?"

Celeste paused in the act of handing Lewis his coffee.

"Yes. I didn't mention it on the telephone, Anton, but Audrey called the police upon discovering the crime scene. But by the time they arrived, it had all been cleaned up, and the body had vanished."

For the briefest of moments, Lewis could have sworn Petrov looked amused, but then his nostrils flared and he took a sip of coffee.

"Extraordinary," he said, lowering his cup. "They must be very skilled people, these criminals. What did the police say?"

"The first officers told me I was making it up," said Audrey. "The second—a detective—she took a swab of the only drop of blood we could find and said she'd run it through the system. There wasn't anything else she could do."

"A drop of blood?" Petrov frowned. "Have they had the results?"

"Not yet. It will take a while."

"Celeste told me that you saw them put the body in the river?"

"They took a large suitcase out of the house and drove to the river," corrected Lewis. "We're assuming it contained the body, but we didn't actually see them drop it in. And the police aren't prepared to search."

Petrov and Celeste looked at each other, and Lewis got the distinct impression there was another conversation taking place. Petrov wasn't reacting at all as he'd expected.

"Can you describe the dead man?" asked Petrov at length.

"White," said Audrey. "In his early sixties, maybe. Light brown hair, a bit shaggy. Clean-shaven. Stocky build." She smiled apologetically. "A bit nondescript, really."

"No. He sounds very . . . forgettable."

"He doesn't ring a bell then?" said Lewis as Audrey winced. "Doesn't sound like someone you know?"

Petrov shrugged, seemingly relaxed about the entire situation. Suspiciously relaxed, in fact.

"Maybe, maybe not. It's hard to be sure. These details are not exactly specific."

"Any idea why someone would commit murder in your house?"

"None at all." He took another sip of coffee. "Perhaps it was a random act?"

But Lewis shook his head.

"They knew your alarm codes," he said. "And where to hide the body. If it was random, they'd have had to crack your security system and clean up on the fly. Nobody could have done it that fast."

"On the fly?" repeated Petrov, puzzled.

"Without planning," explained Celeste.

"Then I am at a loss." He shrugged again and Lewis let out a huff of frustration.

"You don't seem very bothered," he said, and Audrey and Celeste turned to him at once. "A dead body in your house, blood everywhere. Aren't you worried? I would be."

Petrov's nostrils flared again, and he looked hard at Lewis, eyes flashing darkly beneath the white brows. Then he smiled.

"There is no body and no blood. It is hard to be worried about things you cannot see. But you are right, it is troubling. Perhaps . . . perhaps I should move my clocks?"

Lewis felt his mouth drop open, and Audrey coughed, shooting him a warning look.

"I think you're missing the point, Anton," said Celeste, gently. "Audrey walked into a potentially dangerous situation, and we need to get to the bottom of it. Your clocks, delightful though I'm sure they are, are not really the focus of our concern at the present time."

"Of course." Petrov looked at Audrey. "My apologies. I forget. Celeste tells me that you both are investigating. I would be grateful if, once you have found the culprit, you would advise me regarding my clocks."

Now it was Audrey who looked stunned.

"I . . . yes. Of course." She took a sip of her tea, and again, her nose crinkled, although whether that was at the Earl Grey or the clocks, Lewis couldn't tell.

"Do you have security cameras?" he asked, trying to keep the conversation on track. "Any logs for the alarm system?"

"Yes." Petrov nodded. "The Trinity people have the feeds. I cannot monitor the house from Antibes, and I travel also. You should talk to them. I will tell them it is okay."

That, at least, was something.

"How many properties do you have?" asked Lewis, thinking back to the millionaire or billionaire question.

"Only half a dozen," said Petrov. "In the places I visit most often. Otherwise it is a waste."

Even Celeste raised an eyebrow at that. Lewis took an annoyed slurp of his own coffee, which turned out to be delicious. Celeste had never given him this before.

"Are you going to stay at the house?" asked Audrey, setting down her cup. "Only Trinity said I should stop cleaning for now."

"I will go and see it," said Petrov, smiling round at them all, "and check my clocks, but I think perhaps I'll stay in a hotel. It would not do to interfere with your investigation."

Which was, to Lewis's mind, the only sensible thing Petrov said for the entirety of his visit.

26
Audrey

Much to Audrey's relief, Lewis didn't speak again until they were outside in the courtyard. His palpable irritation had made the meeting with Anton Petrov rather awkward, but either he was becoming more polite or fear of having the investigation stopped had kept his comments in check, because he'd eventually stopped speaking, and Celeste had suggested they run along home while she and Anton talked about the good old days, whatever those were.

"Was that guy shady, or was that guy shady?" Lewis grumped as the door shut behind them. It was cold again, and beginning to get dark. "He barely reacted at all to hearing about the murder and was only worried about his clocks! He just went right to the top of my suspect list."

"It was strange," said Audrey, not wanting to badmouth the man who technically paid some of her wages. She fastened her coat. "And he did react to the discovery of the drop of blood we found, did you notice? But Celeste had already called him, so maybe he'd just had time to process?"

"I hardly think—" began Lewis, but he was cut off by someone shouting Audrey's name. They turned and saw the Captain walking down the garden path towards them, heels clicking on the flagstones, with Muffin following along behind. The two had barely been apart since the Captain had brought him home from Battersea.

"Good evening!" said the Captain as he reached them. "I hear you two are finding bodies again." Taken aback, Audrey didn't immediately know how to respond. "Our esteemed landlady told me all about it. Quite the conundrum."

"When?" was all she could think of to say. "When did she tell you?"

"Yesterday evening." The Captain put his hands in his blazer pockets. "Dixon was out, so we had a visit. Tell me, do you think they were hiding in the house while you were there, or did they leave and come back later?"

"I . . . don't know." She looked at Lewis, who was turning a funny colour.

"Mmm." The Captain's moustache twitched as he thought. "I don't suppose you took any pictures of the crime scene, did you? Or the body?"

"No!"

"No, quite. Not the done thing. But you see, a professional would most likely have cut from behind. Better angle that way." The Captain mimed pulling someone's head back with his left hand while his right swept across an imaginary throat. "Whereas an amateur might have gone in from the front, probably with more than one cut. Any idea which it might have been?"

"I don't know," she said again, horrified. She really didn't want to think about that part of it.

"How can you tell?" asked Lewis, suddenly interested. "And how do you know? I didn't think the army went in for throat-cutting."

"I've seen all sorts of things in my time," said the Captain, drawing himself up a little. "Not just an old duffer, you know."

"We didn't think th—" began Audrey, but Lewis cut her off.

"There was blood spatter, if that helps?" he said. "But without a body . . ."

"Quite, quite. Very tricky." The Captain's eyes narrowed. "I wonder where they'll dispose of it. River too obvious, I suppose?"

"Actually . . . " began Audrey, and Lewis glared at her. "What? He knows the rest."

"Fine," snapped Lewis. "We know where they dumped it. Tower Bridge."

The Captain's eyes widened.

"Tower Bridge? My God." He smoothed his moustache. "Cheeky beggars."

"That's what I thought," said Lewis.

"They've got some nerve, these fellas. I suppose it *was* chaps?"

"We think so," said Audrey. "But we never saw their faces."

"No, and you can't be sure these days, can you?" said the Captain. "I mean, look at that club Victor works at. The chaps there . . . some of them, you'd have no idea. No idea at all."

"That's not really the same—"

"And vice versa, of course. In my day, women could do most things a chap could do, but they still looked like women. These days, well . . . "

Audrey looked at Lewis, who appeared equally bemused. Conversations that started with "in my day" invariably didn't end well, but the Captain didn't sound nostalgic. He almost sounded . . . pleased?

"Keep the field open," he went on, nodding. "Clever. Do you know, bodies often get caught in the bends of a river. I shouldn't be at all surprised if that suitcase turned up pretty close to the bridge. Rotherhithe, maybe, or Wapping." He looked from one to the other, then smiled. "We shall see, eh? Keep me posted, won't you?"

He left without waiting for them to reply, and they watched him march down the path to his own front door, Muffin trotting at his heels. It unnerved Audrey how everyone seemed delighted by this hideous situation, but perhaps that was because they hadn't had to see the body, or experience being alone in a house with a concealed killer and a corpse. She shivered.

"I'm going home," she said. "I'm going to have a bath and try not to think about any of this for a few hours. It's all just so . . . "

"Weird," finished Lewis.

"Yeah. We need to go through the vacuum contents too. I'll make a start this evening."

"I want to help," he said at once. "Shall I come over after dinner?"

"Yes, all right. See you later."

The air felt damper than it had the last few days, and as Audrey crossed the courtyard, heading for home, a hacking cough from somewhere on the street outside the square made her pull her coat tighter. She couldn't afford to catch a chill, on top of everything else. All the flats in their block had their lights on now, Victor in Flat 3 and Sarah next door, no doubt nice and cosy inside. Even the Captain had left a light on.

She climbed the steps to Flat 7 and let herself in, hanging up her coat and realising too late that she'd left her cleaning bag at Celeste's. She sighed. She'd have to go over and collect it tomorrow, but maybe she could get in a few extra questions about Anton Petrov while she was there. Lewis would like that.

Half an hour later, as she lay in the bath, bubbles gently hissing around her, she thought about the cleaning problem again. Someone, somewhere, would know the tricks of this particular trade, and Audrey wanted that knowledge. It was a matter of professional pride, if nothing else.

She reached for her phone and began Googling crime scene cleaning. Some of the first results were for forensic cleaning specialists, and after searching for local firms, she sent an identical email to the four closest companies, saying she was interested in entering the field and asking if they'd be prepared to speak to her. It couldn't do any harm, and she was genuinely interested in seeing how people cleaned more challenging messes than finger-paints and ovens.

She dropped her phone back onto the towel and was just relaxing into the suds when she heard the soft bang of a door downstairs. She sat up again, water sloshing around her.

"Mei?" she called but was met with silence. She was about to lie back down when she heard another noise, this time sounding like the front door.

"Mei?" she called again, straining to hear. "Is that you?"

Again, there was no reply, but it had sounded so close and so much like their door that Audrey stood up, grabbing a towel and stepping out of the bath onto the mat, heart pounding. She wrapped the towel around her and put her dressing gown over the top, knotting the belt tightly. Then, finding nothing more dangerous in the bathroom than a pair of nail scissors, she put her phone in her robe pocket and slipped through the door, tiny scissors held in front of her.

She crept downstairs, listening hard. Holding her breath, she sidled up to the kitchen door and pushed it open, scissors at the ready, but found everything just as she'd left it. Then she did the same for the living room, easing the door open without a sound, only to find the room dark and empty.

She exhaled, cursing herself. She was getting jumpy, just like last time. She was safe, at home, in the square. There was nothing at all to be scared of.

Nevertheless, as she passed through the hall on her way back upstairs, she put the chain on the front door.

Better to be safe than sorry.

27
Lewis

Lewis reached for the mug beside him, one hand still hovering over the keyboard. He took a swig of coffee, realising mid-gulp that it was stone cold. He looked at it in disgust. Hadn't he just made that?

The light in the room suggested otherwise, and he was surprised to find, when he looked away from the screen, that he was in virtual darkness. With the curtains open, the stark white light from the halogen streetlamps on the road behind the square shone onto the living-room wall, while the Victorian lamps in the square gave his tiny kitchen a warm glow.

He scrolled up to check the chapter number and realised with delight that he was a quarter of the way through his edits. He stretched, the leather of his desk chair creaking. Time to have some dinner and then get over to Audrey's to look through the evidence.

He got up and went into the kitchen, taking the last ready-meal out of his fridge. He'd have to go shopping tomorrow, another boring admin job getting in the way of his work. Annoyed, he stabbed a fork through the plastic cover on the container, then put it in the microwave.

After a few seconds of watching the lasagne go round and round, he went back to his computer, opening up his investigation document. He scrolled past the list of questions and down to his suspects list. It was short. And weak.

Suspects:

Anton Petrov: Didn't have a straight answer for anything. Didn't seem worried about the crime scene or the dead man, only his clocks. Claimed to have no idea why anyone would be murdered in his house. Amused by the quick cleanup, but rattled by the blood trace found.

Felix Casetti: More bothered by Audrey going in early than by the crime scene. Didn't like the mention of the police. Trying to keep her away from the property. Not inclined to be helpful.

Stranger: Who is the man Audrey saw in the residents' garden? Witness or perp?

He didn't like that the list was so short and lacking in substance. Motive was the thing he needed.

With a sigh, he deleted the title and replaced the word "Suspects" with "Persons in the case" and began adding more names.

Roland Waverley: Casetti's boss. Concerned, but also didn't like that the police were called. Is this because he's looking to expand his business?

Julian Thingy-Ross: Neighbour. Saw nothing, heard nothing.

He stared at the screen, then amended it:

Julian Thingy-Ross: Neighbour. Says he saw nothing and heard nothing.

The microwave went ping, and he abandoned the case notes.

There was always the swab, he thought as he slid the lasagne onto a plate. Assuming Larssen had sent it for analysis like she'd said, there was a chance, albeit a small one, that it would return a match.

Plate in one hand, fork in the other, he returned to his desk.

With Audrey going in to clean every week, whatever they'd been using the house for could realistically only be carried out between her visits. That ruled out anything like a meth lab or a squat.

Gambling ring? Brothel? Audrey would surely have noticed if someone were using the property for anything like that. No one could leave a place so clean and tidy afterwards that she wouldn't notice. Not unless they were a cleaner too.

He paused, a forkful of steaming lasagne halfway to his mouth.

Except they *were* a cleaner, weren't they? The neighbour, Mr. Double-Barrelled, what had he said? Something about keeping to her time and it not mattering when it was an oligarch house . . . What if this wasn't the first time something similar had happened in Beaton Gardens?

Lewis had made a joke about it, saying there could have been a crime there every week, but what was there to stop someone from using Petrov's unoccupied house whenever they wanted? London was famously full of empty properties owned by absentee Russian businessmen. If you could hack the security and knew the cleaner's routine, you could go in as and when you needed to. And it would be especially easy if you had someone on the inside of the management company who had told you exactly when the property would be empty. Someone who definitely would not be happy with a cleaner turning up and mentioning murder to his boss . . .

He put down the plate and reread his case notes. Perhaps the cleanup crew had been there before, which was how they'd known the alarm codes and where to hide the body. Maybe they'd cleaned up other murders. Or other crimes.

He and Audrey needed to get their hands on that security footage. And fast.

28

Audrey

One look at Mei as she walked through the door that evening, and Audrey could see that things were not all right. Her friend looked pale and drawn, the shadows under her eyes darker than ever. Even her hair looked dull and lifeless.

"Hello," said Mei, flopping onto the sofa. She didn't even glance at the television, which was showing her favourite quiz show. Audrey reached for the remote and muted it.

"I thought you'd be at Sofia's for the weekend."

"Me too, but I was lousy company, and we both had work to do, so I came home. Sometimes you just want your own bed."

"This about your troublesome client? Any news?"

Mei heaved a deep sigh before answering.

"Baxter Cole has completely and utterly vanished. What started out as irritating has now become a full-blown manhunt. Something must have happened to him."

Audrey sat up.

"Like what?"

"Cole has enemies," said Mei. "A lot of them. He's a spoiled man-child, so it didn't seem that unlikely he'd have disappeared for another little holiday while the rest of us were busting our chops on his behalf, and then I thought maybe he'd got scared and absconded. But there's absolutely no trace of him, not one. Dominic's filed a missing-person report."

She leaned her head back against the sofa and closed her eyes.

"Your idea from the other night didn't pan out then?" asked Audrey.

"Nope. He'd mentioned a place belonging to an uncle, down in Southend, but he wasn't there. I hired a detective we use, out Essex way. He checked every rental place in the area, and all the hotels too. Cost a fortune, and he found absolutely nothing." She sighed again. "I was so sure too."

"When did you last see him?"

"Wednesday. We had our morning briefing, as usual, when he was unusually obnoxious. He had two other meetings that afternoon, and everyone he was supposed to meet, he met; his PA checked. But he never showed up for work the next morning and hasn't been heard from since."

"How much money did he—" Audrey caught herself. Mei was never that indiscreet. She rephrased the question. "Are there many people affected? Sums big enough to make a person . . . angry?"

Mei smiled at her gratefully.

"Quite a few people. The amounts vary, but some of them are high, yes." She stretched again and glanced at the TV, where the credits from the quiz show were now rolling. "Shall we open some wine?"

"Not for me, thanks," said Audrey. "Lewis is coming over in a bit to go through the vacuum bags from the house."

"Vacuum bags?"

"Yes, we emptied the vacuum at Beaton Gardens so we could see if the killer had left any evidence behind."

Mei frowned. "You should give them to Sofia."

"Sofia can't investigate until we have something solid, remember? And there probably won't be anything anyway. They were so thorough." Before Mei could protest further, Audrey jumped to her feet. "I'd best go prep an area to work in, actually. I'll open a bottle for you at the same time, shall I?"

She went through to the kitchen and cleared the counter to make room for her and Lewis to work, assuming he actually deigned to show up. It was half past seven already, but he was probably lost in his edits. She got the antibacterial spray out from under the sink and cleaned the countertop, wiping it down thoroughly in readiness for sifting through the bags of dust. Then, automatically, she began to clean the rest of the kitchen, and as she sprayed and wiped, she felt the last of her tension drain away. Not for the first time, she wondered whether it was normal to find cleaning as therapeutic as she did, but a happy place was a happy place, and at least this didn't cost her anything.

When she was done, she got a bottle of white wine from the fridge and opened it with practised ease, putting the foil in the recycling bin under the sink and returning the cleaning spray at the same time. She'd already turned to get a wine glass from the cupboard when she registered what she'd seen.

Or hadn't seen.

She opened the cupboard under the sink again.

They were gone. The plastic bags of vacuumed dirt they'd gone to such trouble to collect from the Petrov house were missing.

"Listen, about this case—" began Mei, walking into the kitchen, then stopped when she saw Audrey's face. "What's wrong?"

"They're gone," said Audrey, starting to open more cupboards.

"What's gone?"

"The plastic bags with the dirt from the vacuum cleaner. I brought them home from Beaton Gardens. I put them under the sink this morning but they're not there now. You didn't move them, did you?"

"Of course not," said Mei. "Maybe you put them somewhere else?"

"No," said Audrey, opening cupboard after cupboard, just in case. "I definitely put them under the sink." She turned around in the middle of the kitchen, looking for somewhere, anywhere else she could check, but she knew with stomach-churning certainty that she had not moved the bags. "They're not anywhere."

She looked at Mei, swallowing down nausea and fear. "They're gone. We've been robbed."

29

Lewis

The door to Flat 7 opened before Lewis could knock.

"Hey," he said, looking at Audrey's flushed face. "You okay?"

"Not really." She ushered him inside. "They stole the evidence from the vacuum cleaner. This afternoon, after work. The killer was here."

They went straight to the kitchen, where Mei was sitting at the counter, a glass of wine in front of her. She looked washed out.

"Why do you think it was this afternoon?" he asked.

"Because I was here," said Audrey, with a shuddering breath. "Upstairs. Mei was out, but I thought I heard a door. I went downstairs and there was no one, but there must have been, mustn't there? They'd come in and had a root around the kitchen while I was in the bath . . ."

She looked like she was going to be sick, and Lewis was at a loss for what to do.

"Petrov," he said, and both women looked at him. "He was with Celeste, wasn't he? Dixon wasn't here to see him out, so he could easily have watched which flats we went into, then snuck around later."

Mei sat up straight, a grim expression on her face.

"That doesn't exactly fit with him being a friend of Celeste's," she said.

"You didn't meet him," said Lewis. "He couldn't have been more suspicious if he'd tried." He groaned. "You gave him your address."

Mei glanced at Audrey, who turned pale.

"He asked if I lived with Celeste, and I corrected him, told him I lived in Flat 7. He just seemed so nice. Grandfatherly. Not like a killer."

"Nice has nothing to do with it," said Lewis, trying not to get annoyed. They were both clearly freaked out. "You don't get to be as rich as he is without being ruthless too."

"You've got that right," said Mei bitterly, raising her glass.

"Maybe he brought someone with him." He remembered the town car with no driver. "There was a man outside earlier, hanging around. Dirty hair, black coat. Possibly a black eye."

"Blond?" said Audrey, paling even further.

"Could have been, it was hard to tell. Why?"

"Sounds like the man I saw in Beaton Gardens. And that definitely wasn't Mr. Petrov."

"How would that guy know where you live, though?" Lewis sat down at the kitchen table. "Wonder how they got into your flat."

"There are a couple of tiny scratches on the lock," said Audrey. "They must have picked it. I don't put the chain or the bolt on when Mei's out."

Lewis made a mental note to watch some lock-picking videos when he got home, but the method of entry didn't really matter. Their evidence was gone, and with it, any chance of finding something incriminating.

"Have you called the police?"

"Sofia's on her way," said Audrey, looking at Mei. "But mainly for moral support. She said she could get Forensics in if we made an official report, but I'd cleaned the kitchen to examine the bags." She let out a laugh, although it could also have been a sob. "I cleaned up after them. Again!"

"Well, if you must be so obsessively neat . . . " he began, then stopped when he saw her expression. He searched for something comforting to say. "It has to have been Petrov. He had means and opportunity, and the motive is self-explanatory."

"But it's too obvious," said Audrey. "He'd know at once that we'd suspect him."

"He wouldn't care about being suspected. Only what could be proved. And if a little breaking and entering would help him get away with murder, why wouldn't he risk it?"

The intercom for the gate chimed from the hall, and Audrey went to answer. She came back a few seconds later.

"Sofia," she said. "She's on her way up."

Mei took another glug of wine.

"You sure you're okay?" asked Lewis. Not only did Mei always look well put together; she was also usually talkative and sharp, sniping at him at every opportunity. This quiet version of her was somehow even less fun.

"Peachy," she said, toasting him, and they both went quiet.

A minute later, they heard the front door open, and then Sofia Larssen entered in a draught of cold air. She was wearing jeans and a sweater beneath a woollen coat and carried an overnight bag. She dumped the bag beside the door and went over to Mei at once.

"Hey," she murmured into Mei's shoulder, black and blond hair overlapping as they hugged. "How are you doing?"

"Fine," said Mei, reaching for the wine bottle. "Drink?"

Sofia glanced at Audrey, who gave a tiny shrug. "Uh . . . in a minute," she said. "I want to make a report, if that's okay? Officially. I know you said the break-in was this afternoon and you've cleaned since then, but it's worth having it on record. Then I can talk to the neighbours, request security footage, get Forensics in, et cetera."

"No security cameras in the square," said Lewis. "Celeste won't allow it. And it's not going to be a priority, is it? Audrey saw a blood-soaked crime scene, and no one was interested."

Sofia glared at him.

"This is a domestic break-in. Something was stolen."

"Same at Beaton Gardens," said Audrey, frowning. "Except an entire *body* was stolen. Lewis is right. I appreciate your wanting to help, but all that's gone missing is dust."

Now Sofia looked uncomfortable.

"Well, it won't be high priority, no, if the only thing missing is . . . well, dust, as you say. But it doesn't really matter what's gone. Somebody broke in."

Mei patted Sofia's hand.

"I love that you're taking it seriously, Sofe, but we know how it'll turn out."

Sofia didn't speak for a minute, looking embarrassed.

"I know you've been investigating," she said at last. "Has anyone been hanging around? Following you?"

Audrey, Mei, and Lewis exchanged a look.

"The only stranger in the square that we know of," said Audrey, "was Anton Petrov, a friend of Celeste's. He was visiting her for tea. He owns the house in Beaton Gardens."

Sofia's eyebrows went up.

"Does he indeed?"

"And Lewis saw someone outside. A man. Similar description to the man I saw at Beaton Gardens."

"They were both wearing a black coat, anyway," he said. "Was there any luck with the swab?" He wondered if she'd actually put it in for processing.

"The lab work came back this morning. It's human blood, but no match for anyone in the system."

"How about the stolen minivan? Any fingerprints?"

"No. The vehicle was returned spotless. The owner said it was cleaner than when he'd bought it."

Lewis glanced at Audrey, who closed her eyes. "Of course it was."

"Is that all?" asked Mei, getting to her feet. "Because I'm starving. It's been a terrible end to a terrible week, and I want . . ." She paused, fingers pinched in front of her mouth, as if trying to taste something.

"You want a kebab," Audrey finished for her. "You always want a kebab."

"I do not."

"You do, babe," said Sofia, smiling.

"Shall I order?" said Mei, the menu that was usually magneted to the fridge already in her hand.

"Any more news on your client?" asked Sofia.

Mei pulled a face and handed her the menu.

"Nothing good. He had two meetings on Wednesday afternoon, then vanished, seemingly into thin air." She sighed. "His assistant's frantic, his wife's furious, and my boss is absolutely livid. Either he's done a bunk or someone's done him in."

"Who are we talking about?" asked Lewis, confused.

"Mei's been working on a big trial with her senior partner," Audrey explained. "But the client's disappeared."

"Baxter Cole?" he asked. "The Ponzi scheme guy?"

"*Alleged* Ponzi scheme guy," said Mei. "And yes. How did you know?"

"Saw it online this morning."

"Ugh, seriously?" She looked appalled. "Brilliant. Dominic's going to lose his mind."

"It wasn't a big article," said Lewis, helpfully. "Bottom of the Courts feed."

"Now I really need a kebab."

"Why don't I pop out for you?" He stood up. "It's only round the corner. It'll be quicker than waiting for delivery."

"Really?" Mei was surprised. "That's very kind. Thank you."

As Sofia studied the menu, Lewis tried to catch Audrey's eye, jerking his head towards the door. She frowned.

"Shall I . . . come with you?" she asked, and he nodded at once.

"Yes, good idea."

Mei looked up, wine bottle in hand, tilting her head in a "What's this?" gesture. In response, Audrey looked pointedly at Sofia. Mei rolled her eyes but gave a small smile, and Audrey smiled back. Lewis sighed. Another conversation where no one said a word.

Lewis took Sofia's order—Audrey already knew Mei's—then they put their coats on and stepped out into the freezing night air. The square didn't bustle as much as it used to, even on a Friday night, although the air was filled with the sound of London at its busiest, horn blasts and sirens coming from every corner of the city. Fewer people coming and going, he supposed.

"Either you really want a kebab," said Audrey, buttoning up her coat as they walked along the path towards the gate, "or else you had something you didn't want to say in there."

"I do not want a kebab." He stopped and turned to face her. "How did the burglars know that we'd taken the contents of the vacuum?"

"I . . . don't know." She looked nauseous again. "You think they were watching us."

"What if we're overthinking this?" he went on. "What if Petrov's lying about not having access to the camera in his house? Or else he could have been there the same time as us, watching from wherever the body was hidden. From the plastic on the floor, I thought maybe someone had hired a professional, but what if Petrov himself actually did the murder?"

"Why would Mr. Petrov kill someone in his own house?" she said. "That's insane. Why would he kill anyone, full stop?"

"That's the question, isn't it?"

"We need to tell Celeste. About the break-in here. She'll want to know."

"Not yet," said Lewis, firmly. "She'll only worry. And if Petrov really is her friend, it could make things difficult. Let's see what else we can uncover. We don't want to upset her, do we? Not after last time."

He held the gate for Audrey as they headed out of the square.

Definitely not after last time.

30
Audrey

Audrey didn't sleep that night, and not just because of the late-night kebab. She'd been unable to stop imagining someone creeping through the flat, going through their cupboards, treading on the stairs. She heard creaks and clicks she'd never heard before and turned her lamp on several times to chase away sinister-looking shadows in the corner of her room.

Now she stood by the kitchen window, hands cupped around a steaming mug of tea, gazing out over the square as the sun rose. Her eyes drifted up to the windows of Celeste's apartment. How would she react, knowing her safe haven had been intruded upon, possibly by someone she considered a friend?

Lewis was convinced Anton Petrov was the culprit, but while Audrey agreed he had reacted strangely, he hadn't given the impression of being foolish. To have committed murder in his own house on the day he knew Audrey was due to clean, and then to break into her flat while he was known to be in the square, he'd have to be very stupid indeed.

Well . . . either very stupid or supremely confident. The kind of person who would drop a body into the Thames beneath one of London's most famous landmarks clearly did not lack confidence.

She turned back to the kitchen, automatically looking for something to clean. The fridge, maybe? She couldn't remember the last time she'd cleaned out the fridge. That would be a nice bit of decompression, give her mind time to work through things.

But then she remembered that even her cleaning therapy had been tainted, and her anxiety turned to anger in a flash.

Twice now she'd cleaned up after the bad guys, and once in her own home. Not to mention that she'd been suspended by Trinity even after she'd done them a favour and reported the scene at the house. How dare they do this to her? What had she ever done to them except turn up a few minutes early?

Her phone pinged with an email, and she snatched it off the kitchen counter, ready to be annoyed at what was almost certainly an unsolicited sales email, but her anger died immediately.

> Dear Miss Brooks,
>
> Thank you for your inquiry.
>
> We're always on the lookout for new people to join our team of forensic cleaning specialists, and I'd be very happy to meet with you and discuss what we do in more detail. Unfortunately, due to the nature of our work, our hours aren't strictly Monday to Friday, 9–5. I expect to be in the office next Friday, if that suits? Or, if you don't mind meeting on a Sunday, my team and I will be at a scene in Clapham tomorrow. You'd be very welcome to drop by and see what we do in person.
>
> Let me know which would work best for you.
>
> Kind regards,
> John Keane
> JTK Forensic Cleaning, Summerstown, London SW17

Astonished, she read the email twice before putting the phone down. She hadn't expected to hear from anyone until Monday at the earliest, least of all at seven thirty on a Saturday morning, but Sunday would be perfect.

She texted Lewis.

> **AUDREY BROOKS:** I emailed some professional crime scene cleaners yesterday, and one of them has offered to let me drop by a "scene" in Clapham tomorrow, to see what they do. If you have any questions you want me to ask, let me know.

The reply came back in an instant.

> **FLAT 5 GUY:** A scene? Count me in. Let me know what time, and I'll be ready.

Oh, God, he wanted to come with her. She didn't know whether to be relieved or worried. She definitely wasn't keen on going to a random crime scene to meet a complete stranger on her own, but on the other hand, how many people brought a friend to a job interview? Especially a friend like Lewis. It would be embarrassing, to say the least.

But as she began to type out her reply to John Keane, she realised she had a totally legitimate excuse for that.

> Dear Mr. Keane,
>
> Thanks for your prompt reply. I'm happy to meet you in Clapham tomorrow, just let me know the address.
>
> If you don't mind, I'd like to bring a friend with me. He's a crime writer and very interested in forensics, so if you're amenable, he'd also love to find out more about what you do. But if it's not appropriate, he'd be fine to wait for me nearby.
>
> Best wishes,
> Audrey Brooks

The first part was definitely true, and while the second part definitely wasn't, Lewis would have to like it or lump it. She needn't have worried, however; the response was immediate.

> Dear Audrey,
>
> That's no problem at all. Probably a good idea to bring a friend anyway, as your first crime scene can be rather shocking!
>
> The address is the Victoria Hotel, Wandsworth Road, Clapham. Room 110. I look forward to meeting you both any time after 9 a.m.
>
> Best,
> John

First-name terms already, and he sounded very chill and understanding, which was a good sign. Plus, she'd get to spend some time talking to other people who appreciated the art of cleaning.

She smiled. Now that was an investigative angle she could get behind.

31
Lewis

The sound of Audrey's text arriving had woken Lewis early. He'd forgotten to draw his bedroom curtains again, and the dawn light coupled with a gnawing hunger and his excitement about visiting an uncleaned crime scene meant he couldn't go back to sleep. He got up and went into the kitchen in search of breakfast, only to discover he was out of food again.

This was not in itself a bad thing, because he only forgot about food when he was writing, so it probably meant he'd done some good work, but Saturday mornings were different. On Saturdays, he needed a decent breakfast with a decent cup of coffee, and today especially, he needed brain food. He was working on a case as well as a book.

Annoyed with the preoccupied past version of himself, Lewis went out into the freezing, misty morning, returning an hour later with two bags of fast and lazy shopping and a bag of fresh croissants. He was just crossing the road on Pickering Lane when a cough sounded from somewhere nearby. He stopped at the gate to the square and glanced around. A dark-clothed figure was standing at the entrance of the side street opposite. Lewis peered into the mist. It was a man, quite bulky from the look of it, his head covered by a black beanie hat. Lewis couldn't see his face, but he was sure it was the same man he'd seen watching Petrov's car.

"Can I help you?" Lewis called.

The figure took a step back into the side street and Lewis, still carrying his shopping, went after him. By the time he reached the junction, however, the man was already running, a black shape disappearing into the mist at the end of the street.

Lewis stared after him. Was this man their killer? Or an agent of Anton Petrov's? Had he broken into the square to rob Audrey? If so, why had he returned?

With a sigh, he crossed back over the street and began rooting for his keys. He needed coffee first, then he'd get back to his case notes.

His mind already on his coffee machine, it took Lewis a moment to realise that Marchfield Square was not as he had left it.

He was only a few steps through the gate when he spotted Philip Hetherington from Flat 2, his wheelchair parked up beside one of the benches. His wife, Mekhala, was sitting on the bench alongside him, and they were both wrapped up against the elements, Philip in a hat, scarf, and fingerless gloves, Mekhala in a thick, brightly patterned shawl.

Unusual for that time of the morning, however, Captain Gordon sat across from them on the opposite bench, and beside him was Victor DeFlore from the flat below Audrey's, the Captain's ugly little dog nestled on his lap. Surprised to see the garden so full so early, Lewis stopped dead at the sight of them.

Philip and Mekhala went out to sketch at least once a day, and Captain Gordon did his sudoku outside every afternoon, wind and rain excepted, but it had only just past nine. And Victor hardly ever sat outside in winter.

"Lewis!" called the Captain, his cut-glass accent slicing through Lewis's thoughts. "Join us!"

He approached warily. Talking to one resident at a time was plenty. Four at once felt like trouble.

"Lewis, nice to see you," said Philip, smiling up at him. His sketchbook was in his lap, but it wasn't open. "We've not spoken in a while. How're the edits going?"

"Uh . . . " Lewis didn't remember mentioning his edits to the Hetheringtons. "Fine, thanks?"

"Good, good."

"And work?" asked Victor, draping an arm over the back of the bench in what struck Lewis as a most unlikely gesture. "Still recruiting, are you?"

"Sadly, yes."

There was a pause.

"And how is Audrey?" asked Mekhala, her brown eyes warm and interested.

"Fine, I think."

Another pause. *Oh, no.* He realised in an instant. *Gordon's told them.*

"We heard she found another body," said Victor, and everyone turned to look at him. "What? You weren't fooling the boy. Speak your minds!" He looked straight at Lewis. "Is it true? Did she find a body?"

"A body that then disappeared?" prompted Mekhala.

"And you followed the killers to Tower Bridge?" asked Philip. "On Thursday night?"

Lewis looked accusingly at the Captain.

"Word may have got around," said the Captain, lightly. "But I didn't tell Manny and Joe, they already knew."

"Manny and Joe? What the hell . . . ?"

"I don't think Sarah knows," put in Victor, helpfully.

"Don't think Sarah knows what?" said a female voice from behind, making them all turn. "Is this about the body Audrey found?"

"Ah," said the Captain, finally having the decency to look embarrassed. "Hello, Sarah."

Sarah—a tall, thin woman with ash-blond curls who lived next door to Audrey and Mei—was standing on the lawn between two paths. She was from somewhere up north and had a little boy, although Lewis couldn't for the life of him remember his name.

"Yes, it's about the body," said Victor. "We were just asking Lewis about it."

"Is it true they put it in a suitcase?" asked Sarah. She had a heavy coat on, like she was going somewhere, but he had a sneaking suspicion she'd also just come out to be nosy.

They were all staring at him, waiting for him to answer.

"You can't blame us for being curious," said Philip, sounding entirely reasonable. "Some of us don't get out much."

"And a murder mystery is always interesting," added Victor. Lewis glared at him, remembering how unhelpful Victor had been the last time he and Audrey had had a case. "What? It's different when it's happening in your own back yard."

"Why don't you sit down and tell us all about it?" suggested the Captain, smoothing his silver moustache. "I'm sure everyone would like to hear the details, eh? Not just the edited highlights. We might be able to help."

The others nodded their agreement, looking at Lewis hopefully.

"Uh, sorry," he said, hefting his shopping bags. "I can't right now. I've got stuff to do. I'm . . . uh . . . just on my way to see Audrey."

"With your shopping?" asked Sarah, clearly amused. He ignored her.

"See you later," he said, walking off towards Audrey's side of the square, then added under his breath, "Much later."

He stomped up the steps as heavily as safety would allow and pounded on Audrey's door. She opened it a few seconds later, dark shadows under her eyes.

"What's wrong?"

"That," he said, turning and nodding down to the square below. She leaned past him and looked down to where the group of nosy parkers were staring up at them, and when they saw Audrey, they each raised a hand and waved to her. Every single one.

"Ah," she said, smiling and waving back. "You'd best come in."

She stood back to let him inside, and he put his bags down in the hall.

"They all know and want to help. Can you believe it?"

"Oh, that's sweet."

Lewis stared at her.

"It isn't sweet, it's stupid. Thirteen people can't solve a murder."

"Fourteen, if you count Tom."

"Tom?"

"Sarah's little boy."

"He probably knows too," said Lewis, rubbing his eyes. "I'm not equipped to deal with this. I've not even had coffee yet."

"I'll put the kettle on, shall I?" Audrey paused in the doorway to the kitchen. "Bring those croissants."

Lewis looked down at his shopping and saw the bulging paper bag exposed. Damn it.

Reluctantly, he carried the pastries to the kitchen, where Audrey was filling the kettle.

"Where are Mei and Sofia?" he asked as he walked in, wondering how many people he'd have to share his croissants with.

"They went out for breakfast."

"That man was back," he said, taking off his coat. "The one I saw outside the square while Petrov was here."

Audrey turned to him in horror.

"He's watching us?"

"Seems like it. He ran off when I tried to talk to him."

"Great. Stalked by a killer. This case just gets better and better."

Her tone was sarcastic, but she looked sick to her stomach. She busied herself making coffee while Lewis took a seat at the counter, cradling the pastry bag as he watched her take mugs and plates from the cupboard. Then she put a small French press on the counter in front of him, along with milk and sugar, and took a seat opposite, fishing the paper bag out of his hands.

"Patisserie Hercule?" she asked, taking out a croissant.

"Yes."

"Perfect."

He watched as she began to break up the pastry, pulling apart the buttery layers and folding one into her mouth.

"Don't tell me," she said, rolling her eyes. "I'm eating it wrong. I bet you just wolf it down, don't you?"

"Actually, I eat it the exact same way." He grinned. "You have to savour croissants from Hercule's."

"Right?!" She placed a flake of pastry on her tongue. "If the murder *was* a planned hit, do you think they wanted me to see the body? Timed it deliberately?"

"I doubt it." He reached for his own croissant. "What if the police had been quicker? Or believed you and called in Forensics? They'd have been discovered immediately. I wish we knew who the victim was. It's going to be hard to get anywhere without knowing that."

"Agreed. And I'm determined to get to the bottom of the cleaning. That crime scene firm I texted you about . . . They work for the police, among other people. I emailed a few companies yesterday, asking if they'd talk to me, and this one replied right away. I'd like to find out how the professionals would have done it."

"I'm interested, obviously," said Lewis, teasing apart his pastry. "But I don't see how it'll help. What does it matter how they cleaned?"

She frowned.

"It's important. I don't think many people could have done that. Not so well or so fast. If there was an expert cleaner, then we might have another way to identify the killer. Someone must have arranged everything."

"Fair enough." He shrugged. She had a point. "I doubt they'll be on Google, though. More dark-web stuff, that."

She ignored him, lifting flakes of pastry off her plate with a finger.

"Do you ever wonder about the people here?" she asked suddenly. "In Marchfield?"

"I try not to," he said, taking a second croissant out of the bag and offering her the last one. To his relief, she shook her head.

"No, thanks. I just mean . . . sometimes they say odd things. Like Celeste the other day, knowing about bodies in rivers. And Dixon. I know he's ex-military or something, but what exactly? He never mentions his family or a partner or anything personal, but I'm pretty sure he could do something more exciting than wait on an old lady all day. Then there's the Captain. Not only did he know about throat-cutting and body-dumping, but I think Celeste knew that he'd know. It seems weird."

"What I find weird is how interested they are. When there was a murder here, right under their noses, they all told us to leave it alone."

"Well, we know why that was, don't we?" said Audrey. "When you consider—"

She stopped abruptly.

"What?"

"Mekhala. She does portraits, right?"

"That's right." He remembered the Monet homage that Philip had given him last year, hanging as proudly above his desk as if it were the real thing. "Philip does landscapes."

"Do you reckon she could do a composite sketch?"

He stared at her, a smile creeping across his face as he caught up with her thinking.

"The victim," he said, nodding. "It's worth asking, isn't it? Can you remember him clearly enough?"

Audrey closed her eyes for a moment, then shuddered.

"Yes," she said. "I think so."

"Excellent." He lifted his coffee and toasted her. "They want to get involved, then let's get them involved. Nosy neighbours, here we come."

32
Audrey

"The bridge of the nose was just a little bit wider," said Audrey, as Mekhala made soft pencil strokes on the page. "But the hair is right."

They were sitting side by side on a squishy sofa in the open-plan living area in the Hetherington apartment, which took up the entire ground floor of what used to be the big house. Adapted by Celeste and the late Leonard van Duren to accommodate Philip's wheelchair, it was light-filled and spacious, with smooth wooden flooring and wide pathways between zones of furniture. Much like the house in Beaton Gardens, the walls were white and hung with even more paintings than Audrey remembered. Portraits, landscapes, sketches and oils—everywhere she turned, there was something beautiful to look at.

Lewis sat in an armchair opposite, while Philip had positioned his wheelchair beside him, watching his wife work with unconcealed admiration. Mekhala rubbed out a few lines and added some new ones.

"How's that?"

"Yes, that's it." Audrey moved her head about, looking at the picture. The man's eyes were, by necessity, closed in the picture, and the angle of the tipped-forward head in her memory was making it difficult to be precise, but the forehead and nose were right, she was sure.

"What about the jawline?" asked Mekhala. "Square? Narrow?"

Audrey closed her eyes again. The scene was becoming more vivid but somehow less distressing every time she brought it to mind. It didn't seem healthy.

"I'm not sure," she said, frowning. "The way it was pressed down onto the chest made it hard to tell." She opened her eyes. "Sorry."

"Don't worry," said Mekhala. "Pip, Lewis, would you put your heads down?" The two men did as they were told, dropping their heads forward. Audrey studied them. Lewis's jawline was squarer, without being harsh, while Philip's was softer, with laughter lines at the corners of the mouth, but a more defined chin.

"More like Philip than Lewis," she decided. "But less . . . " She sought the right word. "Soft?"

Mekhala smiled.

"You can say 'jowly,'" said Philip, patting the underside of his chin. "I know what I look like."

"And the face?" prompted Mekhala. "Could you see the cheekbones or not?"

"Yes, but just a bit," said Audrey, running her fingers across her own face. "And I think there might have been a cleft in the chin. Not very pronounced but . . . "

Mekhala continued sketching, rubbing out and adjusting while Audrey made suggestions, until finally, the image on the paper matched the image in her memory. An older white man with a broad, straight nose and heavy brows, his hair thick and on the messy side.

"Yes! That's what he looked like." She beamed at Mekhala, who put her pencil down and turned the pad around for Lewis and Philip to see.

"Wonderful, darling," said Philip.

"Wow." Lewis sounded doubtful. "You're sure you can remember him that well?"

"I'm not saying it's perfect," said Audrey, defensively, "and I only saw him for a few seconds, but that's what I see when I close my eyes."

"All right then." He nodded. "It's a good place to start."

"We should make some copies and give one to Sofia," she said, as Mekhala tore the sheet away from the pad. "That way, when the body washes up, she'll know it's ours."

"It might not be recognisable by the time it washes up," said Lewis. "Depends how long it stays in the river."

The Hetheringtons exchanged uneasy glances. Lewis could be very off-putting at times.

"Well, let's hope not," Audrey said, briskly. "I wonder where it will end up. Imagine if the Captain's right and it ends up in Wapping."

"That really doesn't seem likely," said Lewis.

"Ah, you never know," said Philip. "He's a clever man, Gordon."

Lewis got to his feet.

"I should go," he said. "I've got work to do."

"Me too," said Audrey, trying to sound more regretful than Lewis. "But thanks for this." She looked down at the picture in her hands, feeling better for having something tangible at last.

"You're most welcome," said Mekhala.

"And if you need any more help," added Philip, "you know where we are."

Lewis collected his shopping from where he'd left it in Audrey's hallway, then went home to continue work on his book, grumbling about defrosted food as he went. Left alone, Audrey sat at the kitchen counter, studying Mekhala's portrait of the victim.

The picture made him look slightly younger than she remembered, but otherwise, she was sure it was a good likeness. When she saw him in her mind's eye, however, the clothes still bothered her. He'd been dressed all in black, wearing a close-fitting top with long sleeves and trousers that had a utilitarian sheen to them, like wet-weather gear or sportswear. They just didn't seem like regular clothes.

The sound of a key in the lock made her drop the picture, and as Mei and Sofia clattered into the hallway, she called out.

"Hello, I'm in here."

Mei entered the kitchen, looking much better than the night before. She still had shadows under her eyes, but the cold air had pinked her cheeks, and she wore the trace of a smile. No doubt Sofia had cheered her up.

"Hey," said Mei when she saw her, and held up a paper bag. "Brought you back a pastry."

"Oh." Audrey smiled, remembering Lewis's poorly disguised crossness at her sharing his breakfast and momentarily feeling bad. "Thank you. I'll have it for lunch."

Mei's eyes fell on the sketch in front of her on the counter.

"What's that?"

Sofia walked in behind her, ponytail swishing as she went.

"That's a sketch that Mekhala did for us," said Audrey. "Of the murder victim."

Mei reached for the drawing, but the smile fell from Sofia's face at once.

"Who's Mekhala?"

"She's our neighbour," said Mei.

"Mekhala Hetherington in Flat 2," explained Audrey. "She's a portrait artist. Lewis and I went round this morning. We thought it might help."

Sofia let out a huff of frustration but said nothing as Mei handed her the picture. She studied it carefully, and Mei gave Audrey an apologetic smile. She and Lewis had clearly done the wrong thing. Again.

"I . . . wow, okay, this is a really good picture," said Sofia. "But it's less than ideal, having it done by an amateur. I'd have preferred it to be a police sketch artist." She held the paper away from her and her frown deepened. "I feel like I know this guy."

Audrey sat up straight.

"Really?"

"He's familiar anyway. Hard to be positive with the eyes shut but . . . you're sure this is what he looked like?"

"Yes."

They watched as Sofia gazed at the picture, blue eyes becoming unfocused and distant as she tried to remember. Then she pulled out her phone and dialled a number.

"What's happening?" asked Mei.

"I don't know." Audrey watched as Sofia paced up and down, her mobile pressed to her ear.

"Hey, Vaseem, are you busy? I need a quick favour. Can you pull up a file for me? Name of Grishin. Last August, I think it was." A pause while Sofia listened. "Yes, that's him. There should be an eyewitness e-fit in the file. Can you send me the picture? Yes, if you can. Thanks."

She disconnected the call and looked up.

"I expect I'm misremembering," she said, with a shrug. "Probably just a similar hairstyle or something, but might as well check while we're all here."

"I thought Mei might recognise it," said Audrey, and Mei looked at her in surprise.

"Me? Why would I—? Oh." Mei relaxed and let out a short laugh. "You mean my missing client. No, it's definitely not Baxter Cole. He's not your body at Beaton Gardens."

Disappointed, Audrey got up to put the kettle on, and Mei went to hang up her coat while Sofia took a seat at the counter. She accepted the offer of a cup of tea, but even after Mei returned, her eyes kept drifting back to Mekhala's sketch, her agitation increasingly apparent.

Then Sofia's phone pinged and she picked it up, unlocking it with her thumbprint and tapping through to the message. Another tap and a sharp breath in, then she held Mekhala's picture up alongside the phone. Eventually, she turned it round and showed Mei and Audrey the photo on the screen.

The image was a computer-generated composite, but it was lifelike and startlingly similar to the sketch in Sofia's other hand. Same shaggy, wavy hair and thick brows, same wide, straight nose and rounded jaw. In the computer image, he had dark eyes and a more distinct cleft in his chin, but they were undoubtedly the same man.

"Bloody hell, Auds," breathed Mei. "You nailed it. Who is it?"

"That," said Sofia, tapping the phone, "is Don Tyler. At least, that's one of his names. He's wanted in connection with half a dozen murders that we know of. Most likely more."

"A serial killer?" Audrey was stunned.

"A professional," corrected Sofia. "He kills people for money. He was originally a long-distance shooter, then he disappeared for a couple of decades. Last year, we got word he was back in London with a new M.O. Suspected of three murders by garrotting last year, and at the last one, we had an eyewitness to someone leaving the scene."

"Now you have another one," said Mei.

"Except he wasn't leaving the scene," said Audrey. "He *was* the scene."

They looked at each other, Mei looking as green as Audrey felt.

"Shit just got real," said Mei softly. "Who kills a hitman except another hitman?"

"I know," said Audrey, her mouth suddenly very dry.

"Might be time to rethink the investigation?"

"Yeah." She turned to Sofia. "Will the police look into it now? Is the sketch enough?"

Sofia sighed and ran a hand through her hair.

"If Don Tyler is in that suitcase, then we won't have a choice. Until he turns up, though, all we've got is an eyewitness to a vanishing crime scene; an inconclusive blood swab; three eyewitnesses to a suitcase possibly going into the Thames, which may or may not have a body in it; and now an amateur sketch of a man who looks like a composite of someone we suspect of being a professional killer." She shook her head. "Banham's going to go ballistic when he hears about all this."

Mei looked more stressed than ever.

"You should definitely back off, though, Auds. Please. For me."

"I know." Audrey nodded. "There's nothing more we can do until the body turns up, anyway, and this is way outside my comfort zone. I'll tell Lewis."

But as she reached for her phone, she knew that Lewis was not going to step back, regardless of what she decided for herself. Murder, burglaries, crime scene cleaners, and now hitmen . . . he'd probably be even more invested than before.

She knew exactly what he was going to say.

33
Lewis

Lewis was staring at his computer screen, wondering how on earth he was going to implement one particular editorial comment without unravelling the entire plot, when his phone pinged. He sighed when he realised it was Audrey. He'd only just left her, for crying out loud. Didn't she know he was busy?

> **THE CLEANER:** Sofia recognised the sketch of the victim. She thinks it might be a hitman called Don Tyler.

He spun his chair away from the computer. He hadn't expected Audrey's sketch to provide such fast results. If he was honest, he hadn't expected it to provide results at all.

> **LEWIS MCLENNON:** Good work! It means we were right. It was a professional job. I wonder whether Tyler was attempting a hit and it went wrong, or he was always the intended victim.
>
> **THE CLEANER:** Given that this proves it's organised crime, and the killer knows where we live, maybe it's time to hand over to the police?

He frowned at his phone. She was getting cold feet again. He recognised this from last time. All he had to do was keep her focused on the puzzle, and she'd forget about the danger.

Assuming there was any danger. If they'd wanted her dead, they could have killed her at the time, at the pre-prepared crime scene. Or later, in her flat, when they went in to steal the vacuum bags. It would have made the killer's life a lot easier.

The thought made something worm in his brain, however, and so he tried another angle.

> **LEWIS MCLENNON:** Until that suitcase washes up, what can they do? If we can help speed things up, that's ideal, right? You can get your job back faster. Besides, you said you'd meet those crime scene cleaners tomorrow. It would be rude not to show up. I bet they have all kinds of products you don't have.
>
> **THE CLEANER:** If you're trying to manipulate me, it's not going to work. I had no intention of not showing up tomorrow, because unlike you, I'm polite. It has nothing to do with cleaning products!

He grinned, then put down his phone and turned back to the computer, clicking away from his novel and into the *True Crime Reality Check* forums.

He ran a search for the name Tyler and came up with a few results, but nothing more recent than twenty years ago. The posts were related to unsolved crimes, alleged to have involved professional killers, but half the usernames were marked as deleted, and all the links to the original news articles were dead.

> **[Account Deleted]**
> Another member of the Barnes crew taken out last week. Only half a column in the *Standard*, pg 13, 11/7/2000. Sounds like Quinn from the description, or else Tyler or Macdonald.

~JohnDoe~

Civil servant found dead in Soho warehouse. *The Times*, 3/3/2001, page 2.

Article suggests she was meeting a boyfriend and doesn't say how she was killed, but I heard from someone in the force it was a professional job. Long shot from an AW rifle. Who uses an AW?

[Account Deleted]

For a high profile, they'd have used Tyler, or else Jones/Carr/Quinn, or whatever name he's using now. Unless there's a new kid on the block.

[Account Deleted]

There usually is. Don't last long though!

[Account Deleted]

New hit over in Clerkenwell. Media blackout, but cops reckon Jackson or Tyler.

OldManTrouble62

Word is Don Tyler's not been around since 2003. Jackson most likely. Or Macdonald, if he's still operating.

Outdated gossip from those with underworld contacts wasn't much help, but the dates were useful. The posts strongly implied that Tyler was an experienced killer twenty-odd years ago. Audrey had said the victim looked to be at least in his sixties, maybe older, and if this guy already had a reputation back in the early noughties, then that would comfortably put him at fifty or older.

He wrote his own post.

CrimeWriter159

Wondering if anyone knows what became of a professional called Don Tyler, back in the noughties? Been researching different M.O.s and discovered his name in some archived posts on here. Seems he was a big name who might have vanished abroad. Retired or dead?

At the exact moment he hit the button to post his message, he felt a twinge of apprehension that openly enquiring about a recently murdered hitman might not be the wisest thing he'd ever done, but Tyler was dead, and Lewis had written many similar posts in the past. People would be able to see that from his profile. It was totally normal for a crime writer to ask questions like that.

He smiled then, remembering that tomorrow he was going to be able to ask a real-life crime scene cleaner all kinds of questions that could be useful for his books. It was a shame Audrey had had to tell the guy he was a writer, though; that always led to embarrassment, as people either felt awkward that they'd never heard of him or else remembered his first—and only—successful book and assumed he'd gone into retirement. Informing them that he had, in fact, written two more novels, neither of which anyone had wanted to buy, was a humiliation that never seemed to fade.

He sighed, closed the forum, and went back to his novel. Time for things to change.

34
Audrey

At ten o'clock on Sunday morning, Audrey met Lewis at the side gate, and together they walked to the Royal Chelsea Hospital to catch the bus to Vauxhall. London on a Sunday morning always had a different feel. Nothing opened until late, if at all, and the traffic eased as much as it ever did, leaving the roads clearer for taxis and buses. It was quiet enough that you could hear church bells ringing all over.

"Any news from Sofia?" he asked as they waited at the bus stop. "Have they found the body yet?"

"No, nothing." Audrey tucked some stray hair under her hat. "She'll take the sketch in on Monday and tell DI Banham what's been going on. She's not looking forward to it."

For a moment, Audrey thought Lewis looked worried, but then he nodded and pointed down the street to where a red bus was trundling towards them.

The air wasn't as cold as it had been, but the damp had increased, and as the bus stopped and started along its route, she watched condensation trickle down the windows. She much preferred the cold.

Google said the address was a low-rent hotel, and they found it easily enough, stopping outside just as the door opened and a woman carrying a small suitcase exited the building.

"They still have guests?" said Audrey, confused.

"They gave you a room number, right?" said Lewis. "Must be localised. No point closing down the entire hotel."

She felt nervous, unsure of whether it was because of the crime scene she was about to see or the quasi job interview she was about to go through.

"I suppose we'd better take a look then," she said.

Lewis followed her inside to a small and shabby lobby with generic blue-patterned hotel carpet and off-white walls. A tired-looking concierge looked up but didn't greet them. They walked past the lift towards a corridor, where a sign on the wall directed them to either Rooms 101–110 on the left or the Conference Suite to the right.

"Not very big," said Lewis in a low voice, as they passed half a dozen white doors. "Who'd want to have a conference here?"

They followed the corridor round to the right to a room at the end, beside the fire door. Room 110. Audrey took a deep breath, then knocked smartly on the door.

Two seconds later, it opened, and a petite woman with olive skin and large dark eyes above a filtration mask looked up at them. The rest of her was covered in a white paper hazmat suit, which she wore with the hood up.

Audrey opened her mouth to speak, but the woman turned away.

"John," she called, her voice muffled behind the mask. "For you."

The woman walked away from the door but left it open, and a second white hazmat suit appeared, taller this time, with broad shoulders and a close-shaven beard. He pulled his mask down with a gloved hand, then did the same for his hood, revealing an attractive man with light-brown skin and tightly curled hair who was already smiling at them.

"Audrey?"

"Yes." She flushed immediately. "John?"

"That's right. John Keane." He looked at Lewis and held out his hand. "You must be the crime writer?"

Lewis looked down at the hand, and John laughed.

"Don't worry, it's clean. We've not got started yet."

Lewis grinned and shook his hand.

"Lewis McLennon. Thanks for letting me tag along."

"Hey, any time. Your name's familiar. Would I have read anything of yours?"

"Doubtful," said Lewis, his voice tight now. "*Place a Candle on My Grave*?"

"That was you?" John took a step back. "Whoa. So you wrote *Stone Rites* too? Man, I loved that one."

"I—what?" Lewis blinked, and even Audrey was surprised. Lewis never mentioned his third book.

"Yeah, that final scene at the mausoleum?" John shook his head in what appeared to be genuine admiration. "Brilliant."

Seemingly at a loss, Lewis glanced at Audrey before replying.

"Thanks," he said, actually blushing. "I didn't expect you to be a reader."

Oh, *God*. Audrey cringed inside. Lewis was Lewis-ing again. Fortunately, John looked more confused than insulted, tilting his head to one side and frowning.

"Sorry?"

"Of him," Audrey put in hurriedly. "Of Lewis's books. Not books in general."

She gave Lewis a look, and he turned a deeper shade of red.

"Yes, yes, that's what I meant." He began to stumble over his words. "I mean . . . I just . . . I've never met anyone who's even heard of that book, let alone read it and liked it. Very kind of you to say."

There was an awkward pause.

"Great!" said Audrey, trying to rally. "I was worried this would be awkward."

"Oh, not at all," said John. "I'm very happy to talk about what we do. People are always interested in the crimes, not so much in the cleanup, but it really is fascinating."

"So I'm told," said Lewis, glancing sideways at her, and John laughed.

"There speaks a man not yet convinced. Well, buckle up, because this might get nerdy. You guys all right to put suits on? Then we can get started. You'll have to step inside first. We're under strict instructions not to make the other guests nervous."

He stood aside to let them both into the room, an off-white–painted box with a brown-striped carpet and a double bed with a mattress zipped inside a protective cover. The carpet was stained with several patches of dried blood, and the wall opposite the bed was covered in spatter. The air smelled strange: a dry, fusty scent of synthetic lavender faintly tinged with chemicals.

John handed them each a paper suit and a pair of overboots, along with a pair of gloves and a mask.

"No one died here, just to be clear," he said as they suited up. "But it was a nasty fight, and it's left quite a mess."

"I'll say," said Audrey, looking at the bloodstains.

"They stabbed each other," said the woman from over near the window. She had a bottle of cleaning spray and a wad of paper in her hands, but she wasn't working; she was watching them closely. Audrey wondered what the product was.

"This is Laila," said John. "She's my best cleaner."

"Hi," said Audrey, giving her a little wave. Laila nodded in response.

"And they're both still alive?" asked Lewis, also looking at the floor. "Seems like a lot of blood."

"Apparently," said John. "We've been hired by the hotel to make the room usable again."

"Not the police?"

"We work for the police sometimes too," said John, "but not today. And it's not our place to ask questions beyond what we need to do the job properly and safely. Whether drugs were involved, what debris there might be, any other circumstances that may be relevant. When dealing with blood, we do wear masks to avoid any pathogens, but as you won't be doing any cleaning, you'll be okay in the disposables." He smiled, and Audrey couldn't help but smile back. "Any more questions? No? Well, now that you're both suited and booted, we can get started."

35

Lewis

Lewis and Audrey put on what Lewis recognised as a particulate mask, while John took off his respirator and put on a disposable.

"Easier for you to hear me," he said by way of explanation. "The first thing we do is an assessment of the scene and the space. What trace is where, and how much of a risk it poses. You can see here, we have blood in a lot of places—the carpet, the walls, the bedframe—and there's lots in the bathroom, too, where I assume someone went to get a towel to try to stem the flow of bleeding. We'll use ultraviolet light to check for invisible trace too. Right from the start, I can tell that the carpet can't be saved. That amount of blood, sitting for this long . . . those stains won't come out, so the hotel will need to replace it."

"Is that always the case with carpet?" asked Audrey.

"Not always, but often, yes." John turned to the bed. "Now, the mattress is zipped into two separate protector covers, plus it had a topper, a sheet, and a duvet over it, and we've already disposed of the bedding. When we're done, we'll remove the covers, and the hotel can replace them but save the mattress. The bedframe looks like wood, but it isn't, so that can be cleaned and disinfected easily."

"Is wood easy to clean?" asked Lewis, seeing an opportunity to get the lowdown on their own crime scene.

"Depends on whether it's varnished or not," said John. "It can be difficult to get all traces out of the grain, though, and you might need to sand it down afterwards, to fix any discoloration."

"What are you going to use on the walls?" asked Audrey, crouching down to examine the blood spatter. "Do you have one product that cleans and sanitises, or do you use multiple products?"

"Zabimax to clean it off," said Laila, from over near the window. "Then we spray with Detergise to disinfect. Let that soak in. Then we do that again, and then clean it off."

"I just got some Zabimax," said Audrey, sounding way too enthusiastic to be talking about a cleaning product. "I've never heard of Detergise, though."

"It's specialist," said Laila, turning back to the windowsill.

"Very specialist," said John, laughing. "Laila's own creation. Now, regardless of whether we can see any trace, we clean everything. Walls, windows, furniture, ceilings. Just in case. Now in the bathroom"—he walked over to where the bathroom door opened off the tiny hallway—"things are a bit different. Much easier to clean and sanitise, and easier to spot any trace too." He held the door back with one hand, allowing them to see inside. There were smears of blood on the sink and countertop, and a few splashes on the floor.

"Zabimax and Detergise in here?" asked Audrey. "Or would you use bleach?"

"Bleach isn't actually that effective in removing blood. We have several specialist products we use, depending on the surface."

"So what's the easiest surface to get blood off?" asked Lewis. "If you were planning a murder and you had to clean it up, what would you choose?"

Audrey frowned, but John's eyes crinkled at the corners, and Lewis could tell he saw the funny side.

"Plastic," he said, and a thrill went up Lewis's spine. "Plastic sheet in a bathroom with white tiles. Plastic is easy to remove, tiles are easy to clean, and with white, you can spot any trace more easily." He laughed. "I hope this is for a book!"

"It is," said Lewis, and it wasn't even a half-truth. He was already mentally filling in scenes for his next DI Harding book. "You're right, it is interesting."

"Glad you think so." John turned to Audrey. "This scene is pretty straightforward in terms of what we do. Others are more complex, and when they're in a family home, more sensitive. The police Forensics teams are pretty good and take away the worst of the matter, but some of them can be a bit . . . " He paused, searching for the right word.

"Gross," finished Laila from the other side of the room.

"Gruesome," said John, shooting her a look.

"I was thinking about doing a course," said Audrey. "Would that be useful?"

"That's not a bad idea, although if you did decide to come and work for us, we'd provide training. And obviously, we don't put anyone on a job they're not ready for. I can email you some links for accredited programmes, though."

"Thanks. Any chance I could look at your products? I've seen a couple of new enzyme-based solutions on the market lately, and I'm just wondering what you use."

"Be my guest." John indicated two plastic crates of cleaning stuff that had been tucked into an alcove in the hall. Sprays, bottles, gloves, and paper towels all stuck out from it, and Audrey kneeled down and began going through it. At the first "ooh," Lewis turned away, walking over to the corner by the window to get a better view of the room.

As John crouched down beside Audrey and they began to chat about bleach or whatever, Lewis tried to take a mental snapshot of the room. The number of steps between the bed and the walls, where the blood had dripped onto the carpet, the direction in which it had spattered up the wall.

"You can take pictures if you like," said Laila, who was now wiping over the wall beneath the dressing table with something that smelled medicinal and fruity at the same time. She spoke in a low voice. "I won't say anything. Just put it on silent."

"Really?" said Lewis, immediately unzipping his suit to retrieve his phone and switching it onto silent. He didn't need to be told twice.

"Get the bathroom, too, if you can. It's a good one."

Lewis looked at her curiously. "Purely professional interest, you understand."

"See that there?" She pointed to a cracked, circular indentation in the plaster of the wall opposite, just level with Lewis's eyes. "Someone had their head bashed into that."

He immediately stepped over to take a picture of it.

"And that brown mark there?" she went on. "Dried blood. You can see a few hairs sticking out of it."

Lewis could hear his own interest reflected in the tone of her voice. He hesitated, finding himself in the unusual position of wanting to know more about someone.

"How long have you been doing this?" he asked.

"Eight years."

"Were you a regular cleaner first?"

"No. It's always been bioremediation."

"Bioremediation," he repeated, typing that into his phone. "That's cool."

"Yes."

She carried on cleaning, and Lewis floundered, not used to being the one in charge of small talk.

"Did you go to university?"

"Yes."

"What did you study?"

"Chemistry with forensic science."

"And you didn't want to go into lab work? Or the police?"

"No, I like cleaning."

"Weird."

It slipped out before he could stop himself, but although he braced for her to take offence the way Audrey usually did, she didn't react. He wished very much he could see her face.

"Any other questions?" said John, getting to his feet. "Laila and I need to get stuck in, I'm afraid."

"Just one," said Audrey, also standing. She looked from John to Laila and back again. "How long will it take you to clean this room properly? To make sure you remove every single trace?"

Laila straightened up, appearing to watch John closely as he thought.

"I think . . . three to four hours?" he said. "Not including the carpet removal, which the hotel will do. What do you think, Laila?"

She shrugged.

"Not long then," said Audrey, her gaze flicking over to Lewis. "You must be very good at what you do."

Lewis could tell by the way John's eyes twinkled that he was pleased by the compliment and was glad. He'd hoped these people might be useful; it hadn't occurred to him he might like them.

As he and Audrey removed their protective coverings in the tiny hall, he took a surreptitious photo of the blood-stained bathroom. He pretended not to notice Audrey glaring at him.

John showed them to the door, once again removing his hood and mask to say goodbye.

"Email me if you have any other questions. Or text." He smiled down at Audrey. "You've got my mobile, haven't you?"

"Uh, yes." She smiled back. "Yes, thanks. I will."

"And Lewis." They shook hands again. "Great to meet you, man. Can't wait to read your next book."

Nobody had said that to Lewis in a really long time, and he tried not to grin too widely, lest he look like a maniac.

"Thanks." He tried to sound casual. "Thanks very much."

As they walked down the blue-carpeted corridor and away from Room 110, neither of them spoke, and it wasn't until they'd left the hotel altogether that they looked at each other. The traffic had picked up, as had the wind, and they both fastened their coats as a bus roared by.

"That was *great*," said Lewis, and Audrey burst out laughing.

They got the bus home.

36
Audrey

Audrey spent Sunday afternoon in an armchair in front of the television, processing her exhilarating morning with John and Laila. Sofia and Mei had still been in bed when she'd left for her appointment, and now they were settled in for an *Antiques Hunt* marathon, snuggled up on the sofa while Audrey played third wheel in the armchair.

Her laptop sat on the arm of the chair, the browser open at her favourite YouTube channel. CrochetSteve was a genius, although his voice was a bit annoying, so she tended to watch him with the sound off, hypnotised by the movement of his hands as he crocheted an astonishing array of toys, jackets, and blanket squares. Tonight he was making a stuffed dragon, and she found the methodical way he worked very soothing, allowing her mind to wander and process the last few days.

As she gazed at the laptop, she thought through the cleanup of the scene at 35 Beaton Gardens yet again. Even assuming she could carry the body out by herself, Audrey couldn't have done it in the time. There had to have been more than one person, right from the start. But that meant that wherever in Mr. Petrov's house they'd been hidden, the space had to fit no fewer than three bodies as well as all their cleaning equipment. And would the cleaner have brought a mop? Their own vacuum?

The vacuum. She'd left the vacuum on the landing when she'd run out of the house. If you were hastily cleaning and a vacuum was sitting exactly where you needed it, would you go to the time-wasting trouble of getting out a new one? Or would you use what was already there?

With a witness waiting outside and the police already on the way? She knew what she'd have done. That must have been why they'd broken in to steal the bags of dirt, because they knew there'd be proof in them.

She cursed herself for not locking them away safely or else hiding them better, but it hadn't occurred to her that anyone would know she had them. How long had the burglar rooted about in their belongings before they found the bags under the sink? She hadn't been in the bath that long, yet they'd gotten in and out with terrifying efficiency.

Which was starting to be something of a habit with these people.

She thought again about what Lewis had said, about the killer watching as she'd cleaned. If so, then they'd have known she'd put the vacuum contents in her cleaning bag, and where did everyone keep their cleaning products? Under the sink. It was obvious, really.

Her cleaning bag.

She'd forgotten to get it back from Celeste's. Audrey groaned and hit pause on the video. She'd better get it before Celeste settled in for the evening. What an id—

She squeaked, and Mei looked up, alarmed, startled out of her TV binge-induced fugue state.

"What's wrong?"

"My cleaning bag. I left it at Celeste's."

"Is that all?"

"It had a bag in it. Of dust."

Now Sofia sat up.

"I thought you said they were—"

"I know, and they were. But I missed one. I found it when I was at Celeste's. It might still be there!"

Half a minute later, she was urgently pressing Celeste's doorbell. Dixon didn't even greet her through the intercom, just buzzed her straight up, and she took the stairs two at a time, arriving at the door out of breath and barely able to speak.

The minute she was inside, she located her cleaning bag, tucked neatly into a corner of the hall. She fell down beside it, shuffling through her cleaning products while Dixon looked on.

"Audrey? What's all this?" said Celeste, coming into the hall. The smell of roasting meat drifted in with her.

"Hoover bag," said Audrey, breathing hard. "In here." *Where was it? It had to be here, it had to be.* But Mr. Petrov had been at Celeste's all Friday afternoon. He'd have had plenty of time to search her bag if he'd wanted. Then she remembered. "Pockets!"

She unzipped the front pocket and, with a cry, held her prize aloft.

"What is that, Audrey dear?" asked Celeste, wrinkling her nose at the sandwich bag of grey dirt labelled "Second Floor."

"That," said Audrey, "is evidence from the crime scene. We were burgled, me and Mei. Friday afternoon. They took the vacuum dust Lewis and I bagged up from every room at Beaton Gardens. All of them, or so I thought."

"Friday?" said Celeste, pale blue eyes boring into Audrey's. "You're quite sure?"

"Yes. I put the bags in the cupboard on Friday morning, and later, when I was in the bath after work, I heard strange noises downstairs. Later that night, I found the bags were gone. But I missed one, and so they missed one." She shook the bag at them. "The bag from the murder floor! Hah!"

Celeste and Dixon, who were concerned and angry, grilled her to within an inch of her life about the break-in, but eventually she managed to escape, taking both her cleaning bag and the evidence bag home.

She carried the sandwich bag to the kitchen and, after putting on a pair of gloves and with Mei and Sofia looking over her shoulder, put the bag in the kitchen sink, where she began to sift through the contents, trying to keep everything contained by the plastic.

"We should really get the lab to do this," said Sofia, sounding unhappy and excited at the same time. "You don't know what might be in there."

But she didn't stop her, so Audrey carried on sifting, combing through dust, hair, and carpet fibres. A couple of long strands of hair, which were most likely hers, plus some shorter dark ones, which could have been from Lewis, or maybe the victim. Some short blond-looking ones, which she thought was interesting, but then Sofia had been there, too, and hair broke all the time.

What she was hoping to find, however, she found: white fibres from a woven cotton dust sheet. She knew from experience that dust sheets had a tendency to drop strands when moved, so if someone had bundled the body up in the one on the chair, it was likely they'd have shed some during removal. Evidence that the sheets had been moved. Hopefully there'd be some sort of trace.

She took a piece of paper towel and laid it beside the sink, carefully placing each fibre she found on top. She was up to six when she caught a glimpse of red on white, and her heart skipped a beat.

"Is that what I think it is?" asked Mei, eyes wide.

"Blood," said Audrey, trying to stay calm. "It must be."

Soon, she had a dozen cotton fibres laid out on the paper, each about half an inch long, two of them with delicate red tips. The third was longer, and fully half of it was soaked in blood. Perhaps the weight of the blood had pulled the fibre out, or perhaps it had already worked its way free and so had reached further into the pool beneath the chair, but it was definitely proof that there had been a sheet and that it had been in the presence of blood.

She took a picture of the blood-soaked fibres and sent it to Lewis.

He replied right away.

> **FLAT 5 GUY:** Bloody hell! That was a bit of luck. Can you get Sofia to send them for testing?

Exhilarated and triumphant at having finally gotten one over on the thieves, she turned to Sofia.

"Can you get those tested?" she asked. "You can take the whole bag, but I had to see if I was right. Dust sheets are a nightmare; they drop threads everywhere."

Sofia nodded.

"Of course. Let's get them in some clean Tupperware, though, before they're contaminated." She took a deep breath. "I'll talk to Dean tomorrow. Open a case, explain what all this is about. He's not going to be happy."

"I didn't realise DI Banham *could* be happy," said Audrey, placing the fibres carefully into a little plastic pot. "But thank you."

And when she told Lewis, a few minutes later, he also expressed his gratitude.

> **FLAT 5 GUY:** About bloody time.

37
Celeste

From her armchair in the gallery nook, Celeste watched as London turned its lights on. It was getting on to half past five, and night was falling, turning the damp, grey sky cluttered with damp, grey buildings into a glittering spectacle.

London, as far as Celeste was concerned, seemed to be growing uglier and uglier, with increasingly few pockets of beauty unadulterated by crass modern development. At sunrise and sunset, however, and particularly at night, it seemed more beautiful than ever. How lucky she was to have this view.

A soft clink from the room behind made her lean around. Dixon had begun to lay the table.

"Nearly ready," he said without looking up.

Celeste rose and took a last look at the view, then, after a stroll around the room to stretch her hips and back, took her seat at the table.

Dixon placed a steaming bowl of roast potatoes in the middle of the table, along with a small jug of gravy, then returned with two plates of roast chicken and green beans. They'd simplified their meals since Leonard had passed, as well as their portion sizes. Leonard had had a bigger appetite than even Dixon, and the reduction in food bills still gave Celeste a pang. She wondered if Dixon missed him.

He sat down opposite her, and they reached for their napkins.

"I were thinking beef next week," said Dixon. "It's been a while since we've had Yorkshire pudding, and I've a hankering."

Celeste smiled. They were, as ever, in alignment. Roast beef and Yorkshire pudding had been Leonard's favourite.

"Good idea," she said, helping herself to potatoes.

They ate in silence for a minute or two, but thoughts of Leonard began to bring a lump to her throat, threatening to spoil her appetite.

"I shall ring Anton after supper," she said to distract herself. "Ask him to get onto the Trinity people about Audrey and Lewis and get Audrey reinstated. I shall suggest that he owes her a favour. See what he says."

Dixon swallowed his mouthful.

"Where's he staying?"

"Brown's."

"Has he been to the house?"

"I'm not sure. He said he would but didn't mention when. He was very vague."

Dixon snorted.

"Stock in trade, isn't it?"

"But not with me, Dixon, not with me." Celeste took another mouthful and chewed.

"There was nothing suspicious in the gate logs," said Dixon, after a minute. "On Friday. Before or after he left."

"I didn't think there would be," she said. "But it doesn't mean he didn't do it."

"Accomplice?"

"Possibly. Someone young and spry."

"Could he have done it himself?"

"Oh, I should think so. He's not as slight as he was, admittedly, but he had light feet and lighter fingers. He could easily have done it." She felt a prickle of anger that Anton thought he could use her to facilitate a break-in, on her own property, no less. "I won't stand for it, Dixon."

"'Course not. If it was him, we'll deal with it."

She nodded.

"He has a château in Antibes and seems to be enjoying his life very much. He has a lady friend, and they travel. He sees both his children, has a grandchild on the way. In all other respects, he was an open book."

"But?"

"When I first spoke to him on the telephone and told him about the murder, he seemed rattled. Discombobulated. But when he got here, he seemed more concerned with his clocks. Evasive. Almost stupidly so."

"He was hiding something."

"Exactly. But if he was in France when the murder happened, then what could he possibly be hiding? I stopped short of asking to see his passport to check the stamp, but it crossed my mind."

Dixon didn't reply, and she knew he was working over the problem.

"What're the options? That he arranged the killing himself? Seems unlikely if he were shocked, like you say. That he let someone else use his place for it? Also unlikely, for the same reason. Mebbe he knows who it was in the chair. Made a few calls of his own before he got here and knows something we don't. Or else he knows the killer and it's all been squared away, privately."

Celeste thought for a moment, then laid down her knife and fork.

"I think you've hit the nail on the head," she said, slowly. "He had plenty of time, after all." She pursed her lips, playing back her afternoon with Anton Petrov, reviewing his attitude in line with this theory. Dixon helped himself to more potatoes.

"Yes," she said at last. "I think that's it. The trespass on his property at the very least should agitate him, if not the murder. The fact that he's so unmoved by either must mean that he approves the killing, albeit after the fact. He knows either the victim or the killer."

"Any chance he arranged the killing? Don't let yer dinner get cold."

"I don't think so," she said, lifting her cutlery again. "Anton left all that behind a long time ago, and was glad to do so. He may have done what was required, but he preferred the planning. The machinations. The dirty work was never to his taste. He was rather like you in that respect."

Dixon didn't react.

"By that reckoning, then," he said, squeaking his knife across some beans, "it means either the killer's a friend of his or the victim's an enemy. Sound about right?"

Celeste smiled. How she missed conversations like this.

"Sounds spot on."

"So how do you get him to talk?"

"Ah, now that's the problem. How indeed? He'll want to play the game, I'm sure."

"You could set Audrey on him."

"That might work, although I rather fancy Lewis might stand a better chance. Evasiveness always crumbles in the face of irritation. Bless his heart."

They finished their meal quite cheerfully, and as Dixon stood to clear the table, Celeste's mind went back to the heavy suitcase, currently travelling along the depths of the Thames.

"Of course, if the body doesn't surface soon," she called through to the kitchen, "I might have to take a crack at him myself."

"I'd like t'see that," said Dixon, returning for the serving dishes. "I think you would too."

"Cheeky. I don't suppose there's anything we can do to expedite it?"

Dixon clattered the bowls in surprise.

"Finding the body?" He shook his head. "You'd need a boat with scanning equipment, a couple of divers, a skipper, and a permit, most likely."

"Pft," said Celeste, batting away the details. "And I thought bureaucracy was bad in my day. It's positively Orwellian now."

"Aye," said Dixon, his expression turning to one of amusement. "It's shocking how they won't let the general public search the Thames for bodies anymore."

"I'm hardly the general public, Dixon. If they'd just do their job, I wouldn't need to."

"It'll surface," he said, walking off with the dishes. "Be patient. Let nature take its course."

As she waited for Dixon to return with her ice cream, Celeste's gaze fell on the photograph of Leonard on the sideboard, then on the one of Madeleine. She sighed. That was the problem with being eighty-two. Patience was no longer a virtue.

38
Lewis

Monday was always a comedown for Lewis, returning to work after the weekend, but this Monday was proving more hideous than most.

Not one, not two, but *three* of his candidates had landed the jobs they'd interviewed for, one of which was a very senior position at a major communications firm. Lewis had made a concerted effort to keep his head down at work, and now, not only was he having to deal with this unexpected paperwork, but Steve was prowling around his cubicle, looking pleased as punch and muttering about management.

He glared at his screen. His mind couldn't be less on his job these days, so how on Earth was he suddenly succeeding at it?

He distinctly remembered thinking that the woman who'd kept trying to ask him about his job while he was trying to ask her about hers seemed perfect for human resources. It had been a casual suggestion on his part, but she'd taken it seriously and, a few months later, had apparently knocked her first interview out of the park. Steve had always said there was a lot of instinct involved in recruitment, but where had these hideous instincts come from?

His phone vibrated on the desk, and he hastily turned it to silent.

> **THE CLEANER:** Message from Dixon. Mr. Petrov got onto Trinity this morning, and they've agreed to get

> the camera footage ready for us to look at. When's good for you?

Lewis looked forlornly at the screen. There was no way he could get out of work again. She'd have to go without him.

> **LEWIS MCLENNON:** I can't get out of work again. Sorry.

He sighed and went back to filling out the form, but five minutes later, his phone flashed again.

> **THE CLEANER:** No worries. I just called Felix, and apparently Mr. Petrov said he was to meet us "at our convenience." I told him 5:30. I'll wait for you outside.

His heart leaped. It hadn't occurred to him he could ask her to wait. Maybe today wouldn't be completely awful after all.

By five past five, he was striding down a rapidly darkening Piccadilly in the direction of the bus stop, with his arm stuck out for any passing taxi. If he could get one, a cab would be marginally quicker, but failing that, a number 19 bus would take him almost door to door, if he could bear the frustration of it stopping every sixty seconds. The roads were damp, and Lewis was grateful for the dusk, making the illuminated taxi signs easier to see.

He'd just reached the bus stop when a cab pulled in, and fifteen minutes later, he got out on Lower Sloane Street, a few yards away from the Trinity offices. Audrey was nowhere to be seen, so he stood to one side, away from the door, and waited.

Over the course of the next few minutes, almost a dozen people exited the building, men and women of all ages, dressed in smart office attire. He waited for them to leave, then leaned round to look through the window.

Casetti was deep in conversation with the receptionist—Jess, was it? His elbow was on the counter, and he was leaning down towards her, his face close to her ear. She didn't look happy about it.

Of course Casetti was that type. Lewis wasn't even surprised. He was just about to open the door and go in when someone touched him on the shoulder.

"Hello," said Audrey. Her cheeks were pink, and her hair was windswept, auburn strands flying outwards and glowing in the light of the streetlamps. "Have you been waiting long?"

"Just a few minutes. Where have you come from?"

"Home," she said. "My last job finished at four, but I caught the bus, and I forget it always takes longer at this time."

He wanted to thank her for arranging the meeting to suit him, but it sounded weird in his head, so he just nodded towards the door.

"Shall we? I think Casetti's putting the moves on Jess, and she doesn't look too happy."

Audrey peered around the doorframe and her expression changed at once.

"Steph. And no, she doesn't. Come on." She opened the door quietly, no doubt intending to surprise the creep.

"—forget about it," said Casetti, his voice just loud enough to be heard in the otherwise-quiet room. "Trust me, you've nothing to worry about."

Lewis shot Audrey a confused glance, but as they neared the desk, Steph looked up and Casetti turned around.

"Hello," said Audrey, cheerfully. "Thanks so much for waiting."

"Audrey, hey," said Casetti, agitatedly running a hand through his hair. "No problem at all, thanks for coming by. And, uh . . ." He looked at Lewis. "Lewie, was it?"

"Lewis," said Lewis, more annoyed than he knew he had a right to be. "McLennon."

"Of course, Lewis." Casetti smirked. "Shall we go up to my office? I've got it all set up for you. Steph, could you let Roland know our guests are here?"

He walked away from the receptionist without a backward glance, and Lewis and Audrey followed him up the stairs, his shiny black shoes clicking against the metal edging.

They turned a corner and kept climbing, emerging onto a landing with a watercooler and a plasticky-looking sofa. Casetti led them through double doors into an open-plan office, not unlike the one Lewis had just left. The desks in the middle were wide, separated from each other by low felt-backed walls, while on either side of the room, several private offices were walled off, their doors frosted glass. Two people remained at work, a few desks apart, one on the phone, the other tapping away on their computer.

"In here, please," said Casetti, guiding them towards the first office in the nearest row. He held the door, directing them to the two seats in front of his desk, then sat down behind it.

No one spoke for a moment, then Casetti steepled his fingers and pressed his forefingers to his lips.

"This is a very strange situation," he began, smiling his fake smile. "We downloaded the security footage from the last month. I've gone through it, and I can't see anything untoward at all."

Lewis heard Audrey hiss as she sucked in a breath.

"I advised Mr. Petrov of that, but he insisted we show you. For everyone's peace of mind, he said." Casetti patted a drive encased in rubber sitting in the middle of the desk. It was connected to his monitor via a cable. "I'll just play it for you, shall I?"

He clicked his mouse a few times, then turned the monitor towards them. Lewis had been expecting the camera to be trained on the outside of the house—the front step or the path, perhaps. Instead, the screen showed the inside of the Petrov residence, the front door clearly visible at the end of the hall.

"Wait, so that's . . . " Audrey squinted at the screen, as if trying to get her bearings. "There's a camera above the kitchen door?"

"That's right. Looks a bit like a smoke alarm."

"Is there sound?"

"No, just video. You can see from the time stamp in the corner that we're starting at eleven o'clock. I'm going to speed it up, so shout if you want me to pause."

Lewis sat forward, watching closely as the timer ticked on. Nothing moved in the hall, not even the light, and then suddenly, at 11:33, there was Audrey in the hall, entering the alarm code. With a click, Casetti slowed the recording.

They watched as Audrey dropped her bag, hung up her coat, and took off her shoes. Then, for some reason, she crouched down and put her hands on the floor.

"What on earth are you doing?" demanded Lewis, looking across at her. "Why are you on the floor?"

"I'd been outside freezing for ages," she said, her face turning red. "I was so cold, I couldn't feel my fingers, and Mr. Petrov has underfloor heating."

Casetti looked amused but said nothing. After a couple of minutes, the Audrey on screen put on a different pair of shoes and stood up, walking down the hall towards the kitchen. Then she came out again, this time carrying a vacuum cleaner, and picked up her bag from the hall. After pausing at the bottom of the stairs for a moment, she disappeared from view.

Another mouse-click and the timer sped on until, at 12:04, Casetti slowed the recording again. Thirty seconds later, they watched as Audrey slid into the hall from the staircase, grabbing her coat from the coat stand and bolting out the front door.

Lewis looked at her, and she shifted in her seat, looking embarrassed and uncomfortable. He didn't blame her.

Casetti sped the tape up, and now it was 12:10, 12:15, 12:20 . . . Audrey's frown deepened the more time wound on. At 12:22, Casetti slowed the tape again, and they watched as absolutely nothing happened.

Then, at 12:24, the light behind the door changed. It opened, and in came Audrey and two police officers.

"Go back," commanded Audrey, her voice tight. "Eleven thirty again. Normal speed, not fast."

Casetti glanced at Lewis, evidently surprised by her tone, but did as he was told. A few mouse-clicks later, and there was the hall, empty.

The time ticked on, slowly . . . 11:31, 11:32 . . .

"There."

Audrey pointed at the front door on the screen, and Casetti paused.

"What are we looking at?"

"I'm not there. Can't you see? When the police approach, you can see the light change behind the glass panels in the door. It gets darker before the door opens. But here, there's nothing. I was so cold, my fingers wouldn't work. I dropped my keys twice. I should be there, outside the door, but I'm not. Keep playing."

Click.

"Stop," said Lewis, almost immediately. It was 11:33, and the door was open. He pointed, a tingle running across his scalp. "The door doesn't start to open. One second it's shut, no shadow outside; the next it's half-open, and Audrey's behind it. They bloody looped it!"

Casetti's mouth dropped open, but Audrey looked at Lewis, her relief evident. He nodded. She wasn't going mad.

The door to the office opened, and Roland Waverley walked in, pulling up short when he saw their faces.

"Everything all right?" he asked, looking at Casetti, who'd turned as white as a sheet.

"Um, I don't know," said Casetti, hand flying to his tie, nervously smoothing it down. "They say . . . they think . . . that the video's been looped."

"Looped?"

"The security footage," said Lewis, trying not to sound happy about it. "Someone's run a loop of an empty hallway to cover their tracks. You have a bit of a problem, Mr. Waverley. Your system's been hacked."

39
Audrey

Audrey's heart was beating uncomfortably fast. She felt sick and clammy, embarrassed too. She'd felt that Felix was laughing at her, right up until they realised they'd been hacked, at which point everything suddenly became very serious indeed.

Now Waverley perched on the corner of Felix's desk, his arms crossed, frowning. Felix had played the tape for him too.

"We can't be sure, of course," said Waverley. "It might just be a glitch. A delay. That happens sometimes, yes?" He looked hopefully at his associate.

"I'm sure it does," said Felix, who'd recovered admirably and regained some of his composure. "But the point is, there's nothing on the recording of any use."

"Can you forward to about eleven that night?" asked Lewis. "We know someone was in the house then because we watched them leave."

"What?" Felix and Waverley spoke in unison.

"Mrs. van Duren," said Audrey, hastily, trying to sound as if this should explain everything. "After she'd spoken to Mr. Petrov, we returned to the property, to see if anything else happened, and it did. Two people left the house with a big suitcase, put it into a van, and drove off."

"A suitcase?" repeated Felix, the colour draining from his cheeks again. "You're sure?"

"Very sure. So if you wouldn't mind . . . ?"

She gestured for him to start the recording again. He now looked as sick as she felt. The tape sped on, the hall remaining empty of both people and suitcases, the light gradually changing from grey to black, until eventually the only visible features were the glass panes in the front door and the fanlight above, as well as the occasional flash from the alarm panel on the wall.

"Stop," said Lewis at 10:55. "Let's watch it from here."

The recording played. The glass remained a lighter shade of grey than the rest of the hall, but otherwise nothing happened. The recording went on. Eleven o'clock, five past, ten past . . .

Audrey shook her head.

"It must be another loop," she said. "We were there. We watched them come out of the front door."

Felix and Waverley looked almost relieved, and Audrey couldn't blame them. This wasn't going to reflect well on the company, was it?

"Well," said Waverley at last, "if you're right and someone was in the house the entire day, then they must have some sophisticated hackers. We'll need to talk to our IT experts and get this looked into."

"What about the alarm logs?" asked Lewis. "I assume you have those?"

Felix spoke up. "They . . . uh . . . I'm afraid they're gone."

"What?" said Waverley, his expression darkening. Felix shrank back in his seat.

"There are no logs in the file. They look to have been deleted . . ."

"Deleted by who?" demanded Waverley. "Who else has access?"

"Everyone in the office." Felix shrugged. "But the audit log wasn't configured to record deletions. And if we have been hacked . . ."

Audrey looked at Lewis. Was this incompetence or a cover-up?

"Are there any other properties on that drive?" she asked. "Can we check if they've seen similar activity?"

"Just Beaton Gardens on there," said Felix, "but I can assure you—"

"Great!" Audrey snatched the drive off the desk. "We'll get this to our IT guy, and he can look it over."

Lewis blinked at her in confusion. *Don't say it*, she willed him. *Do not say it.*

"Whoa, hold on," said Felix, reaching across the desk towards the drive, but she was already putting it in her pocket. "You can't take that."

"But Anton—that is, Mr. Petrov—told you to give us the footage, didn't he?" She sounded more confident than she felt, worried they'd insist on her returning it. "He'll be concerned to hear about your system being hacked. He'll want his own experts to take a look, see if they can explain the loop."

"I don't think—"

"Mr. Petrov is *very* worried, as I'm sure you'll understand, about the house and his belongings. About his clocks, in particular. You know how he is about his clocks. He'll be very glad to learn how helpful you're being. How seriously you're taking the safety of your employees." She smiled. "That will mean a lot to him, as it does to me. It does so much for a firm's reputation, an attitude like that."

Her tone was breezy, but the steely glint in her eye dared them to say otherwise.

"Well, of course," said Felix. "Nevertheless—"

"And in spite of this very serious breach, I'm sure Mr. Petrov won't feel the need to take this any further, since you're being so helpful. After all, even the best companies get hacked, don't they?"

"Uh . . ."

"I'm sure our IT department is up to the task, Miss Brooks," said Waverley.

"Nevertheless," said Audrey. She stood up, and Lewis also jumped to his feet. "Don't worry—if our expert finds anything, we'll report back. Will you do likewise?"

Felix looked helplessly up at Waverley.

"This whole situation is very strange, Miss Brooks," said Waverley, shaking his head. "But if that's the way Mr. Petrov wants it . . . "

"It is," she said, firmly.

"Then there's nothing more to be said."

Felix escorted them back downstairs, all his swagger gone. As Lewis opened the front door, Audrey noticed Steph gazing anxiously at them from behind the reception desk.

"Sorry if you had to stay late on our account," she called.

"Oh . . . no." Steph gave Felix a worried glance. "I always work a bit later than everyone else."

"Thanks again, Felix," said Audrey. "Mr. Petrov really will appreciate it."

"Hmm, well. That's the main thing, I suppose."

As they stepped out into the chilly darkness of the evening, Felix shut the door behind them and locked it, flipping the WELCOME sign to CLOSED in a way Audrey felt was rather pointed.

Four paces later, out of sight of the windows, Lewis turned to her.

"What was *that*?" He sounded impressed.

"That was me getting fed up of being patronised."

They began to walk, Audrey automatically heading for the nearest bus stop.

"Who's our IT guy by the way?" asked Lewis.

She laughed.

"Manny. Flat 9. He's some sort of software engineer. I have no idea if he'll actually be able to help, but I had to get that drive off them, and that was all I could think of."

"You did good," said Lewis, grinning at her. "Couldn't have done better myself."

She presumed he meant it as a compliment.

40
Lewis

"Of course I know about the body in Beaton Gardens," said Manny, sounding annoyed. Lewis and Audrey had gone straight home after leaving Trinity and now stood shivering on the gallery outside Flat 9, while Manny leaned against the doorframe, the interior beyond looking warm and cosy. He narrowed his eyes at Audrey. "Although I had to hear it from Celeste."

Emmanuel Moya lived with his boyfriend, Joe, in the flat above Lewis's. Lewis had exchanged nothing more than casual pleasantries with them for the first three years after they'd moved in, but now, thanks to Audrey, they were on proper speaking terms.

"Honestly, I thought she'd wait until we'd at least found the body before circulating the newsletter," said Audrey. "When did you see her anyway?"

"We lunch," he said shortly. "What do you need?"

"Help," said Audrey, taking the drive out of her pocket. "A hard drive full of security footage from the crime scene. We think it's been tampered with."

Manny grinned.

"Well, in that case, come on in." He stood back to make room. "You officially have my attention."

Lewis had never been inside Manny and Joe's flat before. Like Audrey and Mei's, it was a two-floor maisonette, so had a good-sized lounge and a kitchen-diner. Manny was tall and ducked slightly to pass through the doorway to the kitchen, where, it turned out, he'd been sitting at the table watching something on his laptop.

"Sit down, sit down, tell me everything," he said, waving at the highly polished oak chairs. There was a cushion on each, embroidered in turquoise, yellow, and hot pink, and the whole place was light and bright, with pops of colour in the pictures on the walls and the dishes on a large farmhouse-style dresser.

"I like your place," said Lewis, almost without meaning to. His own flat had no interior design to speak of, but since the addition of Philip's homage to Monet, he'd started wondering if other nice things might improve his home.

"Thanks," said Manny. "Interior design is a hobby of mine. If you ever need any help styling your own, let me know." He looked at Lewis with an appraising eye. "You're a black-and-grey kinda guy, yeah?"

"I've never really thought about it."

"Exactly. Decor by default."

Feeling faintly embarrassed but unsure why, Lewis shrugged.

"Joe at work?" asked Audrey, looking around.

"No, he's gone to dinner with his dad." Manny picked up the drive and started examining it. "Source?"

"The property company that looks after Mr. Petrov's place," said Audrey. "Trinity Property Management. There's a security camera inside the house, trained on the front door. There's nothing on the recording for the day in question, but there should be."

"We think it's been looped," said Lewis. "There's at least two points that we know of, possibly more, where there should be people and there aren't."

"Well, alrighty then," said Manny, cracking his knuckles. "This sounds fun. One sec, I'm going to need a cable."

He got up and left the room. A second later, Lewis heard him jogging upstairs.

"Manny's office is on the next floor," said Audrey, by way of explanation. She seemed comfortable, like she'd been there a lot. More footsteps and then Manny was back, holding a cable and another laptop.

He sat back down at the table and opened the second laptop, plugging in the hard drive.

"What have we here then?" he said. He clicked the mouse a few times, and the security video opened on the screen. "Right then. What's the first time you know is wrong?"

"Eleven thirty-two," said Audrey at once.

He pressed play, watching the video carefully. Almost at once, he clicked, then clicked again, frowning. He'd noticed the discrepancy immediately.

"Yep, that's pretty clear," he said, pointing to the bottom half of the screen. The video was visible only in the top half, while underneath there were a whole load of horizontal bars.

"What are we looking at?" asked Lewis.

"See this line here?" Manny pointed at a place where a long green bar suddenly stopped and a new one began, just underneath. The two overlapped, but only just. "That top one is where a recording was being fed in. That one underneath—that started about eight seconds before the first one stopped and then took over as the primary recording."

"What time was this?" asked Lewis.

"About eleven on Wednesday morning. It seems to have run for the entire day."

"You're kidding."

"Nope. See these numbers here? It's a twenty-four-hour recording, and it had just started to loop again. This is it starting on Wednesday, and this is where it looped again on Thursday, same time. It stopped at eleven thirty-three, as you saw, and switched to what I assume is the live feed."

"You can't tell?"

"This is a recording," said Manny. "It records what came in through the camera. What I think's happened here is that someone's hacked into the Trinity system, copied twenty-four hours of footage from the drive, and then fed it back. The camera itself was doing nothing."

Lewis looked at Audrey, her expression turning to one of horror as she started to compute what this meant.

"So they recorded an entire day of nothing to cover up for an entire day of . . . " She tailed off with a shudder.

"It's a clever way of doing it, if you can," said Manny. "As long as you align the start times with the recording, it'll track daylight and match almost perfectly."

"Unless a freezing-cold cleaner decides to break the rules and turn up early," said Lewis, thinking. "They planned a full day to do what they needed to do, but it wasn't enough. They had to keep the loop going. That suggests something went wrong, doesn't it?"

"That's a *you* question," said Manny. "Would you like to know something else weird?"

"No," said Audrey.

"Yes," said Lewis, and Manny smiled.

"The camera wasn't on on Monday."

Lewis sat up straighter. "How can you tell?

"See this green line here? That's the loop. It starts at eleven on Wednesday, but before that, there's barely any live footage. It runs from five on Monday afternoon until the loop takes over on Wednesday morning. If I follow the timeline back before that, it's empty. No footage from about ten on Friday morning."

Audrey put her head on the table and groaned.

"I don't understand," she said, voice muffled.

"So the camera was working fine up to Friday morning, when it suddenly cut out?" said Lewis, trying to get it straight. "It was out all weekend?"

"Yes."

"Then the live feed came back on Monday at five, cutting out again at eleven on Wednesday morning, when it went to a recording fed into the system, a copy of the last day it was working?"

"I think so," agreed Manny.

"Why do both, though? Why not just cut the cameras again?"

"Another you question," said Manny. "But when Audrey showed up early on Thursday, someone stopped the loop and hastily switched to the live feed again. I'll go through the rest of what's on here, see what else I can find. The loop is interesting. Someone must have known Trinity didn't have live monitoring, only playback. This is quick and dirty. If they'd looped the camera in situ, this would be a continuous line, and nothing would look amiss. Seems kinda weird to do it this way."

"Maybe they expected to be out clean, so no one would even know to look," said Lewis. "Only Little Miss Coldhands here scuppered their plans."

Audrey raised a hand and waved sadly, her head still on the table.

"Ah," said Manny, nodding and smiling. "He has underfloor heating, your Russian boss? I wondered what you were doing on the floor."

"Thank you!" said Audrey, sitting up again and turning to Lewis. "See? Perfectly normal."

"Two words I would never apply to you," he replied. "How did you know Petrov was Russian?"

Manny rolled his eyes.

"Everyone in the square knows about the empty Russian house with the clocks and the dead body. Sarah and I were talking about it with Victor yesterday. He and the Captain have been doing their own research."

This time, it was Lewis who groaned.

"Nope, not this again," he said, standing up. "Thank you for helping with the drive, but I'm going home."

Manny laughed and also got to his feet.

"We'll get you in the end, Lewie baby," he said, showing them back into the hall. "Just you wait."

"Not if you call me Lewie, you won't," said Lewis. He opened the front door, suddenly desperate to leave, and a rush of freezing air filled the hall.

"Thanks, Manny," said Audrey, giving him a hug. "You're a star."

"I know, I know." He smiled. "Now get out, you're letting the cold in."

Back outside on the gallery, Lewis sighed.

"This is going to be my life now, isn't it? Everyone knowing my business."

"I don't know what you're complaining about," she said, her footsteps clanging on the stairs down to the courtyard. "I thought you loved talking about crime."

"I love writing about crime. And reading about crime. I never said anything about talking."

"Think of it as a healthy range of perspectives," said Audrey as she reached the ground. "And you can't say it hasn't been useful. We have a picture of the victim, and some insight into the camera hack, which must have come from someone either in Trinity or close to them. I bet Celeste knew it would be helpful to involve everyone."

"I doubt it," said Lewis. "I think she's just a gossipy old lady."

"Celeste isn't *just* anything," said Audrey. "But I'll concede the point about the gossip. Right, I'm off home. Plans for tomorrow?"

"Work. Edits. Waiting for a suitcase to wash up in Wapping. You?"

She laughed.

"Cleaning. And waiting for a suitcase to wash up in Wapping. Or possibly Rotherhithe."

As he let himself into his flat, Lewis realised that he didn't really care where the body washed up, as long as it did. And soon.

Their case was going to sink without it.

41

Audrey

At eight o'clock on Tuesday morning, Audrey found herself manoeuvring about the small kitchen with Mei and Sofia, all trying to eat breakfast and get themselves ready for work, the air scented with fresh coffee and different shampoos.

"I dropped the fibres off at the lab yesterday," said Sofia, in between mouthfuls of muesli. "Should be a decent sample on them, at any rate. I've also written up the case as we know the facts so far. Dare I ask if you've done any more investigating?"

Audrey could hear the subtle emphasis on the word *investigating*.

"Do you want me to answer that?" she said, forcing a smile.

Sofia glanced at Mei, then back to Audrey.

"I don't know. Do I?"

"Mr. Petrov asked the property company to hand over the security footage from inside the house. Their system was hacked. Manny in Flat 9 is looking into it for us."

"Manny? Oh, good!" said Mei. "Keeps it in the family, so to speak."

Sofia's frown deepened, the crease in her otherwise unlined forehead becoming more pronounced.

"This is not a secure evidence chain," she said. "What am I supposed to do when this gets to court? Tell the judge the footage was given to the cleaner, the crime writer, then one of the neighbours before it got to us, but don't worry, it's definitely kosher?"

"As a private citizen, Mr. Petrov is entitled to do what he wants with footage of his property," said Mei, primly. "A break-in is suspected, and he's looking into it, using whatever resources are at his disposal."

"I'm not saying you're not capable," said Sofia after a beat. "Just that a court would prefer the evidence chain to be the owner to the police, and that's it. The more hands on it, the less integrity it has."

Audrey sighed. She assumed that professional private detectives also had this problem, although to hear Lewis talk, you wouldn't think so.

"Lewis and I watched the footage at Trinity. They hadn't spotted the tampering. I merely transported it from their offices to Manny, who's a software engineer. He's just going to take a look at it, not interfere with it."

Sofia didn't exactly relax, but the furrow between her eyebrows lessened.

"Tampered how?"

"The cameras were off all weekend and came back on Monday. Then on Wednesday, the Trinity system was fed a loop of prerecorded footage. It kept playing until I arrived on Thursday, when it suddenly switched to live again. Manny thinks the hack must have come from inside Trinity, or else someone close enough to know how they operated."

"Shit," said Sofia, dropping her spoon and pressing her fingers into her temples. "Are you sure?"

"Yep. One minute the hall's empty, the next I'm half-inside it, turning off the alarm. Plus, you know how we watched two people leave with the suitcase Thursday night?" She shook her head. "Not on the tape. Just a dark hallway, all night."

Mei smirked.

"Good thing we were there then," she said, staring studiously into her coffee cup. "Or there'd be no trace of their exit at all."

"You sound like Lewis," said Audrey, and Sofia groaned.

"Every time we talk about this, I imagine myself in court, having to explain how my girlfriend, her best friend, and their neighbour are the key witnesses in the case, with another neighbour providing a sketch of the victim. And now there's another neighbour involved. Dean might have to take me off the case."

Audrey and Mei exchanged looks. When put like that, Audrey had to admit, it did not sound good.

Sofia opened her mouth to say more, but her phone rang and they saw Dean Banham's name on the caller ID.

"Dean, hey," she said, leaping off the stool and walking out into the hall. "I'm just about to leave."

Mei turned to Audrey.

"I thought you were going to back off," she said, although her tone was more gentle than Audrey expected.

"I know." She smiled apologetically. "But Mr. Petrov told Trinity to release the footage to us. I couldn't not go and get it, could I? What would you have done?"

Mei sighed.

"Exactly the same. But surely now you have enough evidence? Blood swab from the scene, the blood-soaked fibres, a sketch of the victim, and now the video loop . . . you don't need to keep on."

"I know." And she did know. Audrey had no desire to put herself in danger, any more than she already had, at least. "But nobody really believes me. In spite of all that stuff you just said, they still don't believe me. I can't let it go. Any word on your missing client?"

Mei grimaced.

"None. At this point, I almost wish he was the man in your suitcase. At least then I'd know what happened to him."

They fell silent as Sofia returned, phone still to her ear. “Understood,” she said. “I’m on my way.”

She clicked the phone off and put it in her pocket, then took a huge breath.

“Looks like your crime scene just came to us,” she said. “A suitcase has been found on the shoreline in Rotherhithe. And guess what? There’s a body in it.”

42
Lewis

The bus was by far the most efficient route to work for Lewis, if not the fastest, but that morning he'd decided to take the one that went through Beaton Gardens instead of the one that went through Victoria. It meant a bit more walking at the other end, but from the upstairs of the bus, he'd be able to see across the private garden to the houses, where he hoped to spot some neighbours heading out and about, or indeed anyone who could be a potential witness to the crime, including the mysterious man Audrey had seen, who may or may not have been lurking around Marchfield Square.

He was sitting on the top deck of the bus, looking out of the window, when he got Audrey's message.

> **THE CLEANER:** They found the body. Sofia got a call this morning. Suitcase washed up in Rotherhithe!

Lewis almost jumped out of his seat with excitement.

> **LEWIS MCLENNON:** Definitely our guy?

> **THE CLEANER:** Don't know yet. There are protocols when a body's found in the river, apparently, but it's being transferred to the police morgue. Should know soon.

> **LEWIS MCLENNON:** Hopefully it won't be too decomposed by its time in the water.

Audrey didn't reply to that. This was going to change things. On the one hand, the police would now be involved, which would make their investigation more difficult, but on the other, it confirmed that Audrey hadn't imagined it, and even Lewis was relieved to be able to add a body to the evidence they'd collected.

The traffic stopped at the junction, the lights on red, and Lewis looked down into the residents' garden, where a man in a Barbour jacket and raspberry-pink trousers was standing in the middle of the grass, pointing. Was that the man they'd met the other day? The neighbour? What was he pointing at?

He tried to see the dog, which was presumably running about somewhere, but even though Horace-Watts—or whatever his name was—kept gesticulating at something in the bushes, no dog reappeared.

Lewis looked through the trees towards the houses, and a flash of yellow caught his eye. A police car was outside thirty-five. He wiped his arm over the window, soaking his sleeve in condensation, but could see nothing beyond the trees but blank windows and an empty street. Nothing seemed to be amiss. As the bus started up again, his eyes fell once again on Morris-Potts and his fruit-coloured trousers.

The bus moved off, driving past the garden just as a man in police uniform stepped out from behind some shrubbery.

Lewis turned around and kneeled on the seat, craning his neck to see more and attracting a few strange looks from his fellow passengers, including a man in a beanie hat who stared at him from under blond brows, but the bus took him further and further away from Beaton Gardens, which a minute later had disappeared from view.

Lewis considered the policeman for the rest of his journey. It wouldn't surprise him if the über-wealthy residents of that exclusive address regularly called the police in for all sorts of spurious reasons, but was there a chance this visit was connected to their case? The car had been outside the house, after all.

He took out his phone again.

> **LEWIS MCLENNON:** Did you call that guy yet? The neighbour who needed a cleaner?
>
> **THE CLEANER:** Not yet. Why?
>
> **LEWIS MCLENNON:** I just saw him talking to a policeman in Beaton Gardens. Might be nothing, but might be something. Sooner rather than later, if you can.

He then added, as an afterthought:

> **LEWIS MCLENNON:** Please.

43
Audrey

Audrey didn't really like Tuesdays. First, she had to clean the penthouse flat of a model living in Notting Hill, which was not only a two-bus schlep but also awkward and boring. White-and-chrome airport chic with polished concrete floors and clothes scattered everywhere. At least half the time, the model was home, padding around barefoot in a cropped vest and leggings while listening to some podcast or other on her earbuds, and while she was nice enough, her ability to relax while a stranger cleaned around her both impressed and offended Audrey at the same time.

Then in the afternoon, she cleaned a flat in Hyde Park Gate owned by a professor of historical linguistics. It was a nightmare of papers and books, wooden floors and antique furniture, and sash windows that, she assumed from the musty smell, were rarely opened. She'd only met Professor Mitford once, but he'd described his work as "important," his flat as "the old homestead," and the dark and twiddly dust-collecting knickknacks as "gewgaws," which told her everything she considered it pertinent to know.

By the time she got home, she was cold and tired, and annoyed that she had to call Forrest-Ross when she wasn't feeling at her most client-friendly.

She looked at her diary. The only space she had was late on Tuesday afternoon, but that would mean she'd likely be there when they were preparing dinner, which wasn't ideal. Most clients wanted her gone by four at the latest. Really, it would be more convenient if she could do it the same day as Mr. Petrov's.

Assuming she was still going to be cleaning Mr. Petrov's, of course. With the performance she'd given at Trinity yesterday, her suspension might well turn into a sacking.

She made herself a cup of tea, then sat at the counter, trying to get herself together. God knew how she was going to work in questions about the police. Sometimes, she wished she could be like Lewis, just able to blurt out whatever she wanted to know without worrying what people thought of her.

She typed in the number from Forrest-Ross's card and put the phone on speaker, positioning it in front of her as she listened to it ring.

"Ross," barked a man's voice.

"Mr. Forrest-Ross?" asked Audrey, leaning into the speaker. "It's Audrey Brooks, the cleaner. You asked me to call?"

"Ah, yes, good of you to remember. Just let me get the wife in."

She heard rustling, presumably as he went to find his wife, then a woman's voice in the background and a crackle.

"It's the cleaner," came Forrest-Ross's muffled voice. "From next door." Another crackle. "All right," he said, more clearly. "We're both here. I suppose the first thing is, do you have any references?"

"Yes," said Audrey. "Lady Macintyre over on Cadogan Place would be happy to provide a reference, or else there's Mrs. Channing in Kensington." She was only half-sure that Mrs. Channing would give her a decent reference, given she was still sulking about the two weeks off Audrey had taken last year. "Or perhaps Mr. Petrov, from next door?"

"Petrov, eh? Is that his name?" Forrest-Ross chuckled. "Cannae ask him if we never see him, but if Clem'll vouch for you, that's good enough for us. Did you hear that, Evelyn? She works for Clem."

"Of course I heard," said Evelyn Forrest-Ross, clear as a bell in the background. "I'm right here."

It took Audrey a second to remember that Lady Macintyre's first name was Clementine. She wracked her brains, trying to think of a way to ask about the policeman Lewis had seen.

"I'll be honest Mr. Forrest-Ross, I don't have a lot of gaps in my calendar." She took a risk. "Unless you wouldn't mind an evening? I wouldn't mind coming over late, if it was a safe area, of course."

"Call me Ross," said Forrest-Ross. "And this is London. How safe is safe?"

"But, I mean . . . " She floundered, searching for a way in. "There's nothing specific going on in Beaton Gardens? Only I've seen a few police cars in the area lately." *I called one of them*, she added silently.

"Aye? Well, we get them in to move the homeless people outta the garden from time to time. One had been skulking about last week and left a knife behind, so the police came tae collect it. Can't be too careful."

"A knife?"

"Aye. You know how the police are about knives. The guy was long gone, though, so nothing to worry about."

Audrey's heart quickened. The man she'd seen had left a knife behind, meaning the police now had the murder weapon!

"No evenings," said Evelyn in the background, firmly, bringing her back to the matter at hand.

"Well, the only other time would be Thursday afternoon, after I do next door," she said. "About three? That would save on travel time."

There was a pause.

"Is there no way you can come earlier?" asked Ross. "Or switch with the other girl? The one who comes in the morning sometimes. Three would be a bit late for us, on account of our tea."

"I'm afraid not," she said. "I have an hour here and there, but my days are fully booked—" She stopped short. "Sorry, what other girl? Who comes in the morning?"

"The other cleaner."

Audrey picked up the phone, holding it closer.

"You've seen another cleaner? Going into thirty-five?"

"I thought it was you, but the wife says she's got fair hair, and you've red, aye?"

"Aye. I mean, yes." Audrey clenched the fist of her free hand. Another cleaner? Why would Trinity pay two people to clean an empty house? Did Felix not trust her? "What time does she come in, Mr. Ross? And for how long?"

The phone crackled, and she heard a murmured conversation taking place. Then, suddenly, Mrs. Ross was on the line.

"Hello, it's Evelyn Ross here," she said, her accent softer and posher than her husband's. "The other cleaner usually comes on a Monday lunchtime, but not every week. We thought it was you until Julian said he'd met you and you weren't the same girl. She stays a couple of hours and does the laundry too."

"Laundry?" Audrey's blood was rushing in her ears. "On Monday?"

"Yes, the sheets and things. She takes them away and brings new ones. Did you not know, dear?"

"No," said Audrey, through gritted teeth. "I didn't. I didn't know the house was being used."

"Oh, yes. We go up to the Cotswolds most weekends, but we've seen people shipping out on a Monday morning several times recently. Bags and cases."

"People stay there?"

"A holiday lease, we supposed. Or friends of the owner's. There was one last Thursday too. I saw him leave."

She could barely breathe.

"What time last Thursday?"

"About eleven, or just after."

"What did he look like?"

"Seventy, maybe? With white hair and a beard."

"This doesn't make any sense."

"The cleaning? It never has to us either, dear, but you know what these oligarchs are like."

There was an uncomfortable silence as Audrey tried to process this new information, and Evelyn Ross eventually filled it herself.

"You should talk to your employer, dear. If he's no need of you next door, perhaps we could have his space?"

"Uh, yes. Yes, that might be possible. I'll let you know. Thank you both, this has been very helpful."

She hung up on the Forrest-Rosses and stared furiously at the phone.

What the actual hell?

44
Lewis

Lewis left work at five and was already on the bus when he got the text from Audrey, requesting he come round for a debrief, although it sounded like more of a demand than a request. When he stepped off the bus half an hour later and began the freezing walk down Flood Street in the dark, he was wondering what on earth the neighbour could have said to warrant his being summoned.

The temperature was dropping again, and his walk home was quieter than usual, with fewer people to dodge and just a single pedestrian behind him. By the time he reached Pickering Lane, the damp cobbles were becoming icy, and his stupid work shoes slipped and slid on his way down to the square.

Lewis opened the gate to the square and immediately came face-to-face with Roshan Jones, the caretaker, who was sweeping yet more salt across the courtyard with a coarse broom.

"Good evening, Lewis," said Roshan, without breaking rhythm. "Mind how you go, it's freezing up again."

"Thanks," said Lewis, relieved to feel the salt beneath his feet. He walked down the path towards Audrey's block, then climbed the steps to Flat 7. He'd just raised his fist to knock when the door flew open, and she yanked him inside.

"You are not going to believe what Ross said," she began.

"Who?"

"Forrest-Ross," she said impatiently. "The neighbour!"

He unwound his scarf, suddenly hot in the tiny hall. "Well?"

"There's another cleaner."

"Where?"

"Where?! Are you mad? Beaton Gardens!"

He stared down at her, confused.

"Ross and his wife, Evelyn, have seen another cleaner going into number thirty-five. Mondays, apparently, different times. A woman with blond hair. They thought we were the same person. And get this: She does the *laundry*."

The emphasis was lost on Lewis.

"So?"

"No one's living there. What laundry could there possibly be?"

Her green eyes were wide and sparkling with excitement, but Lewis took his coat off before answering.

"Sorry, it's boiling in here." He hung it up. "Okay, so there's another cleaner going in on Mondays, cleaning the place and doing laundry. Curtains? Beds?"

"Beds."

"Then you—the official cleaner, hired by Trinity—come in every Thursday and clean it again?" He was starting to catch up now that he could breathe. "Meanwhile, we know that this weekend just gone, the camera went off on Friday morning and didn't come back until Monday . . . " He breathed out. "Someone's staying there. On the weekends. Someone who knows the alarm code and can turn off the camera."

"Exactly. Now come and see this." He followed her to the kitchen, where an ancient laptop was open on the dining table. "Sit down, take a look."

Dodging the pendant lights over the table, he sat down in front of the computer, unable to hide his disdain for her crappy machine. He looked at the screen. It was a news article from last year.

Sharelets subletting website "flooded with scam properties," claims former employee

A former employee of Sharelets has claimed that the popular subletting website has no safeguards or checks in place to protect properties or their owners.

Sharelets, which has taken the short-term rental market by storm since its launch last year, allows members to list spare rooms on the site for rent by registered users. While the original premise of Sharelets was to offer homeowners the chance of making extra money by renting out their spare rooms on a short-term basis, the site was quickly populated by second-home owners offering entire properties for rent, keen to benefit from the lower fees offered by the new platform.

However, former Sharelets developer Raoul Marquez has since accused the company behind Sharelets of "playing fast and loose with the safety of its users" by failing to vet listed properties or run checks on owners.

Marquez estimates that more than 20 percent of listings on the site are fraudulent, placed there by people who do not own the properties. "People are reporting this, they're making complaints, but Sharelets just removes the listing. In one week, we had more than 200 complaints about fraudulent listings. They know there's a problem and are choosing to ignore it."

Lewis looked up. "You think someone at Trinity's listing Petrov's place without his permission."

"The Rosses think it's a holiday lease. Mr. Petrov didn't mention that, did he?"

"I think there's a lot he didn't mention."

"But he's perfectly entitled to rent out his own house, so why not just say so? And he'd hardly let strangers off the Internet stay in a house full of art and antiques, would he? Never mind the clocks. They could steal stuff. And why pay two cleaners?"

"It would explain some of what Manny found on the drive of security footage too." Lewis tapped his fingers lightly on the keys as he thought. "Have you looked for a listing? On the Sharelets site, I mean?"

"Yes." She sat down next to him. "I couldn't find anything, but it could have been taken down."

"So," said Lewis, leaning back in his chair and folding his arms, "it's an inside job. Felix, most likely. You're responsible for all these properties, half of them empty, you're in charge of the monitoring . . . all you need is an off-the-books cleaner to do a changeover service, and then when the client's official cleaner goes in, everything looks as it should."

"She does one hell of a job." Audrey frowned. "I didn't notice anything. It always looked like nothing had changed."

"Too busy vacuuming the skirting boards," he said, remembering how boringly forensic Audrey's cleaning had been.

"That's true." She nodded, inexplicably reassured. "Yes, that must be it. And there's something else too. The policeman you saw? In the garden? He was there to pick up a knife left behind by someone sleeping in the park."

"What?!" Lewis was momentarily dumbfounded. "The police have the murder weapon, and you led with the *cleaner*?"

"It was on my mind!" she said defensively. "*And* the Rosses saw an older man with white hair and a beard leaving the house just before I got there on Thursday."

"Really?"

"About twenty minutes in it. Could be Mr. Petrov, except he doesn't have a beard."

"He had plenty of time to shave it off," said Lewis. He blew out a breath, trying to take it all in. "If this is all true, then the killer could have rented the property for the entire weekend. We keep coming back to this, but why wait until the middle of the week to murder someone when you're twice as likely to be caught?"

"I know." Audrey rubbed her eyes. "It's stupid."

Lewis reread the article on the computer. It did make sense, and maybe it also explained how the killer had the alarm code.

"Maybe they rented it in the past," he said out loud. "Specifically so they couldn't be linked to it for the week in question. They'd have had the alarm code and a key. Don't those places usually have key boxes outside?"

"The one in Sloane Square does," said Audrey. "Kind of discreetly positioned, but accessible. There's nothing like that at Mr. Petrov's, though."

The sound of a key in the front door made them both jump. A moment later, they heard voices in the hall.

"We're in here," called Audrey, and the voices stopped. Then the door opened, and Mei walked in, Sofia Larssen close behind.

"Hey," said Mei, nodding at Lewis.

She stood aside to make room for Sofia, who, judging by the suit, had come straight from work. Her long blond hair was drawn back into a ponytail, her fringe grazing her eyes as she looked at him.

"Hi," she said warily.

"Don't suppose there's any news?" asked Audrey. "About the body. Bit soon?"

"Ordinarily, yes," said Sofia, taking a seat at the table. "But we jumped the queue because of information received."

"What information?" asked Lewis at once.

"From you," said Mei, looking at him like he was an idiot.

"From both of you," said Sofia, leaning forward. "I showed Dean a photo of your sketch and said I had reason to believe the body in the suitcase was the hitman we've been looking for. We went straight down to the morgue. The suitcase was an expensive one, and surprisingly little water made it inside, so the body was still identifiable."

"And?"

"And the man in our witness composite, the man in your sketch, and the man in the suitcase are one and the same: Don Tyler."

Audrey began chewing her lip. She probably wasn't sure if a dead hitman was a good thing or not.

"Preliminary cause of death seems to be exsanguination," Sofia went on. "One major cut across the neck and throat. I put a rush on testing the blood from the fibres you gave me against the samples from the corpse, and they match, which means we can confirm that the dead man you saw at Beaton Gardens is the same one who was fished out of the river this morning." She looked from one to the other. "It's now officially a murder investigation."

45

Audrey

"It's always been a murder investigation," said Lewis, frowning, and Audrey shot him a look.

"But we get it," she added hastily. "Vanishing bodies, et cetera. Not easy to explain."

"No. Which is why I'm here. Dean—" She paused to look at Lewis. "That's DI Banham to you. He wasn't happy about me running samples through the lab without an open case, but I squared away the situation at the house. Said Audrey called the police and the patrol didn't take it seriously, so I was just covering our bases, but he was pretty mad about you guys staking out the crime scene and following the body drop."

Audrey grimaced. DI Banham disliked them enough as it was without adding new tensions into the mix.

"We were testing a theory," said Lewis, unperturbed. "We just happened to be right."

"That's how I put it," agreed Sofia. "But he wants me to take your official statements, and he'd like to interview you himself."

"Interview?" asked Mei, raising her eyebrows. "Or read them the Riot Act?"

Sofia smiled sheepishly. "A little of column A . . . "

"The knife," said Audrey. "The one found at Beaton Gardens. Did it have blood on it?"

"How on earth do you know about that?" asked Sofia, eyebrows shooting up. "It was only logged into evidence this afternoon. It's been sent for testing."

"What about the first swab?" asked Lewis. "Where did that blood come from?"

"We don't know yet, but it doesn't match the other samples. We're treating that as belonging to a second person of interest. Possibly the killer."

Audrey nodded. "Who could also be the victim."

"What?"

"The intended victim, I mean. If the dead man is a hitman, then maybe he was planning to kill someone, but they killed him first. I thought his clothes were odd, like work clothes. The victim could have become the killer and the would-be killer the victim."

Now Sofia pulled a face.

"Oh, good," she said. "I was hoping this would get more complicated."

"Sorry, just thinking out loud."

"No, you're right. My first thought was one killer taking out another. You get that sometimes, revenge killings or turf wars. Or the person who hired Tyler silencing the only person who could identify them. But, equally, it could be a hit gone wrong." She paused, her gaze drifting as she thought. "That might explain how you ended up seeing the crime scene. Tyler meant to clean it himself but, for obvious reasons, couldn't. It also explains the state of the body."

"What do you mean?" asked Audrey. "I thought you said it wasn't too . . . damaged."

"Yes, but a professional will often cut off the hands or damage the teeth of a victim postmortem to prevent identification. And dispose of the body in a way that makes it less likely to be found. This disposal was efficient, but not professional. Could be a red herring, but it would tie in with the theory that this is an amateur trying to clean up."

There was silence for a moment.

"Is there anything else you've not told me?" asked Sofia.

"Yes, what were you two discussing when we walked in?" asked Mei. Then, when she saw Lewis and Audrey exchange a look, "You can't hold anything back now."

Lewis nodded, which Audrey took to mean, *go ahead*.

"You know how I told you that the neighbour—Mr. Petrov's neighbour in Beaton Gardens—was looking for a cleaner? Well, I called him when I got home this afternoon. He's the one who told me about the knife, but his wife told me they saw a man leaving the house just before I got there on Thursday. An older man with white hair and a beard. Then Mr. Forrest-Ross said something about the *other* cleaner at thirty-five."

"The other cleaner?" repeated Mei. "What other cleaner?"

"That was my question. It turns out they've noticed a second cleaner going in and out of the property on Mondays. Stays a few hours, takes laundry in and out . . . a woman, with blond hair."

"Laundry?" Sofia looked confused. "I thought you said it was empty?"

"The Rosses think it's a holiday lease, but Mr. Petrov never mentioned that. Lewis and I were just talking about it, and we think it might be a scam."

"A scam? Like on that app?"

"Exactly like that," said Lewis, turning the computer around to show Sofia the news item. "If you put that together with the camera outage over the weekend . . . "

Sofia scanned the article.

"Sharelets, right." She pursed her lips, thinking, and brushed her fringe out of her eyes. "So someone is illegally renting out Petrov's place, turning off the camera over the weekend, and having their own cleaner cover their tracks on Mondays?"

"Yes. So it's possible either the killer or our corpse rented the property from them at another time," said Lewis, "remembered the alarm code, and decided to use it for the hit." He ran a hand through his dishevelled curls. "The access is terrible—only one way in that we could find—and they took the body on a good old drive to get rid of it. Beaton Gardens makes no sense as a purely random location."

"No, it doesn't," said Sofia. "But we'll get to the bottom of it. We're working on a list of Tyler's known associates, trying to work out whom he might have made angry enough to take him out. And I'll see if any of our informants have heard of a recent contract Tyler may have ended up with." She looked at Audrey and nodded. "It's a good angle."

Audrey smiled.

"I need to say one more thing," went on Sofia. "This is a police case now. A dead hitman means organised crime, and Petrov himself has some interesting business associates, so we'll be interviewing everyone, including the people at Trinity. Stirring things up. You've already had one break-in, and if these people feel threatened, they will respond in a much more dangerous way. Witnesses have been silenced for less. Do you understand?" She looked from one to the other, her gaze lingering on Lewis.

"We understand," said Audrey, all too aware that she was the witness in question, but when she looked at Lewis, he simply shrugged.

"We'll do our best," he said, and Sofia glared at him. "Celeste and Petrov both asked us to look into it, so we can't let them down. In fact, we're . . . uh . . . giving Celeste an update later this evening, aren't we?"

Audrey narrowed her eyes. *What was he up to?*

"But we'll stay out of trouble," he said, "and share anything we get. We won't tread on your toes."

Sofia looked at Mei, who looked at Audrey, who sighed. It seemed it was easier to start investigating a murder than it was to stop.

Looked like she was in this to the end.

46
Celeste

Celeste and Dixon were playing cards after dinner when the doorbell rang. Dixon looked up from his hand, and the corner of his mouth twitched.

"I think the children have come to play again," he said.

"Well, don't keep them waiting, dear," said Celeste, smiling.

Dixon laid his cards down and put his coffee cup on top to stop her peeking. Quite right too—Celeste never missed an opportunity to cheat. As her mother used to say, those with strong habits never go out of luck.

She laid down her own hand and waited patiently while Dixon buzzed Audrey and Lewis upstairs. They arrived in the usual flurry of coats, cold air, and out-of-breath complaints.

"Hello," said Dixon. "Another visit, is it?"

They both looked over to where Celeste sat at the table, Audrey embarrassed, Lewis decidedly not so.

"We'll be five minutes, tops," said Audrey.

"We need to ask you about Petrov," added Lewis.

"Come and sit down," said Celeste, waving them over to the table.

They pulled out chairs to left and right of her while Dixon remained standing, doubtless intending to hold them to their five minutes.

"We have news," began Audrey. "The suitcase washed up in Rotherhithe, and the body inside is the one from Beaton Gardens. His name's Don Tyler, and he's a hitman."

Celeste glanced at Dixon, his surprise as evident as her own must have been. Her mouth went dry, and it took her a few seconds to reply.

"The victim was a professional?"

"Yes," said Lewis. "Which is why we're here. Either Tyler was the subject of a hit himself, or he was attempting a hit and it went wrong. Is there anything you can tell us about Anton Petrov that would explain why a hit would be carried out in his house?"

Celeste hesitated, trying to think of too many things at once. "How do you mean?"

"According to the last Census, over eight percent of London properties are either second homes or permanently empty," said Audrey. "There has to be a reason they chose Mr. Petrov's house. It's a fancy area, and the access wasn't good, plus they clearly knew people were going in and out. Why pick such a difficult location?"

"Petrov has to be the reason," said Lewis. "I know he's a friend of yours, but is there any chance he might have called in Tyler to deal with someone? Someone who was causing him problems? Or perhaps he took out the contract on Tyler? Petrov matches the description of a man seen leaving the house on Thursday morning, shortly before Audrey arrived."

"Apart from the beard," added Audrey, earning a scowl from Lewis. "It's just so strange."

"Yes," said Celeste softly. "It is."

She was quiet for a moment, and when she looked up, she saw Audrey watching her carefully.

"The neighbours believe the place is being used as a holiday lease," said Audrey. "They think people are staying there on weekends. No one's ever mentioned that to me, and the place is always just as I left it. Has Mr. Petrov ever mentioned renting it out?"

This also surprised Celeste.

"No, never." She took a breath to steady herself. "I can't see why he would need to do that. And you know how he feels about his clocks."

"We don't even know what Mr. Petrov does for a living," Audrey went on. "Everyone says he's an oligarch, but I don't really know what that means."

"Pft, Anton's not an oligarch," said Celeste, latching onto something she did know. "He had to leave the Soviet Union in the seventies due to political differences. His mother was British, you see, so when he moved here, he naturalised and became a civil servant."

"A civil servant?" asked Lewis, immediately suspicious.

"Yes. He worked out of the British Embassy in Paris. That was where he met Madeleine. Then, when she died, he quit to raise the children and start his own business."

"Madeleine? That was his wife, your friend?"

"Yes. She was also a dual citizen—French mother, British father. They hit it off immediately and were very happy together. He's been a different man since she passed."

"Does he have any links to organised crime?" Lewis was grilling her now. "How did he get so rich if he's a civil servant?"

"Well, Madeleine was already wealthy, so he married into money. And later on, his firm became very successful."

"Is there any other reason he might be targeted for this? Any detail might be relevant."

Celeste was, most unusually, at a loss.

"I'm afraid I can't think of anything right now," she said, which was both true and untrue at the same time. Her mind was whirling.

"What exactly *is* Mr. Petrov's business?" asked Audrey.

"Something in finance, I believe," said Celeste, giving a little shrug. "I'm afraid it's too complicated for me, and, I confess, I was never particularly interested. But Anton is coming to dinner on Friday night, so I can do a little digging then."

Audrey's gaze held Celeste's for just a beat too long.

"Thank you," she said, and not for the first time, Celeste wondered if Audrey was a little too sharp for Celeste's own good.

Sensing that intervention was needed, Dixon began to loom. Audrey and Lewis exchanged another look and stood up at the same time.

"I shall report back on Saturday," she said. "I trust that will suit?"

Her tone, deliberately, brooked no argument, even from Lewis, and the two departed quietly, although the looks that passed between them spoke volumes.

Dixon returned to the table, ignoring the cards and cold coffee.

"Don Tyler," he said, quietly. "Thought he'd changed his name."

"He did, when he went to Italy. And again in the States. But he was always Don Tyler in London."

Dixon rubbed at his beard.

"I didn't think he'd dare show his face again."

"Nor I," said Celeste, the chill of a familiar, steely rage creeping down her spine. "If I'd known he was in town, I'd have dealt with him myself, but as it stands . . . " She shook her head. "I don't believe it was Anton."

"Why not?"

"Why wouldn't he tell me? I'd be as happy about it as he would."

"It's possible, though. You did say he'd shaved his beard off."

"Of course it's possible," said Celeste, "but why here? Why now? Twenty-five years is a long time to wait, and to do it in his own house . . . "

She trailed off, unable to imagine what possible circumstances could have created such a dramatic and farcical situation. People like Anton, Dixon, and Celeste didn't forget their training, whoever the target.

"Why would someone else kill him in Petrov's house?"

"That's what I want to know."

"You know you have to ask him," said Dixon. "To be sure."

"Yes."

Celeste used the table as support to get to her feet and went to stand in front of the picture window. She'd been looking forward to dinner with Anton, but now the game would have a new edge. An intricate combination of mutual affection and shared grief, amusing anecdotes and conversational trickery, old reminiscences and polite interrogation.

To see if Anton Petrov had finally killed the man who'd murdered his wife.

47
Lewis

"She definitely wanted us out of there," said Lewis, from his sofa. They'd walked back to his flat in the darkness to debrief, given that Audrey's place was no longer safe to discuss the case, and she now sat in his desk chair, twisting gently from side to side in a way that seemed designed to make him seasick.

"Mmm," she agreed.

"Maybe we shouldn't have barged in again. Dixon seemed a bit off too."

"He did."

"But I thought Celeste was sharper than that. Not to know about Petrov's business . . . "

"Quite."

"And, I mean, civil servant! Everyone knows that's code for spies. And political differences . . . defected, I bet."

"Yeah."

He looked at her.

"What's up?" he asked. "What are you thinking?"

She swivelled the chair to face him.

"I think she was upset."

"Who? Celeste?"

"When I said Don Tyler's name, she reacted. Not to the hit-man bit, to the name. Specifically. She knew it, and it upset her."

Lewis opened his mouth to argue, then paused. He'd known Celeste for years, since before Leonard died, before the murder of Richard Glead . . . She was a tough cookie, but she'd been different lately. Not her usual self. He replayed the scene in his mind.

"Not upset exactly . . . " he said slowly, picturing Celeste's face in the cosy light of her apartment. "Angry, perhaps?"

"Or in pain," said Audrey. "A bit like when she talks about Leonard, but more like—" She stopped, realising what she'd been about to say.

"Like when she talks about what happened last November."

"Yes."

She stood up and went over to the living-room window, which had a partial view of the street behind the west side of the square. The curtains were open, the light from the streetlamp outside brighter than the lights inside.

Lewis opened his case notes, reading them back and adding new information where he had it.

Persons in the case:

Anton Petrov: Didn't have a straight answer for anything. Didn't seem worried about the crime scene or the dead man, only his clocks. Claimed to have no idea why anyone would be murdered in his house. Amused by the quick cleanup, but rattled by the blood trace. Was previously a civil servant, which might be code for intelligence work, before moving into finance. Fits the description of the man seen by Mrs. Forrest-Ross, minus the beard. We know the murder was either a hit or a hit gone wrong, which means at least one professional killer specifically picked Petrov's house. Why? Was the location important? Is Petrov involved? What does Celeste know that she's not telling us?

Felix Casetti: More bothered by Audrey going in early than by the crime scene. Didn't like the mention of the police. Trying to keep her away from the property but worried by the discovery of the looped security cameras. He must be either running the scam or else covering up for the person who is.

Roland Waverley: Casetti's boss. Concerned but also didn't like that the police were called. Worried about the camera hack and wanted his IT people to look into it. Gave way to Petrov's wishes.

Mr. & Mrs. Forrest-Ross: Neighbours. Mrs. Forrest-Ross saw an older man leaving the house on Thursday, just before Audrey arrived. They believe the house is being run as a holiday lease on account of weekend visitors and a second cleaner visiting the premises.

Stranger: Who is the man Audrey saw in the residents' garden? Witness or perp? A resident or someone else?

He glanced at Audrey, still standing by the window, then proceeded to add more people to his list.

Don Tyler: A known hitman found dead in an empty house. Was he the intended victim or the intended perpetrator?

Person or persons unknown: Whoever Tyler met at the house. Possibly another professional, hired to kill him, or a potential victim. Did they clean up the crime scene themselves?

Person or persons unknown: Whoever hired Tyler or paid for the contract on him. Was he even hired at all? It's possible he was working for himself and the killing was personal.

Second cleaner: An unknown woman with fair hair has been cleaning 35 Beaton Gardens on Mondays, as well as doing the laundry. Is she running the holiday lease scam or working for someone else?

On the one hand, he didn't like putting all these unknown people on the list, but on the other, it made it clearer. More logical. Something about the victim being a professional helped, in his mind. It made it more of a professional problem than an emotional one. He rather thought he had an advantage there.

"How do you think the holiday scam fits in?" he wondered out loud. "If we can find out who's running the sublet, we can find out who's rented the place. Might be Tyler rented it in the past and figured out it'd be empty when he needed it for a job."

"More likely than it being a coincidence," she agreed.

"What's most likely is that either Petrov or Trinity is involved," he said. "Of all the empty houses in London, there has to be a reason they picked this one."

"I'm not sure about that," she said. "I was thinking about the second cleaner. Maybe she arranged it. Or maybe she's the killer. Being a cleaner makes you invisible to most people, plus you gain access to a lot of places. It would be a great cover for a professional."

Lewis stared at her for a moment.

"Yes," he said thoughtfully, "yes, it would."

He started typing, faster now, intrigued by the idea.

"Are you writing that down as a case note or a book idea?" she asked suspiciously.

He grinned, still looking at the screen. "Both."

"It could answer the question of why, couldn't it?" she said. "Why Mr. Petrov's house, I mean. Because of the cleaner, not because he's involved."

"I'm not taking him off the list," said Lewis firmly. "Everything about that guy is suspicious. And this is only a theory."

"Okay, so what do we need to prove?" she asked, taking out her phone. "Let's make a list."

"We need to prove that the place is definitely being rented out on the quiet. We need to find out whether Trinity's involved, and if not, who's running the scam. I'm meeting Roland Waverley tomorrow about recruitment, so maybe I'll get another chance to dig a bit. We need to identify the second cleaner and work out if she could be a killer. Any links to organised crime that might suggest she'd know Tyler. That should help us figure out whether it was a hit gone wrong or a hit gone right. Do you think Larssen might tell us about Tyler's M.O.? That's—"

"If you're about to explain what 'modus operandi' is again . . . " she said quickly, holding up a hand, "don't."

He closed his mouth.

"Sofia said he garrottes people," she said. "Is that strangulation?"

"Yes. With a wire, usually."

"Ugh. And that's not too messy, right? The plastic sheeting wasn't huge, which suggests they weren't expecting too much blood."

"Maybe," he said, after a beat. "Perhaps Tyler set the room up, expecting to make a clean kill, but was taken by surprise."

She wrinkled her nose. "Delightful. I suppose I should be glad it was only an amateur killer in my flat that day." She paused. "Sofia's right, you know. First the body dump, then the fibres. They are cleaning up. And I'm the only witness."

Although her tone was light, Lewis saw the fear in her eyes and tried to think of something reassuring to say.

"The killer knows where you live. Where we both live, probably. If they wanted to hurt you, they could have."

She didn't seem reassured at all.

48
Audrey

Audrey didn't sleep well that night either, haunted by visions of men in dark coats creeping around the square. When she woke the following morning, she felt drained and miserable.

After finishing her first job on Draycott Avenue, she went home for lunch, checking behind her every couple of minutes. She saw no one, however, and was relieved to get back to the flat, putting the chain on the door for extra security. She read her emails at the kitchen counter and was briefly excited to see a reply from the last forensic cleaning firm she'd emailed, but then realised their response was the same as the others: politely declining to meet with her and suggesting she monitor their website for vacancies. She was a little disappointed, but she'd only been enquiring in the hope of some cleaning insight, and John Keane had been very generous with that.

By half past three, she'd finished her second job, a pretty little house on Bywater Street. One of the many benefits of being able to live in the area she worked in was that, with the exception of the Notting Hill job, she was rarely more than a half-hour walk from home, and a short bus ride when the weather was awful. Today, however, it was merely cold, the sun painfully bright in a clear blue sky, and in her new warm coat and walking at a brisk pace, she wasn't bothered by the cold at all. The blinding winter sunshine seemed to burn away some of her paranoia, too, and she only checked for shadows two or three times on her way home.

Back in the flat, she took a mug of hot chocolate to the living room and curled up on the sofa, thinking again about John

Keane. He'd been so encouraging, and not at all weird, in spite of enjoying cleaning up blood for a living, and in spite of being one of Lewis's fans.

She didn't know which should concern her more.

On a whim, she sent him a message.

> **AUDREY BROOKS:**
> Hey John,
> I just wanted to say thanks again for showing Lewis and me the ropes on Sunday. It was really interesting, and I appreciate you taking the time.
> Audrey

She shoved her phone away immediately, worried she was going to look unprofessional or overly friendly. She didn't want anyone getting the wrong idea.

Which it definitely would be.

A knock on the door interrupted the thought that had threatened to surface, and she leaped up to answer it, peering through the peephole before removing the chain.

It was Manny and Joe, both wearing thick sweaters, Manny wearing a scarf too. He held up his laptop.

"Hey, Auds, can we come in? I have news."

"Of course."

She stood aside to let them in, and they went straight to the kitchen, seating themselves at the dining table and looking at her expectantly.

"Tea? Coffee?" She checked the time on the microwave. "Something stronger?"

Manny perked up at the suggestion, but Joe shook his head.

"I have to work later. I'm only here because I've not seen you since you found another body, and Manny has been so excited about the whole situation." He ran a hand though his thick brown hair. "Washed up in Rotherhithe, the Captain told us."

Audrey laughed.

"That's right. Has Manny given you the whole story?"

"I think so, but he may have been exaggerating." Joe lowered his voice even though Manny was sitting right beside him. "You know how he gets."

"*He* is right here," said Manny, pursing his lips, "and every word I said was true."

"The blood disappearing?"

"True," said Audrey.

"You staking the place out at night?"

"Also true."

"The body dumped at Tower Bridge?"

"Definitely true."

"Bloody hell." Joe looked impressed. "Who knew you had it in you, Audrey?"

"Oi!"

"Oh, please," said Manny, waving a hand. "We all know this is Lewis's influence. And it's working both ways. That boy is much improved."

Audrey grinned.

"So what have you got for me?"

Manny opened the laptop and tapped a few keys before turning it to face her. Just as before, the screen showed lots and lots of horizontal lines, all stacked up on top of each other, some grey and some green.

"I went back through all the footage on the drive, which is about a month's worth. I saw you arriving every Thursday and then leaving again a few hours later—you're very punctual, by the way—but there are two anomalies. The first is the one I showed you, starting last Wednesday and ending on Thursday, just as you arrive.

Then it kicks in again after you and Lewis leave and runs until eleven o'clock on Thursday night, which is when you said they left the house? They must have turned off the feed just after they left."

"How?"

"Remote access. Not to the camera but to the Trinity system. You can control it from a laptop or a phone. It's the only way they'd have been able to turn it on and off so quickly, especially when you arrived unexpectedly early. But!" He held up a finger. "There are multiple instances of the cameras being turned off. Always for the same amount of time, always the same days."

"The weekends?"

"Exactly."

"Every weekend?"

"Nope. The footage covers five weekends, and three of them are blank. The other two, the tape runs as usual. No breaks."

Joe looked from Audrey to Manny and back again. "That's weird, right?"

"Not if someone's secretly renting the place out on weekends," said Audrey. "How long are the outages?"

"From ten on Friday to around five Monday afternoon."

"The same time every week?"

"Roughly," said Manny, shaking his hand to indicate there was a variance. "A few minutes' difference, which suggests it's manual, not automated."

Audrey considered. The cameras being off Friday to Monday would strongly support their weekend-leasing theory. Checkout for most holiday properties was midday at the latest, and some of the ones she'd seen listed on Sharelets had mentioned checkouts as early as ten. If the guests vacated at midday and you needed a cleaner to go in and change the bedsheets, clean the house so thoroughly no one could tell anyone had ever been there . . . for someone working alone, that would be at least a three-hour job, possibly four, depending on the guests. Add an extra hour for anything unexpected . . .

"There was one other thing," said Manny, turning the laptop and tapping a few keys. "Last Thursday, after you fetch the vacuum and put on your weird little cleaning shoes . . ."

"They're not weird, they're professional."

Manny ignored her, turning the computer back around.

"Here. You're about to do something, and then you stop, looking around. Why?"

Audrey watched as Manny played the footage back to her, deeply uncomfortable at seeing herself on the screen. She saw herself walking back into the hall from the kitchen, carrying the vacuum cleaner, then bending down to pick up her cleaning bag. Then she stopped, straightened up, and looked towards the stairs.

"I . . . don't know," she said, puzzled. The screen version of herself paused for more than ten seconds, chin tilted upwards. Then she remembered. "I heard a noise. I completely forgot!"

"What kind of noise?" asked Joe.

"I don't know. A sort of . . . metallic bang? No, 'bang' is too strong a word. It was softer than that. I thought it was upstairs, but then I realised it must be outside. Like a car or something."

"You're sure it was outside?"

"I was," she said, then bit her lip. "But only because I didn't know there was someone else in the house. I'm not sure of anything anymore."

There was another knock on the door, three sharp raps that echoed through the flat. Surprised, she got up to answer it and found the Captain and Victor standing on the gallery, looking very pleased with themselves.

"Hello, you two," she said. "What's up?"

"Hi," said Victor, smiling broadly. Audrey couldn't remember him ever knocking on her door before.

"Hate to be rude, but could we come in?" asked the Captain. "Got something to run up the flagpole, so to speak."

"Sure." She stood back to make way. "Manny and Joe are here too. Just go on through."

She shut the door and followed them to the kitchen, where Manny and Joe looked up from the computer.

"Ooh, look," said Manny, eyes twinkling. "Surprise neighbour coffee morning!"

"Don't be ridiculous, boy," said Victor. "It's practically evening."

Audrey gestured to the dining table.

"Take a seat. Shall I put the kettle on?"

"Not for me, Audrey," said the Captain, remaining standing. "We'll get to the point, shall we?"

She looked from one to the other and recognised the gleam in Captain Gordon's eye as the same one she occasionally saw in Celeste's.

"All right. Have you got something?"

"Gordon and I have been talking," began Victor, "about your vanishing body, and we think we have an idea where they might have hidden it." He held up a roll of papers.

"Oh?" She nodded encouragingly. "Where? Because it's been driving me mad."

"Panic room," said Victor, firmly. "Rich people all have them, and they're always secret."

"We called it a bunker in the old days," added the Captain. "But Victor and I have been looking at specifications on the Web all afternoon, and they're a bit more high-tech now, he says. More comfortable. I presume you checked the basement?"

"The basement's just a wine cellar," she said, slowly. "But we never checked for secret doors. A panic room. Of course!"

Victor unfurled the papers and put two floor plans down on the kitchen counter. Manny and Joe crowded round too.

"What are we looking at?" asked Joe.

"Floor plans of 35 Beaton Gardens," said Victor. "We found them online, in a council planning archive. There are two listings, about ten years apart. The floor plans have some differences. There was clearly a lot of work done before your mysterious Russian bought the house."

"Like what?"

"Like the utility room off the kitchen—that's not on the earlier plan—and this living room was knocked into one from two." Captain Gordon jabbed a finger onto the plan. "Lots of possibilities for an extra room."

Audrey studied the plans, and something else caught her eye.

"The study too," she said. "It looks the same, but the measurements are different."

The Captain stroked his moustache.

"Worth a second look, I'd say," he said, sounding pleased. "Don't you think?"

"Yes," said Audrey, nodding. "Absolutely. Thank you both, that's really helpful."

"Glad to be of assistance," said the Captain, standing even straighter as he and Victor exchanged proud smiles. Could she love this community more?

"Sure you don't want a cuppa?" she asked, but they both shook their heads.

"No, no," said Victor, already edging towards the door. He wasn't quite as antisocial as Lewis, but he was close.

"And I need to get back to Muffin," said the Captain. "But let us know how the search pans out?"

"Of course," said Audrey, seeing them out to the hall. "Thanks for all your help."

"It's brain exercise," added Victor, tapping his temple. "Isn't it, Gordon?"

"Absolutely," said the Captain. "At this age, you've got to keep the mind active. It's good for us, this detective work you and Lewis are doing. Keeps us all busy."

"I second that," said Manny, when she returned to the kitchen. "It's fun having an activity to do together."

"Better than a picnic any day," laughed Joe.

"I'm starting to think Lewis is having more of an effect on us than we are on him," said Audrey, folding her arms. "I'm going to need to keep an eye on that."

49
Lewis

When Lewis arrived at the Trinity offices that afternoon, he was feeling jittery. Audrey's fear was starting to get to him, and the more he thought about it, the more he realised she was right. The only reason to keep tabs on them was if you wanted to silence them, and as the key witness, it would be Audrey the killer would come after. He hadn't slept well, and now he had to do some real work on top of everything else.

He held the door for two people leaving the Trinity building, pulling up short when he realised who they were.

"Lewis, hi," said Sofia, looking flustered. "What are you doing here?"

"Uh . . . " Lewis turned from Sofia to DI Banham, who looked just as Lewis remembered him: shorter than Sofia, with a buzz cut and a scruffy-looking suit. "Roland Waverley called a meeting. He has some recruitment requirements."

"I should say he does," snorted Banham. "But why call you?"

"Because I work in recruitment," said Lewis, wondering what that first bit meant. "We met the other day."

Banham scowled.

"So I hear. You've been interfering again."

"It's not interfering when the police aren't investigating," replied Lewis, and saw Sofia close her eyes. "Don't worry, we'll share everything we get."

Banham's expression became thunderous.

"Damn straight you will." He jabbed a finger at Lewis. "I want to interview you and your little cleaner friend. I'll be over this evening. Make yourselves available."

Without waiting for Lewis to respond, Banham strode off and, after a quick shake of the head that was clearly meant to be a telling off, Sofia followed.

Now in a bad mood, Lewis went inside. Jess—or was it Steph?—was on the phone.

"No," she was saying, "I'm afraid there just isn't anywhere else. I'm so sorry . . . Yes, yes, I know, but there's an issue with the boiler, and we just can't lease an unsafe property . . . We don't know when it might be fixed, which is why we've removed the listing."

Lewis leaned on the counter while he waited, keeping an eye on the stairs in case Roland Waverley should make an appearance.

"How about a hotel? . . . Oh, I see. Well, why don't I ring around for you and see what I can do? Maybe I'll have more luck." A second phone started ringing. "Yes," she said hurriedly. "Yes, that's no problem. I'll call you back before the end of the day. Bye."

Lewis turned just in time to see Jess-or-Steph put a mobile phone down and pick up the desk phone. He frowned. That hadn't sounded like a personal call.

"Good afternoon, Trinity Property Management, how can I help you?"

As she listened, she glanced up, eyes widening when she saw Lewis standing in front of the desk. Then she scowled and went back to the call.

"Of course. Putting you through." She pressed a button on the phone, dialled a number, and waited a couple of seconds. "Mrs. Jenner for you," she said, then pressed another button and put the phone down. She took a deep breath, then looked up at Lewis. "Hi."

"Hi." He tried to appear friendly. "Bad day?"

To his astonishment, her lip trembled, and for a horrible moment, he thought she was going to cry, but then she took another breath.

"Just busy," she said. "Are you here to see Felix?"

"Roland Waverley," he said, and again, her eyes widened. "He asked me to drop in."

"Oh. Right. What name please?"

"Lewis McLennon of Page and Hall Recruitment."

Looking somewhat discombobulated, she picked up the phone again and informed someone of Lewis's arrival, then put it down.

"He'll be a couple of minutes."

Sensing an opportunity, Lewis tried to imagine what Audrey would do to get her talking. She'd do that sympathetic big-eye thing probably.

"Worked here long?" he asked.

Immediately on her guard, the young woman frowned.

"About two years," she replied warily.

"Do you like it?" he tried. Then, still channelling Audrey, "Looks like it might be a bit stressful."

The frown relaxed a little.

"It can be."

"Well, if you're ever looking for another job . . . " He smiled in what he hoped was a cheeky way. It seemed to do the trick, and her eyes locked onto his.

"I might be actually," she said suddenly. "I mean . . . it's just . . . "

"Hey, you don't have to explain," he said, and now he was channelling Steve. "A change, a step up the ladder . . . sometimes the road to advancement is blocked, and you need to step sideways." *Oh, God, it was happening again. He was doing recruitment.*

"Yes." She nodded emphatically and lowered her voice. "I'm just the dogsbody. I used to just be on reception, but now I'm everyone's secretary, fetching coffee, tidying up, changing—" She stopped abruptly. "I was hoping to move upstairs, but I don't think I want to now."

He rooted in his pocket, looking for another business card. He hadn't given one out in four years, and now two in one week. "Here." He passed it over the desk. "Call me any time."

She took the card and was suddenly all smiles, lowering her head and looking at him from under her lashes.

"Any time? I wouldn't want to upset your . . . wife? Girlfriend? Who was with you before?"

Ah.

"Uh, no. Neither of those. She's just a friend."

The smile broadened, and Lewis felt increasingly uncomfortable. He hadn't meant to flirt, but flirting was definitely now happening to him.

"Great. And in case you were wondering, I wouldn't upset anyone either."

"No?" He gulped, then added, feeling like a cad, "That seems surprising."

She blushed, and now the smile was a little bit sad.

"No, not anymore." The phone chirruped, making them both start. She lifted the handset. "Yes? Okay, I'll tell him." She put it down again. "You can go up. Do you know the way?"

"Yes. Thanks . . . uh?"

"Steph," said Steph.

"Steph. Nice to speak to you."

"You too."

He walked off towards the stairs, feeling horrible. By the time he reached the landing, however, and discovered Roland

Waverley waiting for him, he immediately forgot about Steph and remembered why he was here.

"Mr. McLennon, hello," said Waverley, holding out his hand. "Good to see you again."

"Lewis," said Lewis, shaking hands. "Thanks for getting in touch."

"No problem. Let's go into my office."

Instead of going through the double doors to the left, Waverley took Lewis to the right, where a handful of doors led off a wide off-white hallway. Waverley's office was at the end, beside a door marked "Boardroom."

"Just in here," said Waverley, ushering him into a large, equally off-white room, decorated with framed illustrations of famous London buildings. A big mahogany desk, not unlike the one in Petrov's study, stood between two windows. Waverley closed the door behind them, then sat behind the desk, gesturing for Lewis to take a seat opposite.

"Thanks for coming," began Waverley. "I prefer to do business face-to-face. I think it's important to look someone in the eye, don't you?"

"Sure," said Lewis, who preferred not to look anyone in the eye. He took out his phone. "I'll be making notes on this, if you don't mind?"

Waverley nodded.

"I was rather taken aback when you gave me your card the other day, but it got me thinking, and I've realised we're overdue a few internal changes here at Trinity."

"Great," said Lewis, wondering how long it would be until he could ask his own questions. "What kind of role are you looking to fill?"

"More than one, actually," said Waverley, leaning back in his chair. "First of all, we need to expand our IT team. Recent events have shown we've grown lax and haven't been keeping pace with the industry. We're looking to hire a cybersecurity expert—I'm not sure what the exact job title would be—but someone who can help us upgrade our technology, futureproof our systems, and protect us against hackers."

Lewis sat up straighter.

"This is about Beaton Gardens? You confirmed the hack?"

This was a shock. He'd half-expected Waverley to deny anything had happened, either because Casetti had sufficiently covered his tracks or to protect the reputation of his business.

Waverley nodded, looking grave.

"It certainly looks that way. You and Miss Brooks were right: There was some interference with the security feed. Our IT guy didn't spot anything awry while it was happening, and based on the footage, the loops ran more than once and for some time. I assume your own experts found the same?"

"Yes," said Lewis, noting how the Trinity IT experts had become just one guy. "As well as the gaps over several weekends."

"Which brings me to another point. We'd like to hire a specific security camera operator, someone to keep an eye on the properties in real time. We made the mistake of assuming this was being done, but it seems that our staff are busier than we realised, and things have fallen through the cracks. I take full responsibility for it, but we need to address the situation. I don't know if this is a viable solution, given half the properties are empty much of the time. I imagine it would be dull work, but I think we have to try. Perhaps you could advise us of other duties that could be performed in conjunction with this role? To make it more interesting for the employee and productive for us?"

"I'll have a word with some colleagues," said Lewis, typing that into his phone. "See what they suggest."

"I'd appreciate it." Now Waverley looked uncomfortable and leaned forward, arms on the desk. "There are two other positions I'd like you to look into. This is strictly confidential, you understand."

"Of course."

"We may be looking to hire a new receptionist," said Waverley, and Lewis looked up. "Pending the outcome of an internal inquiry. Or perhaps two on a job-share basis. Our current girl works Tuesday to Saturday, with someone else covering on Monday, but I feel we've overstretched people. We might also need a new senior property manager."

Lewis paused, his thumbs hovering over his phone's keyboard. Waverley was about to sack Steph *and* Casetti?

"An inquiry?" he repeated.

"Yes. We've seen some . . . irregular behaviour from some of our staff, which we've only recently uncovered. Potentially irregular, anyway. We don't want to make a fuss, but we'll be cleaning house, so to speak. Making sure we're above reproach." He waved his hand in an attempt to make it sound casual. "Even if it proves unfounded, we don't want people to say there's no smoke, eh?"

"Right," said Lewis, typing all that into his phone. He kept his eyes on the screen as he decided to take a risk. "I imagine that's important in the property business."

"Yes, indeed. It's an industry based on trust."

"I remember reading about illegal sublets with that app—Sharelets?" Lewis glanced up at Waverley just in time to see him flinch. "You don't need that sort of scandal."

"Quite."

There was an awkward pause in which Lewis pretended to type while Waverley shifted in his chair.

"Were you able to explain the gaps, by the way?" asked Lewis, eyes on his phone. "The camera seemed to go off most weekends, but we couldn't tell how it was done, or by whom. Any ideas?"

"No," said Waverley. "At least, nothing we can prove. The office is closed on Sundays, with only a few people in on Monday. Oversight is limited. The . . . uh . . . police are now aware. We're hoping to get to the bottom of it."

"Ah." Lewis tried not to react. "So that's one security camera operator, one cybersecurity expert, one or two receptionists, and one senior property manager. I'll get some job descriptions drafted and emailed over to you. Any particular date you're hoping to fill the positions by?"

"As soon as possible for the technical people," said Waverley, standing up. "And I'll be in touch regarding the other two. I expect to know by the end of the week."

"Great." Lewis put his phone away and stood up too. Waverley clearly wanted him gone now, and Lewis didn't blame him. It sounded like Felix and Steph were up to their eyes in this, and about to get the boot. "One last question. I don't suppose you'd like to reinstate Au—I mean, Miss Brooks, to her regular cleaning slot, would you? Now that you've identified the root of the break-in there. Mr. Petrov was very worried about his clocks."

"Oh. Yes, I'd forgotten about that." Waverley coughed. "Please do tell Miss Brooks that she may resume cleaning and offer my apologies for the inconvenience. I appreciate her patience. And her diligence, of course. And please tell Mr. Petrov that we have everything in hand. His trust in us is not misplaced, I assure you."

"I'll pass that on."

"I'll see you out," said Waverley, holding the door. He escorted Lewis back down to reception, where Steph looked up eagerly, blanching when she saw Waverley. He didn't so much as look at her but offered Lewis his hand. "Thanks again."

"No problem," said Lewis, shaking it. "I'll be in touch."

He left without a backward glance, feeling elated as he walked away. Felix and Steph had been subletting Petrov's place to vacationers and had embroiled Trinity in a hit! Waverley would be trying to keep it quiet, but he wanted them out as soon as possible.

He walked down to the corner of Sloane Square and waited at the crossing for the lights to change, a crowd of tourists jostling for space around him as the early-rush-hour traffic sped past. He'd told Steve he'd go straight home, and he couldn't wait to tell Audrey his news.

A backpack scraped against his shoulder as the tourist next to him turned around, and Lewis took a step sideways to make room. A black cab beeped its horn at a cyclist, and as Lewis turned towards the noise, someone slammed hard into his back, propelling him into the traffic just as a bus rounded the corner of the junction.

Lewis barely had time to register he was in the road before he was yanked back onto the pavement. The bus squeaked to a halt a millisecond later, the driver looking through the passenger doors at him in horror. A moment later, he shook his head and drove off again, apparently too shocked and relieved to even beep his horn.

"That was a close one," said a man with a Polish accent, letting go of Lewis's jacket. "You could have been killed."

"Yes," said Lewis, nodding his thanks even as his heart hammered painfully in his chest. "I think I nearly was."

50
Audrey

"Do you think it was him?" asked Audrey, when Lewis told her what had happened. "The killer?"

"I don't know," he said, running a hand through his hair. He looked stressed. "There were a lot of people about. It could have been an accident."

"But you don't think so. You should tell Sofia and Banham when they come to interview us. We're clearly *both* in danger."

They were sitting at the kitchen counter, Lewis's coat and scarf draped over one of the dining chairs behind them. He'd recounted his interview with Steph first, then the visit to Waverley, then the incident on the crossing, while she in turn had told him about Manny's findings, the strange noise at Beaton Gardens, and the theory about the panic room.

"No," he said, firmly. "There's nothing the police can do after the fact, and they'd just tell us to back off. Which is not happening."

She nodded.

"I feel bad that Steph and Felix are going to get the sack."

"Why?" He was incredulous. "They're committing fraud. They were going to be found out eventually. They're lucky if they only get sacked and not prosecuted."

"Do you think they might be?"

He shook his head.

"I don't think Waverley will want a fuss. He's looking to expand Trinity, and this would be a big reputational problem. He was worried about Petrov and what he might think."

"They need to be worried. They're happy to spy on their lowly cleaners, but senior property managers can do whatever they want?"

"You felt bad he was getting the sack a second ago."

"Yeah, well. It's horrible losing your job. Trust me."

"Oh, I have good news on that front. I asked Waverley about your job, and he reinstated you immediately. You can go back to cleaning tomorrow."

He smiled at her, clearly glad to be the bearer of good news, and she was genuinely touched by his efforts on her behalf, even if the thought of going back to Beaton Gardens made her suddenly feel sick.

"Wow," she said, forcing a smile. "That's brilliant. Thank you for speaking to him, I appreciate it."

Lewis looked pleased.

"And it's good for us, too, because now we have access to the crime scene again. That idea of Gordon and Victor's about the panic room is a good one. I reckon we'll be able to find it, no problem. If it exists."

She tried to quash the nausea.

"I feel bad for Steph," she said. "You think she's the second cleaner?"

"I do. We need to confirm, but it sounded like she'd been pressured into it. Maybe she and Felix were a thing at some point. I don't think she's a killer anyway. She seemed nice. Friendly."

He looked embarrassed, and Audrey raised an eyebrow.

"What?" The pink spots on his cheeks turned red. "She was flirting a little, maybe."

"And yet you don't think she's a psychopath? Fascinating."

He glared at her, and she giggled, just as her phone pinged.

> **MEI CHEN:** Baxter Cole has resurfaced! Off to an emergency meeting. Might not be home til late. Will keep you posted. x

She smiled.

"What is it?" Lewis asked.

"Mei. Her missing client just reappeared."

> **AUDREY BROOKS:** That's great! Hopefully you can get the case back on track now. Lewis and I are waiting for DI Banham to drop round. Catch you up later. x

She'd just put her phone down when the intercom by the door sounded, and they both jumped.

"Oh, God," said Audrey, hopping off the stool. "They're here. Whatever Banham says, will you try not to antagonise him? Please?"

"I don't do it on purpose," Lewis protested. "He just hates people doing his job better than he can."

"Okay, do not say anything like that." She shook her head. "Just . . . don't."

She went into the hall and pressed the button on the intercom.

"Hello?"

"DS Larssen and DI Banham," came Sofia's voice through the speaker. "At the side gate."

"Come on up," said Audrey, pressing the gate release, then stuck her head back into the kitchen. "Seriously. Just be nice. Please."

She returned to the front door before Lewis could respond and opened it to find Sofia and DI Banham at the top of the gallery steps. Banham already looked angry.

"Miss Brooks," he said, scowling at her.

"DI Banham." She held the door for him. "Please come in."

Banham marched in, heading straight for the kitchen, while Sofia paused on the doorstep, looking tired and apologetic.

"He's in a foul mood," she whispered. "Try to stop Lewis from . . . you know."

"Being Lewis?"

Sofia nodded.

"I'll do my best," said Audrey, closing the door. "But you know what he's like."

"I know what they're both like," said Sofia, and sighed. "Come on, let's get this over with."

51
Lewis

Sofia led the interrogation, starting with Audrey turning up early at Beaton Gardens and highlighting the first 999 call, the follow-up call to herself, and every step at which they had tried, unsuccessfully, to involve the police, before moving on to the suspected body dump, as she insisted on calling it, and the official report she'd filed about the burglary in Audrey and Mei's home.

Lewis tried as hard as he could, to simply answer the questions as they were put, but every now and then, Banham would bark out such a rude comment that Lewis couldn't help but jibe back.

"We're now in the process of unfucking the chain-of-evidence custody," complained DI Banham, directing this at Sofia. "The only thing we've got that hasn't been handled by amateurs first is the swab from the crime scene, which is currently useless."

"I know," said Sofia, sounding like it wasn't the first time they'd been over this. "But the hair and fibres from the vacuum cleaner were handled properly, and that's good physical evidence, and a constable found the murder weapon, which matches Tyler's blood. Plus we've got Tyler's phone from the suitcase and a download of the security footage from Trinity. The loops match the network logs on the phone."

Phone? Network logs?

"That may be," said Banham. "But after these two blundered in to demand the footage, who knows how else it's been tampered with? Whoever's running this thing could have tidied up after themselves, knowing the original export would be inadmissible once it had passed through Petrov. Waverley thinks it's Casetti behind it, and I'm inclined to agree. He was too smooth by half considering everything that's occurred on his watch, but he's had days in which to cover his tracks."

"We've got the original download though," said Lewis. "Why would it be inadmissible?"

"Because Anton Petrov is a person of interest, and you requested the footage on his behalf. Apparently, you're a personal friend of his?"

"Uh . . . "

"We may have exaggerated a little," said Audrey, and Banham glared at her. "Mr. Petrov is a friend of Mrs. van Duren. She asked us to look into it."

"But we have met him," added Lewis. "He wanted us to continue asking questions."

"We'll see if he corroborates that when we talk to him," said Banham darkly.

"What about the body?" asked Lewis, trying to steer the DI back to ranting about evidence. "That must have some clues?"

"I'd hardly call a clumsy stab wound and some plastic wrap with the victim's blood all over it a clue."

Clumsy?

"Not professional, then?" he asked. "An amateur job?"

Banham scowled.

"I didn't say that."

"Is there anything else you've not told us?" asked Sofia, her eyes locking onto Lewis's in a way he didn't much like. "Nothing you're keeping to yourselves? These are dangerous people. You can't hold anything back."

"But if the killing was an amateur job," Lewis argued, ignoring Audrey's pointed tilt of the head, "then they might not be so dangerous. Right? It could have been self-defence. The victim fought back and is now trying to cover up their involvement."

He wasn't stopping his investigation for anyone.

"Will you be searching the house now?" asked Audrey. "I'm supposed to clean again tomorrow."

Banham looked at Sofia, who shook her head.

"Warrants are taking a week at least," she said. "Unless Petrov gives his permission, we'll have to wait."

"Have we heard from him yet?"

"No, sir."

"It's been cleaned at least twice already since Tyler died," said Lewis, helpfully. "I doubt there'll be anything left to find."

Banham's nostrils flared.

"Our Forensics people can find a breath on a needle in a haystack," he said. "If something happened there, they'll find it."

"Why does everyone keep saying 'if' something happened there?" snapped Audrey suddenly. "I know what I saw! You've got the blood, you've found the body, you've even got the murder weapon—what more do you need?"

Banham narrowed his eyes.

"Eyewitness testimony is the least reliable evidence," he said shortly. "Stay out of the property."

"I can't," said Audrey, sounding unusually firm. "I have to wind the clocks."

"What?"

"Mr. Petrov pays me to clean the house and wind the clocks. Some of them are eight-day mechanisms."

"So?"

"So I can't not wind them. They'll stop."

Lewis enjoyed the look on Banham's face as he stared at her.

"Are you mad?" he asked, then turned to Sofia. "Is she mad?"

"No," said Sofia, and Lewis was sure she was suppressing a smile. "She's conscientious. Petrov pays her to wind the clocks, so she does."

Banham opened his mouth like he was about to say something else, then looked again at Audrey, who glared at him. Probably because he'd called her mad.

"Fine," said Banham at last, through gritted teeth. "But. Don't. Clean. Got it?"

Audrey didn't reply, just continued glowering in his direction.

"I think that's all, sir," said Sofia, standing up. "We should go."

"Fine," said Banham again, also getting to his feet. "But you two need to get a new hobby. Take up knitting or something, will you? Because this," he pointed a finger, first at Lewis, then at Audrey, "is starting to get on my nerves."

52
Audrey

"Did you hear what Sofia said?" asked Lewis the minute Audrey returned to the kitchen. "The knife *is* the murder weapon. And Tyler was the one who set up the loop, but Banham said the killing was clumsy, which suggests he was killed by his own intended victim!"

"That's not as comforting as you seem to think," said Audrey with a sigh. "Whoever they are, they're a killer, and they've been in my house *and* tried to throw you under a bus. Nobody else would want the evidence from the crime scene, would they?"

"No . . . " he said, although he looked puzzled. "That would mean there were three people involved—Tyler, his victim, and someone trying to clean up after them both. Casetti, perhaps? But if another professional killer was in the house at the same time as you, it makes no sense to let you walk out of there to alert the police. The person who saw you didn't want or need to hurt you, which makes it more likely it was the cleaner, not the killer."

"You think the killer and the cleaner were different people?"

"I do. But there was a mistake somewhere, I know it. That's why you interrupted the cleanup."

Audrey thought about this. Whoever had planned the hit had hacked Trinity to give themselves a twenty-four-hour window in which to commit murder and clean up. They knew about the camera, which was more than Audrey had done, and they knew about the property being leased out over the weekend. They knew about the second cleaner coming on Monday afternoon, and they also knew about Audrey and her shift pattern, a thought that made her want to lock her doors and never leave the house again. Lewis was right. It was too difficult, too complicated. The location wasn't random. It had been chosen for a reason.

"If Tyler was the intended victim," she said, "then what was the mistake? The timings went wrong?"

Lewis nodded.

"Perhaps he turned up late."

"But if he wasn't the intended victim," she said, "then the mistake was that the victim fought back and killed Tyler. He was meant to clean up and couldn't, on account of being dead, so someone else had to arrange it. Either the person who'd hired him or the person illegally renting out the house."

They looked at each other and spoke at the same time.

"Felix Casetti."

"But we need proof first," added Lewis. "You heard what Banham said, he's a slippery customer. We need something irrefutable to force him to tell us the truth."

"Well, someone told Tyler about the security camera," said Audrey. "Because even I didn't know about that."

The sound of keys in the lock made them both turn, and a second later, Mei's voice carried through to the kitchen.

"Only me," she called. The kitchen door opened. She glanced at Lewis as she walked in. "Hey. How'd it go with Banham?"

Audrey had expected Mei to look better now that her client had reappeared, but instead she looked worse, her skin so pale that her deep brown eyes looked almost black in comparison.

"It went fine," she said. "What's wrong? What's happened?"

Mei, usually so cool and collected, looked as though she could crumple up right there on the kitchen floor. Audrey got up and went to her.

"Tell me."

"He fired us."

"What?"

"Baxter Cole. His assistant called a meeting this afternoon, and when we got there, he marched into the room and fired us from his case, citing *me* as the reason."

Audrey blinked.

"I don't understand."

"He said that we were underhanded and untrustworthy, and he didn't want us defending him anymore. Then he pointed at me and said he knew what I'd done and wouldn't rest until I was in prison. I asked what he was talking about, and he just said, "You know," and walked off. Dominic refused to believe I didn't know what he was going on about, and now the whole team are looking at me like I'm guilty of malpractice, and I just don't know what"—she faltered, then went on,—"what I've done to deserve it."

Audrey wrapped her arms around Mei, who collapsed into sobs. She looked over at Lewis, sitting awkwardly at the table, and shook her head. They couldn't talk any more tonight.

He stood up.

"I'll head on home," he said, and Mei turned to him, her eyes damp and swollen. She looked mortified and brushed away tears with her sleeve.

"Sorry," she said. "I didn't mean to run you out."

"No worries. I'm sorry about your client. He sounds like an arsehole."

"He is." She sniffed and smiled weakly. "But even so . . . "

Audrey left Mei in the kitchen, searching for some tissues, and saw Lewis out to the hall.

"Back to the edits?" she asked as he put his coat on.

"Yes, while I can." He grimaced. "I have to write up those vacancies for Waverley tomorrow."

"Better than me," she said. "I have to go back to the murder house."

"Lucky you." He sounded envious. "See if you can find that safe room, will you? We won't get another chance if the police have their way."

"Sure," she said, sarcastically. "No problem. Let's hope I don't find any killers behind any secret doors."

"Hah, yeah."

On his way out though, he hesitated, turning back to her with a troubled expression.

"What Banham said about hobbies . . . Do you have a side hustle?"

"A what?"

"A side hustle. Some sort of side project you're working on in your free time. Something that's not cleaning."

"Like you and your books?" He frowned, and she realised she probably shouldn't have implied it was a hobby. "Not that that's a side hustle," she added hastily. "I just meant it's not your main job. Anymore."

"Yeah, like that."

She thought for a minute.

"No," she said eventually. "I read, watch TV, do yoga sometimes, although not really. I used to do crochet, but I prefer to watch other people now. There's this guy on YouTube who can crochet stuff you just wouldn't believe—CrochetSteve. I love watching his videos, but I'm just not that good. Maybe if I didn't like my job, I'd be looking for something else but . . . " She shrugged. "Why?"

He shook his head.

"Just something someone said. Not important."

After he'd gone, she returned to the kitchen and cooked spaghetti carbonara, listening as Mei recounted the entire meeting with Baxter Cole while nursing a glass of wine.

"When Dominic asked where he'd been, he looked at me and said, "Why don't you ask her?" Like I hadn't been searching half the country for him. And then that parting shot . . . " She shook her head and gazed sadly into her glass. "I just don't understand."

Audrey heaped some pasta into a bowl, twizzling it into a neat pile.

"Sounds like he's had some sort of episode," she said, grinding black pepper over the top. "Become paranoid and delusional. Has he got any history of that?"

"I don't think so," said Mei, looking thoughtful. "But you could be right. He didn't seem like himself, that's for sure. He had a nasty cough and looked like he hadn't slept in days." She looked down at the dish Audrey placed in front of her. "This looks amazing. Let's change the subject. Tell me what happened with Banham."

Once Audrey had relayed their interview, they retreated to the living room to watch some *CSI*. After Mei dozed off for the third time, however, Audrey sent her to bed and then went up herself, pausing only to check that the deadbolt and chain were on the front door.

She snuggled beneath the duvet and thought about what Lewis had said.

Was it sad that she didn't have a creative outlet? Or some other outside interest? It didn't feel sad to her, but maybe it looked it from the outside. She thought about Mei and her yoga, and the retreats and courses she'd do on her holidays. And Lewis and his books, although if your side hustle became your main hustle, did that mean you needed another hobby?

Maybe crime-solving could be her hobby. It certainly got the adrenaline flowing, although she didn't think she'd like to do it *all* the time.

Her phone buzzed on the bedside table.

JOHN KEANE:

Sorry for late reply, was working and in full gear. No problem at all re: Sunday, it was great to meet you. If you have any more questions, just ask. Happy to talk cleaning any time! And if you do think you'd like to work for us, let me know. We'd love to have you on the team. Maybe we could chat over coffee soon?
John

She smiled. In spite of her nagging fear, her worries about Mei, and her dread of revisiting Beaton Gardens, maybe not everything was awful.

She slept.

53
Lewis

Lewis spent the evening trying to focus on his novel but found himself unable to concentrate. Had someone really tried to kill him? Or had it been an accident?

As a distraction, he began to flick around various social media sites, looking up his colleagues. Chris, who specialised in finance roles, had more than twenty thousand followers on Instagram, a feed that consisted mostly of selfies and pictures of him posing in different outfits in different locations around London. Descending the steps of a hotel in Mayfair, lounging against a red telephone box in Parliament Square, standing beside a window looking out over a park with tall trees and iron railings. How had Lewis not known about his modelling aspirations?

He looked up Ken then but couldn't find any books under his name or an author profile that seemed to match. He must be using a pen name. He kept searching, discovering that Lucy had almost as many followers as Chris, posting pictures of what she called "fusion pancake wraps." Tasha was doing courses in film makeup, while Sameer was about to audition for the *Bake Off*, whatever that was, and Lewis realised with a start that the batch of mini vegetable pastries he'd devoured in the break room last week had been baked by his colleague. He couldn't find Steve's YouTube channel though. Whatever it was, he clearly wasn't using his real name. Perhaps he'd ask Audrey to do some Googling. She was disturbingly good at social-media detective work.

Feeling suddenly uncomfortable but unsure of why, he returned to his case notes. His priority had to be his book and the investigation, not whether his colleagues were interesting and complex human beings.

He clicked to the tab he'd left open on the crime forum to see if there'd been any replies to his message about Don Tyler.

CrimeWriter159

Wondering if anyone knows what became of a professional called Don Tyler, back in the noughties? Been researching different M.O.s and discovered his name in some archived posts on here. Seems he was a big name who might have vanished abroad. Retired or dead?

> **SmileyLives**
>
> The name died in London, but the M.O. kept on abroad. Europe mostly. Probably changed his name.

LilNarco

Cops think he's back in the UK now, though, using the same name. Person of interest in a death last year.

> **SmileyLives**
>
> Really? Not heard that. London again?

LilNarco

Yup.

> **TruCrimeFan99**
>
> Why would he use the same name?

LilNarco

Maybe he wants people to know. Bit of a coincidence, someone posting on here not long after he gets back. Pays to advertise?

Lewis hadn't really considered the implications of Don Tyler returning not just to his old operating ground but also to his old name. Why would a professional do that, if he'd long ago moved on? Was it advertising, as the comment suggested? Tyler knew the name had a reputation worth reviving, and what better way to let all your old contacts know that you were back in town and back in business? Or could it be something else? A message he wanted to send, perhaps?

Perhaps it was the message that had gotten him into trouble.

He opened up his case notes, rethinking his suspect list. Who were the persons in the case, really?

The victim and the killer, whose roles may have been reversed. The cleaner, who could be the killer, but most likely was not. The burglar at Audrey and Mei's, who could be the killer, but who could also be the cleaner. And the man Audrey saw in the garden, who could possibly be all the above.

Why steal the bags of dirt at all? The body of Don Tyler had been bound to surface eventually, and so the only reason to take the contents of the vacuum cleaner was to remove any evidence of someone who shouldn't have been there, or else to discredit Audrey naming Beaton Gardens as the crime scene. That would put Casetti firmly in the frame, although perhaps, and to a lesser extent, Steph.

And, of course, Anton Petrov.

He scrolled down to the bit about the stranger in the garden.

Audrey had seen the guy in the garden, watching the house, on the morning she saw the body. If he was the other cleaner, he could have been lying in wait for the coast to be clear, although Lewis didn't think cleaners should be that grubby. However, he could also have been the killer and watching because . . .

Why *would* the killer stay in the area to watch the crime scene? Surely you'd leave as soon as possible? Why hang around and risk being caught?

To see who came to collect the body. If Tyler had been carrying out a personal hit, the guy would know. You don't piss someone off to that degree without knowing who they are. If, however, you knew someone had been paid to kill you and you'd somehow gotten away, wouldn't you want to know who'd taken out a contract on you? If he'd been in the park before Audrey got there, he'd have seen the man with white hair leaving the house, and he'd have seen Audrey going in. He'd have seen the police, he'd have seen Lewis . . .

With so many people coming and going, it'd be hard to tell what role everyone played. With the exception of Audrey, that is, who arrived with her cleaning bag, came running out on discovering the body, and called the police. She'd be the only one who looked innocent.

So why burgle her house?

He exhaled slowly, heart beginning to thump.

Tyler was the victim but was supposed to have been the killer, while the guy in the garden was their killer but was supposed to be the victim. So how the hell did they identify him? And who had taken out the hit?

He imagined standing in the private garden, hidden in the bushes and watching the house through the railings, those tall bare trees swishing above him as he wondered who hated him enough to want him dead.

Lewis blinked.

The trees . . .

He clicked back into his Web browser and pulled up Chris's photo grid again, scrolling through the endless pictures to find the one he wanted.

There. Chris beside a tall, open window, long sheer curtains billowing around him while he looked wistfully out over a park. They were so common in London, those small areas of greenery surrounded by railings, that Lewis hadn't really paid attention to the background, but the trees . . .

He'd seen those trees before. That exact view.

He clicked on the photo, and it filled the screen. It had been taken in summer, and the view matched perfectly: the wide street below, the iron railings, the hedging and shrubbery, and, most notably, the cluster of tall trees on the right. There was even a glimpse of a red bus through the leaves.

And in case there was any doubt, Chris had helpfully tagged the location.

Beaton Gardens, London.

Lewis zoomed in and examined the photo, grateful to whoever the photographer was for using such high definition. He needed something—anything—to prove that the photo had been taken in Anton Petrov's house.

The shot had been positioned specifically to showcase Chris's face and physique, the filmy curtain wafting inward, with just a glimpse of bookshelves behind. But to the left, on the other side of the window, was the edge of a clock. A distinctive Chippendale grandfather clock that Lewis recognised.

He smiled with grim satisfaction.

Got you.

54
Audrey

The following morning, Audrey set out into an icy wind to walk over to Cadogan Place. More than once, a glimpse of a dark figure made her head turn and her heart stop, but this was London in winter, and men in dark coats were everywhere. The fear was exhausting. At lunchtime, after finishing up at Lady Macintyre's, she decided to pay for an expensive coffee-shop lunch so that she didn't have to spend an hour outside, freezing half to death.

Somehow, though, she still reached Beaton Gardens earlier than intended and now stood beside the garden railings opposite the Petrov house, stamping her feet on the pavement. Her cleaning bag was heavy in her hand, and she walked up and down, trying not to imagine someone peering through the shrubbery at her. She remembered the night of the stakeout and the constant feeling of someone unseen nearby. She shook it off. All seemed quiet and empty now.

The bells of St. Peter's began to toll twelve, so she took a deep breath and crossed the road to number thirty-five, her hands shaking as she put the key in the lock.

"Audrey!"

She turned around in a panic, then spotted Lewis striding down the street towards her.

"What are you doing here?"

"I took an early lunch," he said, climbing the steps to join her. "I have some news. Plus, I thought you might not be so keen on going back in on your own."

He sounded unsure, but she beamed at him, delighted to discover he wasn't terminally insensitive.

"That's an understatement," she said. "I'm very glad you're here."

"Oh." He looked relieved. "Good."

"What's the news?"

"I'll tell you in a minute. Can we go in? It's freezing out here."

Feeling suddenly much braver, Audrey unlocked the door, and the alarm started beeping. She entered the code, then dropped her bag in the hall, turning to look at the kitchen door.

"What are you doing?"

"Looking for the camera," she said, examining what she'd thought was a smoke alarm. "I always felt there was one, but I never knew where it was. I hope Trinity won't mind you being here."

"We told them we were looking into this for Petrov, and he did say he'd vouch for us. Besides," he turned to her, dark eyes flashing, "no one's monitoring the cameras."

"How do you know?"

"Waverley told me. He wants to hire someone to watch the Trinity security camera feeds because no one's actually been doing it. He also wants a cybersecurity expert. They had no idea Tyler had hacked them until we told them."

She paused.

"I wonder why he called you then. There are millions of recruitment people in London, and none of them would be running off to tell Mr. Petrov that Trinity had been negligent. Seems weird he'd choose you, of all people, to confide in."

Lewis opened his mouth to reply, then closed it again. He frowned.

"He didn't give me the details. Just hinted."

"But Mr. Petrov knows something's happened that shouldn't have, so he'll probably sack them and get another company in. Wouldn't you?"

At that moment, the doorbell rang. Surprised, she looked at Lewis, who grinned.

"Shall I get it?"

He opened the door before she could reply, revealing a stunningly handsome man standing on the doorstep. Lewis greeted him with a "Hello, mate," and Audrey watched, open-mouthed, as he ushered the man inside.

"Audrey, this is Christopher Gao. He's a colleague from work. Chris, this is Audrey Brooks."

"Hey," said Chris, smiling and holding out his hand. He had a strong jawline, cheekbones that Audrey would have killed for, and a neat beard that looked like precisely a week's worth of stubble. She smiled back, feeling her face heat, and shook his hand, suddenly worrying about clamminess and whether her hair was smooth or staticky.

She looked at Lewis.

"What's going on?"

"Chris is a model," he explained. "I only found out the other day."

"Trying to be," said Chris modestly, clapping Lewis on the back. "Not as clever as our writer boy here, but I like it."

"Uh . . . " This appeared to take Lewis by surprise. "How did you know I was a writer?"

Chris laughed, displaying perfect white teeth to go with his perfect everything else.

"I Googled you, man! Don't you Google everyone?"

"No. Anyway, Chris has been trying to boost his portfolio lately, and a group of his . . . uh, fellow models . . . clubbed together to rent a couple of weekend places in the summer, as shooting locations."

Audrey nodded politely, then realisation hit.

"You rented this place?"

"Sure did! Got some great shots." Chris took out his phone and, a few seconds later, held it out to her. "These were taken here."

She looked at the photos. Chris standing by the window next to Mr. Petrov's Chippendale clock, looking romantic . . . Chris sitting at Mr. Petrov's desk, looking serious . . . Chris sitting in the murder chair looking pensive . . .

She shivered.

"Yeah, I like that one too," he said, misunderstanding her reaction. "Moody, yeah?"

"Mmm. So . . . who did you rent it from?"

Chris put his phone away.

"It was a bit weird, actually. Normally you just book these things online and they email you the codes for a keysafe, but this was a Sharelet, and we had to pick up the key from an office."

At that moment, the doorbell rang again. Audrey narrowed her eyes at Lewis, who smiled with nothing short of pure glee as he went to answer it.

"Felix, Steph, hi," he said, opening the door wider. "Come on in. Hello again, Mr. Waverley."

Felix ushered Steph in, then stepped into the hall, glancing down to where Chris and Audrey stood. He faltered at once, half-turning to leave, but Roland Waverley was standing behind him.

"Stay, please, Felix," said Waverley.

The colour drained from Felix's face, and he looked at Steph, who whimpered and closed her eyes, leaning against the wall for support. Lewis, meanwhile, took up position in front of the door, clearly determined not to let anyone leave.

"What is all this?" asked Felix, sounding surly.

"Chris," said Lewis, "are these the people who leased you the house for the weekend?"

"Yeah," said Chris, looking at Steph with concern. "Everything all right?"

"You picked up the key from Trinity Property Management?"

"That's right. Sloane Square." He pointed at Steph, whose lip began to tremble. "I picked it up from her on Friday and returned it to this guy on Monday. What's going on?"

"That's what we're trying to sort out," said Lewis.

"There's been some irregularity," said Waverley, his face grave. "My apologies to you, Mr. . . . ?"

"Gao," said Chris, bewildered.

"Mr. Gao. I appreciate you coming down here."

"I don't want to get anyone in trouble," said Chris, looking accusingly at Lewis. Audrey didn't blame him. The whole confrontation was unnecessarily humiliating, especially for poor Steph, who looked like she wanted the earth to swallow her.

"There'll be no trouble, Mr. Gao," said Waverley. "But we will be making some changes to ensure this doesn't happen again. Please don't worry about it."

Chris looked mortified but nodded.

"Can I go now?" he asked. "I need to get back to the office."

"'Course, mate," said Lewis, standing aside to open the door for him. "Thanks again. Can you tell Steve I'll be back in a bit?"

Audrey watched as Lewis saw Chris out, exchanging a few quiet words with him before saying goodbye. He closed the door again.

"Roland," began Felix, but Waverley held up a hand.

"Please don't," he said. "I knew you and Steph were involved, I just couldn't prove it. So please tell Mr. McLennon what he wants to know, and then we can all go. I hope he'll persuade Mr. Petrov not to press charges."

Felix's expression rotated through anger, fear, and back to anger again, his face turning red as it struggled to keep up with his emotions, but Lewis was already rooting inside his jacket. He took out a piece of paper Audrey recognised as the sketch of Don Tyler and unfolded it, holding it out to Felix.

"Did this man ever rent this property from you?"

If looks could kill, Lewis would have dropped down dead right there.

"Yes," said Felix.

"When?"

"January. Just after New Year."

"Just the once?"

"Yes."

Lewis put the picture back in his pocket.

"You were turning the cameras off on Friday," he said, "and turning them back on on Monday, after Steph cleaned. Did you delete the alarm logs after our first visit?"

Felix folded his arms. "Yes."

"Why didn't you want Audrey in before twelve?"

"What?" This confused him.

"When you found out Audrey went in early, you were angry. Why? Did you know about the murder? Did Steph find the body first?"

Steph whimpered again, and Audrey went to stand beside her.

"No!" Felix looked at Waverley in a panic. "Roland, I don't know anything about that."

"The place was fine when I cleaned on Monday," said Steph, in a quavering voice. "I swear it was."

"But when we mentioned that we saw people coming out with a suitcase on Thursday night," said Lewis to Felix, "you thought it might be your guests, didn't you? That they'd committed the crime and had been hiding in the house."

A pause.

"Yes." Then, after a fierce look from Waverley, Felix added, "We only change the alarm codes when we change staff—cleaners and so on. And Petrov was very particular about his cleaner, so I couldn't change the code for Beaton Gardens without raising suspicions. I was worried that people who'd stayed could potentially come back without me knowing, so I set the system to ping me whenever someone entered. It was useful anyway, to check that guests were leaving on time, but last Thursday I didn't get pinged, and I was surprised." He glanced at Audrey. "You were always very punctual."

"Did you try to kill me?" Lewis stared hard at Felix, while Waverley's mouth fell open. "Did you shove me in front of that bus so I'd stop asking questions?"

Felix's face went from red to purple and back again. His breathing quickened as he tried to keep his temper under control.

"It was just meant to be a warning, that's all," he said at last. "The bus was going too fast."

Silence fell, the only sound Steph's snivelling as she rooted in a pocket for a tissue.

"Is that all?" asked Waverley. "I'd like to get back to the office and deal with this properly. Without all the theatrics."

"One more thing," said Audrey to Felix. "The alert you get when someone goes in. It's from the alarm?"

"Yes. As soon as someone turns it off, it lets me know. Same with turning it back on. It's the same in all the properties I manage."

"The alarm was on when I arrived last Thursday. Why didn't you get an alert when I came in?"

"No idea," he said, and there was no trace of charm left in his manner now. "Maybe it got turned off when the alarm logs were deleted. It's separate from the camera system. I never told any guests about it."

"So how would the killer know to hack that too?" asked Lewis.

Felix shrugged.

"Not a clue," he said. "But all the system-access logs had been wiped too." He shouldered past Lewis to the door. "I guess you'll just have to figure that one out yourselves."

55
Lewis

"Was there no other way you could have done that?" Audrey demanded, the second the door closed behind Waverley. Lewis spun around, surprised. He'd been rather pleased with how it had gone.

"Not efficiently, no," he said. "Why?"

"You humiliated them," she said. "Chris too. He felt terrible about it, I could tell."

He felt uncomfortable then, remembering Chris's parting shot as he left. *Not cool, mate. Not cool.*

"Casetti needed to be cornered so he couldn't wriggle out of it. I spoke to Waverley this morning. He said he was sure Casetti was responsible, but that he was trying to pin it on Steph. He couldn't fire anyone without proof. We were helping each other. He did nearly kill me!"

She bit her lip, and he knew she'd be angry on Steph's behalf.

"Well, it wasn't nice," she said, after a beat. "And you should apologise to Chris too."

The thought hadn't occurred to him, but he nodded.

"I need to get started," said Audrey, slipping off her outside shoes and pulling on her indoor ones. "Make yourself useful and check upstairs for murderers, will you? Oh, and take your shoes off first."

He gave her a look but did as she asked, feeling weird about walking around someone else's house in his socks. He started on the top floor and worked his way down, checking the back bedroom twice before returning to the hall.

"No murderers," he said. "No dust, dirt, hair, or blood either, so no need to feel bad about not cleaning." He smiled, hoping she'd forgiven him.

"I'll do the clocks," she said, turning away. "And you can check for secret rooms. Gloves first, though."

She gave him a pair of latex gloves and put some on herself. If the covert cleaners had returned, they might have left a print somewhere.

He followed her around, checking behind every door and every piece of furniture, even running his fingers around the fireplaces where they joined the chimney walls. He had no idea where the safe room might be, but he was leaving no stone unturned.

When they reached the second floor, they both looked down the landing to where the door of what he now thought of as the "murder room" was standing open. They gravitated towards it.

The room looked just as clean, but somehow seemed fresher. Why was that?

He watched as Audrey went over to the wall and swiped it with a gloved finger. Then she sniffed, frowning.

Lewis sniffed too. The room smelled sharp and citrusy, like grapefruit, and the scent was familiar.

"Why do I know that smell?" he asked.

"From before," she said. "It's the same smell as last time, only stronger. The cleaners must have come back, like we thought they would."

He sniffed again.

"They went to town, if the smell's anything to go by."

She went over to the bed, where the sheet still showed the package creases. Their thoroughness didn't extend to ironing, evidently. Lewis then checked the fireplace, crouching down in front of the painted cast iron. Here, the smell was even more powerful, the notes of disinfectant plain beneath the citrus, and he examined the fireplace carefully. Not only had the remaining flecks of blood been removed; there were bits of cast iron showing through, especially around the raised decorative parts. Someone had been aggressively thorough and dislodged some of the old flaking paint.

"Nothing," he said, standing up. "No blood, no hidden doors."

The last thing Audrey examined was the clock, and she picked it up, looking dismayed.

"It's been corrected," she said. "I didn't do that, and I didn't wind it either. It should still be four minutes slow. And the paint chip's gone too." She sighed. "It's like nothing ever happened."

She turned the clock around to show him the back. Through the glass door, they could see the engraved brass backplate, the thin brass pendulum swinging as it should. No smudges and no fingerprints. Lewis shouldn't have expected any less.

But as she was turning it back, she sniffed, frowning again.

"Zabimax?" she said out loud. "They used Zabimax on the clock?"

"Okay."

"No, Lewis, it's not okay. It might be fine on a shabby hotel wall or kitchen paintwork, but you don't spray it on a seventeenth-century rosewood and brass table clock. It's a Massy, for crying out loud! Who are these people?!"

He raised his eyebrows.

"Cleaners?"

"Don't start, McLennon!"

He held his hands up.

"I just meant that whoever did this was clearly an expert in crime scene cleanup, not antique clocks. I bet even John and Laila would struggle with the antiques in this place."

She glared at the clock, then turned her back on it and left the room, closing the door firmly behind them.

After checking the other bedroom, they went down to the first floor, where Audrey wound yet more clocks and Lewis continued looking for secret doors, following the floor plans provided by Victor.

"This is crazy," he said eventually, turning away from a sideboard. "How is there nowhere you could conceal a body?"

"I don't know," said Audrey. "Have you checked the study yet?"

Ten minutes later, they were standing in front of the bookshelves in the study, which were now in complete disarray. They'd moved every book and ornament from every shelf, gone over every inch of the desk looking for a button, but nothing triggered the opening of a secret door.

"It has to be here," said Lewis, pushing again against a section of bookcase. "There's no access from any other place."

He was frustrated. Discovering a secret door to a secret room hidden behind a bookcase was top among Lewis's secret life goals, and to be so near to one and yet so far was beyond disappointing.

"Maybe it's just dead space," said Audrey with a shrug. "Not anything."

"Don't be ridiculous. There's no dead space in London properties; they use every inch. There has to be a switch somewhere."

She began tidying the bookshelves, putting everything back as it was. What was he missing? Where else could it be?

He turned to look around the room, yet another of Petrov's blank spaces, with just the clock on the shelves and the coin in the frame on the wall. He squinted at it. A man with a sword and what looked like a snake. It looked familiar, but he couldn't place it.

"Perhaps we're overthinking it," said Audrey, moving on to the middle section where the clock stood in its glass case. "Perhaps it's not a switch at all. Maybe it's just a door."

"We tried that," he said, pushing against the end unit again. "See?"

"Well, maybe it's a pull." She ran her finger along an empty shelf, then grasped the edges and pulled to demonstrate. It was a small movement, but she leaped away as the bookcase swung outwards a couple of inches, then swung itself shut again.

"Oh my God," said Lewis, lunging forward. "You did it!"

He pulled hard on the shelf, and the bookcase came towards him. It was heavy, and he had to force it back on its concealed hinges, revealing a stainless-steel door set into the wall behind, bearing a keypad and a small screen.

They stared at it.

"I can't believe this was here all the time," said Audrey.

"I can. Lots of rich people have them. I should have thought of it before." He examined the metal door, annoyed they couldn't open it. "This opens inward. They must have pulled the bookcase closed behind them before shutting themselves in. I wonder how they knew it was here."

"Maybe that's the noise I heard when I arrived," said Audrey, and he looked at her, confused. "When I got here that day, I heard a sort of metallic noise. A thud. I thought it was outside, but it could have been this door closing, couldn't it?"

"They're usually pretty thick," said Lewis, knocking on it. It made a *thunk* sound.

"They've wiped this down as well," said Audrey, pointing to some marks on the edges of the door. "It's really hard to clean metal without leaving smears, but they almost managed it."

Lewis leaned in to get another look. The scent of cleaning products filled his nostrils.

"Yeah, and they used that spray. The one John and Laila used."

"Zabimax?" Audrey sniffed. "I don't think so."

"No, the other one. Laila was using it on the walls."

"Detergise?"

"That's it. They must have got some blood on the door when they put the body in. I wonder how they got in. I can't imagine Trinity has the access code for . . . What?" Audrey was looking at him oddly. "What's the matter?"

She put her face close to the door and sniffed again.

"You're right," she said, turning pale. "It's Detergise. It's all over the murder room too. It wasn't any of the products I knew, but I couldn't place it."

"So? They said it was specialist, and these guys are clearly specialists."

"*Laila* said it was specialist," said Audrey, her eyes wide. "But John said Laila invented it. He said it gave them an edge. I thought it was familiar, back in the hotel room. I smelled it here, after the first cleanup. It was them. John and Laila. They cleaned up our murder."

56

Audrey

Audrey thought she might be sick. A legitimate business, with clients including the police themselves, had a sideline in cleaning up contract killings?

"How many employees do they have?" asked Lewis.

"It's just them," said Audrey. "They're a new firm. That's why they were hiring, he said. Oh, *God*." She groaned. "I'm supposed to meet him tomorrow."

"Are you?" Lewis sounded surprised. "About the job?"

She flushed.

"Maybe. I'm not really sure. It was supposed to just be a chat."

"Like . . . a date?"

"No!" She put her gloved hands to her cheeks. "I don't think so. I don't know!"

Lewis sat down on the edge of Petrov's desk and folded his arms.

"How many companies did you email about crime scene cleaning?"

"Four."

"And they were the only ones who replied?"

"Two said they wouldn't meet unless I was called for an interview, and the other one hasn't replied at all. Why?" She closed her eyes. "John and Laila wanted to meet us, didn't they? To see what we knew."

"To see if we were on to them, more like. So let me get this straight." He began ticking things off on his fingers. "We've got a dead hitman, a missing victim-slash-murderer, a scam run by

Felix, a pair of dodgy forensic cleaners working for criminals as well as the police, and a shady Russian businessman who doesn't seem to care about any of the above, even when it takes place in his own house." He looked at her. "Maybe I should become a cleaner. Your work is way more interesting than mine."

"A bit too interesting, if you ask me," said Audrey. "What do I do? I can't meet John now! What if he's the killer? Isn't that sometimes the case? That a person can be "cleaned" as well as a scene?"

"John isn't a killer," said Lewis, taking out his phone.

"Why not? Just because you like him." She narrowed her eyes. "Why *do* you like him? You don't like anyone."

"I like people," he said, taking a picture of the safe-room door. "Just not most people."

"Is it because he liked your books?"

"No." He said it too quickly, and she noticed the shifty look in his eyes. He pushed the bookcase-door back into place. "Listen, I was thinking about it last night, and I'm pretty sure our killer is the guy in the garden. He was lured to a trap where Tyler was waiting to kill him but somehow got away. He lies in wait in the garden opposite, watching to see who comes to clean up the mess, figures it might be whoever called the hit. He sees the man with the white hair, then he sees you arrive, but you run out and call the police, so he bolts. Leaves the knife behind and disappears."

"Okay," she said. That did sound plausible.

"We need to work out whether Petrov called the hit. Celeste said she was having dinner with him, right?"

"Tomorrow, yes."

"For my money, John and Laila are likely just the cleaners, but someone had to hire them. We can talk to them first, try to get some answers. Something to confront Petrov with."

"It's still a crime, Lewis! Hiding a murder, or whatever. We'd have to tell Sofia." She paused. "What if Mr. Petrov isn't involved?"

"Then we cross that bridge when we come to it." He looked at her, and she saw her own conflicted feelings reflected in his eyes. "Look, I'm almost positive this was a hit gone wrong. I don't think you've anything to fear from John and Laila. We're close to unravelling it, I know it."

She chewed her lip, unconvinced, and now the air between them felt strange. Whether they were dangerous or not, John and Laila had committed a crime, yet Lewis seemed totally relaxed about it. He glanced at his watch.

"I should head off," he said. "Need to do some work before the end of the day."

"All right." She was suddenly glad he was going. "Thanks for coming over."

He nodded. "I'll let myself out."

A few minutes later, Audrey changed out of her cleaning shoes and put her coat on. She set the alarm and stepped out into the gloomy afternoon with a sigh of relief, her cleaning bag in her hand. The sky was grey, oppressive with heavy clouds, and she set off down the street in the direction of home. The wind had picked up, the icy edges of it focussing her chaotic thoughts, and as she crossed over, the trees and shrubs blew about beside the railings, allowing her another glimpse through to the garden and reminding her of the blond man in the dark coat.

The killer.

It wasn't two o'clock yet, and the streets were quiet. She walked with unusual speed, fuelled by anxiety and confusion. She was conflicted. She'd liked John, she really had, but if he'd cleaned up a crime scene, not to mention disposed of the body, then she had to tell Sofia, no question. She barely knew the man; she had no reason to protect him.

A beep made her jump, and she stopped, looking around. A cab pulled in just behind her, and Clayton stuck his head out of the window.

"All right?" he called. "Returning to the scene of the crime?"

"I'll be returning every week until I get fired," she said, sighing. "Which might be pretty soon. How are you?"

"Good, yeah. Just ran a guy over to Elizabeth Street. Can I give you a lift?"

"Thanks, but I'm okay to walk."

"It's no problem. I'm picking up at the Chelsea Hospital. You can hop out there. No charge."

She smiled and got into the cab, settling back onto the leather seat. She was happy not to be alone with her thoughts.

"How's the investigation going?" he asked as they turned off Beaton Gardens. She pulled a face. "That good, huh?"

"Complicated," she said. "How's your brother?"

He looked at her in the rear-view mirror, expression suddenly serious.

"You remembered. He's not so good, actually. Had to take him to the clinic again, and he missed some school. It's the weather."

"Yes, it's either freezing or damp, or both. Terrible for mould. Does your mum work?"

"Yeah. It plays havoc with her shifts."

Lower Sloane Street was clear at that time of day, and a few minutes later, Clayton was pulling in outside the Royal Chelsea Hospital, where a red-coated Chelsea pensioner was waiting near the gates, leaning on a cane.

"Here we go," said Clayton, turning around in his seat. "Saved you a bit of a walk, anyways."

"Thanks," said Audrey, opening the door. "You're a star. Hope your brother gets better soon."

"Cheers. Me too."

Clayton got out of the cab, saying a few words to the pensioner before escorting him over and helping him inside, while Audrey began to walk the last half-mile back along the Chelsea Embankment.

The wind off the river was freezing, but it only made her walk faster, her hair whipping around her face. She didn't miss the trials and tribulations of the rental market, that was for sure. In spite of everything, she still felt a sense of peace when she walked through the gates of the square, knowing she was safe and sound in Celeste's private enclave.

A final turn onto Pickering Lane, and then she was back in Marchfield Square. The tension in her shoulders released, and she sighed with relief.

Home.

57
Lewis

It was five o'clock on the nose when Lewis turned off his computer, but instead of bolting for the door as usual, he sat and stared at the black screen for a moment. He'd been in a funk for the rest of the afternoon, and now he just wanted to get home.

He knew that he and Audrey approached things from a different angle, with Audrey looking for justice, while Lewis liked the puzzle. They'd disagreed about almost everything in their first case, including what to share with the police and when, but once it came to it, there'd been no question of hiding anything completely. But shopping John and Laila to the police, most likely sending them to prison . . . he didn't want to do that. He was sure Audrey didn't either, but he was equally sure that she'd do it in a heartbeat if the law said it was right.

She needed to be more flexible, he decided. She was too black-and-white, that was her problem, unable to process the grey areas.

"Night, Lewis," said someone, walking past his cubicle.

"Night, Ken," said Lewis, then turned abruptly. "Hey, Ken!"

Ken paused, looking bemused, and Lewis realised they'd never had a proper conversation before.

"Yes?"

"Steve told me you're a writer."

Ken immediately looked nervous.

"Just a side thing."

"I'm a writer too. I was just wondering what you wrote."

"Oh." Ken looked both pleased and embarrassed. "Historical mainly. Under a pen name. How about you?"

"Crime fiction," said Lewis, suddenly aware that Ken might now Google him, as Chris had done. "How's it going for you?"

"Can't complain," said Ken, and Lewis couldn't tell if he was being modest or not. "Although I'd probably go mad without the day job. I need the regular income, plus it's good to get out and see people. You know what I mean?"

"Uh, yeah," said Lewis, who certainly understood about the income. "Yeah, I do. What's your pen name?"

"Oh, um, it's a woman's name. Better for the genre." Ken's face went red, and he shrugged. "Probably not your kind of thing."

"Oh. Right. Fair enough." Lewis immediately ran out of things to say. "Well, good luck with it all. Have a good evening, yeah?"

"Cheers, you too."

Ken walked away, looking as bewildered as Lewis felt. He wondered how long it would have taken Audrey to learn about Ken's secret career as a female novelist. Seconds, probably.

He put his coat on and was within two feet of the door when Steve stuck his head out of his office.

"Lewis, mate, can I have a word?"

Lewis stopped, his hand already on the door handle. That would teach him to hang about. He turned, forcing a smile.

"Sure."

He followed Steve into his office, watching jealously as half his colleagues filed out to freedom. The other half would work on until six, hoping to catch potential candidates on their way home, when they'd be free to talk openly about other opportunities.

"I spoke to Chris earlier," said Steve, when Lewis walked in. "Apparently, you used him to get a couple of people from Trinity sacked this afternoon."

Shit, is that what Chris thought?

"It wasn't like that," he said, wondering how much he could say. "Two people at Trinity had been working something off the books. Renting out houses they shouldn't have. Waverley couldn't prove it, but he wanted them gone, so when I realised Chris had rented somewhere from them . . . "

Steve folded his arms.

"Look, I appreciate you going all out to get the contract, but that was too far. You're not a detective, you work in recruitment, and we don't get involved in internal matters like that. We've got a reputation to think of."

"It was technically fraud," said Lewis.

"You should have told Chris the situation. He could have had a quiet word with Waverley himself, without all that fuss. Sounded like a bit of a performance, dragging him out to Belgravia. He was embarrassed."

"Sorry."

"Don't say sorry to me," said Steve, sounding like his mother. "Make it right with Chris." Worse, he sounded like Audrey.

Lewis left Steve's office feeling hot and bothered. He hadn't expected Chris to take it like that or to run off and tell Steve about it. Had he really gotten that wrong? How else was he supposed to have cornered Casetti?

He looked across to Chris's cubicle, where he was just putting on his coat to go home. Lewis went over and Chris stiffened when he saw him.

"Chris."

"Lewis."

"Look, mate," he began, wondering what to say. "About earlier . . . I was trying to help Waverley out. What Casetti's been doing is fraud, but Waverley couldn't prove it. He was hoping to deal with it quietly, without involving the police." *In this particular issue*, he added silently. "I should have told you before you got there, but I couldn't be sure. Not until you saw them. I'm sorry."

Chris hesitated, buttoning his coat before replying.

"All right," he said at last. "Apology accepted. But next time, leave me out of it."

"Never again," said Lewis. "I was trying to land a client, but honestly, I'd rather just keep my head down."

"You can do better than Waverley," said Chris, as they began to walk towards the door.

Lewis grimaced. "Not sure I can. Why do you say that, though? Steve's desperate to get the Waverley Group on the books."

"Word is, they're having audit problems. I've just put a few of their people in the system, who're hoping to move on quickly. Latest this afternoon, in fact."

"Trinity?"

"No, the hotel group. Might just be rumours, but . . . " Chris shrugged. He held the door for Lewis, and they left the building together, walking down to the end of Swallow Street, ready to turn onto Piccadilly. He had no idea where Chris lived, he realised, and hoped they wouldn't have to walk too far together.

"By the way," said Chris, and he seemed to have relaxed a little, "that friend of yours—Audrey?"

"What about her?"

"Are you and she . . . y'know?"

"What?" Lewis looked at him blankly for a second. "Oh. No, nothing like that. Just friends."

"Ah, great." Chris grinned. "She seemed nice. Can you ask if I can have her number?"

"Oh." Lewis was taken aback. "Uh. Sure. I guess. Sure. Yes, cool." He nodded. "I'll ask."

"Thanks." Chris clapped him on the shoulder. "Have a good evening, mate. See you tomorrow."

Lewis watched him go, striding off down Piccadilly with his hands in his pockets, men and women alike turning to look at him as he passed.

Audrey could probably do worse.

58

Audrey

"Don't be absurd," said Audrey later, as they sat once again at her kitchen counter. "He's far too handsome; I can't give him my number."

Lewis had come over straight after work to tell her that he'd apologised to Chris. He'd looked windswept, his cheeks pink with cold, and his curly hair free from whatever product he used to tame it. She'd been surprised—first that he'd apologised as he'd said he would, but also that he'd felt the need to come and tell her. Perhaps her good opinion mattered to him after all.

"I'm confused," said Lewis. "He's handsome, but you don't want his number?"

"Correct."

"Why not?"

"Because Chris Gao looks like Gregory Peck."

Lewis frowned. She should have known he wouldn't get it.

"I don't understand."

"You don't *text* Gregory Peck, Lewis. You don't go to crappy London pubs with Gregory Peck, or watch *Columbo* reruns with Gregory Peck, or eat pizza out of the box on the sofa with Gregory Peck. You do those things with . . . " She paused, thinking. "With Jimmy Stewart. Or Cary Grant."

"Clark Gable?"

"Don't be ridiculous."

"Yes," said Lewis, nodding. "That's what I was thinking the whole time you were speaking, that it was me that was being ridiculous."

She rolled her eyes but smiled anyway.

"Please thank him for the compliment," she said, "but tell him he's far too handsome. He'll understand."

Looking baffled but amused, Lewis shrugged.

"All right. I said I'd ask, and I've asked. And he's dodged a bullet, if you ask me." She threw a tea towel at him. "Now, speaking of men whose numbers you *do* have, can we talk about John Keane?"

She stopped smiling at once.

"There's nothing to say."

"You just want to report him and Laila to Banham, do you? Let the police interrogate them on the basis of you smelling a custom cleaning product?"

She didn't want that at all, but it was the right thing to do.

"Yes, actually," she lied. "They committed at least one crime, maybe more. And what if they did do the murder? What if we let them get away with this, and then they go on to kill again? I'd never forgive myself."

He thought about that, tipping his head to one side and looking at her with concern.

"Don't you want to be sure of the facts first?" he said eventually. "What if it wasn't John? What if he was coerced into it? What if someone forced him?"

She hadn't considered that.

"Won't the police take that into account?"

"They might. But they'll still get a conviction. And you don't really think he killed Don Tyler, do you?"

He said it earnestly, with no trace of contempt or annoyance, and she chewed her lip, imagining DI Banham shoving John into a police car on her say-so, sending him and Laila to prison, with proper hardened criminals.

"If there's so much as a hint they committed the murder, we can turn them in," Lewis went on, and she winced at the idea.

"Someone hired them, most likely the same person who hired Tyler, and if we can figure out who that was, we can work out who he was meeting at the house and how it was Tyler who came to die. This may be our only chance."

"And if they do this all the time? If they're professional 'cleaners' for killers?"

He didn't even comment on her use of air quotes.

"Then we can still report them, although I personally think it's kind of cool."

She stared at him, thinking, her eyes fixed on his. She did not think it cool, she thought it was terrifying, but she supposed it was fair to give them a chance to explain.

"Fine," she said at last, sighing. "I'll go. But I am not going by myself. I chose a café on Piccadilly to meet him at, so you can be there too. There's no way I'm questioning him on my own."

Lewis nodded.

"Of course," he said, and smiled. "I wouldn't miss it for the world."

Which, she felt, was rather missing the point.

59

Celeste

At eight fifteen on Friday morning, Celeste left the breakfast table and sat down in her armchair in the gallery nook. It had rained in the night, ruining the picturesque spectacle of Marchfield Square in sparkling white frost, replacing it instead with dripping leaves, muddy-looking grass, and glistening grey flagstones.

She scanned the square with her binoculars, catching a glimpse of Audrey moving around in her kitchen, of Sarah doing likewise in hers, no doubt getting little Tom ready for school. The Captain's curtains were still closed, while Victor was already crossing the courtyard and heading out. She wondered which local café would be serving his breakfast this morning.

On the other side of the garden, she saw almost no movement. Lewis rarely stirred in his apartment until he burst from the door at 8:25, combing his hair with his fingers. Manny and Joe above were night owls, rarely opening their curtains before ten, Joe's late shifts at the restaurant dictating their routine.

She sighed and put the binoculars back into the drawer of her tea table. Audrey would be here soon, and then she would be distracted. Dixon had been very good, all things considered, about leasing the empty flats, but she met with each of her residents at least once a week, and they'd all mentioned the two unoccupied properties, one way or another.

She felt they were starting to talk.

"Anything you need?" asked Dixon, walking into the room. He was dressed in his civvies, as he liked to call them, ready for his day out.

"No, thank you, dear. Audrey will be here soon. You get yourself ready."

As Dixon wandered off, Celeste's mind returned, unbidden, to where it had been dwelling the last few days: Madeleine Petrov.

In spite of their age difference, Madeleine and Celeste had been close, and their friendship had lasted for fifteen years. Madeleine had been gifted, excelling at her work in the same way Celeste had excelled at hers, and they'd complemented each other, carrying out operations all over the world. Celeste had relied on her like no one else. When she'd married Anton and had the children, Celeste had suggested it was time for her to get out, but Madeleine wouldn't hear of it. She loved her work, and it wasn't inherently dangerous.

Or at least, it shouldn't have been.

Fortunately, Audrey was punctual as ever, her arrival shaking Celeste from her thoughts. She and Dixon exchanged a few words in private before he left, reminding Celeste yet again that whatever she'd been in the past, she was now, first and foremost, an old lady, someone who needed looking after.

She sighed again.

"Everything all right?" asked Audrey, coming to perch on the second armchair.

"Yes, of course." Celeste forced a smile. "Just a little tired. Let's have an update on your case. Have you learned anything more?"

Audrey had just opened her mouth to reply when the doorbell rang again, and she went to answer it, speaking a few words into the intercom and returning seconds later.

"It's Mr. Petrov."

"Buzz him up, dear," said Celeste, somewhat apprehensively. Anton was supposed to be coming for dinner. A surprise visit did not bode well.

Anton took the lift rather than the stairs, and so it was two minutes before he arrived, Audrey waiting by the door.

"Mr. Petrov, hello."

"Audrey." Anton sounded pleased to see her, and no wonder. Celeste couldn't question him closely with witnesses present. "How nice to see you again."

"Come on through."

Audrey ushered him through to the gallery nook, where Celeste rose to greet him. He kissed her on both cheeks.

"Celeste, you are looking tired," he said without preamble. "You are not resting enough?"

"Too much rest is exhausting, Anton," she said. "Do sit down. I was expecting you this evening."

He sat down, looking sheepish.

"I had hoped to come for dinner, but I'm afraid I must go to the police station to be interviewed." Audrey gasped. "They were most insistent. I am on my way to meet with my lawyer and thought I would come and tell you myself the sad news."

"That is sad," agreed Celeste, noting that Anton had chosen the easier interrogation. "But I appreciate your coming to see me."

Anton turned to Audrey, who hovered nearby, awaiting instruction.

"Is there any news on your investigation?" he asked. "The police have requested to look over the house."

"Oh. Um, yes, actually." Audrey seemed nervous. Anton was, after all, a suspect in the case. "They found the body. The victim was a man named Don Tyler."

Celeste watched Anton carefully, his eyes widening just enough to let her know that he was reacting, but not enough to let Audrey realise that he knew the name.

"And who was this man?" he said, after a pause. Not quite a long-enough pause, in Celeste's view. "Why was he in my house?"

"He was a hitman," said Audrey. "A contract killer. But the police are investigating now, which is probably why they need to speak to you. They spoke to me and Lewis too."

"But not, I expect, at the station?" said Anton, with a twinkle in his eye.

"No. Sorry."

He shrugged.

"*Plus ça change*," he said, which Celeste thought was rather cheeky. "A hitman, hmm? That is a surprise."

"We think the house was being rented out fraudulently. An older man with white hair and a beard was seen leaving the house not long before I got there," said Audrey, and Celeste noticed her examining Anton's face. Looking for signs of guilt? Or of a recently shaved beard?

"Oh?"

"Yes. And we think . . . " said Audrey, and Celeste could tell she was choosing her words carefully. "That it was an accident. That Tyler was using your house, perhaps your name, for some specific reason, but his target fought back."

"You think the target killed him?"

"It's possible."

Intrigued—and in Celeste's opinion, genuinely so—Anton leaned back in his chair and folded his arms, muscles straining the fabric of his sweater.

"Then who was this target?"

"We don't know, but we think it was a man in a dark hat and coat seen near the house that morning, watching from the garden. White, blond, scruffy-looking. Not much to go on."

"Perhaps it's someone you know," said Celeste, fixing Anton with a firm look. "Is there anyone you know in London whom people might want to see dead? Any remaining contacts? Business acquaintances?"

"Nobody I can think of."

Celeste tutted.

"Anyone new? Someone you've just met?"

"Most of the people I deal with, I have never met in person," said Anton. "But we run background checks, and I do not deal with anyone who is not legitimate."

Celeste raised an eyebrow.

"Truly," he said, with a wry smile. "I don't need to take risks anymore; I am very rich. Take that man in the news, the one who is missing from his trial. He tried to meet with me many times. Told me about his many clients—bankers, hoteliers, tech people—tried to get me to invest. Offered to come to Paris, even. But I said no. We could see he was a . . . " He paused, searching for the right word. "Madeleine used to say it, about dishonest businessmen. A wise boy?"

She smiled.

"Wide boy."

"Yes. A wide boy. And I do not deal with wide boys."

"No," said Celeste, regretfully. "None of us do anymore, do we? Just out of interest, what was his name, this wide boy?"

"Cole," he said. "Baxter Cole. Now there's a man who has upset many people. If he was dead, I would not be surprised."

There was a hiss from Audrey, and something tickled Celeste's memory.

"That name rings a bell."

"He is all over the financial pages."

"Money doesn't interest me, Anton," said Celeste, who had never read the financial pages in her life. "It's people who do."

"That's because you have always had money." He wagged a finger at her. "For the rest of us, it is a source of endless fascination."

"He's Mei's client," said Audrey to Celeste. "The one that went missing. Only he's not missing anymore."

"Oh? I had not read that," said Anton. "He should go to prison then. Many people lost their money because of him, millions of pounds." He got to his feet. "But I must go. I'm sorry, dear Celeste, for breaking our dinner plans. But we will rearrange, yes?"

Celeste smiled.

"Of course, Anton," she said, looking him in the eye. "You don't get out of it that easily, police or no. We have a lot to discuss, you and I. A lot to discuss."

Anton held her gaze for a moment, then acquiesced with a tip of his head.

"Yes," he agreed. "We do."

60

Lewis

At three fifteen, Lewis met Audrey outside the bookshop on Piccadilly. She'd arranged her meeting with John to be somewhere busy and closer to Lewis's office and left Celeste's early so she wouldn't have to go alone. Lewis was glad. While he was 90 percent certain Audrey was in no danger from John Keane, the other 10 percent nagged at him. He'd never forgive himself if anything happened to her.

She looked pale and tired, although that might have been the yellow hat he'd given her, which, he now realised, didn't really suit her. How had he not noticed that before? Perhaps it was the weather being so damp and grey and miserable. It highlighted the brightness of the thing.

"I've only got an hour," he said by way of greeting. "Then I've got to head over to Trinity again. Waverley called the office this morning."

"I want this over and done with," she replied, ignoring his comment about Trinity and starting to walk. Piccadilly was heaving with tourists, as usual. "And I have to get back to Celeste. Dixon likes me to stay until he gets home, and this is the second time I've left early."

"Wants a full report, does she?"

Audrey smiled then.

"You know it. Mr. Petrov came over this morning."

"I thought it was tonight?"

"It was, but he's had to cancel. The police have asked him to stop by the station this evening to be interviewed. He was on his way to meet his lawyer."

"They think he did it too!"

"We don't know that. If Mr. Petrov arranged all this, why would he allow us to investigate?" she asked. "Why tell Trinity to give us the security footage? Why meet with us at all?"

"To throw us off the scent."

"He was telling Celeste that he doesn't take risks these days. Apparently, Mei's client was trying to persuade him to invest in his Ponzi scheme, but he was having none of it. Cole was too much of a 'wide boy' for Anton Petrov."

Lewis narrowed his eyes.

"Did he actually say that?"

"Yes! Well, he said 'wise boy,' but Celeste corrected him."

"Hmm."

The coffee shop was close by and very crowded, with no free tables. Lewis left Audrey waiting near the door, ready to nab a table should one become free, while he bought tea and coffee.

By the time he got back, she'd bagged a table by the window and was gazing anxiously out of it.

"Good work," he said, putting the tea in front of her and sitting down. He checked his watch. Nearly half past.

Audrey took off her hat and tried to smooth down her hair. She was fidgety, her eyes darting to the window every few seconds, and soon her nervous energy started to get to him too.

"For crying out loud, relax," he said, and she shot him a look. "You're fine. Public place, millions of people. I'm here. Calm down."

"Easy for you to say. I feel like a catfish."

He bit back a laugh. He supposed it was something of a sting. Audrey's phone pinged, and she grabbed it at once, probably hoping that John had cancelled their meeting. Her face fell, however, and she put it down again.

"Mei," she explained to his questioning expression. "Her boss has called an emergency meeting to iron out whatever's been going on with Baxter Cole. She said she'll probably be home late and need a kebab and some wine."

Ah.

"Do you think they'll fire her?"

"I don't kn—"

She stopped talking, eyes widening. He followed her gaze and saw a figure he recognised walking past the window, a tall man in a white jumper and jeans, who paused by the door to let a couple of people exit before coming inside.

John Keane had arrived.

61
Audrey

"Audrey, hey," said John, as he reached the table. "And Lewis." His smiled faded, just a little. "I didn't realise you'd be joining us."

He sounded friendly, if a little wary, but he smiled his easy smile and sat down, taking off a knitted hat. He looked better than Audrey had remembered, his eyes warm and twinkling, while his white fisherman's sweater emphasised the broadness of his shoulders.

"Hi," she said, her palms becoming clammy. "Can I get you a coffee?"

John looked from Audrey to Lewis and back again.

"I think maybe I won't," he said, at last. "You're not here to talk about a job, are you?"

"Uh . . . " She glanced at Lewis. Now would be an excellent time for him to jump in and start being direct. "No, not exactly."

"The thing is, John," said Lewis, and even he sounded awkward, "we know."

"Know what?"

"About Beaton Gardens. We know you and Laila were the ones who cleaned up the crime scene, then took the body of Don Tyler and dumped it at Tower Bridge."

John froze, the twinkle disappearing from his eyes.

"I don't know what you're talking about," he said flatly.

"Look, man," said Lewis, leaning forward across the table. "We know, okay? We know that you did it, and we know how you did it. We just want to know why."

John forced a laugh.

"I honestly have no idea—"

"Don't," said Audrey, sharply. "Don't do that. When you made that body disappear, I thought I was going mad. The police said I was making it up, and the detective thought I'd imagined it. Even my flatmate didn't believe me at first. If you sit there and tell me what I know happened *didn't* happen, then so help me . . . "

She glared at him with such ferocity that he pulled back in his seat. He didn't speak for some time, his eyes fixed on Audrey, his expression flickering between fear and concern. Then he took a deep breath and laid his palms flat on the table.

"All right," he said, sighing. "From the outset, though, I want to make it absolutely clear that I have no idea what you're talking about. But . . . if what you're saying happened happened, and you're asking me, as a professional, how such a situation could have come about, then I suppose I could hypothesise."

"Hypothesise," repeated Lewis, glancing at Audrey.

"Yes. I'm not saying it happened like this, you understand. I'm just saying that in a hypothetical scenario like that, this is hypothetically how it could have worked."

"Okay . . . "

John exhaled.

"Imagine you're about to head off to work when you get a call from someone you know. A friend, maybe, or a family member. And they have a problem. They've been away and come home—and I'm not saying it *was* their home—and found a terrible scene. A dead body in a chair. Blood everywhere. But . . . plastic sheeting on the floor. Someone had planned to murder this man in their house.

"Now this is bad enough, but imagine if this dead man is someone they know. A killer. He's killed many people, including someone they love. And here he is, years later, dead. In their house. They're not sorry he's dead—they're glad, in fact—but they didn't kill him. But they do have a motive, and now they have a very big problem."

Audrey and Lewis looked at each other. John had to be talking about Mr. Petrov.

"Now this person," John went on, "doesn't know why the body is in their house. They don't know who's killed him, or why, but what they do know is a really good cleaner. They ask you to come and help them clean everything up before anyone can pin it on them.

"Morally, of course, this is wrong. The right thing to do is to report the crime, tell the police the truth, and hope that justice is done correctly. But what if they don't think they'll be believed, because of who they are and where they come from? What if their reputation is important to them? What if they're of an age where they just want to live a quiet life, and they're so glad this man is dead, so absolutely certain that he deserved whatever was done to him, that they don't want to waste a precious minute more dealing with the fallout from this? You can kind of see why they might want to do the *easy* thing, and not the right thing."

"The easy thing!" exclaimed Audrey.

"Easy is relative, in this situation," said John, with a weak smile. "You understand this, and while you half-wish they'd do the right thing and go to the police, you also know that your own name will be tainted by association. And your legitimate, law-abiding business, which you've worked so hard to establish, could be ruined before it's even got started. The other half of you—the admittedly selfish part—also just wants to make this go away.

"So you convince a friend to help you and you head over to the house, but London's London, and the traffic is awful, and by the time you get there, it's late. You have to wait for the coast to be clear before you can go in, and the regular house cleaner comes at midday.

"Then, once you're inside, you find an even more complex situation. The crime scene is fine, you know how to deal with that, although they don't generally still have bodies in them, but the owner gives you the dead man's phone, which is somehow linked up to the management company's security feed. It's playing a loop, and you realise that if it keeps doing that for much longer, the people monitoring the feed will notice, especially when the regular cleaner doesn't appear on camera at midday. You know you're not going to have enough time to get it all done—there's only half an hour left—so you tell the owner to set the alarm and go. There's nothing they can do anyway, and not enough room to hide you all. Not with the body as well. But the two of you should have just enough time to get the body safely wrapped up and hidden and give the place enough of a clean to pass a cursory inspection. Then you can finish the job properly later."

"Which you did," said Lewis.

"No," said John patiently. "I did not. But a hypothetical person could have."

"Go on," said Audrey. "What happened next?"

"But just as they're about to begin cleaning, the alarm starts to beep. The cleaner's early. Our hypothetical person is now absolutely bloody terrified. Talk about being caught red-handed. So he and his friend have to quickly hide themselves, hoping the cleaner isn't too conscientious and perhaps decides to skip a few rooms."

"Hah!" said Lewis. "As if."

"Shut up," she retorted. "Go on, John."

"They wait, squirrelled away in their hypothetical hiding place—"

"The safe room in the study," put in Lewis.

"A hypothetical safe room," agreed John, "where they had intended to hide the body but are now hiding themselves, waiting for the cleaner to find the scene. So they turn on the other cameras."

Audrey's stomach twisted.

"What other cameras?"

"The hypothetical safe room is equipped with state-of-the-art tech, and there are cameras all over the house. Our hypothetical cleaner turns them on and watches as the real cleaner cleans an empty house with such forensic thoroughness that they want to offer her a job on the spot, but of course they realise that she's going to find the body."

Audrey blinked, struggling to process the compliment alongside the rest.

"So," John went on, "they predict what's going to happen next. Any normal person, upon finding a scene like that, will run outside, call the police, and wait somewhere safe. They rely on the cleaner to do just that, and they wait, ready to perform the most extreme clean of their lives."

"You watched me find the body and leave the house?" asked Audrey, feeling such a bone-deep level of ickiness, she couldn't stop herself from shuddering. "On camera? Then you left the safe room and started cleaning?"

"That is what these hypothetical cleaners would have done in that situation, yes. Hypothetically, they could have cleaned the scene in fifteen minutes."

She'd gone through it so many times, trying to factor in an extra pair of hands for the removal of the body, and the closest she'd gotten was twenty minutes. She couldn't help but be impressed.

"Then they squeezed back into the safe room with the body," continued John, "and watched as the police came in and found nothing. But then another person came, and they *did* find something. The hypothetical cleaners hadn't quite got everything. They had to sit and watch while the pair found some evidence and handed it to the police, and then continue to watch while they—very cleverly, I might add—thought to take every speck of dust in the house away with them, just in case. Under any other circumstances, it would have been phenomenal to see. Hypothetically, I mean."

"You and Laila spent three hours in a safe room with a dead body?" blurted out Lewis, and John sighed. No one could frustrate people like Lewis.

"No, I'm saying that in that *hypothetical* situation, our hypothetical cleaner *could* have spent three hours in a confined space with the body of their mother's killer, using his dead face to unlock his phone so they could keep hacking the recording."

Audrey's jaw dropped.

"Your *mother*?" she repeated, and John flushed.

"A person's hypothetical mother," he said, looking away. "Not mine, you understand."

Audrey didn't know what to say. Don Tyler had killed John's mother, and yet John had cleaned up his remains like it was just another scene. She didn't know whether that showed staggering professionalism or a disturbing level of detachment. Both, probably.

"Then what?" asked Lewis. "What did you do after we'd gone?"

"I imagine the hypothetical cleaners would have left the safe room and finished the job properly, then waited for hours, rerunning the loop from the dead man's phone. Then, once it got dark, one of the cleaners would have snuck out of the house at an opportune moment and come back later to help dispose of the body. Once the police had been informed, they couldn't take any more chances."

"Did the safe-room cameras record the murder?" asked Lewis.

"No," said John. "They weren't on. The homeowner only turns them on when he's there."

"Did your mother know Anton Petrov?"

Audrey kicked Lewis under the table. John took a deep breath.

"I think I've hypothesised all I can," he said, reaching for his hat. "What's important for you to understand is that it was done to protect someone. The dead man had no friends, no family. He was a monster. And people had suffered enough at his hands."

"Why did you agree to meet us?" asked Audrey. "Back in the hotel? You must have known who I was. We wouldn't have worked it out if you hadn't done that."

"I wanted to find out what you knew. Besides, I'd seen you work."

Then his eyes fixed on hers in a way that made her heart skip. She swallowed.

"Did you burgle my flat? Or was that Mr. Petrov?" Then, she realised. "He let you in when he left and told you where I lived."

John looked so ashamed that she almost forgave him on the spot.

"Anything that was hypothetically done needed to be done," he said, putting on his hat and standing up. "But I am sorry. We couldn't take a chance that the homeowner had left a trace at the scene."

"One more question," said Lewis, looking up at him. "The body. The suitcase. Why Tower Bridge? Hypothetically, I mean. Seems a risky place."

John shrugged.

"Old stories," he said. "People tell stories about places, and when those people are gone, the stories are all you have left. Then, in a crisis, you get a strange idea, and the next thing you know, you can't think of anything else. It just felt right." He smiled, seemingly at some distant memory. "The body didn't need to disappear forever, just long enough. The suitcase was a miscalculation, I admit, but it was the only one big enough."

He looked down at Audrey.

"If you ever want a job," he said, and this time his smile was only for her, "call me. Or even if you don't. Call me."

And John Keane turned and left.

62

Lewis

They sat without speaking for a few minutes, absorbing everything John had said. Audrey looked flushed and angry, which Lewis admitted was preferable to pale and afraid, but even so, her expression was strange.

"You okay?" he asked, raising his voice to be heard over the hubbub of scraping chairs, whistling coffee machines, and other people's conversations. The man at the table nearest to them was reading a newspaper, and it rustled loudly whenever he turned a page.

"I don't know," she said slowly. "He managed to make it all sound . . . "

"Reasonable." Lewis nodded. "I know."

"Is it reasonable?" She looked at him, brow furrowed. "I don't know what to think."

"Me neither," he said. "But if someone killed your mother, and then that person turned up dead on your doorstep, and then someone else you cared about was at risk of going to prison for it . . . " He considered this. "Honestly? I don't know what I'd have done. I suppose it depends on how much you trust the police."

She didn't say anything to that.

"I wonder if the safe-room cameras really were off," he said. "Petrov could have deleted the footage before John got there. Although I guess there's no point in recording an empty house for months on end. And I wonder how he and Petrov knew each other. He wouldn't reveal that."

"No."

He sipped his cold coffee, giving her a chance to think.

"What do you want to do?" he asked eventually. "About reporting them. It sounded like it was a one-off, didn't it?"

"He could have been lying though."

But somehow, Lewis didn't think John had been lying, and he had a feeling Audrey didn't either. He watched her as she thought, chewing her lip, eyes distant, wondering what calculations she was doing. The sky outside the window grew darker. He checked his watch. It was past four.

"Let's think about it," he said. "There's no evidence against him except for your nose for cleaning products and a hypothetical conversation, so there's no need for him to run. We've got time."

She sighed.

"Yeah," she said. "It would be our word against his." Then she corrected herself. "*Their* word. Laila was involved too."

"Hypothetically," said Lewis quickly. There was no need to bring Laila into this. "He never confirmed that."

She looked at him curiously for a moment, then nodded.

"When we were going through Mr. Petrov's study," she said, "they were less than a metre away, in the safe room, watching."

She shivered. It was creepy, now that he thought about it.

"I have to get back to Celeste," she said. "And you have to get over to Trinity. We don't want you to get fired, do we?"

Lewis didn't answer that but dutifully stood up. Audrey grabbed her hat and began to manoeuvre herself around the table, carefully avoiding the man with the huge newspaper, who had just turned over another page.

They spotted it at the same time, the picture on the back of the newly turned page, but it was Audrey who reacted first. She grabbed the top of the paper, straightening it out.

"Hey!" said the man, trying to shake it free of her hand. "What are you doing?"

"It's him!" said Audrey, jabbing at the page. "The watcher from the garden!"

"And everywhere else," said Lewis. "Who is he?"

"Sorry," said Audrey, smiling apologetically at the man, who was still tugging at his newspaper. "Could I just see that picture? I think I know this guy."

The man—a smart individual in a blue suit—folded the paper and handed it to her, craning in to see who it was she'd recognised.

PONZI SCHEME MILLIONAIRE SACKS LEGAL TEAM, said the understated headline. They hastily scanned the article, but it was the picture they were really studying.

Gone was the well-dressed, over-manicured person from the photos Lewis had seen in the news. This picture was candid, taken outside on the street as he exited a building. His hair looked darker and longer, and he appeared not to have shaved for a while. There was an angry, frightened look in his eyes as he stared at the camera.

"You know the Ponzi scheme guy?" said the man, looking at the page as Audrey handed the paper back. He snorted. "Hope you didn't give him any money."

Lewis stared at Audrey, and she stared back. The missing man from the fraud trial was the man from Beaton Gardens. The one who'd been following them. The one they had thought was both the intended victim and the killer.

"It's Mei's client," said Audrey, eyes wide and her voice breathless. "It's Baxter Cole."

"But he's about to go to prison, isn't he? Why would anyone bother to kill him?"

"Mei said Cole was sure he'd get off." She spoke slowly, still thinking. "And Mr. Petrov said people lost millions in his scheme. Cole was desperate to meet with him, probably seeking more investment."

Things clicked into place for Lewis.

"Of course! What better way to trick Cole into a meeting than using Anton Petrov's name and inviting Cole to his empty house? Maybe Cole believed Petrov could bail him out in some way, and Tyler leveraged that. If everything went right, Petrov would never even know his name or that his house had been used." Another thought struck him. "Or . . . if John was telling the truth, and Tyler and Petrov knew each other, it could even have been a bonus for Tyler to implicate him. There must have been a grudge there, right? If Tyler killed someone Petrov knew?"

"Agreed."

"So Cole's the intended victim, but something happens." Lewis was thinking out loud. "He kills Tyler instead and flees the scene. Unsure who called the hit, he stakes out the house to see who comes for the body, then goes into hiding. He doesn't come out until Tyler's body is recovered from the Thames."

"Why, though?" said Audrey. "He could have gone straight to the police, claimed it was self-defence."

"I don't know. And who called the hit in the first place? Because if John was telling the truth and it wasn't Petrov, and if Cole was the intended victim, then we're still missing someone."

"From what he said to Mei when he reappeared, it's possible he thinks she did it. Remember what she said the other night? About Cole accusing her of something? He said she was underhanded, and he was coming after her. He must think she's involved."

"We need to talk to her. Now."

63
Audrey

It took them twenty minutes to reach Mei's offices on Knightsbridge, Audrey sending a flurry of texts to both her and Sofia on the way, and by the time they reached the foyer, they were hot, sweaty, red in the face, and looking about as unprofessional as it was possible to look.

"Mei Chen, please," panted Audrey to a startled receptionist. "She's expecting us."

The receptionist pointed behind her to where Mei was just stepping out of a lift. She scurried over, wearing a security lanyard.

"You'll need to sign in," said Mei, nodding at the receptionist, who put a sign-in book in front of them. "You're sure about this, are you? Because they're up there now, with Cole. Dominic invited him in the hope of persuading him to reconsider, but he turned up with his new legal team and insisted I leave the meeting." She rubbed at the crease between her eyes. "It's been a horrible day, Auds."

Audrey looked at Lewis. *Were* they sure? This could be Mei's career on the line.

"We're pretty sure," he said, sounding confident.

Mei looked at him askance, but then the doors opened again and Sofia walked in, blond ponytail swishing, DI Banham following behind like a model's security guard.

Banham looked daggers at them.

"What did I tell you two?" he growled.

"All we did was recognise his picture in the paper," said Lewis, holding up his hands. "And we called you right away."

"Just like we said we would," said Audrey, giving him her best innocent smile.

Banham's nostrils flared, but he said nothing, just turned to Mei.

"Take us to him, then."

They squeezed into one lift and rode up three floors. Mei led the way down a wide corridor to a room marked *Conference Room 4*. She knocked twice, then opened the door.

They walked into the room to find half a dozen people in suits sitting around a big table, along with Baxter Cole. He was clean-shaven now, and the darkness around his eyes had faded, while his hair was smooth and swept over, just like in the photo Mei had shown her, rather than the dirty and exhausted-looking individual she'd seen watching her in Beaton Gardens. No wonder she hadn't recognised him.

Everyone turned to look at them.

"You!" said Baxter Cole, turning pale.

"What's going on?" barked a tall, distinguished-looking man with white hair. "Mei, you're not supposed to be here. And who are all these people?"

"Apologies, Dominic," said Mei. "This is Detective Inspector Banham and Detective Sergeant Larssen. They've come to see Mr. Cole."

Cole stood up and began to edge away from the table, something immediately noticed by Banham, who narrowed his eyes like a terrier.

"There's an awful lot of solicitors," said Banham. "Do they all need to be here?"

There was some muttering around the table, and the two youngest-looking people stood up and left, leaving just three people in suits and Cole looking like a cornered dog.

"Who are your solicitors, Mr. Cole?" asked Sofia, and the two suits sitting opposite Dominic raised their hands.

"We are. Brayford and Khan."

"Very well." Banham turned to address Cole, looking delighted to have an audience. "Mr. Cole, have you ever been to 35 Beaton Gardens, Belgravia?"

"No."

"I have a witness who saw you there last Thursday afternoon."

Cole looked at Audrey.

"She's mistaken."

"Is she?" said Banham. "I think not, not least because I didn't tell you the witness was Miss Brooks. I didn't even say it was a woman, and yet you looked right at her."

Cole turned pink and then white again.

"That was the same day a dead body was seen there," Banham went on, and Audrey was gratified to hear it finally stated as fact. "A dead body that promptly disappeared and then turned up in the Thames, in a suitcase."

"What's that got to do with me?" Cole waved at his solicitors. "Can't you do something about this?"

The two lawyers looked at each other.

"You're under no obligation to answer," said one.

"Quite right," said Banham. "We also heard that you've been keen to make the acquaintance of one Anton Petrov, is that correct?"

"Never met the man," said Cole at once.

"I didn't ask if you'd met him," said Banham. "I asked if you *wanted* to meet him."

"Thirty-five Beaton Gardens belongs to Mr. Petrov," said Sofia. "We have reason to believe that a man named Don Tyler lured someone to the address last week with the express intention of committing murder. We think that person was you."

"Based on what?" asked one of the lawyers. "A single eyewitness?"

"Two eyewitnesses," said Sofia. "One of the neighbours also described a man fitting the description of your client skulking in the residents' garden opposite. That was his word, by the way, *skulking*. We also have DNA evidence from the scene."

At this, both of Cole's lawyers turned to him. He blanched.

"What DNA evidence?"

"Blood, Mr. Cole," said Banham. "And hair. Neither of which match our victim, so we're hopeful they'll match the perpetrator. Under the Criminal Justice Act, we can order you to provide a DNA sample for elimination purposes."

"Only if he's arrested," said the other lawyer.

"But he's already been arrested," said Banham. "He is, in fact, on bail right now, is he not? About to face trial? For fraud?"

The lawyers looked at each other. Cole looked at the door.

"I . . . I wasn't there. I don't know Petrov. I've never seen this woman before in my life!"

"Mr. Cole, please," said Banham. "Let's not make this any harder, eh? All you need to do is come along to the station and give us that DNA sample. If you weren't there, this'll all be over quick as a wink. Your solicitors can accompany you."

There was a pause during which Cole looked from Banham to Sofia to his lawyers, his breathing becoming more erratic by the second. Then he cracked.

"It was her!" he wailed, pointing at Mei. "She set me up! It was self-defence, you can't get me for that!" He looked wildly at his lawyers. "They can't, can they?! She tried to have me killed!"

"Mr. Cole, don't say anything more!" instructed one of them, while everyone else looked at Mei in shock.

"I did not!" said Mei, sounding baffled and horrified in equal measure. "I've nothing to do with this!"

"I heard you!" Cole screamed, his face now looking like a mottled ham. "The night they took the body. I was in the garden, waiting to see if whoever set me up would come back for it, and I heard a woman talking into an earpiece. Talking to you. She said Mei Chen was sitting in a taxi, and then I crept about a bit, and I heard you on the other side of the railings. She was hanging about, watching the house, just like I was."

"Oh, *God*," said Mei, burying her face in her hands. "I was there for the same reason you were!"

"That's what I just said!"

"No, Mr. Cole," said Audrey, trying to keep calm. "I'm the one who found the body, as I think you know. When it disappeared, we went back to watch the house to see if someone would come for it. Me, Mei, and Lewis here. Mei is my friend. She was helping me figure out what was going on. We had no idea you were involved."

Cole was breathing heavily, his eyes swivelling in their sockets. Audrey thought he might be about to have a heart attack, but then he sank onto the carpet and started to sob.

Banham glanced at Sofia, nodding towards the man on the floor. Sofia sighed but went over to Cole, crouching down beside him.

"What happened, Mr. Cole?" she asked gently.

"Don't answer that," barked one of his solicitors as Sofia handed Cole a tissue. "We need to speak to our client in private."

"I got an email," said Cole through shuddering breaths, ignoring the lawyer. "From Anton Petrov, like you said. I'd been trying to get a meeting with him for a couple of years, and he'd always declined, but he said he could help with my situation. You know, the trial?"

The solicitors slumped in their seats.

"It seemed kosher, but I got a friend to check the address of the meeting, just in case. He confirmed the house belonged to Petrov. So I went along with the money on Wednesday evening, just before eight. A man answered the door, all dressed in black, and he said Petrov was upstairs in his study."

"Hold on," said Lewis, earning more daggers from Banham. "What money?"

"Uh . . . " Here, Cole did look at his lawyers. "The email said that Petrov could help, for a price. Two million. Cash."

"You took two million in cash to Beaton Gardens?" asked Banham, incredulously. "Where'd you get it? Aren't your assets frozen?"

"I always keep plenty of cash around," said Cole. "Anyway, I trotted on after him, up and up, and then he opened the door to a bedroom. I walked in, and the room's empty, just a bed and a chair under a sheet, and then . . . "

"Then what?" prompted Sofia.

"I don't know really. All these clocks started to chime, loads of them. It made me jump, but he was right behind me, and I knocked into him. We both fell back, and when I turned around, he was standing there, holding a wire. Stretched out in his hands, you know? I backed up but knocked into the fireplace, and he punched me. Just smashed his fist right into my nose. Blood everywhere. Then he pulled a knife instead and came at me, so I tried to dodge, but he slashed me, and I slipped on something on the floor. Hit my head on the bedstead, made my vision go funny. He came at me again, and I tried to kick him, but his legs kind of went out from under him, and he went backwards, onto the chair. When I got up, he was clutching his throat. He dropped the knife, so I grabbed it, but then he just looked at me and . . . gurgled."

"Gurgled?" repeated Lewis.

"Blood started spurting out of him, and I felt a bit faint. I hate the sight of it. My ears were ringing, and I couldn't see straight. I think I passed out 'cause when I came to, my head was pounding, and it was pitch black. I ran, straight outside, but I still had the knife. I climbed the railings into the garden out front and looked for somewhere to get rid of the knife. I buried it."

"Where it was found by a neighbour's dog a few days later," said Banham. "You're trying to tell me that professional killer Don Tyler stabbed himself in the throat?"

Cole looked up at them pitifully. "That's what happened. I swear it."

"Then what did you do?"

"I still felt woozy, so I hid under some bushes until I could get myself together. I figured the guy must be dead, but someone would have to come looking for him, so I waited. I wanted to know who'd set me up. But I must have passed out again because when I woke up, it was daytime, and she was just arriving." He pointed at Audrey once more. "She went straight into the house, so I stayed hidden, watching. I thought she might have come to collect the money or something, but then she came out again not long after, looking terrified. I figured she must have found the body, but when the police came, nothing happened. They left a few minutes later, looking pretty cheesed off, then that guy came"—he pointed at Lewis—"and her"—Sofia looked uncomfortable—"but everyone went away in the end. I couldn't understand it. I kept watching, to see who else would come."

"And?"

"And no one did. Not for hours and hours. I got too cold to stick around and was starting to feel pretty sick, but I was just trying to find a way over the railings when this lot showed up again." He gestured at Audrey. "She was talking to someone in her ear, going on about how cold it was, then I heard her say Mei Chen's name and realised she was there too. I assumed they were working together, so I crept about a bit, trying to find her, but before I could, someone came out of the house, and they all hopped into a taxi and drove off." He looked sheepishly at Mei. "I thought she must have been a plant, someone they'd put on the team to bring me down. But I was in a bad way, so I holed up in this cheap B&B in Victoria until I got better, then started to do some digging. I found out where she lived and went round there, saw them all going in and out. I even saw Petrov show up and go inside! I figured it was some sort of conspiracy, and they were all working together to take my money and get rid of me."

Mei shook her head in disbelief and ran a hand over her face.

"I don't even know what to say," she said.

"Who's 'they,' Mr. Cole?" asked Banham, sharply. "You said someone 'they'd' put on the team."

Cole looked at his solicitors again, who both shook their heads at him.

"I might be stupid," he said, "but I'm not *that* stupid."

"Where's the money now?" asked Sofia. "The cash you took to the house."

"Not a clue," said Cole, glancing at Mei. "I thought she took it."

There was silence for a moment, then Banham walked over.

"On your feet, son," he said. "Let's get you down the station to make an official statement. You can start by making a list of people who might want to kill you."

"Might take a while," said Cole, getting up and blowing his nose. "There's quite a few."

"That doesn't surprise me," said Banham, putting a hand under his elbow and ushering him towards the door. "Look on the bright side though. You're finally going to meet Anton Petrov."

64
Lewis

"I can't believe he thought I'd arranged to have him killed!" said Mei, the instant the door had shut. "I have no words!"

"We'll need to discuss that," said her boss, whose name Lewis had immediately forgotten. He looked so much like a senior partner in a law firm that Lewis was sure he must be the model for any number of legal-based television dramas. "I can't say I approve of our solicitors going on stakeouts."

"No," said Mei, sighing. "I can't say I do either. I'm sorry, Dominic."

"We'll talk," said her boss, heading for the door. "But I'm relieved to know it was all just a misunderstanding. Come and see me on Monday, yes?"

Mei nodded, and they waited until he'd left the room before they started speaking again.

"Three out of four mysteries solved," said Lewis. "Just one left."

"Three?" said Mei. "What else do you know?"

"Oh, uh . . ." Audrey looked at Lewis, who shook his head. No need to mention John and Laila. "I didn't tell you. Victor and the Captain worked out where they hid the body. There's a safe room in the study."

"Is there?" Mei looked impressed. "Good work. So the big thing now is, who hired Tyler? Is Petrov officially off the list? Do you think he cleaned up?"

"A guy like Cole must have a million enemies," said Lewis, before Audrey could say anything.

"He wasn't popular," agreed Mei. "In his initial briefings, Baxter said the first wave of investors had brought in bigger fish, whose money he really didn't want but couldn't refuse. It put pressure on him to increase the yield, he said, and there were a number of implied threats."

"Underworld characters, you mean?"

"I assumed so. He said they all got their money back, and then some, but there was nobody he could ask to stand as a witness for the defence."

"I wonder who got him to bring the two million, then. That seems like a risk to me. What if he hadn't had it? What if he'd said no?"

"Explains why he thought he was going to get off, though," said Audrey, looking at Mei. "You said he'd got overconfident all of a sudden."

Mei nodded.

"He thought he'd bought himself an acquittal. Why did he think Petrov could do that for him, though? You'd need some very dangerous contacts to be able to do that. Does Petrov have that kind of influence?"

"Possibly," said Lewis, thinking back to everything Celeste had said about him—or, rather, everything she'd *not* said. "But everyone thinks wealthy Russians are corrupt. Cole might have just made an assumption."

He walked around the room, running his fingers over the polished wooden conference table. It was a nice big room, albeit as bland as his flat. Good space for pacing.

Two million. Was that the going rate for a hit? Seemed a bit steep. Had the killer been trying to get Cole to pay for his own murder? Or was the amount significant for another reason?

"Was there anyone who invested two million in Cole's scheme?" he wondered out loud. "Maybe someone was trying to kill two birds with one stone, so to speak. Get their money back and shut Cole up at the same time?"

"There were a few," said Mei, looking thoughtful. "Some more, lots less. Not everyone pressed charges, though."

"Really?" Audrey was surprised. "Why not?"

"To receive compensation, victims have to prove their losses, and not everyone can do that. When it's dodgy money, for example. And not everyone wants to. One of Cole's investors had invested half his pension pot and not told his wife. He was hoping for early retirement, and now he'll be working until he's seventy-five. He didn't file because he didn't want his wife to know."

"Why kill Cole, though?" asked Audrey. "Then nobody else gets their money back."

"Enough people got a return on their investment that it would be possible to argue the money was just mishandled," said Mei. "And if that could be proved—or at least not disproved—then nobody would get their money back."

Lewis and Audrey looked at her.

"What?" said Mei defensively. "That's the job!"

"I'll bet," said Lewis. "But is there anyone on the list of investors who didn't press charges for whom two million might cover their losses? With extra for the hit."

Mei thought for a minute. "It's possible. I can check, but I think the people who didn't file were mostly around the million mark or under."

"God," said Audrey. "Can you imagine just writing off a million pounds?"

Lewis walked over to one of the windows and looked across at the building opposite. It was now properly dark outside, and he could see right into the offices across the way, where people were getting up from their desks and putting on their coats, ready to go home.

He checked his watch. It was past five.

Lewis's phone pinged, and he rooted around in his pocket. The only person who usually texted him was Audrey.

> **STEVE GUEST:** Thought you were meeting Waverley? He's just phoned to ask why you've not showed.

"Shit," said Lewis. "I forgot my meeting. I've got to go."

> **LEWIS MCLENNON:** Ran into a police incident on the way. Should be there in twenty.
>
> **STEVE GUEST:** I'll keep an eye out for that in the news, shall I? Get your arse over there.

Steve didn't believe him. He'd pushed it too far. Could he be fired for that?

The thought filled him with inexplicable dread. Why was that? Last week, he'd been almost hoping he'd be fired. Now he was scared of losing his horrible job.

"Where are you meeting him?" asked Audrey.

"Trinity offices. Lower Sloane Street. Assuming he's still there."

"Come on," said Mei, "I'll sign you out."

She hurried them down to the front doors, and as they stepped outside into the freezing night air, she'd thrown out her arm before Lewis had even registered the illuminated FOR HIRE sign heading down the road towards them.

"Amazing!" said Audrey as the cab pulled up beside them.

"Sloane Square?" said Lewis through the open window.

"Hop in," said the driver.

"Thanks," he said to Mei, climbing inside. "Debrief round yours when I get back?"

"Definitely," said Audrey, fastening her coat. "Good luck with Waverley!"

The last thing he heard as he slammed the cab door was Mei's voice.

"What did you just say?"

But the cab was already moving, turning sharply onto Hans Road and driving away from the traffic on Knightsbridge in the direction of Sloane Square, where Lewis might, just might, be able to save his skin.

65

Audrey

Audrey watched as Lewis's taxi cut a tight turn through the stationary traffic and sped off down a side street. The darkness made the lights from the buildings brighter, and the air was filled with angry car horns and the whine of electric vehicles. Brake lights reflected off wet pavement, and she shivered as an icy gust of wind ran through her.

"What did you say?" asked Mei again, grabbing Audrey's arm. "Who's he going to meet?"

"Roland Waverley," said Audrey. "He runs Trinity Property Management. Why?"

Mei was looking worried.

"There was a Waverley on Cole's initial investor list," she said. "I assumed it was Martin Waverley, the hotel guy."

"How much did he lose?"

"Not sure. He didn't file charges in the end, so he's not part of the suit. I expect it would have been quite a bit, though."

Audrey stood frozen to the spot, her brain suddenly so full that she couldn't follow a single thread properly.

"I can't think straight," she said, moving around on the pavement. "Why would a legitimate businessman invest in a scheme that was obviously too good to be true?"

"Often it's a recommendation from a friend or business associate," said Mei. "The new money is paid down to the earlier investors, so they think the fund is strong and doing well and recommend it to their friends, and so on. Baxter said he ended up paying out much sooner than planned in order to keep some of his scarier investors happy, which meant he couldn't invest as responsibly as he wanted to." Mei shrugged at Audrey's frown. "That's what he said. Some people made business investments, all clear and aboveboard, but a quick return is tempting, and, if you keep it off the books, tax-free."

"If Waverley did what Lewis suggested—used Mr. Petrov's name to try to get his investment back from Cole—then why would he also want him dead? Why get a hitman involved?"

"Maybe he knew Baxter Cole wouldn't leave two million in cash with a complete stranger who wasn't Anton Petrov. As he said, he might be stupid, but he's not *that* stupid."

"So he knew the only way Cole would release the money was if he was killed on delivery." Audrey looked at Mei. "But the money wasn't there. Not by the time I arrived. Who took it?"

"There was a gap between Cole leaving the house and you turning up," said Mei. "When the cleaners arrived. Maybe they took it?"

Audrey thought back to their conversation with John. He hadn't mentioned anything about any money, but then he wouldn't have, would he? Not if he'd taken it. And then there was Mr. Petrov. He was already very rich. Would he take dirty cash, if it was conveniently lying around? She wouldn't put anything past anyone at this point.

Mei wrapped her arms around herself. "Can we go back inside? I'm freezing."

As they returned to the foyer, it all started coming together in Audrey's mind.

"What if someone else had access to the house?" she said out loud. "Someone whose company managed the property, and had access to the security camera, and could turn off the access alerts? Felix had programmed the system to alert him whenever someone went in, but he said he got no alerts on Wednesday or

Thursday. He also said all the access logs had been deleted. We assumed it was Tyler because he'd hacked one part of the system, but Waverley could have taken care of the rest. Maybe having Mr. Petrov's name on the books even gave him the idea!"

The lift dinged behind them, and Mei's boss walked over, wearing a silk scarf and an overcoat.

"Still here?" he said as he neared the door.

"Dominic," said Mei. "What do you know about the Waverley on the initial investor list Baxter provided?"

Dominic looked taken aback.

"What do you mean?"

"He didn't file charges, and I assumed it was Martin Waverley, but apparently there's another one? With a property company?"

"Roland? I doubt it would be him. Trinity doesn't have that kind of money, not in cash anyway, although it's doing well, I hear. No, I'm pretty sure it would have been his father, Martin. They're having some difficulties, you see. There are whispers about missing money." He looked at Audrey suspiciously. "Hearsay, you understand."

"Roland Waverley is Martin Waverley's son?" asked Audrey.

"That's right. Set to inherit the entire Waverley Group someday. He's been on the board for years, but he's ambitious, and Martin knows it. He keeps Roland on a tight leash."

"Thanks, Dominic," said Mei. "That's very helpful. Have a good weekend. Sorry again for all the trouble."

They watched as he left the building, then turned to each other.

"Roland could have taken the money," said Audrey, thinking back to what John had said about Mr. Petrov's arrival. "Tyler is killed in the evening. Cole's money isn't delivered like it should be, so Waverley decides to investigate. Maybe he turns up later that night or early the next morning, finds Tyler dead and Cole gone, and decides to just take the money. Cole said he was passed out in the park. He didn't see anyone coming or going until I got there, at half past eleven. Plenty of time for Waverley to come and collect it first. What if Waverley Senior had messed up? Invested company money in Cole's scheme and lost it all? Roland tries to get it back, to protect his dad's reputation and prove he's worthy of running the business."

"Sounds plausible," said Mei. "You need to tell Lewis before he meets Roland."

Audrey took out her phone and hastily typed a message to Lewis.

> **AUDREY BROOKS:** Mei thinks there was a Waverley on Cole's investor list. No charges filed. We think it's Roland's dad, Martin!

Lewis replied at once.

> **FLAT 5 GUY:** That makes sense! I heard the Waverley Group were having an audit. They must have been working together to get the money back, and Roland saw an opportunity. Uncovered Felix's Sharelet scheme, put it together with Petrov's oligarch reputation, and the plan wrote itself. It would all have worked perfectly, too, even with the murder being messed up, if you hadn't showed up early. Very clever indeed.
>
> **AUDREY BROOKS:** Roland might have taken the money from the crime scene. Cole was out cold for a long time, and Roland would have had the same access as Felix, John, and Mr. Petrov.
>
> **FLAT 5 GUY:** I'm nearly there. Will see what I can get out of him.

Then she looked up.

"You don't think he's in any danger, do you? From Roland?"

"No," said Mei, slowly. "I wouldn't have thought so. There's no actual evidence against them, nothing concrete anyway. And if they're already being audited, then the damage is done. The loss will be discovered."

"But if Roland Waverley got the money back, then what? Would they still get in trouble?"

Mei shrugged. "They could maybe say it had been misfiled somehow. Or that it was an accounting error that has now been fixed. Tyler's dead, and if they're smart, the money they paid him will be well hidden."

"But if Lewis lets them know that we know what they did . . . ?"

". . . Then they would need to find a way to shut you both up," finished Mei. "You'd be the only fly in their ointment."

They stared at each other.

"So what you're saying is that in order for us to be safe, Lewis has to *not* tell Waverley what he knows? Not do that overexplaining, showing-off, I-know-more-than-you thing that he really, really loves to do?"

"Yeaaaaaaah . . . "

Audrey's spine turned to ice.

66
Lewis

By the time Lewis reached the Trinity offices, Roland Waverley was outside, walking away with his briefcase in hand. Lewis scrambled out of the cab and ran over, heart pounding, his thoughts tripping over themselves as he tried to organise his priorities. He was no longer trying to land a client; he was trying to catch a criminal.

"Mr. Waverley," he said. "I'm so sorry I'm late. I got held up."

Roland Waverley didn't look happy to see him. He hefted his briefcase from his left hand to his right.

"I'm afraid I'm going home," he said, briskly. "I have dinner plans."

Shit.

"I really am terribly sorry." Lewis's phone started vibrating, so he put his hand in his pocket to silence it. "The police wanted to talk to me about the events at Beaton Gardens. It took longer than I expected."

"Oh?" Waverley's expression changed from one of annoyance to one of interest. "What did they want to speak to you about?"

He had to play this carefully. Act like he didn't know about Martin Waverley and what Roland had done.

"They told you about the murder, I take it?"

Waverley sighed.

"Yes," he said, looking suddenly very tired. "One of Felix's customers, they believe."

"That's right. A man named Don Tyler."

Waverley looked thoughtful for a moment.

"Well, now that you're here," he said eventually, "we may as well talk. Walk with me, will you?" And he set off in the opposite direction, heading away from the noise and hubbub of Sloane Square, where the streets thronged with shoppers and tourists and people on their way home.

Lewis's phone began to vibrate again as he fell into step beside Waverley. They were walking down Lower Sloane Street, where the traffic flowed slowly but steadily. He silenced his phone again.

"What did the police want with you?" asked Waverley. "I thought it was the girl who saw the body."

"Yes, it was, but there was a man who'd been following us, and they needed us to identify him."

"Following you?" Waverley's brow furrowed. "Why?"

"Because he'd also been watching Anton Petrov's place. He'd seen us there and wanted to know how we were involved."

"Who was he?"

"Baxter Cole," said Lewis, watching carefully for a reaction. "You know, the Ponzi scheme guy?"

Waverley's face remained neutral, although beneath the light of a streetlamp, Lewis thought he saw the man's jaw clench.

"I've heard the name."

"He was the intended victim, apparently. There was a fight, and Tyler was killed accidentally. Cole was staking out the place, trying to find out who'd organised the hit against him."

"I see."

"Tyler had used Anton Petrov's name and address to lure Cole to the house with two million in cash."

"Really?" Waverley actually did a decent job of acting surprised. "The police never mentioned any money."

"That's because it's missing," said Lewis.

"This Cole person doesn't have it?"

"Nope. Says he left it behind. The police will be looking for it now."

Lewis's phone vibrated yet again. Steve no doubt, angrily chasing him up. He put his hand in his pocket and turned it off. No distractions. This was important.

They walked in silence, reaching the end of Lower Sloane Street and continuing onto Chelsea Bridge Road, where the traffic was queuing up. Mopeds wove in and out of the lanes of buses, taxis, and delivery vans, while cyclists whipped past in the bike lane, creating icy draughts as they went by.

Waverley didn't speak for a long while and, from the look on his face, was genuinely troubled. Lewis wondered how to restart the conversation. Work, perhaps.

"So, what was it you wanted to see me about?" asked Lewis, trying to sound casual. "Are you ready to post the vacancies?"

"Hmm?"

"To replace Steph and Felix."

"Oh, yes. That's right. Sacked with immediate effect." Waverley spoke with grim satisfaction, his eyes fixed on the glistening pavement ahead. They were walking faster now. "Thank you for your help the other day too. You and your colleague. I know it was unpleasant, but Felix wouldn't admit to any of it, nor would he do the decent thing and resign. And once the police had been round, well . . . "

"Will you press charges?"

"What?" Waverley seemed surprised. "We don't want that kind of fuss. We've had to tell the clients, of course. I've had a number of difficult conversations today, as I'm sure you can imagine. But we've managed to convince them it was just a few bad apples that have now been rooted out. We've offered compensation, and they're all happy to take it no further."

"You must be relieved."

"Yes, indeed. Very."

They strode on, going faster than Lewis was now comfortable with, marching down the road towards the traffic lights at the Embankment.

"It was funny about those alerts, wasn't it?" asked Lewis, trying to catch his breath. This guy could give Audrey a run for her money.

"What alerts?"

"The ones Felix had set up for the alarms. It was a separate system, he said. The only way Tyler could have known about it is if someone had told him. Or if someone had changed them from inside Trinity."

Waverley didn't look at him.

"I expect Felix lied. He lied a lot, it seems."

"He told the truth about the rest. Why would he lie about that?"

"Who knows what motivates these people?"

They arrived at the junction and stopped at the pedestrian crossing, Waverley jabbing at the button. Traffic streamed past, and the air became damp, the smell of the river mingling with the fumes from the road. The lights changed, and they crossed, Lewis following Waverley as he walked towards Chelsea Bridge.

He had him, he knew he did—he just needed to push him a tiny bit further.

"The compensation you paid out," said Lewis, "to your inconvenienced clients. Was it more or less than two million pounds?"

Waverley stopped dead, spinning around to face him.

"What are you implying?"

"I think you knew what Felix was up to long before we told you, and you planned to use his scam to your own advantage. If Tyler got away with it, no one would ever know the property had been used for a murder, but if something went wrong, Felix would get all the blowback."

"How dare you?" said Waverley, furious. "You can forget about that contract, McLennon. You and I have no further business."

He strode off, walking onto the footpath over the bridge, but Lewis hurried after him, dodging to avoid the swing of Waverley's briefcase as he drew near.

"Did your dad steal the money, or was it you?"

"I don't know what you're talking about."

"Oh, yes, you do." Lewis tried a partial bluff. "You might not have pressed charges, but it's all in Cole's legal files. It'll come out soon enough."

Waverley pulled up short again, looking at him in horror.

"Everyone knows the Waverley Group has money problems," Lewis went on. "Got the auditors in, I hear. What was it, embezzlement? Or just a bit of sly borrowing for a quick return? Waverley Senior trying to get a little bit richer before retirement?"

"You know nothing about it," said Waverley, starting to walk again. There were only a handful of pedestrians on the bridge, all some distance ahead, and Lewis kept pace alongside him. "Stop talking."

"They say you're the man tipped to take over," said Lewis. "Were you worried your father would destroy the business before you got your hands on it?"

"I don't want his company," hissed Waverley, his voice barely audible above the traffic rumbling over the bridge. "I've got my own business, which I've built from the ground up. All I needed was a small cash injection for expansion, and we'd have been the biggest management company in the city. My father has no vision; that's why the Waverley Group's stagnated. That's why the board wants him gone."

Light dawned.

"Dad wouldn't lend you the money, so you decided to take it! An unauthorised loan to invest in a sure thing. Then, when the scheme came good, you'd return the loan and keep the profits. Except Baxter Cole shafted you."

"Cole shafted us all."

Waverley spoke before he could stop himself, but in that instant, Lewis knew he had him. And from the look in Waverley's eyes, he knew it too.

"What was the plan? Get Cole to return your investment with a bit extra for the lost returns, plus enough to pay Tyler for the job?" Lewis shook his head in admiration. "It's genius, I have to admit. Getting him to pay for his own execution. What happened when Tyler didn't deliver the cash? Did you go to the house? Find the body? You must have panicked then."

Without warning, Waverley turned abruptly, bringing the briefcase up into Lewis's nose. He staggered back against the guardrail, feeling hot pain and warm blood all over his face. He'd only just righted himself when the briefcase came round again, knocking him sideways, and as he felt the metalwork at his back and Waverley's hands on his shoulders, he realised in horror that he was trying to tip him over the railing and into the river below.

He scrabbled to stop himself from being manhandled over the bridge, but his vision was blurry from the first two blows, and in the darkness, he couldn't work out where Waverley was. Waverley landed another hit to the side of Lewis's head, and he kicked out several times, finally making contact, but Waverley was ready for him. With another hefty blow from the briefcase, Lewis was suddenly looking straight down into the dark water of the Thames.

The guardrail dug into his ribcage, and he gripped the railings below with all his might, ready for the inevitable drop as Waverley continued to batter him. Lights began to flash at the edges of his vision, orange, blue, and red. He tried to yell, but his blood was pounding in his ears, and if he made a noise, he couldn't hear it. The lights got closer, as did the darkness. He readied himself for freezing oblivion.

Suddenly there were hands on him again, except now he wasn't being pushed, but pulled. For one moment, he thought he was floating, but then he felt solid ground beneath him, and as his eyes swam into focus, Audrey's face emerged from the flashing lights.

"You're okay," she said, her voice sounding very far away. "You're okay. We've got you."

He looked at her, confused, tasting blood and feeling like he might pass out. He turned his head and saw, a little way along, a mass of black shapes moving about. He squinted, making out a blob of red and another of yellow in amongst all the black, and frowned, which made the pain in his face explode.

"Who'sh dat?" His voice sounded thick and funny.

"Clayton, Sofia, two uniformed officers," said Audrey. She was crouched beside him on the ground, one arm around his shoulders, the other hooked around his forearm. He started to shake.

"Dey got 'im?"

"They did." She pulled him tight.

They stayed like that for a while, until the shaking lessened, then she stood up and helped Lewis to his feet. He could now see a police car with flashing lights parked between the safety bollards, while just in front of it was a black cab with its hazards on.

"Next time you go to meet a murderer, answer your damn phone, all right?" She sounded strange. "We were almost too late."

He realised then that it was Audrey who was shaking and pulled her into a hug.

"Who's 'we'?"

"Me and Clayton." Her voice was muffled against his chest. "Mei had his number. We got to Trinity and found you gone, but Steph was still there, packing up her things. She told us you'd walked off with Waverley in the direction of the bridge. Pretty sure Clayton broke a thousand laws on the way here."

"Well, I abbreciate it," said Lewis, resting his bloodied chin on top of her head. "You did good, kiddo. You did good."

She burst into tears.

67
Audrey

After spending Friday night sitting in the emergency room with Lewis, Audrey spent most of Saturday in her pyjamas before going to see Celeste and Dixon that afternoon. She found Lewis already there, debriefing them over tea and cake, a couple of stitches in his eyebrow, a couple more across his swollen nose, and yet more across one cheekbone.

"How's the concussion?" she asked, weirdly pleased to see his messed-up face. "You look terrible."

"It's fine, I think," he said with a lopsided grin. "It hurts more than I thought it would. All good for the book, though, I guess." Audrey rolled her eyes. "I told Steve what had happened and that I wouldn't be in on Monday, and he wasn't happy. I had to send him a picture of my face before he'd believe me."

She sat down at the table.

"How are you?" asked Dixon, passing her a plate.

"Yes, dear, you look wrung out," said Celeste.

"I'm okay," she said. "I didn't get beaten up with a briefcase."

She saw Celeste and Dixon exchange a look.

"Anyway," she went on, "I came over because I've had an idea I wanted to talk to you about. It's about Flat 10."

Dixon snorted.

"You're too late," he said, nodding at Lewis. "This one's already asked."

"Asked what?"

"About your friend Clayton's mother," said Celeste. "It sounds like a terrible situation for them, poor lambs, and Dixon and I agree that we owe Clayton a favour for looking after you all. I'll invite them for tea tomorrow."

"Lewis asked you about Clayton's mum? *Lewis* did?"

"I'm right here," he said. "And of course I did. Why wouldn't I?"

"I didn't think you'd heard a word he'd said in the cab."

"Just because I'm not talking doesn't mean I'm not listening."

"Well." She folded her arms, annoyed but unable to explain why. "Listening and caring. I don't know what's got into you."

"Oh, I think we do, dear," said Celeste, lifting her teacup and smiling.

On Sunday, Clayton brought his mother, Miriam, and his little brother, Lionel, over to Marchfield Square to have tea with Celeste. Audrey knew from experience that the longer an interview lasted, the better it was probably going, and when the three finally emerged from Celeste's apartments two hours later, it was with Dixon, who took them across the square to Flat 10.

She squealed with excitement and reached for her phone.

AUDREY BROOKS: Dixon's showing them Flat 10! They're moving in!

FLAT 5 GUY: That's good news.

AUDREY BROOKS: I'm going out to say hello. You should too.

FLAT 5 GUY: Nosy neighbour.

AUDREY BROOKS: Move it, McLennon.

Dragging Mei with her, Audrey pulled on her coat and made her way down to the courtyard. The Captain was on his bench, doing his crossword puzzle with Muffin at his feet, and smiled as they approached. Within five minutes, they'd been joined by Philip and Mekhala, Manny, Victor, and, yes, even Lewis.

"The poor woman's going to be terrified," he said, scowling.

"We're a welcoming committee," said Audrey. "Oh, I found your writer friend by the way."

"My what?"

"Ken McKeith? He writes under the name Rosemary Roebarrow. Historical romances. Strong on the bodice-ripping, from the looks of it."

"Right. Ken. Romance." He blinked a few times, then rallied. "That didn't take you long."

"Social-media history is Audrey's superpower," said Mei. "Very useful for dating background checks. Hey." She nodded over his shoulder. "They're coming."

They watched as Clayton, Miriam, Lionel, and Dixon descended the steps to the courtyard. Dixon muttered a few words as they spotted the group, and Clayton laughed, walking ahead to say hello.

"Hey, how'd it go?" asked Audrey. "Are they taking it?"

"Are you kidding?" Clayton grinned. "It's a palace. Thanks, guys, you've no idea what this means."

He gave Audrey and Mei a hug and shook Lewis's hand.

"How's it coming?" he said, pointing at Lewis's face.

"Getting itchy."

"That means it's healing," said Mekhala, touching his chin to inspect his injuries. "You mustn't scratch, though."

"Everyone," said Dixon, joining the group, "this is Miriam Bird and her son, Lionel. As I think you've already guessed, they'll be moving in to Flat 10. I hope you'll make 'em welcome."

"Mimi, please," said Miriam, shaking everyone's hands. "As we're going to be neighbours."

Mimi was a short woman, with natural hair pulled up into a bun and a smile just like her elder son's. Lionel was almost as tall as Clayton, in a gangly, teenage way, with black-framed glasses and a shy expression.

"Mimi, eh?" said the Captain, looking her up and down. "Where are you from? Originally, I mean. I understand you've moved about."

"Hoxton," said Mimi, her smile becoming tight.

"Hoxton?" The Captain stroked his moustache. "I knew a man from Hoxton once. Name of Alec. Bad sort. Drove a hideous yellow car."

"I know him," said Mimi, nodding. "Looks like a squirrel."

"Yes!"

"Last I heard, he was in Wormwood Scrubs for arson."

"Doesn't surprise me. Best place for him, I'd say." The Captain adjusted the pen in his blazer pocket. "I . . . uh . . . don't suppose you bake, do you, Mrs. Bird? Chocolate cake, that sort of thing?"

"Mimi," said Mimi. "And no, not chocolate cake."

"Ah."

"But wait until you try my banana bread."

The Captain beamed.

"What do you do, Mimi?" asked Philip, also smiling.

"I'm an APT."

"What's an APT?"

"An anatomical pathologist technologist. I won't explain, as it can sound a bit gruesome, but I work at Fulham Public Mortuary."

Audrey almost laughed aloud at Lewis's expression. He looked like he might explode with delight.

Clayton touched her elbow, drawing her aside.

"Will you keep an eye on 'em?" he asked. "Until they settle in? I'm worried about Lionel. He's moved so much already."

"Of course," said Audrey. "We look out for each other here. I don't think you need to worry, though." She looked over at the little group and smiled. "I think they're going to fit right in."

68

Celeste

Celeste and Anton smiled at each other across the dining table, which was now set for coffee. The sky outside was clear and blue, and the apartment was lit by bright afternoon sunshine, the picture window projecting golden light onto the wall opposite. They'd had a long and pleasant lunch, but then Dixon had cleared away dessert and made himself scarce, allowing Celeste to begin her interrogation in private. She and Anton both knew it was coming, but they were also both pretending that it was not.

"I am glad that London keeps you busy," said Anton, taking a sip of his coffee. "Although you should try the continent. The weather here is terrible."

"You'll get no argument from me on that front," said Celeste, shaking her head. "I think it rains half the year now. I don't expect you miss it."

"I don't like London anymore," said Anton. "Not for business or travel. I keep a place for the children, as they have dual nationality, but only Jean has any fondness for the place. He seems to get more English, while Sabine gets more French."

"That's only natural, I suppose. Anglo-Russian father, Anglo-French mother, born and educated in England, but raised in France . . . Nationality becomes somewhat fluid in those circumstances, one imagines. Even you, Anton, sound a little French these days."

"Do I? Hah." He seemed delighted. "You should come out to Antibes, Celeste. Meet my girlfriend, Véronique. I think you would like her. And the weather . . . " He held up a hand, his fingers pinched together. "*C'est parfait.*"

"I should like that," said Celeste. "Since my hip replacement, travel is much easier."

More sips of coffee, more smiles, until Celeste could bear it no longer.

"No more games, Anton. Let's have it. When did you really arrive in London? I assume you flew in by private plane?"

He gazed at her levelly, his training still evident in the stillness of his brow and the slow way he blinked. Then he shrugged.

"Last Thursday. Early."

"Why?"

"I received a call. One of my people in London told me questions were being asked. About me. My property. I was concerned."

"You went straight to the house?"

"I arrived just after ten."

"So you found the body." A statement, not a question. "And recognised him?"

"Of course. I've seen that face in my dreams every night for twenty-five years. I kept tabs on Tyler, as you say, as he clearly did on me."

"So you return to that house after two years away and find the body of Madeleine's killer just waiting for you."

He laughed, a short sharp sound without humour.

"Like a Christmas present."

"What did you do?"

Another shrug.

"Stood. Stared at him. I wanted it clear in my mind, a memory to bring me comfort in my old age."

"Then what? You cleaned up the mess?" Celeste shook her head. "I remember how you worked, Anton. You were a terrible cleaner, so your kills were always neat. Tidy. And, of course, you're older now."

Anton half-smiled, his eyes somewhere far away.

"You are right, of course, dear Celeste. I am no cleaner, and we are not avenging angels anymore. I did not know why Tyler was in my house, and I did not much care. He was dead, and I was glad, but nor did I wish to be implicated. I straightened the clock, then I called in the professionals."

"Who?" pressed Celeste, ignoring the nonsense about the clock. "Who did you call? An old contact? A friend?" Then, prompted by a flutter in her stomach, "Family?"

There it was, the flicker under Anton's eye, the tell he could never quite suppress when under stress. Anton had been an orphan when he left Russia, his only family the service and the one who had adopted him when he married Madeleine.

And the one they had created together.

"Jean," she said at last, and now Anton looked at her properly. "Jean came to London to help you? No . . . " She nodded. "He was already here. Your son is a cleaner? How did you allow that to happen?"

The flicker turned to a flash then, his dark eyes glinting beneath the unruly white brows.

"I allowed nothing," he growled. "Children grow up. They develop minds of their own. It is the tragedy of parenthood. Perhaps if Madeleine had been here, she could have stopped him. But I am just his father." He sighed then, his pain showing through. "He takes after her in many ways. She said cleaning up after men, whether it was wet towels or wet blood, was no way for women to live, so she taught him. He liked the work. Sabine is like me. Good with computers. She doesn't like chaos."

"Tell me what happened," said Celeste. "In the house. Why did Audrey nearly catch Jean?"

"She was early," he said, simply. "I spent too long trying to think who could have left the body for me. Then I called Jean, and it took time for him to arrive. London traffic. *C'est abominable.* By then it was past eleven o'clock, and the Trinity people said the cleaner came at twelve, so Jean told me to leave. That he and his friend would take care of it. I flew back to Paris."

"And shaved, presumably." She raised an eyebrow.

"I was seen as I left the house. By one of the neighbours."

"Then you reentered the country later. Eurostar?"

"Yes."

Celeste tapped a finger on the table.

"Audrey and Lewis. They found out that Tyler was hired by Roland Waverley to kill Baxter Cole. I don't know if it was Waverley's idea or Tyler's, but they used your name to lure him to the house. All set up for an efficient kill, by the sound of it, except your clocks went off and surprised them both. There was a struggle."

"That is a thing that Tyler would do." Anton rubbed at his chin as he thought, no doubt missing his beard. "He would enjoy the irony of using me that way. And I would enjoy it, if that was what happened." Then he laughed, deep and from the belly. "I would enjoy that a great deal."

Celeste paused, wondering how to phrase her next question. Madeleine's death still held a lot of pain for them both.

"Why would Tyler hold a grudge against you, Anton? If anyone had cause to take revenge, it would be you."

The smile faded at once, and a hard glint appeared in his eyes. He shrugged.

"You need to stop shrugging, Anton, it makes you look guilty. What did you do?"

"Nothing that was not necessary. Or deserved."

"I'd appreciate it if you told me. Two of my protégés were dragged into this, and I'd like to know why."

"Only one was dragged," said Anton, with a sniff. "The other dragged himself."

She smiled, conceding the point. "Nevertheless."

He held her gaze, then smiled fondly.

"Madeleine was your protégée, too, was she not?"

"At first."

"And then you were friends. Almost like sisters."

Celeste was surprised by the way the emotion rose up inside her, seeing her grief reflected in his eyes, hearing the same pain in his voice.

"Yes," she said softly.

He looked away, eyes trained on the picture window.

"After Madeleine died, I wanted to kill Tyler with my own hands, so I set a trap. But I underestimated him. He was cunning. Slippery. He got away."

"You should have asked me to help," she said. "I would have. What did you do then?"

"Like I said, I'm good with computers. I took his money instead. Every penny he made from every job, I took it. From his Swiss bank account, from his accounts in the Emirates, from Panama and Hong Kong. I took it all, and I kept taking it, until he disappeared."

"Changed his name. Several times."

"I never stopped looking for him. Sometimes I read about a kill that might be him, but I couldn't be sure. He did a good job of hiding from me."

"Then he reappears in London after twenty years, using the same name. It's like he wanted you to know."

"Yes."

"And the two million? The children think it was Waverley who took it, but he denies ever going to the house."

"I told you, I always take Tyler's money."

"Well, this wasn't his. It belonged to the people Cole swindled."

Anton sighed, and she recognised the sound of defeat.

"What would you like me to do with it?"

Celeste smiled.

"I'll have a word with Mei Chen and send you a list. I can trust you to do the right thing."

Silence descended as she drifted into thought, while Anton remained staring into space. One thing she'd always admired about him was that he never felt the need to fill a silence.

"I had no idea Jean was in London," she said at last. "Should I be offended that he hasn't called? I am his godmother, after all."

"I told him he must, but he was worried you would try to interfere."

"Interfere?" Now she *was* offended.

"To try to help him. He wanted to stand on his own two feet." Anton's tone said he disapproved. "He has been here two years, almost, and this is the first time I have been allowed to visit. He has his own business, in forensic cleaning. He works for the police and London councils, all aboveboard. He spells his name the English way and has taken Madeleine's surname."

That startled her.

"Keane?"

"Yes. Not as good as Petrov, in my opinion, but he said for business, it was better." He sighed. "Children. What can you do?"

Celeste smiled politely and took another sip of her coffee.

John Keane, in London. Working as a cleaner. Well, well, well.

When they'd finished their drinks, Celeste stood up and walked over to the window, looking down on her beloved square. She was delighted to see not just Audrey but Lewis as well, helping move the Bird family's belongings into Flat 10. Miriam seemed to be having a good chinwag with the Captain, which was a nice surprise. The man was getting gossipy with old age and loneliness. It would do him good to make new friends.

"The new tenant," said Anton, joining her at the window. "You think she will fit in with the rest of your people?"

"Oh, yes," said Celeste, nodding. "Yes, I think she'll do very well."

She smiled, lifting her eyes to the London skyline, where the winter sun had begun its descent, light glinting off the buildings.

They stood in silence for a moment.

"It is time I was going." Anton spoke with just a touch of regret. "It has been an interesting visit, but I am ready to go home." He turned to her. "What will you do now? Is it time for you to rest?"

"Oh, I shouldn't think so for a minute." Celeste looked back down at the square, where Sarah and Tom had come out to meet Miriam and Lionel. She smiled again. "Not for a single minute."

About the Author

NICOLA WHYTE studied Drama at Aberystwyth University and spent many happy years as a bookseller before becoming a web developer. She now co-owns a digital agency in the southwest of England. Her work has been listed for the Comedy Women in Print Prize, the BPA First Novel Award, and the Cheshire Novel Prize. *10 Marchfield Square* was named as runner-up in the 2023 *Daily Mail* First Novel Competition. She lives near Stonehenge in Wiltshire with her family.